The sky was turning a light yellowish pink when Barkson saw the first movement on the hill. At first she thought the movement a trick of the light—a shadow, passing along some grass, heading in the same direction the windstone vehicle was.

Then she saw another shadow and another, and they weren't normal shadows. The sun hadn't risen yet. There shouldn't have been those kinds of shadows at all.

"How much farther do we have?" she asked Helia.

Helia was gripping the driving sticks so hard that her knuckles had turned white. Barkson doubted that Helia had seen the moving shadows, so it had to have been the approach to her brother's home that had her so nervous. More movement along the hillside.

"Slow down," Barkson said quietly.

"I'd like to get there as—"

"*Slow down*," Barkson snapped.

Helia did. Barkson leaned forward a little. There were no real shadows on the ground that would move like that.

She had a growing feeling that something was very wrong.

THE FEY SERIES
(READING ORDER)

ALSO BY
KRISTINE KATHRYN RUSCH

MORE FROM THE FEY

Destiny: A Story of The Fey

Lessons From The Writing of The Fey

THE DIVING SERIES

Diving into the Wreck: A Diving Novel

City of Ruins: A Diving Novel

Becalmed: A Diving Universe Novella

The Application of Hope: A Diving Universe Novella

Boneyards: A Diving Novel

Skirmishes: A Diving Novel

The Runabout: A Diving Novel

The Falls: A Diving Universe Novel

Searching for the Fleet: A Diving Novel

The Spires of Denon: A Diving Universe Novella

The Renegat: A Diving Universe Novel

Escaping Amnthra: A Diving Universe Novella

The Court-Martial of the Renegat Renegades

Thieves: A Diving Novel

Squishy's Teams: A Diving Universe Novel

The Chase: A Diving Novel

Maelstrom: A Diving Universe Novella

Writing as Kris Nelscott

THE SMOKEY DALTON SERIES

A Dangerous Road

Smoke-Filled Rooms

Thin Walls

Stone Cribs

War at Home

Days of Rage

Street Justice

AND

Protectors

Writing as Kristine Grayson

The Charming Trilogy, Vol. 1

The Charming Trilogy, Vol. 2

The Fates Trilogy

The Daughters of Zeus Trilogy

BARKSON'S JOURNEY

THE SECOND BOOK OF THE QAVNERIAN PROTECTORATE

KRISTINE KATHRYN RUSCH

WMG
PUBLISHING

Barkson's Journey
Copyright © 2024 by Kristine Kathryn Rusch
Published by WMG Publishing
Cover and layout copyright © 2024 by WMG Publishing
Cover design by WMG Publishing
Cover illustration by Echo Chernik
Background art © cappa | Depositphotos
Figure art © Ravven and © Cheshire Studios
Vehicle art © Alina Lytvyn "Vex"
Map art and design © Stephanie Writt | WMG Publishing

ISBN-13 (trade paperback): 978-1-56146-979-6
ISBN-13 (hardcover): 978-1-56146-980-2

A special journey for my wonderful fans.

BARKSON'S JOURNEY

TRINOVANTE

CHAPTER
ONE

Lucinda Barkson slowed her windstone vehicle about three blocks away from the Office of the Constabulary. The fog was thinning, but the visibility was still low. There was a lot more traffic here than there had been on the other roads—large carriages, constabulary on horseback, some people walking.

They all seemed to be headed to or coming from the Office of the Constabulary. Barkson didn't want to attract attention here, so she negotiated the large vehicle through openings in the traffic as if the windstone could break.

It couldn't—not easily—but the vehicle did sit lower than the carriages, so was often hard to see in a crowded area like this.

Until now, Barkson had driven, in Gussie's words, "like a crazy woman." There had been a purpose behind that seeming craziness.

Barkson had to make sure they weren't being followed. A carriage couldn't have followed at the speed Barkson had gone, and a person on horseback would have stood out if they tried to keep up with the vehicle.

Barkson hadn't explained that to Gussie. Gussie, who had gripped the edge of the bench seat with a single gloved hand, and hadn't said much after asking if Barkson always drove like this.

Otherwise, Gussie—Augusta Kirilli, the oldest child of Augustus Kirilli—sat primly in the passenger seat of the vehicle. For the first time, maybe in her entire life, she was wearing pants and a loose blouse that she kept trying to adjust.

The clothes belonged to Barkson, along with the boots. Gussie's clothing was stained with blood. When she had peeled it off before washing down at Barkson's apartment, Barkson had quietly gathered the pieces and tossed them in a pile behind the building to be burned.

Barkson made herself pay attention to her driving. She needed to get Gussie to the Office of the Constabulary in one piece. It was probably the only place Gussie would be safe right now.

The neighborhood around the Office of the Constabulary had once been cheap rentals and tiny homes. Now, it consisted of offices and businesses related to the Constabulary.

There were several Offices of the Constabulary throughout the city of Trinovante, but this office serviced one of the richest areas in the entire city. Most of the Old Families lived nearby, in stately estates with massive amounts of land and servants.

Nothing much happened in this neighborhood except petty theft. Until the last few days.

Barkson had heard tell of massive destruction at some of the manor houses, and that was before Gussie had located her at Mallankam's Public House. Gussie had told her a horrific tale that seemed to get worse as more details emerged. Gussie had sought Barkson out because, as Gussie said, Barkson was the only person she knew who could help.

In the past day or so, Gussie's father had been attacked and murdered, the family estate ransacked, and all of the staff killed in hideous ways.

This morning, Gussie and her driver had found all of the bodies, and had had a strange encounter with her father that had more than a little tinge of magic to it. Gussie hadn't really allowed herself to believe in magic before, even though the Kirillis were steeped in it.

Now, she did, although reluctantly.

Or perhaps what Barkson took for reluctance was utter emotional exhaustion.

Gussie was currently holding herself together with sheer determination. She sat upright, not allowing her back to touch the seat. Even though her hand gripped the bottom of the seat, she wasn't holding herself up with it. She was staring out of the windscreen, as if the road and carriages before her were the most important things in the world.

Barkson admired that. She had never realized just how strong Gussie was. They had gone to school together and had become fast, if unlikely, friends. They were very different—Gussie, prim and proper and concerned with how things looked, and Barkson, breaking every rule as she tried to get through.

Gussie had brought Barkson home several times, mostly on school holidays, until Barkson stopped accepting the invitations because she was so uncomfortable. Still, she had gotten to meet everyone in Gussie's immediate family, including her father.

Barkson hadn't had much time to register his death and how

she felt about it. She knew a lot more about Augustus Kirilli than his daughter did.

Now was not the time to tell Gussie any of those things.

Barkson pulled over across the street from the Office of the Constabulary. It was a huge ugly building, with several stories and too many doors. A wide covered walkway swarmed with people, some in uniform and many in everyday clothes. Large posts at the edge of the walkway made sure that no one drove onto it, either with a carriage or a windstone vehicle.

There was a carriage park to the side of the building, but no place for windstone vehicles. Barkson had noted that curiosity before, but she had never considered it a problem until now.

Gussie stared at the building, her lower lip trembling. She had had an impossible day, and yet she hadn't broken down, not yet anyway. Barkson had given her the opportunity at the apartment, and Gussie had not taken it.

Gussie had been on the move all day. After discovering the destruction and the bodies of the murdered staff, Gussie had sent her driver—a man named Zeitsev—to this Office of the Constabulary to report the crimes. Then Gussie had gotten in her own windstone vehicle and driven somewhere—she wouldn't tell Barkson exactly where—to hide some satchels her father had given her, maybe before or (oddly) after his death.

Barkson didn't understand the part about the satchels, and she wasn't sure she was supposed to.

Gussie had told her almost everything, only holding back the location of the satchels because her father had sworn her to secrecy.

Barkson believed her for a variety of reasons. Gussie had been a physical mess when she found Barkson. Gussie's clothing was covered in blood. She had a bloody handprint on her back. The bottom of her skirts was brown with dried blood, and her hair was coming out of its usually neat bun. Gussie had looked like a woman about to collapse, but she hadn't.

Barkson had taken Gussie home, fed her, clothed her, and demanded that she sleep.

But Gussie couldn't.

I need to get in touch with my siblings, she had said more than once, *and for that I need you*.

That was why Barkson had fourteen letters in the hidden compartment of her windstone vehicle—two letters for each sibling—along with a map that showed her where each Kirilli sibling now lived. Barkson had also brought almost every weapon she owned, from her pistols to nearly a dozen daggers.

They too were in the hidden compartments in the back.

Gussie hadn't seen Barkson pack those. Gussie had been busy writing the letters, calmly penning the same first letter to each sibling, detailing their father's death. The second letter, Gussie had said, was the important one, and she made sure that Barkson understood that no one was to receive the second letter first, ever.

Barkson had had to swear to that more than once, because Gussie seemed able to do only one thing at a time.

That she was still standing after the day she had was a miracle; that she was thinking clearly enough to come up with a plan for her siblings was something that left Barkson in awe.

Gussie still stared out the windscreen, her back rigid. She hadn't moved at all. Barkson wasn't even certain Gussie knew that they were in front of the constabulary.

Barkson put a gentle hand on Gussie's shoulder, hoping she

hadn't fallen asleep with her eyes open. Barkson had seen some of the strongest men she'd ever known do that accidentally in her work for the Shadow Company. Sometimes exhaustion won.

But Gussie wasn't asleep. She blinked, smiled ruefully, and sighed.

"I don't want to talk to them," she said about the constabulary. The rich never did.

Had this been a normal day, with normal events, Barkson would have pointed out that class disparity to Gussie. Barkson had liked jabbing at the class differences between them since they'd met at Bekyce School for Girls nearly twenty years before.

"I know you don't want to go in there," Barkson said, "but you need to inform them. They need—"

"I'm sure Zeitsev told them everything," Gussie said.

They'd had this discussion at the apartment, then again when they had gotten into the windstone vehicle, and apparently they were going to have it again. Barkson tried not to sigh.

She needed to get on the road. After hearing what Gussie had been through—what was going on—Barkson knew that time was of the essence.

She had to reach all of the Kirilli siblings as quickly as possible. The problem was that they were scattered across the Dorovich continent, in several different countries. Emberto, the youngest son, lived near Mount Vitaki, and that was at least a three-day drive from here, nonstop.

Barkson wouldn't be able to go nonstop. Even if she didn't have the other siblings to deal with, she would need some sleep. And those three days didn't count road conditions or other problems she might encounter along the way.

"They need to hear from you," Barkson said of the constabulary. "They need to hear *everything* from you."

She had never said that before.

"I can't tell them about my father. It might be magic," Gussie said, staring out the passenger-side windscreen.

Might be magic. It *was* magic. The man had showed up, injured, at the manor house and then had faded away after he had delivered the satchels to Gussie. No one faded away without some kind of magic.

"Then don't tell them that part," Barkson said. "Just tell them you saw him, and get them to that kitchen."

Where the bodies of the staff were. The constabulary would take it from there.

"You just want them to protect me," Gussie said. "But what if they're involved?"

"They're not," Barkson said.

"You can't know that!" Gussie's voice rose. Barkson braced herself. Was this the much-needed, much-anticipated breakdown?

Barkson had hoped Gussie wouldn't have that until Barkson had left on this long trip.

"I can know it," Barkson said as calmly as she could. "You just mentioned magic, and you're right. The constabulary enforces rules *against* magic. They wouldn't sanction this kind of attack. They wouldn't attack an Old Family, and they wouldn't use magic against your father."

Gussie looked at her, eyes lined with tears.

Barkson squeezed Gussie's shoulder. It was so thin, and so much was riding on it now.

"I know this for a fact," Barkson said. "If I didn't, I wouldn't have brought you here."

That convinced Gussie. She took a deep breath, nodded, and then sighed.

"You have my key, right?" Barkson wanted to remind Gussie that she had a place to go.

"Yes," Gussie said. "And you don't have to give me the instructions again. I know them. I'm to get someone from here to drop me off a block or two away from your place. I should be able to make it from there to your apartment just fine. They can't know where I am."

She sagged a little, finally looking defeated.

"I won't be able to sleep," she said.

"But you'll be safe," Barkson said.

"I'll be safe," Gussie whispered, as if she didn't believe it.

Barkson wasn't sure she believed it either, but she did know one thing: she couldn't make this drive with Gussie in the passenger seat. Not that Gussie wanted to come. When she had been thinking just a bit more clearly, she had mentioned that she planned to go to the families of each staff member, tell them they had lost their loved one, and give them enough money to survive for a few months.

That by itself would take days and an emotional toll that Barkson didn't want to think about.

She had made Gussie promise she would not return to her father's property—indeed, to any Kirilli property—until this crisis had passed.

"I need to get on the road," Barkson said.

Being blunt seemed to be the only way to end this cycle of

indecision. Obviously, Gussie was getting tired. All of the events of the day were hitting her now.

Barkson wasn't the kind of friend who could comfort a person in a time of need. Barkson was a woman who took action.

Gussie had been right to find Barkson, and to send her with the letters to the siblings. Gussie had no idea who Barkson really was or what she had been doing since they left their advanced studies at Serebro Academy, but Gussie did know that Barkson sometimes took on dangerous "odd jobs" that had once been—in Gussie's opinion—extremely unladylike.

Barkson was actually saddened that Gussie had need of her most unladylike friend. Gussie had long belonged to a part of the world that Barkson had thought untouchable by blood and violence.

Barkson had been so very wrong.

"Yes, yes," Gussie said. "You have to leave. Tell them...well, you know what to tell them."

She was referring to her siblings, none of whom lived in Trinovante. Some of them had children. Others...well, Barkson hoped she could find them quickly.

"I do," Barkson said. "I have all that I need. I'll send you letters as well, just to keep you informed, in case..."

She made herself stop. She had almost made a misstep. She had almost said, *in case I don't make it back.*

That had been a goodbye saying for members of Shadow Company. She hadn't expected it to become so rote that she almost said it to Gussie.

Gussie looked at her sharply. Gussie had probably heard the unstated words.

"In case?" she asked.

Barkson made herself smile reassuringly. "In case it takes me longer to return than you expect."

That was also true. Barkson had no idea what she was driving into, nor did she know how long it would take her.

Gussie grabbed her hand so tightly that Gussie's glove rubbed against Barkson's skin.

"You can't die on me too," Gussie said.

Barkson grinned in her most insouciant way.

"Gus," she said, "that's why you're sending me. I'm inde-structible."

A tear ran down Gussie's face. "That's the thing, Lucinda," she said. "No one is. I thought my father was, and you saw—well, you didn't see. You know..."

"I know," Barkson said. She had to stop the emotional breakdown before it happened. "Your father did everything he could to make sure his legacy was protected. I'm going to do everything I can to make sure your family is safe. You have my word."

"I know." Gussie let go of her hand. "You're a true friend, Lucinda."

Barkson laughed, deliberately. "I'm not sure that's true, Gus. You're paying me."

"You didn't want me to," Gussie said.

Trapped by her own words from a few hours ago. Barkson had no response for that.

"Go," she said. "Before someone in the constabulary wonders why we're parked here and their curiosity delays my journey further."

"Right. Yes." Gussie opened the door. Finally. She slipped a booted foot out, then turned.

Barkson half-held her breath, hoping this wouldn't lead to more discussion.

"Be safe, Lucinda," Gussie said.

Since that command contradicted the very point of this journey, Barkson had no option other than a polite lie.

"I will, Gus," she said. "I promise. I will."

FILIPPA

CHAPTER
TWO

ISARA

T he sun had set by the time Barkson made it out of Trinovante. The road narrowed, but the lightstone lanterns on the front of her vehicle lit up the area as if she had captured a small but powerful portion of the sun.

The lights swept the manicured hedgerows that lined both sides of the road like fences. Farther along, she knew, she would find actual stone fences, some of which had blocked off this road for nearly a thousand years.

The country of Qavner was old. It had been conquered twice in its existence, both times so far in the past that only students of history knew all of the details. In ancient times, the Aekwen had come down the Hidden River, and conquered cities throughout the continent of Dorovich all along the way.

The Aekwen were the first to found Trinovante, on the shores of the Tamsi. The evidence that the Aekwen had been that far south, however, lay mostly in the development of these fences, and in the road, which had a stone underpinning.

13

That Aekwen design made this part of the road smoother than other parts. It didn't sink and need to be shored up on the boggier parts of the road, unlike later roads built by Qavnerians.

Barkson would be using Gussie's map a lot on this journey. Barkson had used it the first time to figure out where her first stop would be. She was going to the home of Filippa Kirilli, now Filippa Kirilli Netuno. Filippa had married well, although not the Old Family marriage that her father had wanted.

The Netunos ran the village of Isara. Barkson had come there often, partly for its pubs and partly because she had done some training in the foothills nearby.

Gussie's map showed that Barkson would have to turn off the main road long before she reached Isara. Apparently the estate where Filippa now lived was to the south of the village, in a large area that was Netuno property.

Barkson had never met any Netunos, although she had a history with Filippa Kirilli.

That history had Barkson worried.

Filippa had also attended the Bekyce School for Girls. She had been two years behind Gussie, but socially years ahead.

While Gussie had focused on her studies, Filippa had focused on making connections. She didn't have friends per se— she was too acerbic for that—but she had acolytes.

Filippa had made Bekyce a hellscape for anyone she didn't like.

And she really hadn't liked Barkson.

The windstone vehicle bounced along a road that was growing increasingly more unkempt the farther Barkson got away from the main road. She slowed down tremendously, leaning slightly forward to watch cracks and crevices.

A road this poorly maintained could drop off, or have bits and pieces jutting up. A horse could step over the pieces. A carriage could straddle it.

But the windstone vehicle was low to the ground and anything jutting too high could damage the windstone vents underneath.

She slowed down even more, and finally saw some gaslights flickering in the distance. They were about person-high, and as she got closer, she realized that they were built into some stone columns that marked the gate to what had to be the Netuno property.

She hoped the gate wasn't closed, since no one was expecting her.

The fence itself wasn't ancient stone, like the others here. It was brown and smooth, clearly built for the estate. She reached the top of the rise where the columns were, and slowed to a near crawl, so that she could see the entrance.

The gates were closed. They were of iron, which relieved her. That meant no one with idle magic could get in easily. The ornate scrollwork, revealed in the light from the vehicle's light-stone lanterns, spelled the name *Netuno*.

She parked the vehicle outside the gates. She grabbed her driving gloves from the passenger seat, and slipped them on. Then she got out of the vehicle, and walked to the gates to see if they could be pushed open, when she saw movement out of her left eye.

She whirled.

A man, clutching an oversized candlelighter, peered at her from beside the gate. Some used the tip of a candlelighter to adjust the doors on a gaslight. It was an old-fashioned way of doing things, since gaslights were easier to maintain than candles used to be.

That gave her a sense of his age. Even though he was trim, he had to be old enough to remember when the gate lights were candles instead of gas.

"State yer business," he said, his tone low.

She wondered if he would have said anything if she hadn't seen him.

"I have urgent business with Filippa Kirilli Netuno. I'm here at the behest of her sister, Augusta Kirilli."

"I was na told that anaone would arrive tonight," the man said, holding the candlelighter as if he would turn it into a weapon at any moment.

He probably could. If the gates were made of iron, then the candlelighter probably was too, which made it very strong. The tip, where a long wick used to be, was probably honed to a point now.

"I realize you had no notice, and I'm sorry," Barkson said, deciding to go with polite at the moment. "But Augusta sent me because she's handling a crisis. I have letters for the family that must be delivered immediately."

He held out a hand, as if he expected Barkson to give him the letters.

"I've been instructed," she said, looking at that soot-covered palm, so visible in the light from her lightstone lanterns, "to speak to no one but Filippa herself."

"I'll see if she'll speak ta ya," he said. "Yer name?"

"We don't have time for this," Barkson said. "You'll let me through right now."

"I'm sorry, miss, but—"

She didn't wait for him to talk about niceties. He was a groundsman at best, not a butler, not a guard at the gate, no matter how he presented himself.

She pushed the gates in the very center, and felt them shake.

"Miss, ya canna—"

She pushed harder, noting that his accent got thicker the more distressed he was. She kept an eye on him, so that he didn't run at her or swing that candlelighter.

He did neither. He remained beside the columns, almost as if he was afraid of her. And maybe he was. She doubted many people arrived here unannounced after dark.

The gates groaned, and then, slowly eased open.

"I will be sure to let the family know that you were doing your duty," she said as she walked back to the vehicle, hoping he wouldn't attack it with the point of the candlelighter.

He still didn't move.

She got in her vehicle, maintaining eye contact with the man the entire time. Then she closed her door, and drove forward through the wide gates, which were still opening.

The sweeping light from the lightstone lanterns revealed a manicured lawn that rose and fell in mounds. They did not look manmade, but more a part of the landscape that extended for miles to her right and her left.

Although she saw some shadows toward the village that she suspected were hedgerows, dividing the property. Or maybe marking part of the property that was used for relaxation and leisure, and the other part—the farming part—that stank of manure. The part that the family probably did not want to see.

The drive to the estate cut through the mounds. Sometimes Barkson couldn't see the lawn around her—just the land, rising

—and sometimes, she saw the entire expanse, or at least what the light from her lightstone lamps revealed.

Finally the drive went up ever so slightly, and around a corner, revealing a huge estate building that was wider than most of Trinovante's city blocks. The estate building was four stories high and rectangular, made from the same dark brown material as the fence farther back.

The drive circled around the front of the estate. There were no other vehicles here, not even a hint of one, which made Barkson realize that this estate was one of the wealthier she had seen.

Even to keep up that kind of appearance of wealth—the continual raking of the tire tracks and prints from the horses, the cleanliness that wasn't inevitable when carriages were nearby—would have cost more than Barkson had seen in her lifetime.

And, once her grandparents had died, she had seen quite a fortune.

She pulled up in front of the estate, near the main doors. They were two stories tall, with an arch over them with a design that resembled the design on the front gate.

Gaslights framed the upper part of the doors. She had no idea how those were operated. Maybe from some kind of switch inside.

The estate was built to intimidate. It would have done its job, too, if she hadn't been to several others built with the same purpose in mind. Some estates like this, particularly in the outer regions of Qavner, maintained the exterior, but had entire stories shut down, because the owners couldn't afford the staff to continue the upkeep.

Usually that showed, though, especially upon approach with a vehicle that created as much light as hers did.

This estate seemed to be in much better shape than those others. The suggestion of wealth was probably not an illusion.

She reached over the seat, opened the small compartment. Behind it were the hidden compartments. She opened the one on the right and removed the stack of letters. She had them in order of closeness to Trinovante, but she checked the name on the envelopes anyway.

Filippa.

Barkson made sure she had both envelopes. Then she closed the compartments, and shut the vehicle down reluctantly, because the light from the lightstone lanterns would fade, probably before she reached the door.

She grabbed her coat from the passenger side and removed her goggles, setting them on the seat.

She did not bring a weapon. Most people did not expect her physical fighting ability, and if she needed it, she would have to let it make do somehow.

She let herself out of the vehicle, slipped on her coat, tugged her cap over her eyes, and closed the vehicle's driver's door. Then she walked across the drive. Just as she reached the four shallow stairs that led to the entry, the light from the lightstone lanterns faded, leaving only the dirty, shadowy gaslight.

Her nerves jumped just a bit, and she embraced that. She never got so nervous that she startled at everything, but a small case of nerves would make her a little more vigilant.

The doors looked even bigger up close. They weren't ornate, the way that the doors at the Kirilli manor had been. Those entry doors had been beautiful, carved from some kind of wood from one of Gussie's grandfather's trips.

These doors were flat. The only edges they had were there to cover the weights inside that made them easier to pull.

Even the door knocker was plain. It was a simple ring over a metal plate. On close inspection, it became clear that the knocker was also made of iron.

She glanced at the hinges on the door. Iron. The door handle was iron.

She found that curious. The estate was old, and so, clearly, was the door. The iron trim spoke of some kind of history with the magical—and not good history either.

With her gloved hand, she grabbed the ring and pounded it against the plate. There was the expected bang, followed by a boom that echoed around her. She thought for a moment that she saw sparks flare off the plate.

Someone had added some kind of gong to the door knocker itself, so that sound would reverberate throughout the estate. She had seen that before, but never in Qavner. It was a design that came from one of the northern countries.

She waited and was about to knock again when she heard locks slide back. Then a bang as something was removed.

The door opened inward, revealing little more than some gloom. The faint scent of cloves tickled her nose.

A man leaned out. He was wearing a black suit with a white shirt. His hair was as white as the shirt, but combed back. His face, illuminated by the wavy gaslight, had sunken cheeks and sunken eyes.

He didn't speak, which was a bit of a surprise. She had

expected him to inform her that she was not wanted here, just like the man at the gate had done.

"I'm Lucinda Barkson," she said. "I'm here on an urgent mission. Augusta Kirilli needed me to deliver two letters in person to her sister Filippa."

The man at the door extended a hand, this one covered with a white glove, as if he expected Barkson to set the letters on his palm, just like the man at the gate had done.

"I must deliver the letters in person, and I must watch her read them," Barkson said.

"I will see to it—"

"No," Barkson said. "You will not. There's been a terrible tragedy, and I need to make sure that Filippa understands—"

"Mistress Netuno *will* understand—"

"I will speak to her." Barkson put her own gloved hand on the door and shoved it inward as hard as she could. "You will take me to her."

"I'm not allowed to take uninvited guests to Mistress Netuno," he said.

Barkson could fight this or she could suffer through some protocol.

"Who are you allowed to take uninvited guests to?" she asked, suspecting she knew the answer.

"Master Netuno will see some guests, if I announce them," the man said primly.

"You will take me to him," Barkson said.

The man put his hands on the side of the door, as if he was going to wrestle it closed.

"You will wait here," he said.

"No," she said. "I will not."

She had good leverage on the door. She had learned, over the years, that the best exterior doors opened outward. Whoever had built this place hadn't known that rule.

She could get inside quicker this way, and she did, using her full body weight to shove the door open all the way.

"Miss," the man said, as if he disapproved of her. He probably did.

She stepped inside the entry. It was large. The floor was covered with flagstones. Two tables on either side of the large room had candles burning all along their length, which was where the cloying scent of cloves was coming from.

"You will take me to Mr. Netuno immediately," she said. "Every moment you waste puts the entire family in danger."

"You will wait here," he said, "and I will get—"

"For the love of..." she said, "I'll find him myself."

She pushed past the man into the gloom. This part of the estate was poorly lit. The candlelight wasn't warm and soothing. Instead, it enhanced the dark stone walls and made them look filthy.

As she followed the flagstone down the corridor, the smell of cloves receded, replaced by the smell of mildew.

The man caught up to her, walking beside her.

"This isn't proper," he said.

"Nothing about this situation is proper," she said. "It would be easier for all of us if you just take me to—"

"Lucinda?" A rather plumy voice spoke from the darkness to her right.

Barkson stopped and turned, privately appalled that she hadn't even realized there was a hallway beside her. She was usually good at seeing things, even in the dark, but this estate

22

was lit by filthy gaslight lamps, and the light they gave off was gloomy and brownish.

A woman stood there, hands clutched in front of her as if she had been the one startled. She wore a long dress of a dark color impossible to determine in this awful light. Her hair was up in a bun.

"Filippa?" Barkson asked, even though she knew the answer. Gussie was the only one who could call her Lucinda, but an entire school full of girls who were now women also knew Barkson by that name.

"What are you doing here?" Filippa stepped into the wider corridor. As she stepped into the light, her dress reveled itself to be a wine red, which made her hair look brown by comparison, and gave a sallow yellow color to her skin.

"I have a message for you from Gussie," Barkson said. "Is there somewhere we can talk in private?"

"Yes," Filippa said. "You're dismissed, Woodridge."

The man nodded and started to walk away, but Barkson caught his arm.

"Please bring Mr. Netuno to us," she said. "He'll need to hear this."

Woodridge looked at Filippa, as if waiting for her to approve the order.

"This is serious, then," Filippa said to Barkson.

"Quite," Barkson said.

"Do as she asks, Woodridge," Filippa said. Then, without a second glance at him, she said to Barkson, "Come with me."

Barkson turned and headed into a deeper gloom. What she had taken for a hall was an open door leading into a dark room.

Lamps sat on two different tables on opposite ends, their light flickering.

Judging by the smell, these were kerosene lamps. Barkson had lived in Trinovante so long that being in a home without any lightstone lamps on the walls seemed old-fashioned and odd.

The lanterns made Barkson nervous. If anything knocked them off their perches, the lamps would start a fire.

That was why Trinovante insisted on homes being furnished with lightstone lamps. Lightstone was named for its internal light, which could become quite intense.

But lightstone was just that—stone. It never got hot. The light was cool to the touch, so fires did not happen within the city limits.

This place had stone walls, but that was probably all that would save it from ruin should a fire start.

Filippa walked through the room, and pushed open two more doors.

"Even though it's not appropriate," she said, "we'll use the morning room. No one will disturb us here."

Filippa stepped inside. Two lanterns burned here as well, which was apparently the norm for rooms not being used.

Filippa walked to a wall covered in curtains and pushed them back, revealing large windows that overlooked that manicured lawn. On the horizon, a half-full moon rose, its pale light touching the mounds that made the lawn look like it was flowing river.

Filippa reached up and turned the jets on a gas lamp attached to the wall. She walked around the room, lighting four more gas lamps.

"Woodbridge will be here shortly to light a fire," Filippa said. "He'll bring refreshments."

"I'm afraid I don't have that kind of time," Barkson said. "I need to keep traveling. I have to talk with all of your siblings as soon as possible."

Filippa turned, hands clasped again. She wore rings on both hands, with more jewels than Barkson had ever seen in one place.

"Is it Father, then?" Filippa asked.

"I think you should sit down," Barkson said. "I have two letters for you from Gussie. After you read them, I'll answer any question you might have."

Filippa frowned at her. Filippa's frowns were prodigious things. They always had a tinge of anger, which had been missing from the interaction thus far.

Then Filippa extended her hand, becoming the third person in just a few minutes to want those letters.

This time, Barkson handed one out. Not both. Gussie had given her strict instructions on that. Only one at a time.

Filippa took the envelope gingerly between her bejeweled fingers and looked at the front. Gussie's handwriting was lavish and easily recognizable.

Filippa's frown changed from something directed at Barkson to one that revealed a bit of fear and worry.

Filippa took the letter to a chair near the window, and picked up one of the still-burning kerosene lanterns, setting it on a nearby table. Then she sat down heavily, staring at the envelope as if it was about to attack her.

In some ways, it was.

Barkson turned her back on Filippa and peered at the fireplace. A fire had been laid in anticipation of the next use. All Barkson had to do was find the matches, so that she could light the paper under the wood.

She stood, glancing sideways at Filippa. She was still holding the envelope, her hands shaking.

Barkson wanted to remind Filippa that time was of the essence, but she didn't. Clearly Filippa understood that something was very, very wrong, and was afraid to face it.

Barkson glanced at the top of mantel and saw a small box. She took it, opened it, and found stick matches. She took one and struck it with her thumbnail, then crouched and lit the paper beneath the wood.

The paper sprang to life, igniting the wood quickly.

She put the grate in front of the fireplace and turned, expecting Filippa to chastise her for doing work better left to the staff.

But Filippa was staring at the letter, big fat tears running down her face and dripping off her chin. She held both pages in her hands, and was comparing across.

When she realized that Barkson was looking at her, Filippa said, "Is this true?"

"Yes," Barkson said. She had decided on the drive here that she would not tell anyone that she hadn't seen Augustus Kirilli's body.

A door banged behind them. Woodridge entered with a frown of his own. It grew deeper as he realized that he hadn't set the fire in the fireplace.

He looked at Barkson as if she had sinned.

Behind him, a slender man with a pleasant face stepped into

the room. For a moment, Barkson thought he was another member of the staff until he scurried toward Filippa.

"Darling," he said, "what's wrong?"

She handed him the letter. He moved closer to the light, bowing his head. His brown hair was thinning at the top. His hands shook as he read.

When he finished, he looked up at Barkson.

"You must be this Lucinda person," he said coldly.

So much for pleasantness behind the face.

"She is, Nigel," Filippa said quickly, as if anticipating a tirade. "We went to school together."

"How do we know this is true?" Nigel Netuno asked.

"That's Gussie's handwriting," Filippa said. Her voice was thick with tears.

"We should have received notification from the city of Trinovante," he said.

"I'm sure you will," Barkson said. "I'm ahead of them, at Gussie's request."

Nigel's lower lip curled. "There are procedures to handle such things," he said. "I have no idea why Augusta would go outside of them."

Barkson blinked, startled. Despite his appearance, this man was some kind of domestic despot. No wonder Filippa seemed subdued.

Barkson made herself take a breath and recalibrate. She had dealt with small-time bullies before.

She handed the second letter to Filippa. Nigel tried to grab it, but Barkson wouldn't let him.

"These are intended for your wife," Barkson said. "She will share if she needs to."

Filippa gave her a watery look, but Barkson wasn't sure Filippa was seeing anything.

This time, Filippa opened the envelope quickly. With her head bowed, she read.

"What is this nonsense?" Nigel asked Barkson, as if she had invented all of this as some kind of distraction.

And with that question, Barkson had had enough.

"She just received word that her father is dead," Barkson said. "You could show some compassion."

Nigel glared at her. "Her father has always been a difficult man."

"I'll wager he was, from your point of view," Barkson said calmly. "He didn't want his daughter to marry you, did he?"

Nigel tilted his head a little. "We're a good match. She's from one of the oldest families in Qavner and my family—"

"Has had a tidy little fiefdom on the edge of a big city, unable to cross into the seats of power for the entire country," Barkson said, matching his curt tone. "That's a good marriage from your point of view. Not so good from the perspective of a member of one of Qavner's Old Families."

A flush darkened Nigel's face. Barkson knew, with that look, that her interpretation was the correct one.

She probably should have stopped there, but she couldn't, not while Filippa continued to read.

"I'll wager," Barkson said, "that you thought the match would give you entry. That's not how power works in this country. Too bad you didn't know it."

Nigel clenched his right hand into a fist, crumpling part of the letter. "You don't know who you're talking to."

28

"You have that wrong," Barkson said. "I don't *care* about my conversation with you. I came here to speak to Filippa."

Barkson wished she had never asked for him to join them.

Filippa lifted her head. Her hand was shaking.

She looked directly at Barkson.

"Do you believe her?" Filippa asked, clearly speaking to Barkson about Gussie.

"Yes," Barkson said again. "She's not staying at her home at the moment. She sent her staff away until this gets settled."

"Well, that's ridiculous," Nigel said. "It's an overreaction—"

"Perhaps you didn't understand the letter that you're holding," Barkson said. "Augustus Kirilli *and his entire staff* have been killed, the Kirilli manor the subject of a violent attack. Gussie believes, and I concur, that someone is targeting Kirillis. If you don't take this seriously, you will lose your wife and your children, not to mention anyone who is in the same building with them when the attack occurs."

Nigel frowned at Barkson, as if she had been the one planning an attack on his family.

"Tell me who would do this," he said. "We're a civilized country, and this sort of thing—"

"I don't know yet who did this," Barkson said. "I left before the perpetrators were found. Gussie was afraid that you might be in danger, and considering what's going on, I agreed. That's why I'm here."

Filippa took the letter she was holding, folded it, and put it into a pocket of her skirt. Her face had fallen into lines familiar to Barkson from their girlhood. *This* was the Filippa that Barkson knew, not the somewhat meek woman of a few moments before.

"I'd like my letter back," she said to her husband.

He looked at her as if he had never seen her before.

"Sit down, Filippa," he said. "This woman wants you to overreact. I have no idea what her agenda is—"

"My agenda," Barkson said tightly, "is saving your family."

He glared at her.

"My letter," Filippa said, palm out.

He started to crumple it further, but Barkson took a step forward and grabbed his hand. She held it awkwardly, her thumb underneath his, bending it sideways.

If she bent it too far, it would snap.

He cried out in pain, and tried to pull away. Her grip tightened.

"The letter," Barkson said.

He released it like a child would, letting it fall rather than handing it to anyone.

Woodridge stepped forward and grabbed the letter. He stepped around Nigel and Barkson and handed the letter to Filippa.

She gave him a watery smile.

"Thank you, Woodridge," she said, then cleared her throat. "We're going to take my sister's advice. We're going to clear the estate until she says we're safe."

Filippa was speaking directly to Woodridge, ignoring her husband.

"Wake the nanny," Filippa said. "We'll get the children out of here. You will handle the staff. They need to return to their homes until this passes."

"Some of them live on the grounds, ma'am," he said.

"And they will have to stay with their families offsite. They need to let us know where," Filippa said.

"Fil, you're overreacting," Nigel said.

It would take just the flick of Barkson's thumb to break his. Just a flick. She was tempted.

"Then stay here, Nigel," Filippa said. "The staff will not stay. I will not allow it."

"They're my staff," he said.

"You gave me full authority over them," she said. "They're going to leave."

They stared at each other as if they were alone in the room. Nigel's hand was shaking in Barkson's. She didn't know if that was from whatever emotion he was feeling or if it was from the pain she had not stopped inflicting.

"You have nowhere to take the children," Nigel said. "If you believe this rot, then you can't take them to any of your family's properties."

"I know." Filippa's voice was dry. "I think it would be best if I don't tell you where they're going."

She let her flat gaze fall on Barkson.

"Either break his fingers or let him go," Filippa said. "I don't care which."

Barkson let go, surprised at the change in Filippa. Maybe she had needed permission to do this. Or maybe she had been waiting for a moment that would change everything.

Or maybe the letters had revived the old Filippa, the one who knew how to take charge.

Nigel grabbed his hand, and glared at Barkson. "You didn't have to do that."

"Be glad I didn't do more," she said. "You're being an idiot."

31

He sucked in air, and that sound told her that no one had ever spoken to him that way before, not even the wife who was starting to grow a spine.

He turned to Filippa. "We'll go to my parents," he said. "They have a large home—"

"No," Filippa said. "You will do whatever you need to. I'm taking the children elsewhere."

"Let me know where that is," Barkson said. "I will be the one to contact you when the threat is over."

Filippa stared at her for a long moment, then said, "Why are you doing this, Lucinda? You're not exactly known for your generosity."

Maybe that was why they had never gotten along. They saw each other a bit too clearly.

"I don't consider this generosity," Barkson said. "Something bad is happening, and I'm in a position to stop some possible..."

She almost said "carnage," but she was discussing Filippa's family.

"Something worse from happening," Barkson said.

Filippa nodded. She took the first letter, and folded it like she had folded the second, placing it in her pocket as well.

Then she looked at her husband. He clutched his hand to his chest, his skin a mottled gray now from pain and anger. Barkson might have broken a small bone in his hand.

Filippa said nothing to him, though. Instead, she looked back at Barkson.

"Before the staff leaves, I will have them give you some supplies. Knowing you, you haven't brought enough food."

That was true. She hadn't thought much about food.

"Woodridge, would you see to Lucinda's needs?" Filippa said.

"That's not necessary," Barkson said. "Time is of the essence here."

Filippa blinked, then nodded. "You're in your windstone vehicle, aren't you? That's part of the reason you agreed to this."

"Yes," Barkson said.

"All right, then." Filippa looked at her husband a third time. "Nigel, please leave. You're not going to be useful here."

His eyes narrowed. "I think it's hard to be useful when people insist on overreacting to everything."

He pivoted and stalked out of the room, pretending at a dignity that he had clearly lost.

Filippa watched him go. Then she closed her eyes for a second, as if she was trying to gather strength.

"Woodridge, please talk to the staff," she said, clearly dismissing him.

He nodded. "Would you like the nanny sent here?"

"Yes," Filippa said, then shook her head. "No. I'll go to the nursery myself. I need to oversee everything.

"The sooner you leave," Barkson said, "the better off you'll be."

"I realize that, Lucinda," Filippa said.

Woodridge looked at both of them, as if he was waiting for one of them to instruct him on something else. When no one did, he left.

Filippa let out a small breath. "I don't want anyone to know where we're going. I'll bring the nanny along and the cook, but no one else."

"You're not going to go somewhere connected with your family, are you?" Barkson asked.

"You've made it clear that such a thing would not be wise," Filippa said. "There's a house on the coast where we went during our Academy days. Did you ever come?"

"No," Barkson said, not willing to add that she was never invited to trips that included girls like Filippa. Besides, by the time they had graduated from Bekyce and moved to Serebro Academy, they ran in completely different circles.

"It's an ironwood house. No one knows exactly how it was built, but it's the sturdiest thing I've ever seen," Filippa said.

A strand of hair fell from the tight bun on the top of her head. Filippa tried to tuck the strand behind her ear, but failed because her hand was shaking.

Barkson wasn't sure she liked this idea. A rental would require paperwork. Even though she doubted anyone targeting the Kirillis was monitoring everything, Barkson couldn't rule that out.

Particularly with magic involved.

"Who owns the property?" Barkson asked.

Filippa leaned forward, hands clasped.

"An old wise woman left it to me," she said quietly.

Barkson let out an audible sigh. She had told Filippa—

"And before you say anything," Filippa said, "it's not listed as a Kirilli property. Nor does it use my married name."

"Then how is it registered?" Barkson asked.

"It isn't. It never was. I'd been meaning to register it, but..." She shot a nervous glance at the door, then her gaze met Barkson's. "I never told Nigel about it."

Barkson leaned back slightly. Filippa had been planning an escape from Nigel for some time.

"Do you need help getting away from him?" Barkson asked, her tone changing. She had done this for women several times. She just never talked about it.

Filippa sighed shakily. "I'd like you to stay until he leaves or we do. I realize that keeps you from getting to the rest of the family, and if you don't want to..."

Her voice trailed off. Her marriage must have been a nightmare to change the powerful young woman that Barkson had known into this uncertain creature.

"I'll stay," Barkson said. "I promised Gussie I'd keep you safe. I will do that."

"Thank you." Filippa blinked back tears. "Thank you so much."

My dearest G,

As of late this evening, F. and the children have left their abode, in the company of a few members of the staff. I will not say more here, except to assure you that, at F's request, I waited until all was well before departing the area.

Once I hear from you that all is well, I will alert them, as we discussed.

Your not-so-humble servant,

L.

CHAPTER

THREE

Barkson stood in the shadows near the postal building in what passed for downtown Isara. Isara was smaller than she had realized. In addition to the pubs, it had two markets, some business buildings, and houses that lined the small hill where someone long ago had decided to place the village.

The layout of the streets suggested that once upon a time, Isara had been a larger community, but someone—and she would guess that that someone had the last name Netuno—had torn down buildings and taken over land once devoted to housing.

If Barkson was the curious type (and about these things, she was not, unless she was being paid to be curious), she would have investigated whether the villagers were forced to leave their homes, or whether they had already left when the homes were torn down.

If she was a betting woman (and she was not), she would have placed money on the idea that they had been forced.

The postal building was clearly marked with the seal of the Protectorate—a blue shield with gold trim, and the words *For the Safety of All* in ornate Old Qavnerian. A flickering light in the upper story meant that this postal building was of the original design and had never been upgraded.

Early postal buildings, constructed in countries that were new to the Protectorate, always kept their staff onsite. In those years, the postal buildings were occasionally attacked, as representatives of the Protectorate.

Such things rarely happened anymore, but the old buildings remained, and apparently, in some small venues, like this one, they still served a purpose.

Barkson wouldn't have to give the short letter she had written to Gussie directly to the postal employee. There was a mail slot in the door, high enough off the ground that no one could reach in and pull the letter back out.

There was also a big red sign that informed everyone in big black letters that stealing mail from the Qavnerian Protectorate was a serious crime.

Barkson was waiting to see if anyone had followed her from the Netuno estate. She had been the last to leave, despite her best intentions.

And, ironically, Nigel had been the first. He had taken the best carriage (of course) and four horses, and he had fled with his driver, which Filippa had said was for the best.

I never trusted that man anyway, she had said of the driver. *I think Nigel employed him to spy on us.*

The rest of the family left next, three little girls, all under the age of ten, blinking in the half-light of the slowly emptying estate. The nanny was younger than Barkson would have expected, but seemed competent enough. Three other members of the staff, who had no family to speak of, had decided to travel with Filippa.

Filippa claimed she trusted them, and the driver she had chosen.

They left in a less ostentatious carriage which, Barkson had to concede, was also probably for the best.

The rest of the staff scurried around, shutting down the estate, taking their own belongings, and giving Barkson a sideways glance as they went about their business.

Woodridge had stayed to make sure everything was taken care of properly. Barkson had the sense that, until she had talked with him, he had planned to stay at the estate all by himself, to make sure it was maintained.

Then she had told him what, exactly, had happened to the Kirilli staff.

Woodridge had left last, on his own horse, looking a bit lost.

Barkson had driven toward the village, then pulled over to write the short missive. She wanted to talk with Gussie, to ask if Gussie knew how difficult her sister's marriage was, what a terrible person Nigel had turned out to be, but there was no time for that.

Barkson did feel uncomfortable, being the only person who knew where Filippa had taken the children—until she realized that if no one ever informed Filippa that she was safe to return, Filippa's heart would not be broken.

Barkson had finished the letter, placed it in an envelope,

addressed it, and affixed her own seal on the upper corner, so that the letter would be charged to her postal account.

That was the only flaw in this entire journey—she would be leaving a trail of letters and postal charges. But it would take some time for a savvy investigator to think of examining any of that—and she didn't think that whoever attacked the Kirilli estate had been savvy or subtle.

By the time someone figured this all out, Barkson would be at a new and different location.

Unless she was followed.

Which was why she was standing here, in the dark, as rain began to fall. The rain was slight enough to be annoying. She wasn't going to get wet quickly, but she was going to get wet.

Her vehicle was conspicuous. That was the only problem with it. Not many people had windstone vehicles, particularly outside of Trinovante. She would be remembered.

She could do nothing about that.

But she could make certain that no one followed her from location to location.

Of course, they would need their own windstone vehicle for that.

No one had come by this rather sad building for the past fifteen minutes.

She had waited long enough.

She needed to get to the next stop. It would take another two hours at minimum to get there. She didn't like the idea of arriving anywhere before dawn, but she had no real choice.

She shook the beaded water off herself the way that a dog would when it came in out of the rain.

Then she stepped out of the shadows, and glanced around one final time.

What a miserable little place. She couldn't understand why Filippa had ever thought she could build a life here.

But she had, and it had been ugly.

Barkson hoped that Filippa's new life would be better.

If she survived.

If all of the Kirillis survived, which, at this moment, Barkson still wasn't sure would happen.

CHAPTER
FOUR

It was the darkest part of the night by the time Barkson arrived at Helia's Tower. She had thought Helia's Tower was the name of an estate, like the estate where she had found Filippa.

Instead, Helia's Tower was an actual tower, rising against the night sky. The tower was taller than anything Barkson had seen in Trinovante, taller even than the clock tower at Serebro Academy.

The rain had cleared up about an hour outside of Isara, and clouds floated across the half-full moon. Its light was stronger than Barkson expected, even now, as it was working its way down the western sky.

The moonlight fell across the road, which was no longer carved into the hills. Instead, the road rose with the hills, and there were more of them than Barkson expected. She had never really noticed the terrain going north when she drove in the daylight, but at night, the terrain was quite treacherous.

At least this part of the road was maintained, unlike the road to the Netuno estate. But then again, this was the main north–south thoroughfare.

Right now, her vehicle was the only one on the road, but by dawn, Barkson suspected, the road would be littered with carts and carriages and horses and walkers heading to various parts of the countryside.

The next stop past Helia's Tower was an actual town named Bonna. The road wound its way down to Bonna, which was on the banks of the Hidden River.

Barkson had actually been to Bonna and thought it a pretty little place. But she knew from Gussie's map that if Barkson arrived in Bonna, she had missed the tower completely.

When Barkson had first seen the map, she worried that she wouldn't be able to find the tower, particularly if she got there after dark.

But now she wasn't worried at all. The tower rose like a spire against the night sky. She suspected even if there had been no moon, she still would have seen the spire, jutting up toward the clouds.

It reminded her of something. As she got closer, she realized what that something was: It was the replica of Mount Vitaki at the Mazurka Museum.

The Bekyce School took the twelve-year-olds to the town of Mazurkita and its museum every year, apparently believing that was the point they could most appreciate dioramas, and the point at which they were most susceptible to learning about the size of the Qavnerian Protectorate without asking all of those uncomfortable questions that would come up later on, such as why would Qavner feel it necessary to fold already-existing countries into something called "a Protectorate" and even if such an action was necessary, why did Qavner feel it necessary to install their own government over and above the local one.

Barkson was staring so hard at the tower, that she almost missed the little curl of road that veered off to her right. Gussie had warned her about that road, said that it would be hard to see because it had been designed to be hard to notice.

Barkson had to yank on the steering sticks hard. The tires of the vehicle squealed as it made a ninety-degree turn at a speed designed for cruising not turning.

It took all of her strength to keep from spinning out. The squealing tires made her wince.

She had one extra tire, but if she had to replace more, then she would be facing at least a day in Bonna while she waited for the correct tires to arrive.

She expected this little road to be as bumpy and chopped up as the road to the Netuno estate; instead, this road was smooth, as if something like a grater ran over it, making sure that it remained flat.

She had never been on an unpaved road this smooth. It made her uncomfortable.

The closer she got to the tower, the more its height became apparent. But its width startled her. Its base wasn't much bigger than that of an average house.

The tower was square, even though that had been hard to see in the darkness, and it narrowed the farther up it went. It ended in a point.

The road changed about a half mile out. It was now covered in gravel, which was slippery at the speed she was going. She had to slow down without using her brakes.

Tire marks along the side of the road, visible in the light from the lightstone lanterns made it clear that other vehicles had hit the gravel going much too fast, and had toppled off the side of the road.

That was the point Barkson realized the road was elevated. Not that much—maybe four feet or so off the regular ground—but enough to do damage to anyone driving recklessly toward the tower.

She had the feeling if she looked in daylight, she would see parts of carriages and carts and windstone vehicles littering the roadside.

That rise was more effective than a fence at preventing anyone from traveling off the little sliver of road.

She had to watch the road, since it wound everywhere. She couldn't look up at the tower until she reached a circular drive. The drive was also gravel and as the lightstone lamps swept it, she realized six different vehicles were parked around its edges.

All of the vehicles were windstone vehicles of different makes and models. They also came from different eras. One was relatively new—albeit not as new as the vehicle that Barkson was driving. Two were models that Barkson had owned before this one.

Two more were old enough to be considered obsolete, and then, near the edge of the tower, was the first incarnation of the windstone vehicle, with its flat cart-like body, small wheels and gigantic driving sticks.

The original vehicles had been designed along the same lines as windstone gliders, only without the wings, and tilted upward as if they were going to take off at any moment.

Barkson had driven one on a lark, just once, and found the

vehicle difficult to control. It seemed to want to float, even though it was too bulky for that. The front tires never really did seem to be firmly on the road.

She pulled up on the other side of the circular drive, away from the six windstone vehicles. She also parked her vehicle so that its headlamps faced the road rather than the building.

It was a modicum of caution that she had learned about the hard way. More than once, she had had to race into her vehicle to get away from something or someone. Having to turn around cost time and effort.

She had no idea why she was worried about that sort of thing here, but she was.

The entire tower made her nervous, perhaps because it was not what she had expected.

She reached into the back of the vehicle, popped the compartment with the letters and removed the two for Helia. Barkson stuck them into her coat, which she had not removed since she left Filippa's. The night had gotten cold, and there was no way to easily heat the interior of the windstone vehicle.

Plus, Barkson had been driving at a speed that made the internal chill worse. She was grateful she had brought two pairs of gloves and a second cap, in case she lost the first. This trip was going to be harder on her than she thought.

She took her weapons this time. She hadn't needed them at Filippa's, although who knew what would have happened if Nigel had decided to prevent his family from leaving.

This place was much more isolated. It made Barkson feel unsettled, and she had learned long ago that her instincts were worth trusting.

She got out of the vehicle, gently closing the door behind herself, and looked up at the tower.

She couldn't see the tower's top. She wasn't sure how many stories she could see, because she wasn't sure if the black squares she was looking at on the upper half of the building were decoration or windows of some sort.

Lower down, it was clear. There was at least one window on every floor.

And farther down than that, she noted that the first five windows had lights on.

She didn't remember seeing that many lights on as she drove up to the tower. Someone clearly knew she was on the property.

She headed to the door, her boots crunching on the gravel.

The door was an arch, carved into the bricks that formed the tower. The bricks were an unusual grayish-green color, which made her think of ironwood.

Barkson resisted the urge to touch the bricks. Instead, she inspected the door, which appeared to be made out of the same wood as the door on the Kirilli manor. The door even had some of the same carvings—bas-relief heads and torsos, only here they were smaller.

A chill ran down Barkson's spine. If someone didn't like these designs in Trinovante, that someone would hate the same designs here.

She reached up for the door knocker carved at eye level. It had the Kirilli family crest carved underneath the actual knocker. A broadsword rose from the bottom of the design, with a heart floating above it. Over the top of that, a crown glinted in the light.

50

Some slogan in Old Qavnerian glowed just like the crown, but she didn't have time to translate it.

She pounded the knocker against the wood three times. A boom echoed throughout the lower level of the tower.

"Coming!" a female voice shouted from above. "Didn't you see the lights?"

The blame in those sentences caught Barkson by surprise. She heard some banging, and then a loud resounding curse, followed by a clatter. The door shuddered as locks clicked back, and finally the door swung open, nearly hitting Barkson.

She had to move to get out of the way.

A slight figure stood in the blazing light coming from the interior of the tower. All of that light came from lightstone lamps, and those lamps had clearly been lit for a while. Lightstone lamps got brighter the longer they were operating. Sometimes, Barkson thought, they could get as light as a hot sun at midday.

The figure had short, cropped hair and wore pants and a long coat. But Barkson couldn't discern any more because the light behind the figure put the face in darkness.

"My goodness, Lucy, what are you doing, lurking in the middle of the night?"

Lucy? Barkson felt a jolt. She had forgotten that Helia used to call her Lucy because she felt that Lucinda was too prim and proper.

"Helia?" Barkson asked.

"Of course," the figure said, then turned as she swept a hand toward the interior. "Get in here. It's cold."

As the figure turned, the light hit her face. It was indeed Helia Kirilli. Her face was a bit longer than it had been when she was a girl, and it had a few frown lines, but that was to be expected.

Helia was the strongest personality that Barkson had met in a family filled with strong personalities. Helia had always carved her own path, partly because the family never really saw her as anything but the baby—and a rather difficult baby at that.

Barkson stepped inside the tower, and out of the way of the door. The interior smelled damp, the kind of damp that came from an active water leak, not longtime mold and mildew.

The entry was haphazard, as if it had once been a living area. Several large oak chairs with the Kirilli crest carved into the back and arms were pushed against the wall. A table that had more carvings stood to the right. A lightstone lantern stood on top of it, but that lantern wasn't on.

All of the light came from the lamps affixed to what was clearly a brick wall. Inside the resemblance to ironwood was gone. Now the brick looked like it had been made from the mud near the banks of the Hidden River.

"What is this place?" Barkson asked.

"My home," Helia said. "Be nice."

"Where's the staff?" Barkson asked.

"I fired them all. They talked too much, and I hated all their stupid questions." Then Helia peered at Barkson. "Don't tell my father."

No chance of that, Barkson nearly said.

"You're here because of him, aren't you?" Helia asked. "I've been thinking about him for the last three days. It's almost like he's been standing beside me, helping me work, which is something he would never ever ever do."

Barkson let out a small breath. "Is there somewhere we can go to sit down? I've been driving all night."

That wasn't entirely true, but it was true enough. Besides, Barkson was hungry for the first time since she'd embarked on this trip. She had forgotten to get food at Filippa's.

"Oh, yeah," Helia said. "Manners. I haven't thought about them for a century. I didn't do well in comportment, manners, and rhetoric in school."

Barkson might have known that once upon a time. Filippa used to complain that she would have to monitor Helia when Helia arrived at Bekyce, because Helia never managed the niceties.

"Just a place to sit would be good," Barkson said.

"Well, we have to go upstairs for that," Helia said. She went to the front door, replaced a gigantic bar (also covered with Kirilli crest carvings) and then turned maybe a dozen locks.

Several of the locks had their base on the backside of the door, and arched around the bar itself, holding it in place.

It was a strange way to protect the entry, but it would work, at least in the short-term.

Until someone destroyed the door itself.

Helia tapped Barkson on the shoulder. "This way."

Helia led her to the side of the room, past a small wall, also made of Hidden River brick. A narrow staircase, well-lit with lightstone lamps, wound its way up.

Helia went first. Barkson followed, feeling the weight of the day with each step. The staircase turned only once, leading to the next floor. But Helia didn't stop. She walked across flag-stones and started up another flight, and then another, and another.

Barkson was just about to ask how far they had to keep going when Helia stopped.

"Kitchen," she said, which surprised Barkson. In every building Barkson had ever been in, the kitchen was on the lowest level.

This one looked like no kitchen she had ever seen before. Sure, it had a long wooden table in the middle and more of those oak chairs, but around the table were counters covered with breadboxes, loose knives, piles of silverware, and leaning towers of dishes.

A cast-iron stove, with a fire burning in its center, was against one wall, near an actual fireplace. They probably shared a chimney that must have gone up on the outside of the tower.

Closer to the stairs, an icebox stood behind another stone wall, protecting it from the kitchen's warmth.

Helia opened the icebox. "I can heat up some stew that I had for dinner."

Given the haphazard look of the surfaces inside this kitchen, Barkson didn't want anything that had been cooked here. But her hunger was hard to hide, given that her stomach had growled three times on the climb up.

"Just some cheese and bread would be fine," Barkson said. "Or fruit or carrots."

"All right," Helia said.

She took the top plate off the leaning tower and pulled a towel from another pile that Barkson hadn't seen until that moment. She wiped off the plate (Barkson was hoping that was just for good measure) and set it on the table. Then Helia pulled a cheese plate from behind the mound of silverware. The cheese plate, mercifully, had been covered.

Bits of various cheeses from all over the area were scattered on the plate. It looked like Helia had been snacking on them for a while, which didn't really bother Barkson. It was, perhaps, the first thing so far that hadn't bothered her about this kitchen.

Helia found some rye bread to go with the cheese, and poured some warm mead from a pot over the fire into a mug.

The mead smelled good, but Barkson knew better than to drink it right away. It would be too hot.

"Sit," Helia said, wiping off the seat of the nearest chair.

Barkson did not make a face, although she wanted to. Instead she said, "Thank you."

Helia sat beside her, grabbed the bread, and broke a hunk off.

"So, Lucy," Helia said, "I don't talk to you for maybe ten years, and now you're here? It's important, right? What does my father want?"

She sounded so eager, as if she had been waiting her entire life for her father to want something from her.

And given Augustus Kirilli's relationships with his children, that just might have been the case. He had stopped paying close attention to his children once he realized that Gussie would be able to help him with his various businesses.

Barkson looked longingly at the food. She wouldn't have long with it, before she had to deal with whatever Helia's reaction was going to be to the news.

"Gussie gave me two letters for you," Barkson said. "I'm to give you this one first."

She reached into the pocket of her coat and pulled out a single envelope. Fortunately, it was the correct one.

"Well, that's mysterious," Helia said with a bit of a smile.

Her eyes had tilted down in disappointment, though. Apparently, she really had wanted to hear from her father. "Maybe you can tell me what's in it?"

"No, I cannot," Barkson said.

Helia sighed and rolled her eyes. She set the envelope on the table. "I hate Gussie's rules."

"There's a method to it," Barkson said. "Please, just read the letter."

Helia pushed it aside and leaned on one elbow, looking at Barkson. "You know, I never get visitors here. My family—*my* family thinks what I do is strange. My father gave me this place after I graduated, because, he said, I reminded him of some great-aunt. Do you know how many artifacts there are here? I mean, the Thaumaturgical and Alchemical Departments at Serebro would kill to have—"

"Helia," Barkson said. "Please. Read the letter. I have to get on the road soon, and I can't until you've read the letters."

And we've gotten you out of here, Barkson wanted to add. The news about the artifacts almost made her shiver. Gussie had repeated over and over again that most of the destruction in the Kirilli manor had been the items that were brought back from various trips her grandparents had taken.

Barkson had seen those items on her few trips to the Kirilli manor. Those items had always sent ripples through her—ripples of some kind of latent power.

She didn't feel that here, but she might not have been close enough to the artifacts.

Helia's expression changed. She looked very serious.

"This is something bad, isn't it?" she asked quietly.

"Yes," Barkson said.

"Lucy, please. Just tell me."

"No," Barkson said. If it had been anyone else, she would have thought the person couldn't read. Now, she realized that Helia just didn't want to read the letters, either because Gussie had written them, or because part of Helia already knew something awful had happened.

"You are stubborn," Helia said, and stood up. She picked up the envelope, tapped it twice on the table, and took it with her toward the fire.

Barkson took that moment to break her own hunk of bread off the loaf. Then she cut small pieces of various cheese and placed them on the suspect plate. It had looked clean enough, she supposed. Besides, whatever was on it probably wouldn't hurt the cheese.

She ate quickly, looking down to give Helia some privacy. The food tasted better than she had hoped, the rye a little salty and tangy, the soft cheese she had chosen first the perfect accompaniment.

She ate enough that she trusted the mead, but made herself take only some small sips. It didn't have a high alcohol content, but high enough that combined with her tiredness might cause some kind of disaster.

She had seconds before she realized that Helia hadn't said anything. Barkson finally looked over at her.

Helia was leaning against the stone edge of the fireplace, clutching the letter, tears running down her face. She wasn't making a sound, nor was she wiping the tears away.

She finally realized that Barkson was looking at her.

"You said a second letter," Helia said, sounding calm, as if the tears weren't streaming down her face. "It better not be 'and ha-ha, this was all a joke.'"

"I'm sorry, no," Barkson said.

Helia closed her eyes and swallowed hard. Then, without looking, she folded the first letter and put it into a pocket that Barkson hadn't even realized was in the pants.

Barkson took the second envelope out of her coat. Helia finally opened her eyes.

The tears had stopped but her eyelashes were spiky and her face glistened in the light.

Barkson handed Helia the second envelope.

Instead of setting it aside, as she had with the first, Helia tore the end off the envelope and pulled a single sheet covered in writing out.

"You know what's here, right?" Helia asked as if all of this was Barkson's fault.

"I know what was in the first letter," Barkson said. "Not the second."

"So it could be a joke," Helia muttered in a tone that told Barkson that Helia knew no joke was forthcoming.

Helia tossed the envelope into the fire. The fire flared around it, leaving only the word *Helia* etched in smoke for just a moment.

Another shiver ran down Barkson's back. She had always known that the Kirillis had a powerful magic that they mostly ignored. She wondered if they knew how much of that magic they wasted on a daily basis.

Helia read the second letter, but didn't cry through the reading as she had through the first. Then she folded it and put it in the same pocket, which made the side of her pants jut out oddly.

"She wants me to leave here," Helia said. "To go somewhere away from Kirilli property as if that'll solve anything."

"Almost everything at the manor similar to things here," Barkson said quietly, "was destroyed around the time your father died."

Helia let out a breath. "I thought she was exaggerating the damage."

With the death of the staff? Didn't that sink in? Barkson wanted to ask, but didn't.

"No," Barkson said. "If anything, she's being restrained. It's Gussie."

Barkson didn't know that for certain, as she hadn't read these letters, but she had heard Gussie try to describe what she had seen as she was trying to figure out what exactly to write. Gussie always erred on the side of fewer details rather than more.

"She doesn't want me to take anything with me," Helia said. "I have a cat."

"I'm sure you can bring your cat," Barkson said. "If you have something to transport it in."

"Her," Helia said. "My cat is a her. Her name is Aldena. I can't leave her."

"Don't then," Barkson said, feeling just a bit annoyed.

"And my work. I can't leave my work. I'm doing several things at once. I'm designing..." Helia stopped and looked at Barkson. "I'm working."

"I know you majored in the History of Thaumaturgical and Alchemical Arts at Serebro," Barkson said. "You won't shock me."

Although this set up was a bit of a shock. She hadn't expected Helia to be alone.

"I have to bring them," Helia said.

"You don't have time," Barkson said. "*We* don't have time. I have to wait until you leave, and I still have everyone else to contact. Except Filippa. She was on the way."

"Filippa and *Nigel*, the raging idiot," Helia said. "She married him to make Father angry, you know that, right?"

Barkson didn't, and she didn't care.

"Helia, please. You need to pack a few things, find something to contain the cat, and leave."

"I have nowhere to go," Helia said. "Even if you weren't going to tell the rest of my family to get out of wherever they are, I can't go to them. They don't like me."

"I have money if you need that," Barkson said.

"I don't need money," Helia said as if she was shocked at the suggestion. Maybe she was. Maybe no one had thought her short of coin before.

She ran a hand over her hair. It fell around her face in uneven clumps, making Barkson realize for the first time, that Helia had cut her hair herself.

"I'll help you pack," Barkson said. She was feeling somewhat revived after the food.

"You're going to see Dilshad next, right?" Helia asked. "If you're going north, he's next, and that's good, because he's the only one of us with a great family. They're nice and to have them die like Papa..."

She choked, turned away, and gasped a sob. Then she squared her shoulders and turned back, new tears on her face.

"I can get you to him faster," Helia said.

"You need to take care of yourself," Barkson said.

"You need sleep," Helia said, "but if I drive, you can sleep, and we can be at Dilshad's by midday latest. Otherwise, it might be afternoon, and who knows what's on our tail."

Our tail. That shiver ran through Barkson again. She hated thinking about what might be coming after her.

She hoped she was right: that whatever it was had originated in Trinovante. Both Helia and Filippa lived in the countryside, and weren't that easy to find. But Dilshad worked for the Protectorate, and Emberto helped run the Forbidden Valley Antiquities Service.

They would be easy to find.

"Besides," Helia said into Barkson's silence. "I'm not going to be able to hide away knowing my family is in danger. I might be the only person who can help them. I'm clearly the only one not in denial about our abilities. Well, maybe one of two, but you know."

Barkson didn't know. She didn't know all of the Kirillis. She knew the Kirilli daughters because she'd gone to school with them. She had gotten to know Benedeto at Serebro Academy. But she had never met Emberto. She only knew what his job was because Gussie had told her.

And then there was Corrin. Barkson didn't want to think about Corrin. Not yet, anyway.

"You need me," Helia said.

It sounded like Helia needed Barkson too. She really didn't want to go anywhere with all of Helia's possessions and a caged cat, but she wanted to make sure she found the homes of the rest of the Kirillis.

Maybe Helia would make that easier.

"Can you leave the cat or find someone to care for her?" Barkson asked.

"No." Helia's voice was flat.

Barkson half expected her to plead or make promises about the cat, but Helia was silent after that refusal. If she hadn't been twisting her hands together, Barkson wouldn't have realized how very upset she was.

Barkson sighed. "Before I agree to anything, you have to promise a few things."

Helia nodded. "I'll do what it takes."

"First," Barkson said, ignoring that little outburst, "you'll listen to me."

"I'll listen unless you tell me to get rid of my cat," Helia said.

"Second," Barkson said, "I will be in charge of this journey. In all aspects. If I tell you to remain in the vehicle, you will. If I have to drop you at an inn in some small village, I will do that. You will spend several days alone in that instance."

Helia's lips thinned.

"*I* will impart the news, exactly as Gussie told me to. No telling your siblings anything until they read their letters." Barkson crossed her arms. "If you can't promise that, then you're not coming along. And if you break that promise, I will leave you at the nearest inn. Do you understand all of this?"

Helia nodded. "I promise," she said.

"All right then," Barkson said. "I will help you put things in my vehicle. That cat has to remain in its cage."

"Her cage," Helia said. Then she saw the look that Barkson gave her. "I promise. She'll stay in the cage."

"Let's gather a few things," Barkson said. "We can't take a lot."

Particularly with a cat cage in the back of my vehicle, she almost said. But she didn't. She had the odd sense that there was more to this cat than simple companionship.

The books of magic talked about special relationships between humans and animals, relationships that made the humans stronger and better at what they did.

Given Helia's interest in alchemy and thaumaturgy, and the fact that she lived alone in this somewhat creepy place, she might have imagined that this cat, this Aldena, made her stronger.

"Do we have to take your vehicle?" Helia asked, as if she already knew the answer.

Barkson wasn't going to indulge this kind of thing. Nothing was going to be up for debate.

So she turned the tables just a bit.

"I assumed you can drive a windstone vehicle," Barkson said. "Did I make a mistake?"

"No mistake," Helia said. "It's just I've modified one of mine. It will go faster than yours."

The last thing Barkson wanted was some vehicle that Helia thought she had improved and that she had actually sabotaged.

"We're taking mine," Barkson said. "In fact, we're going to proceed as if you and your cat were not in my vehicle at all. We're going to do what I want when I want and how I want. I thought we were already clear on that."

"I just figured—"

"If we are not clear, I will dr—"

"I know," Helia said, her shoulders sagging. "You'll drop me at the nearest inn."

She gave Barkson a thin smile.

"I know everyone says I'm a nuisance," Helia said. "I try too hard. I know I do. I'm just...different, that's all. I can be useful, really. I know things about things. Please. I can't be alone right now. You've already talked to Gussie and Filippa, and if Filippa's letters were like mine, then you can't tell me where they are, because they're in hiding."

Barkson allowed herself a small nod. She could give Helia that much.

"So that leaves me to go with you, to see Dilshad and Corrin and Emberto and Ghita and Deto." Helia sniffed, then wiped a hand over her face. Apparently tears were starting. "I promise. If you and I don't do well, then I'll try to leave with them to wherever they decide to hide. If they'll have me."

It was that last that caught Barkson by surprise. Helia hadn't added the *if they'll have me* as a rhetorical trick or as fake humbleness. She truly wasn't certain they would.

Barkson supposed that made sense. After all, Helia was living alone in a tower in the middle of nowhere. Gussie had known where she was, but Barkson couldn't imagine Gussie visiting this place.

The comment made Barkson uncomfortable. It made her feel responsible for Helia, and Barkson didn't want to feel responsible for anyone.

"I want to be on the road within the hour," Barkson said.

Helia ran a thumb underneath her eyes. She nodded. "It'll take me less," she said, and then proceeded to prove herself right.

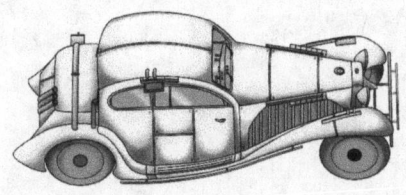

My dearest G,

I located H. It took some convincing for H to vacate the property until the crisis is resolved. H is no longer on the property, and I am heading to the next point.

Since it is the middle of the night as I pen these words, I shall keep this missive brief.

Your not-so-humble servant,

L

G'NZIDIA

CHAPTER
FIVE
DILSHAD

Before they left, Barkson made Helia drive the windstone vehicle around the tower twice. Barkson hadn't been sure Helia could even start the vehicle. When Barkson had purchased the vehicle, the sales office had told her the vehicle was tied to her. She had thought it might only work for her.

But maybe it would only work if she was in proximity.

The only thing that Helia found unfamiliar about Barkson's vehicle was the use of windscreen cleaners. The rain had followed Barkson from Isara, and the drops littered the windscreen. Barkson had paid extra for the cleaners, so that drops could be smoothed off the screen, and she had to show Helia how to use them.

Helia had loved that feature. She hadn't liked how small the back of the vehicle was, commenting on the lack of space behind the driver's side. Barkson didn't yet tell her about all of the extra compartments.

At that moment, Barkson hadn't been certain she and Helia would remain driving companions, particularly as the cat howled its way down the steps, across the drive, and into the vehicle.

The cat was a magnificent, if small, creature. She had silver fur of a type that Barkson had never seen before, and large blue eyes that seemed almost human. The cage was larger than Barkson expected, with a door along the top as well as the side.

Helia said the top was designed so that she could easily insert food and water into the cage, and if to prove her point, she brought two large glass containers, one filled with water and the other with some kind of food pellets that Helia said the cat would eat in a pinch.

Barkson was less worried about the food pellets than she was about the box built into the cage, a box filled with sand. If the cat used that box during the drive, the small vehicle would be overwhelmed with odors that Barkson didn't want to deal with.

She had mentioned that, and Helia had produced a leash. The cat—Aldena—had a collar, and the leash could attach to it. Apparently, when they stopped, Helia planned to walk Aldena around any area as if she were a small dog.

Barkson had decided not to think about that. She was more concerned about the two other boxes that Helia had brought. One was filled with books and documents and maps, all of which gave off a sparking energy that seemed almost physical. The other had small items that didn't look familiar to Barkson at all. Bits of plants and statues and a musical instrument or two, as well as vials of liquids inside more glass jars and tiny lightstone lanterns.

Barkson had been the one to pack food from that unusual

kitchen, even though she hoped they wouldn't have to eat it. The food still didn't look entirely trustworthy. She mostly took what she could trust—the bread, some mead, cheeses, and fruits, all of which looked all right at a glance.

Helia turned out to be a safe enough driver that Barkson closed her eyes, setting her mental clock for two hours of sleep. Also she put one part of her mind on monitoring the drive, so that if anything felt off for any reason, she would come awake quickly, ready to do battle.

She bumped awake as the windstone vehicle eased to a stop. Bright lights stabbed her eyes. She put up one hand, blocking the light.

"Where are we?" she asked Helia.

"Border checkpoint," Helia said. She looked tense.

Barkson ran the other hand over her eyes, waking herself up. Border checkpoint meant they were on the border between Qavner and G'zen.

G'zen liked to believe it was still an autonomous nation, even though it had been part of the Protectorate for more than a dozen years. It had been one of the last countries to join, surrounded on all sides by the Protectorate.

Instead of threatening war or any kind of military attack to convince G'zen to join, the leaders of the Protectorate had simply blocked access for all of G'zen's goods outside of the country.

G'zen controlled a small portion of the Hidden River, but had treaties with the Protectorate to get goods through. The Protectorate canceled all of those treaties unilaterally. It had taken a year or so before G'zen finally acquiesced and decided to join the Protectorate.

By then, many of G'zen's citizens had left, heading to places with abundant food and supplies.

"Let me handle this," Barkson said.

She wished she had awakened sooner. She would have switched to the driver's seat.

"I can tell them—"

"You're not saying anything except to defer to me," Barkson said. "You're not even going to give them your full name. Do you understand?"

Helia blinked at her and suddenly looked alarmed. Apparently, she would need continual reminders to be careful.

"Yes." Helia tensed even more. "Should we switch positions?"

"No time now," Barkson said as the vehicle rolled toward the guard towers.

There were two, and they were the source of the light. Years ago, when the countries were not attached, G'zen had a fully staffed military here, as well as a series of gates that vehicles had to pass through, if they had received approval for travel throughout the country.

There were locks along the Hidden River as well, even though they had been mostly abandoned now.

A thin guard, carrying a musket and wearing the green and gold uniform of G'zen, stepped out of the guard tower, and peered menacingly at the vehicle.

Barkson pulled down the windscreen on the side of her door and leaned out. "Is J'sun here?"

The guard peered at her, as if he had not seen her before. For all she knew, he hadn't. She usually went north on the other side of the river, so that she didn't have to go through G'zen.

"He's in the tower," the guard said, somewhat reluctantly.

"Well," Barkson said with a smile she didn't feel. "Send him out. Tell him an old friend is here."

She didn't have wine. She usually carried at least one bottle and she had forgotten. So as the guard went back to the tower, she turned and grabbed a jar of mead from the back of the windstone vehicle.

"Hey," Helia said. "That's for us."

"Not anymore it isn't," Barkson said. "And you promised to stay quiet. I know of a good inn not far from here."

Helia leaned back in the driver's seat, looking straight ahead. The bright lights of the checkpoint didn't seem to bother her at all.

But Barkson had noticed that, in the back, Aldena had buried her head between her paws.

"Why aren't you driving?" A deep bass voice caught her attention. One of the tallest men she had met outside of Qavner leaned over the passenger side of the vehicle.

"I have been. I needed sleep. My friend Helly offered to during the night."

Helia clearly balked at the nickname, but she didn't say anything. Instead, she leaned over and waved at J'sun.

He crouched, placing a meaty arm against the side of the vehicle.

"What kind of business are you on now, Barks?" he asked.

Barkson didn't want to see Helia's reaction to her nickname.

"You see that cat back there?" Barkson pointed over her shoulder. "I have been cursed with the assignment to bring it to Chiedanna, where its new owner lives."

"Why didn't you just leave it?" J'sun asked, peering around her.

"Money, my friend," Barkson said. "Apparently, someone loves that creature a bit too much. I'm being paid a small fortune. Would you like to see?"

"Yes, I would," he said, a little softer this time.

She reached into the pocket of her coat, and pulled out two gold coins.

"That's not a fortune," he said.

"It is for a five-minute conversation." She smiled at him and held them just below the door, so that his companion couldn't see.

Technically, she should have been able to drive through the checkpoint without bribing a guard, but that usually meant a delay of a few hours to a few days.

The people of G'zen, unable to fight the Protectorate, decided they could harass its people to the very edge of their patience.

Helia leaned toward her and started to whisper something, but Barkson grabbed her arm. Tight.

"Oh," Barkson said without looking at Helia, "is there a good inn nearby that you might recommend?"

He took the two gold pieces and they disappeared into the front of his uniform. "You're only an hour or two from Chiedanna. What do you need an inn for?"

"The way back," Barkson lied. "I'd rather stay in your fair country than that little hellhole."

J'sun chuckled. "You have a very good point."

He named an inn and gave her very precise instructions, then made her repeat them back.

"You should be able to place your vehicle near the stable," he said, "but I would not leave any goods in the vehicle itself."

"Thank you," she said, making a note of that even though she had no plans to stop at the inn.

He tapped on the side of the vehicle, something he'd done many times in the past. She wasn't sure if he did it to let the other guard know that everything was all right, or if he did it to thank her for the bribe.

She was about to tell Helia to drive away, when Barkson thought of one more question.

"Say, J'sun," she said, "have you seen anything unusual recently?"

He stopped and peered at her. "What do you mean by 'unusual'?"

"When we were picking up the cat," Barkson lied, "we heard tell of attacks on some of the homes of the Old Families in Trinovante."

"Couldn't happen to a nicer bunch," J'sun said viciously.

Barkson hoped that Helia didn't have a physical response to that statement or if she did, that she wasn't visible on the far side of the vehicle.

"I agree," Barkson said blandly, "but it is of concern, since the two of us are traveling alone."

"Barks, are you telling me that there's something you can't handle?" J'sun grinned at her.

She made herself grin back. "I can handle anything if I'm prepared."

"On that, I hear you," he said. Then his expression got serious. "I haven't personally seen anything. But I heard about some unusual-looking strangers."

"Unusual how?" Barkson asked.

"You ever hear of the Fey?" he asked.

Barkson felt that shiver that had been haunting her since she started this trip. So that was what had been niggling at her brain. Some history she'd studied back at Serebro Academy.

Helia tapped Barkson's hand, but Barkson ignored her, tightening her grip on Helia's arm.

"I mean who hasn't?" Barkson said. "But they're in Nye, right? That has nothing to do with us."

"That's what I thought, but you know the paintings, right? The famous ones of that attack on Mount Vitaki?"

Barkson frowned. She knew some paintings but they were all different.

"You'll have to be a bit more specific," she said.

"I can't," J'sun said. "I saw them a decade or more ago. I just remember looking at the creatures pouring out of the mountain. They were tall and skinny and had ears like bats. Some of them rode animals if I remember right."

Barkson nodded, mostly to encourage him to continue.

"I saw some people coming through the checkpoint out of Qavner," he said. "Reminded me of those paintings."

Barkson's heartbeat increased. "Reminded how?"

"Bats," he said. "Those long faces, skinny with upraised eyebrows. You know the type."

Barkson did. "They're all over Trinovante. Tall skinny people with strange eyebrows have been part of Trinovante since time immemorial."

"But not with bat ears," he said.

Bat ears? She knew what he meant. He was talking about the shape of the ears, with the point at the top. But she didn't consider anyone to have bat ears. She had never seen anyone whose ears were too large for their head.

"And those people in Trinovante speak Qavnerian, right?" J'sun asked. "These people, they didn't speak anything like Qavnerian or G'zenda. In fact, they spoke a language I'd never heard before, and you know me. I've heard pretty much everything. I couldn't even guess what it was or what it was related to."

That chill had stopped running up and down Barkson's spine. Instead it settled in her heart.

"They were trying to hide too," he said. "Wearing hoods over their heads, keeping their faces averted. They were on a wagon, and the one driving was the only one who spoke Qavnerian. I'd've thought he was one of us, if the others hadn't been with him. His face was...strange."

"Strange?" Barkson asked.

J'sun shook his head. "Maybe I was tired. But I couldn't really focus on it. It was as if—I don't know. As if he was underwater."

Helia flinched so hard that Barkson nearly lost her grip on Helia's arm. It took most of Barkson's strength not to look at Helia.

Barkson didn't want to be distracted. Something about J'sun's concern caught her.

"How many were there?" she asked.

"Eight," he said. "Maybe ten. One or two of them seemed almost invisible to me."

That flinch again from Helia. Barkson shook her arm gently, silently telling her to settle down.

"Where did they go?" Barkson asked.

"I don't know," J'sun said. "We wouldn't let them through for the maximum time allotted."

"When was that?" Barkson asked.

"They left two days ago," he said and then frowned. "This bothers you?"

"I'm stunned that you're calling them Fey," Barkson said. "Are you sure they weren't some gang of kids or troublemakers from Trinovante?"

"If they were, they were still strange," he said. "They couldn't provide any addresses, and they didn't speak the language."

"Do you know what they wanted?" she asked.

He shook his head slowly. "They said they were passing through."

"You didn't believe them," she said.

"It doesn't matter what I believe," he said. "I have no legal right to stop them."

He sounded very bitter. Now, he was talking about the limitations the Protectorate put on him, not about the group he had tried to prevent from entering G'zen.

"You ever see anything like it before?" she asked.

"A group like that?" he asked. "No, I never have."

That chill had made its way through her and almost had become a part of her. She hadn't been this uncomfortable in a very long time.

If what he said was true, it didn't bode well. The Fey were a military culture. She'd studied a number of military cultures. The smart ones always sent an advance team to figure out what they needed to bring on a mission to conquer an area.

She had learned in the Academy, and others concurred, that

the Fey would be fools if they tried to conquer the Protectorate. It wasn't as large as the Fey Empire, but the Protectorate did more to govern its people than the Fey did.

However, the Protectorate had its own problems. The Fey embraced their magic. The Protectorate did not.

"Did this group have magic?" she asked J'sun.

He shook his head. "I'm no expert. But if they had tried anything, I could have detained them longer."

"If you knew about it," Helia said so softly that Barkson doubted J'sun could hear the comment.

"You seem awfully curious about this," J'sun said to Barkson. Clearly he hadn't heard Helia.

"Perhaps it's just my imagination," Barkson said, "but everything seems strange of late. Haven't you noticed that?"

J'sun gave her a small smile. "I just do my job and provide for my family as best I can."

He stood up, glanced over his shoulder at the guard tower, and circled his finger in the air, the *they're all right* symbol that Barkson had seen many times before.

Then he turned back to her.

"You be safe, you hear me?" he said.

Normally, she would have bantered with him, maybe said something snide like *you only care about my gold*. But that wasn't appropriate tonight, for either of them.

"You stay safe as well," she said, then raised the side windscreen. Raising a windscreen was always much more difficult than lowering it. She had to put a knuckle in the small knuckle holder and slowly pull up until the screen caught.

"Ready?" Helia asked.

"Yes," Barkson said. "Drive cautiously. I don't want his companion to stop us for being reckless."

"You think he'd do that?"

"I know he would," Barkson said.

Helia followed her instruction, driving slowly past the guard towers. Barkson blinked as the vehicle moved away from the powerful lights. There were a lot of outbuildings here, which, she had learned over the years, contained contraband seized from someone crossing the border. A few of the buildings that had no windows used to house prisoners, people who were trying to cross into G'zen illegally.

Now that G'zen was part of the Protectorate, there was no illegal entry, but J'sun did tell her that the buildings were still used for actual criminals, those transporting stolen goods or illegal substances over the border.

As Helia drove carefully past those buildings, Barkson realized she hadn't asked enough questions. She should have asked if J'sun and his partner had taken any suspicious characters into custody or if they had picked up some illegal items in the past two days or so.

For a moment, she debated returning, but decided that would really seem out of the ordinary.

The vehicle went down a slight incline, and suddenly they were in darkness. Ahead, lights glimmered. Barkson knew from experience that was G'Nzidia, the largest city in the country.

G'Nzidia was laid out haphazardly. It had grown from a small village and was laid out to avoid the occasional river flood. The flood plain was mostly walled off, although some still tried to build on it.

Unlike Trinovante, which was laid out on a grid pattern, G'Nzidia seemed to be constructed by whim.

They had driven maybe a mile into the darkness before Helia said, "You didn't have to bribe him. I could have handled it."

"I did have to bribe him," Barkson said. "If I ever failed to bribe him, he would stop treating me like a friend."

"Some friend," Helia said.

"And," Barkson said, because she couldn't quite let it go. "You couldn't have handled this. We don't have the time to wait while they screw with us. We have to keep moving."

"I could have sent for my brother," Helia said. "That's all it would have taken."

Barkson frowned. "Which brother?"

"Dilshad," Helia said, then looked over at Barkson. Helia's eyebrows went up. "You don't know, do you?"

"Don't know what?" Barkson said.

"That Dilshad is the second in command at the G'zen Protectorate Office."

Barkson let out a breath. That wouldn't have helped at all. That might have caused a lot more problems, given how the G'zendians felt about the Protectorate.

"Maybe I'll tell him that the border guards are taking bribes," Helia said primly.

"You'll do nothing of the kind," Barkson said. "We're going to deliver your sister's letters, make sure he understands, and then continue onward."

"He's probably not going to want to leave," Helia said. "Dilshad believes he knows better than everyone else."

He's not the only one, Barkson thought but didn't say.

"I'll keep that under advisement," she said. "How far do we have to go?"

"If we get there before dawn, we should go to his home. Afterwards, he might be at the Protectorate offices."

"Then hurry," Barkson said. "We need to get there sooner rather than later."

"Yes'm," Helia said with a touch of humor in her tone. That she could be so light threw Barkson off a bit. Apparently, Helia was as good at compartmentalizing her emotions as Barkson was.

They rode in silence for another mile or so, and then Barkson realized what a resource she had beside her. Helia had studied everything anyone could study about magic and science and the confluence between them. That meant a massive study in the history of magic, not just in the Protectorate or even in Dorovich, but all over the world.

"What do you think about J'sun's mention of the Fey?" Barkson asked.

Helia didn't reply. For a moment, Barkson thought Helia hadn't heard. Just as Barkson was about to ask again, Helia said, "That's all I can focus on. If he's right, something bad is happening, Lucy."

"Something bad *is* happening, Helia," Barkson said. "That's why we're here."

"I know." Helia sighed. "I... No one likes me much because I don't always respond the way people expect. Emotions are messy, you know?"

Barkson nodded. "I know."

She didn't look at Helia at that point, but at the rising and falling hills of the countryside. The lights of G'Nzidia were getting closer.

The city always surprised her. It burned lights all night long, which made it visible from far away.

"I meant," Helia said after a moment, "that things might be bad, not just for me and my family, but for all of the Protectorate."

This was the kind of discussion that Barkson needed. She placed her hands on her knees and shifted slightly in the seat. She hadn't realized just how uncomfortable the passenger side of this vehicle was.

"What do you mean?" she asked.

Helia bit her lower lip, then looked to either side, as if she was making certain they were alone on the road. Almost as if she didn't want anyone to hear the conversation.

"The Fey want to take over the world," she said.

"That's the rumor," Barkson said.

"No rumor," Helia said. "They believe that their Black Throne is meant to rule everything, the entire world, and they've acted on it for centuries."

"All right." Barkson had learned some of this history at the Academy. But she also learned that some people needed to tell stories in their own way and their own time.

"The Fey attacked here—or tried to—centuries ago," Helia said.

"I've seen the art," Barkson said.

"It was more than that," Helia said. "They brought an entire —I don't know the word. Troop? Army? Force?—but most of them died on the way here. We learned that later. Somehow, they managed to get to Mount Vitaki without being seen, and then they started attacking communities in the Forbidden Valley."

Barkson had known parts of this. She knew about the attacks; she didn't know that the Fey had somehow gotten to Mount Vitaki without being seen.

"Do you think they camouflaged themselves somehow?" Barkson asked.

"No one knows," Helia said. "The Fey have magic that we don't or maybe we do, but we abandoned ours and we attack people who study it or use it. Magic is everywhere, Lucy, and we try to deny it, and it's dangerous."

"The magic is dangerous?" Barkson asked.

"It is, you know that." Helia's voice sounded thick. Her face was in shadow, so Barkson couldn't see if Helia's expression had changed. "But denying it is even worse. It makes us unprepared."

Barkson frowned. There was truth to that statement.

Helia seemed annoyed at Barkson's silence. "That's why I was at the tower. My family didn't want me anywhere near them if I was going to study magic."

Her voice wobbled on the last part of that. Now Barkson was beginning to understand.

Helia's family had hurt her deeply. She didn't want to cooperate with them or mourn them, but she was going to have no choice. She clearly still loved them, or she wouldn't have insisted on coming with Barkson.

Helia would have taken one of her vehicles and her now-silent cat and driven somewhere that she felt safe. Alone.

"Somewhere along the way, we confused magic with the Fey and with the threats with some of the other places we were taking over," Helia said, recovering her voice. "And by 'we' I mean Qavnerians. I'm of the opinion that we've built the Protectorate not to protect others, like we say, but because we are protecting ourselves."

Barkson had never heard that theory. "What do you mean?"

"I think we're the most terrified people in the world," Helia said. "We're afraid of other cultures, and we're afraid of each other. And we pretend to be strong so that we have some measure of control."

Barkson frowned. She had no idea what to think of that. Philosophy had its place in middle-of-the-night trips, but might not seem as useful in the light of day.

"What about the Fey?" Barkson asked. "You said this could get bad."

"Oh, come on, Lucy," Helia said. "You know how fighting works. I know you do. You don't go into a place cold. You send in advance troops or whatever. And you destroy as many weapons and leaders as you can before you bring your entire force into the place. Right?"

"That's good military theory and strategy," Barkson said. "We've used it. 'We' meaning the Protectorate."

"Yes, I know," Helia said. She was scanning the road again, but this time Barkson had a sense she was looking for something. "I studied history at the same schools you did."

"Just because we consider it good strategy," Barkson said, "doesn't mean the Fey do."

Helia let out a bitter laugh. "Where do you think we learned it? They've run campaigns longer than the Protectorate has existed. There are military scholars all over the Protectorate who know everything the Fey have done. They've made some mistakes along the way—they nearly lost early on in L'Nacin—but they learned from those mistakes and came back stronger. That's what the Fey do."

"They haven't come here for generations," Barkson said. That was what bothered her about J'sun's claim. The Fey would have to go through Leut to get to Dorovich, and the Fey hadn't come near Leut.

"That's where you're wrong," Helia said. "They've come here ever since. Sometimes it's been innocuous. They've come in ones and twos, as part of a trading company or onboard a ship. Some have stayed here. We have a large community of Fey and half-Fey people throughout the Protectorate. Where do you think the fears of magic came from?"

This was getting too convoluted for Barkson. She thought fears of magic came from practices in the northern countries.

"I just wanted to know if you think what J'sun said is plausible," Barkson said. "I guess you do. What I don't understand is why the Fey, if they're here, would murder Kirillis."

Helia gave her a sideways look, as if she couldn't understand Barkson at all.

"We're the ones who made magical items popular. We're the ones who set up the archives throughout Qavner and kept magical practices alive. And we're the ones who came up with the plans to take over countries all along the Hidden River." Helia cleared her throat. "You know that, Lucy. We studied history in the same place."

Barkson was getting tired of being reminded about that. It made her feel stupid and she wasn't stupid.

But she remembered details other than the ones that Helia mentioned. Barkson thought the Kirillis had lost influence over the past generations, which was why Augustus wasn't in the government. He had been working as some kind of glorified accountant or something.

Then again, Barkson hadn't known that Dilshad was working for the Protectorate. So there was still influence in the family.

It just seemed strange to her that the Fey would go after a family that didn't have a lot of political power. There were other Old Families that were much more active in Qavner's government.

"I'm not sure what to think," Barkson said. She was speaking the truth. "It doesn't make sense to me that a military force from half a world away would come to Qavner and target the Kirillis."

"You told that guard that the Old Families had been targeted," Helia said. "Is that true?"

"I don't know," Barkson said. "I'd heard rumors before Gussie found me. But I hadn't checked any of them out."

Barkson had had no reason to check out the rumors. People hired her or she did what she wanted. And this trip for Gussie was the very first time in her career that Barkson had voluntarily worked for an Old Family.

"Are there other reasons that someone would target the Old Families?" Barkson asked Helia.

Helia shrugged, then moved the sticks. The vehicle spun sideways. For a moment, Barkson thought they were in trouble. Then the wheels found purchase on some kind of side road.

"There's something strange happening with the Old Families," Helia said. "My father..."

Her voice broke, then she cleared her throat.

"...he wanted Gussie to be a Regent."

Barkson nodded.

"It should've been me," Helia said. "I know magic the best, and the Regents are in charge of the study of magic."

But with Helia's lack of interpersonal skills, she wouldn't have been able to persuade anyone, especially not a testy group of Regents.

"My father..." Again, the broken voice, the throat-clearing. "He got more secretive about them over the years. The Regents, I mean. He thought something was going wrong there."

"So there might be dissent in the Old Families about the study of magic?" Barkson asked.

"But that wouldn't lead to murder!" Helia said.

Oh, but it could. Anything could lead to murder, especially where power was concerned.

But Barkson didn't say that to Helia. It wasn't time to say anything like that. Helia was too raw, even though she didn't want to admit it.

"Are we getting close to Dilshad's place?" Barkson asked.

Helia sniffled, then squared her shoulders. "Two rises over, and around a few corners. He lives just outside of G'Nzidia. But I don't know when he goes to work. It might be really early, knowing Dilshad."

"If he's not at home," Barkson said with a confidence she didn't feel, "then we should be able to find him at work."

She hoped. Because there was another possibility, one she didn't really want to contemplate.

She and Helia might arrive to an empty house, and if that was the case, there was a good chance that Dilshad would have been the same kind of victim as his father.

"Is your brother married?" Barkson asked.

She hated the fact that she hadn't been able to research her journey before she embarked. Normally, she would have known everything about the Kirillis before heading out.

She was only going on half-remembered facts and whatever she could pull out of Helia.

"Yes, he's married," Helia said tersely, as if she didn't approve. "And he has a son I've never met."

Barkson was beginning to wonder if she should have brought Helia along after all. It didn't sound like she got along with any member of her family.

"How old is the child?" Barkson asked.

"Baby still," Helia said. "Maybe a year...? Not old."

Barkson felt a surge of irritation. Not at Helia, but at the situation. A baby made things that much more difficult.

"All right," Barkson said. "Once we get there, you're going to have to let me talk."

"I know what to do," Helia said. "But he is my brother."

"Yes," Barkson said. "And for that reason, I'm going to do most of the talking and ordering. I don't want to get in the middle of your relationship."

"Such as it is," Helia said.

Barkson gave her a sideways glance. Helia's mouth was set in a grim smile.

Barkson nodded.

"Such as it is," she said.

G'NZIDIA

CHAPTER
SIX
DILSHAD

The sky was turning a light yellowish pink when Barkson saw the first movement on the hill. At first she thought the movement a trick of the light—a shadow, passing along some grass, heading in the same direction the windstone vehicle was.

Then she saw another shadow and another, and they weren't normal shadows. The sun hadn't risen yet. There shouldn't have been those kinds of shadows at all.

The road wound through the slight hills. There were no trees. They'd been cut down and replaced with grass, as if trees caused problems. Right now, Barkson was grateful for the lack of foliage. She could keep an eye on those shadows.

"How much farther do we have?" she asked Helia.

Helia was gripping the driving sticks so hard that her knuckles had turned white. Barkson doubted that Helia had seen the moving shadows, so it had to have been the approach to her brother's home that had her so nervous.

And Barkson didn't blame her for that. With all of the deaths that Helia had just learned about and the horrors that had happened in Trinovante, of course Helia would be nervous.

Even if her brother and his family were fine, Helia had made it clear in the discussions over the drive that their relationship was not the best.

More movement along the hillside.

"Slow down," Barkson said quietly.

"I'd like to get there as—"

"*Slow down*," Barkson snapped.

Helia did. Barkson leaned forward a little. There were no real shadows on the ground that would move like that.

She had a growing feeling that something was very wrong.

"Pull over near the top of the next rise," she said.

While she liked the fact that there were no trees so that she could see the shadows, that meant whatever was causing the shadows could also see her.

"What's going on?" Helia asked.

"I'm seeing movement," Barkson said.

Helia followed instructions, driving the vehicle slowly up the rise, and then stopping.

"Stay in the vehicle," Barkson said. "And remember our agreement. Do as I say because this could be very dangerous."

Helia nodded. Her skin had gone gray. She looked terrified. She pulled up an extra brake so that the vehicle wouldn't slide back down the road, and then she turned slightly in her seat.

Barkson thought Helia was going for a weapon, but she wasn't. She was checking on the stupid cat.

Barkson couldn't help herself. She looked too.

The cat sat primly upright, looking out the front windscreen as if she could see whatever it was that Barkson had seen.

And maybe she could.

Barkson reached into the pile of coats and items beside the cat, finally finding one of her pistols. She removed it, cradling it, then opened the passenger-side door and slid out.

She didn't close the door all the way, because the sound might carry. The morning was still, without a lot of wind.

She had no idea how sound might work in these hills. Either the hillsides would block sound entirely or it would be possible to hear the slightest cough.

She wrapped her own coat around her, dagger on her hip, and slipped on her gloves, watching the area nearby carefully.

The movements she saw were slight but coordinated. One shadow moved carefully, and then another, and another, all in a forward movement.

And as far as she could see, the only target was a good-sized estate house, nestled in the hills.

Her heart pounded.

The shadows were too far away for her pistol and too far apart for her to do anything one on one.

She counted five shadows, moving slowly across those hills. The shadows would get to the house faster than she would—at least on foot.

She hated this, but she saw no choice.

She scurried around to the driver's side.

"Scoot over," she said.

"What? No," Helia said. "Don't you need me to drive while you shoot or something?"

Barkson didn't have time to argue. "Scoot. Over."

Helia's eyes widened, but she scooted. Barkson climbed in.

"Pull the passenger door closed and slam it as you do," Barkson said.

"But they'll hear—"

"Yes, Helia," Barkson snapped. "They'll hear it. I want them to hear it. If you question every damn thing I say, then we will be too late to do anything."

Assuming these shadows were actually a threat to Dilshad's home. Assuming these shadows weren't some kind of security he had hired all on his own.

Helia grabbed the door and yanked it closed, so hard that the entire vehicle shook. The door slam was muted, which answered Barkson's mental question about sound. Apparently, the air's stillness and these hills muffled sound.

She cursed silently. For the first time, she wanted sound to carry.

So she started the vehicle badly, deliberately spun the tires, and peeled out onto the road, driving like a madwoman.

The road bumped beneath the wheels. She couldn't quite see the shadows.

"I want you to open your windscreen and yell," Barkson said.

"Yell what?" Helia asked.

Barkson was going to slap Helia silly if Helia asked another stupid question. Barkson had a lot of understanding for Helia's lack of social skills, but didn't need it right now. Right now she needed action.

"Just scream," Barkson said. "As loud as you can. Lean out and scream."

Helia brought the windscreen down, sending too much air

through the front seat of the vehicle. Then Helia let out a wail of a scream, something they probably heard in G'Nzidia.

The shadows stopped moving, just like Barkson hoped they would. One of them moved slightly—an arm raise, maybe?—and then the shadows flowed toward the vehicle.

Barkson let out a breath. She had wanted this. And she hoped that Dilshad would forgive her if these shadows were some kind of security.

"Have you ever shot a pistol?" Barkson asked.

"No," Helia said.

"Well, then, we're going to have to stop this thing, and you're going to crawl in back with your infernal cat, and if I die, you will play dead too, both of you, so that whatever is out there will leave you alone. You got that?"

Barkson didn't wait for an answer. She drove to the top of the next rise, which was only one rise away from the house, and stopped the car diagonally, so that it blocked the road entirely.

Then she opened her door, climbed out, and opened the door in the back. She used both doors as a shield. If someone was going to attack her, they had to do it directly.

She hoped Helia listened, because that was Helia's only chance of survival.

The shadows loped up the side of the hill and as they came close, Barkson realized they weren't shadows at all, but tall, thin people, wearing mostly black. She primed her pistol, hands steady.

She didn't have enough shots with this thing to take out five quickly. She could maybe get off two shots before the people arrived.

They had long black hair and narrow faces. Their arms were muscular and their legs powerful.

If she let them touch her, they could easily beat her to death. She could handle one or two of them, but five of that size? There was no way.

She had to push the odds into her favor.

She braced one arm on the side of the door, then placed the pistol on that arm, watching and waiting for one of the attackers to get within range.

They had formed a V, running swiftly now, hair flying behind them. She took a deep breath and pulled the trigger.

The shot boomed, rocking her a little. A puff of smoke clouded her vision. She couldn't wait to see who (if anyone) was hit. She had to prime the pistol again.

She moved steadily when another boom rocked her. And then another, and another, and another.

She looked up. Where the attackers had been, there was a smoking crater with flames pouring out of it.

She didn't stand. She'd fought the magical before, and knew this could be an illusion designed to draw her out. But it felt real enough. The thick smoke smelled of burning flesh.

Barkson's eyes watered. She waited, but the flames weren't going down. If anything, they were rising higher.

"I think I killed them," Helia said from behind her.

Barkson turned. Helia was leaning over the roof of the vehicle, one hand curled around a small box, another flat on the canvas. Her eyes were wild.

"You...killed them?" Barkson asked.

"I thought the boxes would work," Helia said, still looking at the smoke. "I knew they'd explode, but could I get them there? I had made little flying boxes, but I hadn't tested them. I guess they did though."

She emitted a tiny giggle, a panicked giggle.

"You did that?" Barkson asked.

Helia nodded. "I have more. We can use more, if they come out of that smoke."

The hell with the smoke. Barkson wasn't going to wait and see if anything survived it. If the five attackers were injured, she didn't want to get close. Who knew what they could do?

"Get back in the vehicle," Barkson said.

"You're not angry, are you?" Helia asked. "I mean, a pistol is great, but you only took out one and there wasn't time—"

"Get back in the vehicle *now*," Barkson said.

Helia nodded, and slipped back into the passenger side.

Barkson glanced into the back area, saw the cat was still sitting pretty but her eyes were avid, as if the fire intrigued her. Nothing else seemed to be missing.

Barkson couldn't even tell where the boxes had come from, and she didn't have time to figure it out.

She closed the back door, then climbed into the driver's seat, before glancing at the fire.

It was burning even taller, sparking blue and pink and orange with a touch of blackish gray. The smell was growing worse.

She pulled her door closed.

"Make sure your windscreen is up," Barkson said as she moved the driving sticks.

The smoke was crowding around them now, making it hard to see. She had to drive slower than she wanted because she didn't want to drive off the road.

She was operating mostly by memory and a sense of the road's size rather than being able to see anything.

Helia sneezed beside her and wiped at her face, but said nothing.

Barkson drove down the hill and into the low area, which got the vehicle out of the smoke.

There was movement at the house, and Barkson hoped that it was Helia's family, not those attackers.

"Get one of your boxes ready," she said.

"It's not that easy," Helia said, "especially sitting down. It's too dangerous."

"Then be mentally prepared," Barkson said as she drove the vehicle up the rise. Signs on each side of them read *Private land. Keep off*. But she drove past them anyway.

The road smoothed out, and the estate house came into clear view. A man stood in the door. He was round and balding and reminded Barkson of Augustus Kirilli.

"That's Dilshad!" Helia sounded relieved.

Barkson wasn't relieved yet. She wanted to tell Dilshad to return inside where it was safe, but she couldn't, not from this distance.

So she sped up, reaching the house in record speed. She parked at the edge of the drive, not by the door, worried that Dilshad might try something before he realized who was in the car.

She got out, waved a hand, and yelled, "Get back inside!"

He didn't move. "Who are you?"

Helia got out. "Dil! Go inside."

"Helia?"

"*Now*, Dil. We'll be right there." For once Helia sounded sensible.

Dilshad went into the house. Barkson leaned against the vehicle, breathing hard. She scanned the countryside.

The view was great from here. If she stepped away from the house, she could see the entire valley around her, with the Hidden River in the distance.

The sun had come up fully, and the lights of G'Nzidia had faded. Barkson's heart pounded.

The black smoke from whatever Helia had done rose. There was a crater where the attackers had been. One attacker lay farther back. That must have been the one that Barkson had shot. Helia had said she hit something.

But the other attackers were nowhere to be seen.

Barkson had no idea how big the attacking force was. Eight, maybe, like J'sun had said? But what if there were more in the distance who would come to see what the smoke was? She figured they had maybe a half an hour, maybe just a bit more, before they came under siege again—if someone was coming.

"Do you think they're dead?" Helia asked again, as if she didn't want to be responsible for any of it.

"I think we have to assume they are not," Barkson said. "I'm going into the house. You're staying here with Aldena, and keeping an eye out. If anyone comes out of those hills, you get me, you got that?"

"Yes." Helia sounded subdued. "You'll hurry?"

"Yes," Barkson said, because she had absolutely no other choice.

G'NZIDIA

DILSHAD

Barkson grabbed the letters for Dilshad, but left her pistol. She had to trust that Helia had the ability to handle anything that might come up that hill.

Helia had handled five attackers so far.

The top of the hill had no landscaping either—no large or even small spindly trees, no big plants, not even a bed of roses. The house itself looked like it had grown out of the hillside. The driveway butted up against the house's foundation, and slid underneath the stairs that led up to the door.

Maybe that meant that despite its appearance of age, the house was new.

She scurried up the stairs to the man standing there. Dilshad was round just like his father, with similar doughy features. His dark eyes, though, were sharp. He had an intelligence that shone out of them.

He had his back to the doors, his hands on the knobs. The

doors were made of a familiar dark wood, with figures carved into them. The doors looked familiar: Barkson had seen doors like that on the Kirilli manor.

"I don't know who you are," Dilshad said. "But that looks like my sister Helia. If it is, then I need to speak to her."

Barkson was about to answer him, when the air to her left shimmered. The shimmer was the size of a door.

She'd seen something like this before. It was a portal from somewhere to this driveway. The fact that something had portaled here suggested that the five attackers that had died (or at least been stopped) on that hillside had portaled in as well.

Which meant they weren't the eight that J'sun had seen.

Barkson turned, hand on the hilt of her dagger as she waited to see what, if anything, came through that portal. The shimmer parted, revealing the edges of a room with brown wood walls.

A woman, tall and thin, wearing a black hood and black leggings, stepped through. She had upraised eyebrows and pointed ears, and a determined look on her face.

In one hand, she held a silver dagger. Another rested on her hip. She gave Barkson a dismissive glance and turned toward Dilshad.

He appeared startled and confused. He looked at Barkson as if she was part of the attack.

She kept her gaze firmly on the woman who had come through the portal. Barkson couldn't tell if someone was behind her or not, but Barkson couldn't wait.

The woman raised her hands, making fists as she extended her arms toward Dilshad.

Barkson grabbed her knife, and in one smooth movement, flung it at the woman.

The knife hit the woman in the forehead, just above the eyes.

The woman toppled backwards from the force of the blow. She fell to the side of the portal, which shimmered, flared with a brownish light, and then winked out altogether.

The woman lay on her back, unmoving.

"Get inside now," Barkson said to Dilshad.

He didn't have to be told twice. He opened the door ever so slightly and scurried into his house.

Barkson walked over to the woman, wishing for some kind of stick or a longer weapon that would have enabled her to poke the body without getting near it.

But Barkson didn't have that, so she got as close as she could without being within arm's reach.

That at least enabled Barkson to see the woman's face. Her eyes were open and unseeing. The knife had sliced through the front part of the brain, almost cutting it in half.

That was what Barkson had intended to do, and it had worked.

The woman appeared dead. If she wasn't, she was badly injured enough to be out for a long time.

Barkson stepped back, and looked at Helia, who was leaning over the roof of the vehicle, hand over her mouth, eyes wide.

"Leave the body alone," Barkson said. "You stay where you are."

Helia nodded. Apparently, she didn't have to be told twice, which was a nice change.

Barkson backed away from the body, still not trusting what her eyes were telling her, and headed toward the house. As she came up the stairs, the door opened ever so slightly.

Dilshad peered out. "My sister needs to come in," he said.

"Your sister stays where she is," Barkson said.

"It's Helia," he said. "She doesn't know what she's doing."

"She knows better than both of us," Barkson said. "I'm Lucinda Barkson, by the way. Your sister Gussie sent me with two letters for you. You need to read them quickly."

She almost added, *and then you need to leave this place*, but considering how contrary Helia had been whenever she was given a command, Barkson had to assume that Dilshad would be the same.

"I don't know you," he said. "I don't want to invite you in."

"Probably wise," Barkson said. She reached into her pocket and pulled out an envelope. She checked it to make sure it was the first letter for Dilshad.

It was, so she handed it to him.

"You said you have two," he said.

"I have strict instructions to give you this one first, and to watch you read it," Barkson said.

"Gussie's not usually that bossy," Dilshad said.

"You'll understand in a minute," Barkson said.

He glanced at the body on his drive, then at his sister, before tearing the envelope open. He read quickly, just as Barkson had asked him to do, his expression growing more and more grim the farther he got into the letter.

Unlike his sisters, he didn't ask if the information in the letter was true. He probably didn't have to, given the smoke that reeked of burning flesh still rose off part of his land, and what appeared to be a dead body lay a few yards from his front door.

He folded the letter. Then he looked at Barkson, his eyes dry.

"The second?" he asked, extending his hand. It trembled.

She handed him the second envelope.

He tore it open, and read that letter quickly as well.

"Sensible," he muttered. Then he let out a small breath, glanced at his sister, then back at Barkson again. "I take it Helia didn't do what was asked."

"Oh, she did," Barkson said, feeling odd that she had to defend Helia at this moment. "She was supposed to leave the tower and she has. She wanted to make certain her siblings were all right."

Dilshad's lips thinned. "I have to get my wife out of here, my son..."

"Yes, you do," Barkson said. "I can't escort you, since I need to reach the rest of your family, but you have to tell me where you're going."

"Yeah." He had probably gotten that from the letter. Then he waved the letter at the woman on the driveway. "Are those... people...going to come after us?"

"I don't know," Barkson said. "I think that depends on you. You're going to have to go somewhere that they can't trace you, and since they found you here, they seem to know something about you. So no Kirilli property—"

"Gussie said that," Dilshad said, a bit haughtily.

Barkson gave him a pass. Fear made some people difficult.

"—and nothing tied to your wife. If you find a rental, you can't use your identification—"

"Yes, all right," he said. "I know of two places that are owned by the Protectorate and not used much. Maybe that would work."

He wasn't asking her advice. He was thinking aloud.

"You need to pack your wife and child up immediately and get them out of here," Barkson said. "I have no idea how these attackers found you, but they did, and I don't know how many of them there are."

"I don't know how to fight them," Dilshad said, and now he did sound scared.

Barkson nodded. "Most people don't," she said. "That's why Helia will go with you."

"Helia doesn't—"

"Helia saved all of us back there," Barkson said. "You'll need her, and you'll need to be kind to her."

"I thought you said she wanted to make sure everyone else was all right," Dilshad said.

"She does," Barkson said. "But I'm not sure how much of this she's going to be able to take. Especially if…"

Barkson didn't want to say it. She drew a breath. Dilshad spoke into her silence.

"Especially if the attackers have already visited the family farther north." His voice was quiet now. He seemed to have set his fear aside enough to be thinking clearly.

"Yes," Barkson said.

"She's not going to like the change in plans," he said.

"She's the least of your worries," Barkson said. "You have a windstone vehicle or a carriage that can hold the four of you?"

"I do," he said.

"Then get moving," Barkson said. "I'll remain out here."

He shoved the letters into his pocket, and went inside the house.

Helia looked at Barkson, then at the body on the drive.

Now, Barkson walked over to it. The woman hadn't moved, and she wasn't bleeding from the wound. Her eyes had clouded over.

She was dead.

Barkson let out a small sigh of relief, then walked back to the windstone vehicle.

"You're going to send me with Dilshad," Helia said.

Barkson couldn't tell if Helia had overheard or not.

"Yes," Barkson said. "These attackers, they've found him, and he doesn't know how to defend himself or his family. You do."

"You couldn't have handled this on your own," Helia said. "It might be worse ahead."

"It might be," Barkson said, "but the longer we delay, the greater the chance that something will happen to the rest of your family. I work better alone. You're going to have to trust me. Gussie does."

"Gussie would want me to go with you," Helia said.

"Gussie wants her family to live through this," Barkson said. "I don't think Dilshad and his family will survive without you."

"He hates me," Helia said.

"He didn't argue when I told him you were going with him. He just said that you wouldn't like it." Barkson looked at her. "I don't care what you like or don't like. I need to make sure you're safe, and you—and Aldena—will not be safe with me."

Barkson added the cat because the cat seemed more important to Helia than Helia's own life did.

Helia let out a small breath. "Does Dil have a place to go?"

"He says there are some places that the Protectorate owns, so it sounds like he does."

Helia nodded. She twisted her hands together and looked back at the smoking crater.

"I killed some people, didn't I?" she asked. "We don't know if they were really attackers."

"We do know," Barkson said with a bit more certainty than she felt. "This last one portaled in, which meant they knew this location. There was no evidence of horses or carriages, and it's a long way from G'Nzidia by foot to this spot, so the attackers probably portaled in too, but a little too far out. Portaling isn't always exact."

She didn't know that for a fact, but she had to calm Helia.

"They came to kill your family," Barkson said. "You stopped them. For whatever reason, your family is a target. I am not. Right now, these attackers have no idea I exist."

Helia nodded, then her lower lip trembled. She bit it, as if that was going to stop her emotional reaction—and it did for the time being.

"Some warrior I am, huh?" she asked.

"You're a hell of a warrior," Barkson said. "And when this is over, you're going to train me on how to use some of your inventions."

"Then you might need a cat," Helia said. "Because none of mine work if Aldena isn't around."

Barkson looked at her, startled. "Why is that?"

"I don't know," Helia said. "I think it's what the old books say. Magic gets channeled through animals sometimes. I just know that once Aldena showed up as a stray on my doorstep, everything I tried worked better."

Then Helia looked a little panicked.

"But that's not why I brought her. She's my only friend. I told you that."

Barkson reached across the top of the vehicle and took Helia's hand. It was cold.

"She's not your only friend," Barkson said gently. "I'm one, too."

Tears spilled out of Helia's eyes, but she didn't try to wipe her face. Instead, she squeezed Barkson's hand so tightly it hurt.

"Dilshad'll hate having me along," Helia said.

"You saved his life," Barkson said. "I have a hunch that'll make him rethink everything."

She hoped she was right; she didn't know the man. But she had seen him gather himself in the face of fear. People like that usually saw clearly enough in a crisis.

That was probably one of the reasons he had this particular government position.

The front door of the estate house banged open and Dilshad scurried out. He ran like a man who hadn't tried moving fast since he was a child. He glanced at the body, and nearly tripped over his own feet, staggering a little as he reached the vehicle.

"Helia," he said, "we're going to have to take the carriage. We need to get your belongings to the carriage house right now."

Helia wiped her face with the back of her free hand.

"You don't mind that I come along?" she asked, voice small.

"Why would I mind?" he asked as if she had just said the stupidest thing in the world. "Right now, it seems, the Kirillis need to stick together. I want to talk to you about everything you know, and we clearly can't do it here."

Then he turned to Barkson.

"You did tell her what this is about, did you not?"

"The letters told both of you," Barkson said.

"And you elaborated, I'm sure." He waved a hand dismissively. "Come, Helia. We have to move fast."

Helia looked at Barkson.

"Go with him," Barkson said. "I'll drive to the carriage house and we can unload your things."

And that was exactly what they did.

My dearest G,

You made the right decision to send me on this journey. I reached D's home in time to thwart an attack. The attackers got hurt, but we did not. But it is clear to me that haste is necessary, so I will go as quickly as I can.

D and the others have left their abode. Their destination is a good one.

More news when I have it.

Your not-so-humble servant,

L.

Feltingham

EIGHT

Sending Helia with Dilshad and his family had been a smart move. Barkson drove north in the blessed silence. She wasn't feeling calmer, exactly, but she did notice the lack of tension in the vehicle.

She didn't need the tension. She still had to find four more Kirillis, including Corrin. Given all that had happened at Dilshad's, Barkson really needed to focus.

The road curved and widened as it dipped into G'Nzidia. The capital city of G'zen looked less impressive in the daylight. The outskirts were made up of small one-story houses that all looked the same.

They were made of dried river mud with some kind of thatching for a roof. There was more poverty here than Barkson expected, and in poverty there was often opportunity for outsiders to take advantage.

The outer neighborhoods had their own foul odors as well. In some areas, it was the stench of rotting garbage; in others, actual urine. It wouldn't have surprised her to see a urine trough along the side of the road.

She'd seen that in a few other countries—not ones that were part of the Protectorate—but the smell had been the same.

She drove a bit faster, weaving around carriages and riders on horseback. She had to be somewhat careful, since she was on an unfamiliar road in an unfamiliar city, but she also had to move quickly.

The last thing she wanted to do, though, was hit anything, because that would slow or stop her journey.

She didn't miss Helia exactly, but Barkson did miss having someone to back her up. Helia had done a remarkable job for a woman with no fighting training. Her weapons were startlingly effective.

Helia had more magic than Barkson had encountered in a long, long time, and Helia had a sense of how to use it. She had probably terrified her family when she had been a child; she would have come into her magic young and then made the kind of bad decisions that a child would make when she was being ignored or wasn't getting her way.

Barkson looked forward to hearing the stories—from all of the Kirilli siblings.

But part of Barkson worried about what she had just experienced. The attackers had known what they were doing. They had arrived at dawn, when a family was most vulnerable, and had Barkson not been close, those attackers would have succeeded.

And, if she was being honest with herself, the attackers might have hurt her. Helia had been the one who had stopped them.

Barkson was going over the fight in her mind as she drove. While the family had been gathering their things and hurriedly packing the large carriage that was going to take them to the River House, as Dilshad had called it, Barkson was looking at the dead woman on the driveway.

She really did look like the drawings of the Fey that Barkson had seen when she had been at the Academy. Tall, thin, with eyebrows that slashed upwards and eyes so dark that they looked gray as they clouded over.

Her cheekbones had been upswept as well, and her chin pointed. Her hair was pulled back, almost as if the woman never wanted to give it any thought.

Barkson had forced herself to search the woman's clothing for any kind of clue as to who she was. Barkson found another dagger and little else of use.

Barkson couldn't even tell if the woman was the one who created the portal. Magic often died with its user, but that portal was closing even before Barkson had flung her knife at the woman.

In some ways, that had been a good thing, because the woman might have toppled back into the portal, and that might have triggered another force to come through the portal, maybe a force big enough to kill them all.

Barkson had waited until the carriage was packed and on its way before she even considered leaving the hilltop. She had told them she wanted to secure it, but in reality, she wanted to watch them go. If there had been trouble, she would have been able to catch up to the carriage quickly and maybe she could have helped.

But the carriage wended its way along the winding road,

heading in the opposite direction of their final destination, as per her instructions. She didn't want some other group to come in and follow the carriage tracks.

She had given a similar instruction to Filippa too, although that had been less necessary, since Filippa had gone in one direction and that horrid husband of hers had gone in another.

This time, it would be Barkson's vehicle that obliterated at least some of the carriage tracks, at least the ones leading out of the estate house.

If more attackers came—and she had a hunch they might—they would follow her trail into the city rather than the family's trail to the River House.

The family had disappeared before she drove away. At that point, she had to trust Helia to protect them.

Once the carriage had finally disappeared from sight, Barkson had driven down the driveway. She had stopped at the still-burning crater and examined it.

The crater was deep. She couldn't see the bottom because of all the smoke. The stench had faded, but the smoke continued. The flames burned blue with bits of something that looked like diamond glitter.

Magical fire, but of what kind she wasn't certain. Even though the flame should have been hot, it was not. It almost looked like the recreation of a fire.

The grass around it had not burned. The only fire existed in the crater itself.

One body lay further back in the grass, but Barkson would have had to walk near the crater to view it. The attacker hadn't moved since she had shot him, so she was going to assume he was dead.

Certainly, if any of the attackers were alive and injured, breathing that foul smoke would have done them no good.

It was doing her no good either. Her eyes watered and her lungs burned.

She did not have any water or anything else that would have put out the flames, and she did not have the magical ability that Helia had either. The flames would either have to burn themselves out or continue until someone figured out how to stop them.

She hoped that the smoke would serve as a warning to anyone traveling here, instead of as a beacon.

It could have been both, she supposed, and it had been that supposition that forced her to continue moving. She needed to warn the rest of the family.

According to the maps that Barkson had, the next family member on the journey north was Ghita. Ghita had entered school as a seven-year-old just as Barkson was beginning her final year. Barkson had been studying for exams that would get her into Serebro Academy and hadn't had a lot of time for the dramas of the Kirilli family.

Still, she'd shared a few meals with the Kirilli sisters. Ghita had been cripplingly homesick, so homesick, in fact that Gussie had wanted to send her home.

Ghita had stopped that with a wave of her small hand.

You did it, Ghita had said, her voice small. *And you didn't have your sisters here. It was just you.*

Then she squared her thin shoulders in a tiny imitation of Gussie's signature move.

If you can do it, Ghita had said, *then I can do it.*

Barkson had thought the comments weird bravado. She had

both admired them and worried about them. She hadn't liked the fact that a child had been put in that awkward situation. And she hadn't liked the fact that none of the Kirilli sisters had hugged Ghita after that declaration of strength.

The sisters had merely nodded and then continued with whatever they had been discussing.

Only Barkson had commented on Ghita's decision.

It's not easy here, Barkson had said. *You make the decisions that are right for you, not the decisions that you're expected to make.*

Ghita had glowered at her.

You're not a Kirilli, she had said. *You wouldn't understand.*

Apparently, Barkson understood little about being a Kirilli. Ghita had been fierce even as a child. Barkson couldn't quite see how Ghita had gone from that fierce little creature into a woman full-grown with children and a life that sounded—at least as Helia had described it—relentlessly traditional.

Maybe a woman who had been forbidden from going home throughout most of her childhood wanted nothing more than to create a home of her own.

A home that Barkson was going to destroy with one simple visit.

Barkson adjusted the driving sticks, and slowed down ever so slightly. She might have to stop and look at the maps, just to make sure she was on the right track.

She had memorized the ones that Gussie had given her, but Helia had changed them.

Gussie only knows the traditional routes, Helia had said. *Let me show you the best routes.*

She said she had used Gussie's family map as the template

and redrew it. The map Helia drew, quickly and without a lot of supplies, reminded Barkson of the maps she had seen in the antiquities section of the Old Library at Serebro Academy.

Helia's maps floated and moved and seemed to have a life of their own. She had put them in a long round leather case that looked more like a case that would hold a musket or a sword.

Helia had placed it in the back of the vehicle, and part of Barkson wished that Helia had taken the case with her.

But the case remained.

Barkson hadn't paid a lot of attention to the case when Helia had been in the vehicle. Mostly Barkson's attention had been divided by sleep, the conversation with Helia, and the stupid cat.

But now, Barkson could almost feel that case, as if it had a life of its own. She had a sense that it glowed, but she couldn't really tell, because the sun was up.

The road had changed. It had widened and was covered with even, flat stone, as if someone had taken care with the design. A turnout appeared off to her right. She was still on a slight rise, and as she pulled into the turnout, she realized the entire city of G'Nzidia was laid out before her.

It was a green city, with a lot of trees whose foliage, from this height, covered most of the buildings. The roads were visible, working their way in and out of the trees. Some of the trees were clumped together in either green spaces or parks.

The city seemed to be built in a semicircle, with the center of the semicircle facing the Hidden River.

From this vantage, the Hidden River glistened and sparkled in the sunlight, as if it was an easy, comforting river, the kind that punts and paddleboats could glide on.

But Barkson had had a lot of experience with the Hidden River. It lived up to its name. Farther north, it was an obviously angry river, but here, in the center, it hid its anger beneath a placid surface.

Too many small boats had been caught in eddies and currents; too many large ships had gone aground; and too many people had died because they tried to swim here. The river would grab their feet and pull them under, not caring if they were accomplished swimmers or not.

Barkson had seen people drown just a little north of here, and she knew that the river was no calmer here. It branched away from Trinovante, and even that part of the Hidden River was deceptive.

As was the Tamsi. Technically, the Tamsi wasn't a separate river. It was a branch of the Hidden River. Early settlers of Trinovante had thought the Tamsi their river, when, in truth, it was still part of the main river in Dorovich.

There was a lot about the history of this continent that one community or one country believed, and it had turned out not to be true.

Apparently, she was living part of that change right now.

Because whatever was happening to the Kirillis had to be important and, Barkson was beginning to realize, it had a lot to do with magic.

She got out of the vehicle, reached into the back, and removed the leather case. She popped the lid off, and a map floated out.

She nearly dropped the case in surprise. She managed to keep her grip on it, though.

The map unfurled, as if it were on a table and someone was

unrolling it. The map even stopped unfurling, corner by corner, as if that imaginary someone had put a rock or a cup on the edge to hold it in place.

The map pulsed. It was a blur of colors and lines. Barkson blinked, not quite able to focus on it.

She took a step back. The center of the map resolved itself into an image similar to the one she could see from this turnout. The city pulsed before her, in the map and in real life.

Her heart pounded. She was more unnerved than she wanted to admit.

She wondered if she had to ask the map a question. She wasn't entirely sure she wanted to speak out loud to it.

But just as she had that thought, the map focused even more. The image got larger and larger, focusing on a section of G'Nzidia that led around the outskirts of the city.

The map moved, as if a small vehicle was driving along the road that the map was showing her. The map curled and curved through some side streets, then headed back onto a side road that paralleled the river.

From what Helia had told her, Ghita and her family lived in Feltshyon, which was another country in the Protectorate. Feltshyon wasn't as big as Qavner, but it was one of the few countries that had land on both sides of the river.

Barkson had driven from G'zen to Feltshyon many times, but she had never taken this route. This route kept her closer to the river.

When Qavner was trying to form the Protectorate, Feltshyon fought them at every turn. It was an actual war—or wars, really. Because every time Qavner lost, they'd regroup and try again.

The thought made Barkson pause. The Fey had come to Dorovich centuries ago. And now, at least some of them were here again. They had some kind of military purpose, and it had something to do with the Kirillis.

Her hands shook, and she willed them to stop. If this was a war, then she was a cog. But she was an important cog, one that would thwart whatever it was that these Fey were planning.

She made herself focus on the map. Every time she did, it changed. It didn't want her to go through the small country of Chiedanna. The route the map gave her across the border near the Hidden River was circuitous.

But if she went as the crow flies, then the route near the river was the most direct. It looked, to the naked eye, like going slightly east into Chiedanna and then west again in Feltshyon would take much longer.

Chiedanna's roads were the best in the Protectorate. Made of some kind of material that was actually smooth, the roads in Chiedanna encouraged speed. More than once, Barkson had gone through Chiedanna at five times the speed she went anywhere else.

As if it heard that thought, the map focused even more on the roads in Feltshyon. They closed in on a glowing point, one she hadn't seen until moments before. That point, according to the map, was Ghita's home on the outskirts of Feltingham.

That location of Ghita's home made the route the map had shown Barkson much more logical. She would have gone an hour or more out of her way to arrive at that very same spot.

Barkson committed the route to memory, and then started to reach for the map. She stopped halfway, not knowing what she was reaching for, exactly.

That map seemed to be made of light, not of parchment.

As she reached her hand up, the map receded. As her fingers brushed against it, the map turned into parchment and started to flutter to the ground.

She caught the map's right edge. It felt warm. In the corner, near her thumb, was Helia's signature. Above it was a circle with an HK intertwined in the middle. On the edges of the circle were tiny replicas of the Kirilli crest.

Barkson wondered how Helia had had time to create the map while Barkson had been hurrying Helia out of the tower.

Barkson frowned; Helia hadn't had the time.

She had already made these maps. For her own amusement? Or because she knew they would be needed?

Barkson didn't want to think about that. Nor did she want to set the other maps down so that she could roll up this one.

At that thought, the map flapped, making a cracking sound. A puff of air made Barkson momentarily lose her grip. The map then rolled itself up, and slipped back into the leather carrying case.

Barkson snapped the lid into place, as if she had trapped one of the Fey inside.

Her heart rate was elevated, like it had been when she fought that woman who had come through the portal.

Clearly, the map had magic. The question was, should Barkson trust the map or should she go the way that Gussie had told her to go?

Helia had believed that Gussie didn't have the knowledge to get Barkson to the right locations fast enough. Helia had wanted Barkson to trust Helia's maps, not Gussie's.

Helia had saved Barkson's life. Helia had performed some amazing magical feats just in the past several hours.

Barkson had to trust that the maps were another magical feat, one that would help her save the Kirilli family.

Barkson had agreed to this task, thinking all she had ahead of her was a very long ride, with some stops to inform siblings that their father was dead. She had known that something or someone was after Kirillis, but she didn't believe that the danger would have manifested already.

This last stop disabused her of all of it.

Now, she had to hurry because she was terrified she wouldn't get to the four remaining siblings in time.

OLYX

FELTSHYON

FELTINGHAM

FELTSHYON

CHAPTER
NINE

The sun had just reached its zenith when Barkson reached the outskirts of Feltingham. Although it didn't feel like she was in the outskirts.

This part of Feltingham was overgrown and wild. Fences weren't neat little rows like they were in Qavner. Fences were the foundation for overgrown climbing vines from roses to ivy and beyond. Everywhere, the neighborhood was lush and green.

Bugs slammed against the vehicle's windscreen, and more than once, Barkson had had to stop to wipe the thing off. She needed more water; the bug layer had become a smear of yellow, green, and brown goo. She managed to get a lot of it off with a cloth she kept in the back just for polishing the vehicle.

That cloth was going to get thrown out when she returned to Qavner—or maybe, she might exchange it for a new cloth somewhere inside Feltingham.

The air was thick with humidity. The area smelled of overgrown greenery and rich, fertile mud.

Barkson wished she had remembered that about the bugs when she set out on this trip. She was unprepared for the onslaught which was, she had to admit, a lot worse this close to the river.

She'd been hugging it all along, on a road that didn't seem to have any traffic at all. If she were a more fanciful woman, she would have believed that the road created itself just for her.

But there was a lot of evidence that the road had existed here for centuries. The old fences, the large stone posts at intersections, the occasional huddle of cottages against a ridge.

The fact that the air was still and quiet just reflected Barkson's unease and made her think of horrible things.

Like...what if Ghita and her family were not at home? How would Barkson find them? What if Barkson did find them, the way that Gussie had found her father's staff?

Barkson had seen a lot in her life, but she had never seen anything quite like what Gussie had experienced just the day before.

And the fact that it had only been the day before made Barkson even more uneasy. Events were moving rapidly, and she was beginning to feel like she was falling further and further behind.

A road made of yellow dirt lined with red and orange flowers on either side, rose out of the muck like a dream.

The map had shown exactly that, but Barkson hadn't wanted to believe it. She had thought the yellow in the center, each side lined with red and orange, had been an artistic affectation rather than an accurate representation of what Barkson was actually seeing before her now.

Recent carriage tracks grooved the yellow. Fortunately, the

road was wide enough that Barkson could move her vehicle slightly to the right and not get caught in the tracks.

The yellow on the road was dirt of some kind, placed on top of the ground, but not really packed down.

That showed that the road wasn't used as much as other roads that Barkson had traveled along. Carriage tracks should have made her calmer; they didn't, though.

Maybe it meant that the Kirillis were already gone. Or maybe it meant that the attackers had arrived by a completely different route this time.

She had no idea, and the fact that she was alone ensured that she would dwell on all of this rather than find something else for her mind to consider. Her mind was playing with the fact that things could go seriously wrong in the next hour the way her tongue would play with a loose tooth.

She wanted to shake off the feeling, but she was having trouble doing so.

Which was probably logical, given all she'd been through already.

She made sure she was on alert. The vehicle was having trouble in the yellow dirt. It was fine, almost like sand, and a little slippery.

The dirt was getting into the windstone vents. If this continued, she'd have to stop and empty them out.

At that moment, though, the road crested over a hill. The lush greenery continued down the other side, but the carriage tracks went left, instead of following the rest of the yellow dirt down the hill.

The map had shown this as well, without the carriage tracks. A narrow path went between green leafy lumps which,

Barkson had to assume, probably had some kind of fence beneath it.

She followed the carriage path. It weaved around dead tree stumps and gigantic live tree trunks, which were also covered in ivy.

It seemed that everything here, if it remained stationary long enough, would be covered in vines.

And sure enough, once she rounded the next corner, she saw that she had been right. A stone house stood at the end of the drive, and threaded throughout were vines and flowers and greenery.

It looked intentional.

It might have been. The grounds here were certainly cleaner than the area on the drive up.

A carriage was parked to one side. It didn't seem to fit on the property. The coachman sat on his bench, the reins on his lap. Two horses fidgeted in their harnesses. They didn't seem disturbed as her vehicle grinded its way to a stop.

Barkson would have to clean out the vents, and that irritated her. If she had to make a quick getaway, she would have trouble.

She parked. This house looked something like the house on the map. That house had been pristine—no greenery—and it had seemed smaller.

The house before her was probably as big as the estate house that Dilshad lived in. Only this place looked like it had grown out of the ground, almost like a stone mound on a mountainside—not that there was any mountain near here.

Barkson couldn't see a door, or any way to enter the house. There was no path leading away from the drive, nothing to suggest that the house even had an entrance.

The carriage was probably blocking it.

Voices rumbled from a distance. They sounded edgy, shrill, as if someone was upset.

Barkson heard both male and female voices, and a few whose gender she couldn't determine. The mood seemed to quiet any birds that might have been around here, but not the inevitable bugs.

Some of them chittered and buzzed, as if they too were carrying on an important conversation.

A few of them danced around her head, tiny gnats that looked like black dots across her vision.

The gnats decided her.

She hated it up here. It wasn't a haven like some of the other Kirilli homes had been. This was some kind of overgrown nightmare.

She grabbed the letters and shrugged on her coat, even though the air was warm and humid here. She holstered her pistol and made sure she had at least one knife.

She had left one of her favorite knives in the dead woman at Dilshad's. Barkson had been unwilling to pull the knife out of the woman's forehead.

The knife Barkson now took was more accurately called a dagger. It had a mean serrated edge that could cut anyone dumb enough to test its sharpness with the fat part of their thumb.

She placed the knife in its sheath on her belt, but left her coat open, not because of the heat, but so that she could easily reach one of the weapons if she needed to.

Then she gently closed the vehicle's door, latching it carefully so that it wouldn't make much of a sound—not that the conversationalists would have heard it.

Their voices had grown progressively louder.

"I did not!" a woman yelled. "And you have no right!"

A man answered, his voice an angry rumble.

Barkson tensed. This kind of fight was not what she needed when she delivered the letters.

She thought about going the other direction from the carriage, but a tangle of vines and shrubs and greenery stopped her. It looked like she could get trapped inside that area just by stepping inside it.

Instead, Barkson walked over to the carriage. It was black and navy with some sort of official symbol on the side. The symbol had writing in a language she couldn't read. It looked like, though, that the language used the Shyon-Dana alphabet, which meant the language was probably Felttese, given where she was.

Felttese meant that the carriage was official to the county or the city or the country itself. Barkson wasn't exactly certain about the details of the local government.

All she knew was what everyone in the Protectorate knew: in theory, the Protectorate left the local governments intact. In practice, the local governments handled things that the Protectorate deemed unimportant.

The coachman wore a small cap with the same symbol on the side. The symbol also covered the brown sleeves of his brown and gold uniform. The symbol appeared on the whip he had across his lap, and on the horses' harnesses, as well as the side of their blinders.

"You can get off my property!" the woman shouted. "You have no rights here."

"That's where you're wrong, ma'am. We have rights..." The man's voice faded as he started to explain what rights he had.

Barkson made a fist, placing all of her annoyance in the center of it, and released it.

Her booted feet kicked up a bit of yellow dirt. She hadn't realized that the yellow was part of the natural color of whatever kind of soil there was in this part of the Protectorate.

The coachman looked over at her and startled. He hadn't seen or heard her.

He stood, about to call someone, when she shook her head.

"I'm part of the family," Barkson lied.

Then she pushed past the carriage, careful to stay clear of the horses, and rounded the side of the large house. Here the greenery had more order. Orange flowers bent off large shrubs, begging to be touched. The vines had been cut back on the building itself so that it actually looked like the stone house Barkson had seen on the map.

Three men in brown and gold uniforms stood near a cluster of shrubs. A fourth man stood closer to the building.

A young woman stood on a porch, a baby on her hip. Another woman, older and clearly part of the staff, stood behind her, twisting her hands together. A little boy was peeking through her skirts.

The young woman looked startlingly like Gussie had when she and Barkson had gone to the Academy.

"Ghita?" Barkson said, using her *I'm in charge* voice. "What's going on here?"

The young woman turned to her, and Barkson saw the differences. Ghita's face was longer than Gussie's had been, her eyes darker, but filled with an incredible intelligence.

Barkson saw the expression on Ghita's face change from anger to *who the hell are you?* to...

"Lucy?" Ghita asked, sounding almost frightened.

"Yes," Barkson said, glad that Ghita hadn't used her last name.

Barkson stepped slightly to one side, so that the men would think that Ghita wasn't confirming Barkson's identity; they would think Ghita hadn't seen Barkson clearly.

Barkson walked over to the men, allowing her coat to swing so that they could see her weapons without her having to brandish them.

"What is this about?" she asked.

Ghita's eyes narrowed. "They're saying that Rudolfo is dead. They're saying I killed him."

It took a moment for Barkson to remember that Rudolfo was Ghita's husband. Helia had tried to make sure Barkson knew the names of all the relatives, but the children's names in particular weren't sticking. Apparently neither were the names of all of the spouses.

"Where did he die?" Barkson asked Ghita, as if the men weren't there.

"I'm not sure he *is* dead," Ghita said fiercely. "These men want to take all of us into custody, just like they've tried to do several times in the past two weeks. They claim that Rudolfo doesn't represent a government they recognize, and he needs to be in prison. We've been begging the Protectorate for more security."

Barkson blinked, not certain exactly what was going on. She knew there was unrest in several countries—there always was, in the Protectorate.

"Have they ever threatened his life before?" Barkson asked, her heart rate increasing even more. She didn't like the coincidence.

"Yes, of course," Ghita said. "We get death threats every day. That's why Rudolfo wants me to leave the country. He thinks there's an uprising coming."

Ghita glared at the men now, as if they had started the uprising already.

Barkson still didn't look at them. "When did you see him last?"

"This morning," Ghita said, with anger directed at the men. "Two hours ago. He was *fine*. These men are lying."

These men might not be lying, Barkson almost said, but that meant she would take a side. Right now, she had to handle this so that Ghita and the children could get out of here, maybe sooner rather than later.

Barkson faced the men. The one closest to her was older, with some gray lining his temples. His face was square, his skin dark, his expression concerned rather than angry.

The men behind him had the implacable expressions of people who had been brought along, not for their expertise, but because they had to act as security.

Their uniforms resembled the coachman's, with brown and gold, and a lot of symbols.

The older man had a cap under his arm, but his uniform was less of a uniform and more like a slightly official shirt paired with whatever pants he had found in his closet that morning. The pants were navy. The rest of his clothing was not.

His gaze met hers. He had the look of a man who was used to giving bad news.

"What happened to Rudolfo?" Barkson asked.

"Who are you?" the man asked.

"You're the one on the Olvedus's property without permission," Barkson said, using Rudolfo's last name. "You get to answer my questions first."

It was a gamble to approach the man that way. The man's eyes narrowed, and for a moment, Barkson thought she might lose that gamble. Her entire body relaxed, as it always did before a fight. If she tensed, her opponent would notice, and they might take action before her.

Then the man clearly made a decision. He glanced at Ghita, then back at Barkson.

"Lord Olvedus died shortly after he arrived at work," the man said.

Lord Olvedus? Barkson hadn't heard that honorific used in connection with the Protectorate before. Perhaps that was a local affectation.

"He was alone at the time," the man said. "Which leaves us with only one conclusion: the man was poisoned."

Barkson blinked, startled. "Only one conclusion?"

She didn't continue with that train of thought out of respect to Ghita. But dying alone might have meant some kind of apoplexy or breathing issues or even choking on a bit of food.

"Yes, ma'am," the man said. "He wasn't an older man. He had no health problems. He wasn't eating or drinking at the time."

"So you assumed he was poisoned...by his wife?" Barkson asked.

"No one else had access," the man said.

"I beg your pardon," Barkson said in a tone that suggested

she wasn't begging anyone's pardon for anything. And now she would have to be graphic, because she needed this argument to end now. "But he had to go through half a city to get to his office. He had probably greeted a dozen people. You are aware, are you not, sir, that poison isn't just ingested. It can be administered through touch or even in the air. If he is dead, as you suggest, then there is no way you could have investigated everything before coming here to accuse his wife of something heinous."

The man's eyes narrowed even more. "Who are you again?"

"Who are *you*?" Barkson asked. More gambling. "You certainly are not behaving like someone who is a trusted public servant."

He bristled. "You have no right to speak to me that way."

"I have every right," Barkson said. "You're the one without rights. This family represents the Protectorate. At best, if you are who you say you are, you represent a small city. You have no rights on this property and you have no reason to harass the lady of the house."

He sputtered. Ghita shifted slightly, as if Barkson's words surprised her.

The security men didn't move. Apparently they didn't see Barkson as a threat.

Yet.

"If you're here to inform her of a tragedy, then you are doing a piss-poor job of it. *Sir*." Barkson made sure the contempt she felt for him registered in her voice.

"He's gone," the man said to Ghita. "You can come identify the body."

"She will do no such thing," Barkson said. "Not with you,

anyway. You'll be leaving the property. But before you go, you will inform her where her husband's body is being taken."

The man glared at Barkson. "It will remain in the office until we know what exactly happened."

"Ah," Barkson said with a smile she didn't mean. "You concede that I have a point. Good. Now leave. We will be there to talk with Rudolfo or to take him home, depending on the circumstance. But we will use our own conveyance. You may leave now."

He straightened even more. She was shaming him in front of his men, deliberately. She wanted to see what he was really made of.

Finally, he pivoted and stalked down the driveway.

"Come with me," he said to the men. They followed.

Barkson did, too. She needed to move her vehicle so that the carriage could leave, but she also wanted to make certain that the carriage *did* leave.

"Lucy," Ghita called.

"Just a minute," Barkson said. "I'll be right back."

She followed the men, making sure that none of them remained behind. It looked like one of them was considering it until he saw her. Then all four men climbed into the carriage.

Even though she wanted to run, she walked unhurriedly to her vehicle, got inside, and moved it a little farther up the drive so that the carriage could pass.

It did, without anyone acknowledging her. The dust rising from the wheels was yellowish brown, and smelled faintly of saffron.

That tickled a memory—something about spells used in the

outlying countries to control behavior. She might check that later.

She didn't like the thought, though.

She got out of the vehicle and watched the carriage make its way through the overgrowth. Once she could no longer see it, she walked back to the other side of the house.

Ghita remained on the porch but the other woman and both children were gone.

"This isn't a social visit," Ghita said. "You're here for a reason."

"I am," Barkson said. "Gussie sent me."

"I suppose she needs something," Ghita said. "You can tell her that we have our hands full. Ever since Rudolfo took over the Office of the Protectorate for Feltshyon, we've been dealing with protests and attacks by locals and all sorts of threats. These people have no trouble telling us that they will kill our children if we don't leave the country. Which only makes me more determined to stay."

These people. Barkson had heard terms like that before, only farther north. It never boded well.

And if Barkson was in this position, she would have left if someone threatened the children. Or gotten the children out. Or, at least, hired more security—and not of the local variety.

She decided not to step into that thicket at all.

"Gussie doesn't need anything from you," Barkson said. "She asked me to give you two letters. You need to read them immediately."

Barkson handed Ghita the first letter, while keeping a grip on the second.

"Well," Ghita said, "give me the other one."

Barkson shook her head. "There's a procedure."

Ghita's upper lip curled in contempt. "Of course there is."

She opened the first envelope and pulled out the letter. Then she looked around to make sure no one else was watching.

The house might look isolated, but Ghita was clearly worried. She was afraid she was being watched.

Barkson tapped the other envelope against her palm, and surveyed the area. She didn't see any movement in the lush greenery. The flowers were magnificent, reds and golds and pinks and yellows, and looked like they were wild, which Barkson doubted.

All of the blooms faced the house, which suggested that someone had worked on the plants. She just saw no evidence of who.

Ghita made a small choking sound.

Barkson looked at her sharply, remembering the accusation of poison. But Ghita wasn't actually choking. She was trying to hold back sobs.

She waved the letter at Barkson. "Why would anyone do this?"

"I don't know," Barkson said, "but we thwarted an attack at Dilshad's earlier this morning."

"We?" Ghita asked.

"I picked up Helia along the way. She's with Dilshad and his family now. They're safe."

Ghita looked back at the letter as if she didn't believe it. Then she shook it at Barkson.

"Do you think...?" Ghita shook her head, still shaking the letter, as if it had stuck to her hand. "Do you think...?"

Barkson waited, having learned long ago not to finish the sentences of someone in distress.

"...that Rudolfo...that someone did this...?" Ghita swallowed, unable to go on.

"I don't know," Barkson said. "I don't like the coincidence, but as you said, there's unrest here."

"Yeah." Ghita's contempt returned. "The locals hate us. They call us colonizers."

They aren't wrong, Barkson thought but did not say. The Protectorate took over the governance and the economics of every country along the Hidden River, all the way to Mount Vitaki.

"Here's the second letter," she said.

"Leave it to Gussie to make this overly complicated," Ghita said with the same contempt.

What had happened to this young woman that she had become so nasty? Barkson had had no idea that Ghita had turned into someone that, had they met on the street, Barkson would dislike intensely.

Ghita took the envelope and ripped open its edge, then pulled out the second letter.

She stared at it for the longest time. "She wants me to leave? And go where?"

"The letter should tell you," Barkson said.

"Somewhere *safe*? Somewhere unconnected to the Kirilli family? What does that even mean?"

"She doesn't want you easily found," Barkson said.

Ghita was still staring at the letter, but she clearly wasn't seeing it. "And if...?"

The tears started falling again, hitting the paper with soft thuds.

Barkson waited. She thought she knew the direction of this question, but she still waited, resisting the urge to tap her foot and urge Ghita to hurry.

"...if he's...like my father...?"

That was probably a good analogy, because Ghita's father had died in a magical attack. If Rudolfo had died, and it wasn't poison, then dying alone at his young age probably was another magical attack.

And that meant that Ghita had to get out of here quickly.

"I don't know," Barkson said. "If I think I can safely send word, I will. But I still need to reach three of your brothers. They will take priority."

"So no news is bad news," Ghita said.

"Maybe," Barkson said. "I can't exactly answer that."

"Rudolfo said this would protect us." Ghita waved a hand at the property. "Everything here, it's some kind of botanical thaumaturgy. It's supposed to keep bad people away. But it didn't work today, did it?"

So that explained the saffron smell, the overgrowth, and the flowers, which now come to think of it, looked somewhat threatening.

"Those men did not take you from here or harm you," Barkson said. She wasn't going to deny any kind of magic. Not today.

"That's because of you," Ghita said.

"Maybe," Barkson said. "But those men seemed pretty subdued."

Ghita sighed. "If we're protected, then I should stay here."

"I found you," Barkson said. "Those men found you. It sounds like you're under threat from several sides. If it was just you, I'd say that you should stay. But it's not. You have children."

"I could send them with you," Ghita said.

Barkson barely managed to suppress a shudder.

"No, you cannot," Barkson said firmly. "I am going to see your brothers. If I run into the same kinds of problems I had at Dilshad's, then I can't guarantee that your children will survive."

The word *survive* slipped out before she could stop it. Ghita looked like she had been slapped.

"It's that bad?"

What do you think? Barkson wanted to say. *Your father is dead. His staff is dead. Your brother and his family nearly died and would have if we weren't there.*

"Yes," Barkson said without elaborating. "It's that bad."

Ghita tapped the second letter against her chin. All the air seemed to have gone out of her. All the fight, all of the power.

"The woman who is taking care of your children," Barkson said. "Is she local?"

"Why?" Ghita asked.

"Please," Barkson said. "Answer me."

"No," Ghita said. "My father…"

Her voice cracked. She cleared her throat, wiped at her eyes, and took a deep breath.

"My father hired her. He said…"

Ghita had to take another deep breath.

"He said that we needed someone we could trust and he trusted her."

"Good," Barkson said. "Then the four of you need to leave

now. You mentioned a place that Rudolfo wanted you to go to. Where did he want you to go?"

"To my father's." Ghita's voice was small.

She might have been unpleasant, but her entire world was turning upside down. Barkson had to remember that—with all of the Kirillis.

"Is there anywhere else you can go?" Barkson asked.

Ghita kept tapping the second letter against her chin, the first letter half-crumpled in her hand. She was shaking her head as she did so, her gaze moving back and forth as she thought.

Then she shrugged.

"There's a really nice inn in Chiedanna. We spent a week there after we got married." She bit her lower lip. "I know it's still there because we went a few weeks ago, to celebrate our anniversary."

Her eyes filled with tears.

Chiedanna. If Barkson had driven through Chiedanna, she would have arrived too late.

The sense of urgency she'd been feeling just got worse.

"Do you have enough money to pay for the four of you?" Barkson asked. She could give Ghita some of the gold coins that Gussie had given her, if need be.

Ghita started nodding. She sniffled, but kept nodding. "We have emergency funds and some luggage already packed. Rudolfo kept saying we might have to leave fast, so we had to be ready."

"He was right," Barkson said. "Do you have a windstone vehicle?"

"Yes."

"Do you know how to drive it?" Barkson asked.

"Rudolfo made sure that I did." Ghita sniffled again. "He made sure. And I practiced."

"Then you need to leave here," Barkson said, "as fast as you can."

"Are you going ahead of us?" Ghita asked, as if she was suddenly afraid that Barkson would leave them alone.

"No," Barkson said. "I need to wait for you to leave. You'll have to tell me more about that inn."

Ghita nodded again. "I will. Then you'll find Rudolfo?"

"If you tell me where the offices are," Barkson said. She didn't want to go anywhere near a potential investigation, but technically, Rudolfo Olvedus was part of the Kirilli family. She needed to find out if he was killed by locals or if he was the victim of a magical attack. Or if he died of some kind of natural causes.

"I can do that," Ghita said. "But you'll be careful, right?"

"Yes," Barkson said. "I'll do what I can."

If Rudolfo was still alive, if those four men had come for some other reason, she would make sure that Rudolfo got out of Feltshyon and was able to join his family.

Ghita nodded, her lips pursed, her gaze on the letters again, as if the information in them would change.

"What if he doesn't come?" she asked, almost to herself.

"You'll go on," Barkson said.

Ghita looked up at her. "What if I don't want to?"

Barkson had not expected all of these messy emotions when she agreed to take this journey for Gussie. Barkson never thought of herself as particularly wise or empathetic.

She couldn't try right now, either.

"What would Rudolfo say if he heard you admit that?" Barkson said. "Especially since his children were in your care."

"They're my children, too," Ghita said fiercely. Which was probably an automatic response.

"What would he say?" Barkson asked.

Ghita looked at the plants, at the flowers, then at the letters again. She pulled them to her chest.

"He would tell me to straighten up," she said. "He would say there's time for emotion later. He would tell me that if we act, everything will be all right. He would tell me...he would tell me..."

She shook her head.

"I can't do this, Lucy. I can't."

Barkson's heart sank. She hadn't expected this from a Kirilli either, particularly not from Ghita the fierce.

"Of course you can," Barkson said. "If Gussie could handle seeing your father and the staff dead, and still manage to write letters to her entire family and send me on the way, then you can take your children out of here."

Ghita let out a small surprised "huh." "You remember that I used to use Gussie as my role model? You still remember that?"

Barkson smiled. "The fierce little girl who said she could get through the Bekyce School for Girls because her sister had done it? Sure, I remember that."

Ghita nodded. "I'm older now. Maybe a little dumber."

"Maybe," Barkson said. "If you don't get out of here fast."

"Right." Ghita turned and looked at the door. Whatever she saw made the tears flow harder. "Do I tell them about their dad?"

One of them was a baby, but Ghita clearly wasn't thinking about that clearly, which worried Barkson.

"No," Barkson said. "You have no information right now. You tell them that I'm searching for him, which will be true. If you leave this place as fast as possible."

"All right." Ghita went into the house. Barkson stood outside for a moment, trying to decide what to do, since she was not invited in.

Then she decided that it didn't matter. She had to hurry Ghita through this. Barkson would talk to the nanny or the maid or whoever that other woman was, and get her to help.

The faster they moved, the better off they would be.

Barkson had to make sure everyone in the household understood that.

CHAPTER
TEN

Somehow, Barkson got Ghita, the nanny, and the children out of the house within the hour. Ghita had been moving by rote, going through motions that she had clearly learned through repetition.

Barkson silently thanked Rudolfo, and hoped that she would get the chance to thank him in person.

After Ghita left, Barkson drove to the edge of the drive where she could see the rest of the property, more or less. It wasn't like Dilshad's property, which had been barren and had visibility for miles.

This property had hiding places everywhere.

Barkson watched until she couldn't see the cloud of dust from Ghita's carriage any longer. Barkson hoped they would get to Chiedanna without a lot of problems.

Her only consolation was that Chiedanna wasn't that far from Feltingham. Ghita, the nanny and the children would get to Chiedanna—and maybe to safety—within a few hours.

If they didn't stop.

Barkson hadn't warned them about that, but she had managed to put some fear into the nanny. Maybe the nanny would keep Ghita on the right pace.

After they were out of her view, Barkson handled the next problem. The yellow dirt. As the day warmed, the air smelled more and more of saffron.

The dirt had gotten into everything, and it coated her boots. Barkson had to remove the vents and use one of the tools from her kit to blow the dirt out. The dirt was fine, almost like powder, and it took several attempts to clear the vents.

She had to do so again, after she had gotten off the drive and onto the main road. Her windstone vehicle left yellow tracks on the paving stones. She almost stopped to blow the dust off the paving stones, and finally decided that she didn't need to.

If someone was going to try to track Ghita, then they might follow Barkson's windstone vehicle tracks instead.

The drive into the main part of Feltingham took less time than Barkson expected. The Olvedus property felt like it was far outside of town, but it really wasn't—not taking the route that Ghita had suggested.

The buildings went from estates built far apart to narrow houses to dilapidated huts within the space of a few miles. The saffron smell left, finally blowing out of the vents, to be replaced by the stench of a hot city, overrun by horse manure, garbage, and days-old cooking smells.

Maybe if there had been more of a wind, Feltingham would have smelled better, but the air was still, as if it were waiting for something.

Barkson was trying very hard not to speed through the city

streets. They were filled with well-dressed people on horseback, people in faded clothes walking near the edges, and strangely shaped carts with people sitting in the back being pulled by a single person, running.

The runners could almost keep up with the horses.

Barkson didn't see a lot of carriages this way. She was clearly on a back road, not the main road.

This road turned slightly to the right and then opened up onto a large plaza, filled with merchants hawking wares. She had to turn to the right to avoid driving into the plaza, and then she found herself on narrow streets again, only these streets were lined with buildings so old that some of them had turned a kind of gray instead of the sunlight-reflecting white walls that some of the other buildings had. All of the roofs were made of red tile.

In the very center, a tower rose off the side of a round building that was made of riverstone. The building had clearly been built as a fortress, and the city had grown up around it. That explained the winding roads.

The Office of the Protectorate for Feltshyon was apparently in that building. And although she could see it, she had no idea how to get there.

The winding road she found herself on was filled with people, all of whom—male or female—wore linen robes of varying colors, matching pants, and sandals.

These people had to be locals. No one from Qavner would dress like that. She slowed the vehicle to a crawl and wended her way around people, wishing she had the top down so that she could apologize.

Most of the people got out of her way, but several of them glared at her as she crept by them. As much as she could, she kept her gaze on that tower. Finally, she rounded another corner, and found herself on a wider street, filled with carriages like the one that had come to Ghita's home earlier.

Barkson wasn't about to park her windstone vehicle this far away from the tower. Fortunately, windstone vehicles didn't seem to be common here, so she had been able to get people to move, just from the novelty of it.

Now she managed to creep between the carriages, praying she wouldn't spook horses. These horses were hardy, used to city streets and surprises. A few nervously raised a leg or shook their heads, but none bolted, for which she was very grateful.

She managed to stop right in front of the tower. A series of stone steps, painted red like the roof, climbed to the entrance. The steps were wide on the bottom, growing increasingly narrow until they reached the door itself.

The door was open, and people wearing the uniforms she had seen that morning were scurrying in and out.

Then she saw the man she had seen at Ghita's. He was on the landing, two rows up from the street, watching his people carry items out of the tower.

Barkson had a hunch this action was not sanctioned by the Protectorate.

But she couldn't worry about local politics right now. She leaned out the window and yelled at him, wishing she had caught his name.

He didn't turn at first, until she shouted, in Qavnerian, "I am here for the Kirilli family!"

He looked around, then finally focused on her. He hurried down the stairs and stopped at her window.

"Say that much louder and you will find yourself under

attack as well." He spoke as softly as he could. That was when something registered for Barkson.

The crowd was a quiet one. She hadn't heard them do much more than talk and murmur as she drove her way here. Even when someone was angry at her, they shook a fist. They didn't yell.

"Where is Rudolfo?" Barkson asked.

The man's face changed. It didn't soften, exactly, but it had lost some of its aggression.

He waved a hand at a white wagon, with a single horse attached to the front. In back, there were bodies, covered in red blankets with sunrise shaped patterns across the top.

"His body is there," the man said.

Barkson's heart sank. She didn't know what Rudolfo looked like, but she had to pretend that she did.

"Show me," she said, and got out of the windstone vehicle. Then she turned toward it. "Before I go with you, though, I need some of your people to guard this."

His expression flattened. She recognized the look. It was one of those looks people used when someone had crossed a line, but no one could call them on it.

"That's not our job," he said.

"Make it your job," she said, knowing she was behaving badly. But she couldn't tell him why she needed that vehicle or why she needed to get out of here quickly, with everything intact.

She was going to have to trust him, and she didn't want to.

He continued the flat look for a long moment. "We didn't kill him," he said.

"Neither did we," she said.

"Something else happened here," he said. "I have a feeling you know what that is."

"I don't," she said. "Not until I see him, and I'm not going to look at anything until I know that I have a vehicle to return to."

"You do not trust my people?" he asked.

"I arrived when you were trying to arrest Rudolfo's wife. So why should I trust you? She says there has been some discontent among the locals."

"Discontent." He snorted. "Discontent."

Barkson waited, feeling very vulnerable, even inside her vehicle. Driving out of here would be very difficult. If the crowd turned on her, she would have to scare them with her pistol or drive through them. She didn't want to do any of that.

She kept her expression impassive as she thought of it all, though. She didn't want him to know that she could be lethal if she had to be. But she also didn't want him to think of her as a victim.

"You would not like it if we overtook your home and tried to make it our own," he said.

It would help if I had a home, Barkson almost said. But she didn't. She understood his point.

"I'm not part of the government," she said. "I'm here as a representative of the family."

"Representative," he said. "Not part of the family?"

She wasn't sure how to answer that. She wasn't going to tell him who she was.

"Rudolfo's wife did not feel safe after your stunt this morning," Barkson said. "She sent me."

He looked at Barkson long and hard. "So, not a family member," he said after a moment. "But trusted."

You have no idea. Barkson wondered if he could hear those unspoken words. She didn't try to say them though. All she did was wait, quietly, for him to say something more.

"I will make sure your vehicle is protected," he said after a moment. He snapped his fingers in the direction of the tower.

Barkson couldn't see who the snap was directed at until two men, not from the morning, left their posts at the base of the stairs and joined the man.

They were tall and thin. Their age difference appeared only as they got closer. One was about Barkson's age; the other had to be twenty years older. They both wore their hair long but tied back.

"They will watch your vehicle, and if something happens to it, I promise you, they will not work for me or the community ever again." The man wasn't looking at her as he said it, but at the other two.

They didn't seem cowed by the threat. She wasn't sure she wanted them to be.

She got out of the vehicle, and knew that even with the guards, she didn't dare be away from it for very long.

The air was warm and humid. She wasn't sure if it was normally warmer here in Feltingham, since it was at a lower elevation, or if the sun had finally reached its zenith, and was making every part of Feltshyon warm.

She kept her coat on, though, because she hadn't removed her weapons for the drive.

The man led her to that wagon. She caught a faint whiff of death, which was fast if Rudolfo had died that morning. But heat sometimes sped up decay, and she wouldn't have been surprised if that had happened here.

Nine bodies were stacked on top of each other in the back of the wagon. They were wrapped in light cloth.

The man stopped on the far side of the wagon and peeled the cloth back from the face of the body closest to him.

The body belonged to a man. Someone had closed his eyes. He was young enough to be Ghita's husband, and he had the pale skin of someone who was from the coastal towns of Qavner.

The man who was helping Barkson continued to pull down the cloth. The dead man was wearing a tunic that the Protectorate gave to all of its senior officials. The tunic seemed to fit perfectly, so no one moved it or changed it.

There was no blood and the skin—at least on the face— looked like it was intact.

"What killed him?" she asked.

"We don't know," the man said. "The others, though, we found them dead the same way. It was as if something had simply reached inside them and stolen the life from them."

She suppressed a shudder. She wasn't going to suggest that the deaths had a magical component. She didn't dare mention the word, when she didn't know the magical history of Feltshyon.

"We have one survivor," he said. "She saw it. I did not know that when I came to the house. Nor did I know about the other dead. Would you like to speak with her?"

"Yes," Barkson said. "But first, answer me a question."

He stared at her, chin jutting out defiantly.

"If you had no idea what had happened, why did you really come to the house?"

He moved his jaw, just a little, as if he was trying to answer, but wouldn't allow himself to do so. Then he looked down at Rudolfo (if, indeed, that was Rudolfo) and finally looked back at Barkson.

"The house does not belong to them or to the Protectorate," the man finally said. "It is ours. It is a historic house, like this tower is a historic place. The Protectorate has confiscated not just our buildings but our history."

"And you were going to take it back," Barkson said.

He pulled the cloth back over Rudolfo's face.

"Would you like to speak to the survivor?" he asked.

"Yes, if you bring her to my vehicle," Barkson said.

His lips pursed as if he had eaten something sour, but he didn't argue. Instead, he beckoned someone at the edge of the crowd.

Barkson walked back toward her vehicle. The guards stood next to it, but they didn't seem to stop people from circling it, gawking at it, peering at the interior.

"Back away from the vehicle," she said as she approached. She hoped they all spoke Qavnerian. They were supposed to be able to. It had been taught in schools since the Protectorate took over the country, but that didn't mean everyone learned it.

There was a backlash against learning and speaking Qavnerian in some countries. She had no idea if this was one of them.

Still, the people closest to the vehicle backed away. One of the guards—the younger one—flinched and would have moved too if the other one hadn't spoken softly to him.

Barkson stalked toward them, wondering if she should offer them coin for their efforts or if she should just let them be.

Before she could make a decision, the man brought a stout woman with him. The woman wore a long dress of thick material and her graying black hair was piled on top of her head.

She clearly didn't belong here any more than Barkson did.

"This is Ma'am Makelli," the man said. "She was your man's assistant."

Barkson's man. Rudolfo.

Barkson leaned against her vehicle, making sure she was standing so that she could see the entire length of the vehicle and the woman.

Barkson wasn't sure, but it seemed like this part of the road had even more people in it than it had just a few moments ago. Many of them were focused on her.

She didn't like this at all.

But the woman—Makelli—she was not some kind of ringer, as far as Barkson could tell. Makelli's eyes were red, and she was shaking.

"I understand you were in the building when Rudolfo died," Barkson said.

"When they all died, yes, ma'am," Makelli said, her eyes downcast. She wasn't looking at anyone.

"What happened?" Barkson asked.

Makelli shook her head, then looked at the man. She seemed more frightened of him than Barkson.

"I can't say, ma'am," Makelli said.

Barkson looked at the man, too. "Thank you for bringing her here. Now, let me talk with her."

His eyes narrowed, but he stepped back. He snapped his fingers again, and the guards left with him.

Barkson wasn't sure if that was a subtle threat against

Makelli or against Barkson and the vehicle, and she wasn't going to worry about it. She was going to get her answers and leave this place.

"Can I take you somewhere?" Barkson asked Makelli, knowing she might talk more if there was privacy.

To Barkson's surprise, Makelli shook her head. "I sent for the Administrator of this Region. He should be here soon."

The Administrator of the Protectorate for this Region. Barkson had no idea what soon meant or even if the word would reach him, and she wasn't going to speculate. She needed this woman to talk, and then Barkson had to leave.

She was, frankly, relieved that Makelli did not want any assistance.

"What happened?" Barkson asked again.

Makelli took a step closer. She smelled of sweat, the kind of flop sweat someone got when they were terrified.

"I have to use words that the Protectorate doesn't like," Makelli said.

Barkson nodded. "I thought as much. Don't worry. I won't report you."

As if there was anyone to report to. But Barkson didn't add that.

"I think it was magic," Makelli said. "And not the kind they practice here. Here it's all flowers and potions and botanicals. But this—it was aggressive."

"Meaning what?" Barkson asked.

"A window opened and a light came through," Makelli said. "It was so powerful that it carved into the stone wall."

"Tell me the rest of it," Barkson said.

"It wrapped around everyone in that cart." Makelli waved

her hand at the cart. "I was just off to the side, but see? It singed my dress."

She held up her skirt, and sure enough, an edge had been sliced through. Barkson wondered what she might see if she pulled those cloths around the bodies all the way down. Maybe the deaths were as benign as that man wanted her to believe.

"They all—every one of them—cried out at the same time, and then they fell." Makelli clasped her hands over her chest, clearly distraught. "I didn't move. Not till the light went away. And that window. It went away too. Then I went over to Lord Olvedus. His eyes were open. He was dead. Maybe if I went sooner..."

"You would have died as well," Barkson said. She wasn't offering sympathy. She was just trying to get through the story. "This window. Was it a window inside the tower?"

"No, no," Makelli said. "It wasn't built anywhere. It just appeared in the air."

"Have you seen something like this before?" Barkson asked.

"No, no." Makelli said. "I just read about it, you know, in school. History of the Purges. The idea that someone could just enter a room with the wave of a hand, well, I used to think it was laughable."

She shook her head.

Barkson focused her gaze on Makelli. "Did you see anyone walk through that window?"

"I've been trying to remember," Makelli said. "It was just the light. I'm certain of that."

Barkson frowned. "Was Lord Olvedus always in that spot at that time of day?"

"His desk?" Makelli asked. "Of course. And he usually was hearing petitioners."

"So everyone knew he would be there," Barkson said. "It was advertised."

"I suppose you could say that, yes," Makelli said. "It was known if you had a complaint you came at that time."

She waved a hand at the people around her.

"*They* always came, more and more of them all the time, to complain about the Protectorate. Not something that we could do, mind you. Just the fact of it. As if we were in charge of the government. They apparently don't understand cogs."

Barkson wasn't sure she did either, until she focused. Cogs in a wheel. Underlings.

Either Barkson was getting tired or she was being incredibly distracted by the people milling around her. All of them seemed tense. None of them seemed to care about the bodies, though.

The wagon with all of the bodies hadn't left yet, either. No one seemed to be guarding it.

Barkson wasn't certain, but it seemed like more and more people were filling the plaza.

"You'd say that there's been a lot of unrest?" Barkson asked.

"Yes, yes, of course. I thought everyone knew," Makelli said. "Feltshyon never liked being part of the Protectorate. They tolerated us for a while, but lately..."

She let her words trail off.

"Do you think what happened today was because of the unrest?" Barkson asked.

Makelli shook her head. "Almost all of the dead are Felttesons. If anything, I think they blame us for that today. I've felt this kind of tension before. It leads to riots."

She wrapped her arms around her torso, as if hugging herself would make things easier.

Barkson hadn't looked at the other bodies. It was her own blindness that made her think they were all from Qavner.

"They have to understand that Rudolfo is dead as well," Barkson said.

"I don't think they know that." Makelli was speaking softly. "I don't think it matters."

"Do you think he was the target or they were?" Barkson asked.

"He was, clearly." Makelli said. "It was his office."

"Why then did the constabulary think his wife poisoned him?" Barkson asked.

Makelli sneered. The look made her seem older and a little mean. "They look for any excuse to get the Olvedus family out of that house. If the house is empty, then they'll take it over, the brutes. They think it's theirs instead of the spoils of war."

Barkson blinked. That was similar enough to what the man in charge had told her to be believable.

And now, the house was empty. She wondered if any of the Felttesons had taken it over yet.

"Who do you think attacked Rudolfo?" Barkson asked Makelli.

"Not someone I know," Makelli said. "I don't know anyone who has the ability to...you know. Do you?"

Open a portal? Shoot a lethal dose of light through it? Enough light to slaughter several people?

Barkson did not personally know anyone who could do that. But the attack was similar enough to the one at Dilshad's home to give Barkson an idea as to what happened.

160

The plaza had become wall-to-wall people. Barkson was going to have to push her way out with the nose of the vehicle.

"I can't stay here any longer," Barkson said, "and I don't think you should either. Let me take you out of here."

Makelli shook her head. "I'll be fine."

"Someone just tried to kill you," Barkson said. "You need to leave."

Makelli nodded. "I do. But I don't know you. And forgive me, but after this morning, I'm not going anywhere with someone I do not know."

Fair enough. Barkson probably wouldn't have either.

"All right, then," Barkson said. "Thank you for your time."

Then she let herself into the vehicle, making certain all the windscreens were up. She could no longer see Makelli. People were now shoulder to shoulder, talking, moving, pushing—almost a sea of people—and most of them seemed to have an eye on the stairs leading into the tower.

Makelli had been right; there was going to be some kind of incident.

Barkson couldn't drive forward. She would go into the thick of the crowd.

Instead, she backed up, ever so slowly. People moved out of her way. Some slammed their palms on the side of the vehicle in protest. Others glared at her.

It took nearly five minutes to go half a block—she could have walked it much faster—and by then everyone seemed to realize she was moving. She backed up until she could ease into an alley between buildings. There she turned around, driving out of the plaza the way she came.

Or rather, crawling out. Because she wasn't moving much faster than when she was backing up.

The crowd was no longer eerily silent. People were talking and some were yelling and she thought she heard the cadences of a speech.

She couldn't understand the words, but she could understand the emotion. Fury, anger. Someone was trying to rile up the crowd.

She reached for her cap and her driving goggles, figuring they might make her look less like a Qavnerian. At least she hoped that would be the case.

She had no idea how many Felttesons had windstone vehicles, but she had to hope that some did.

It was almost impossible to move the vehicle forward, but she managed. More and more people were pouring past her. They didn't seem to care about her. They were talking animatedly, a few arguing, and more than a few carried short swords, wicked-looking daggers, sickle swords, and curved swords. A few people carried actual sickles and more than one had an axe.

A shiver ran through her. Something about this morning had been the last straw for the people of Feltingham. The death of so many of their number while only one Qavnerian died? The fact that Qavnerians held their tower?

Or was something more planned? Maybe the man she had spoken to had used the events of the morning as a catalyst to get the Olvedus family out of that house. Maybe that man had planned to go up to the house anyway.

Barkson couldn't quite understand why he had helped her find Rudolfo. She was convinced that the man hadn't played a trick on her. The dead man had clearly been a Protectorate

Administrator. It would make sense that whoever was after the Kirilli family would find Rudolfo first. He was a public figure. His whereabouts during the day were easy to pinpoint.

Barkson continued to focus on the man who had helped her, though. Perhaps he thought that confirming Rudolfo's death would make certain that the family left that house.

And they had. Strange he hadn't asked about it. Maybe he had been planning to go back and check later, after whatever happened here.

Or maybe the events of the morning near this tower meant that his plans had gotten derailed.

She was finally reaching the edge of the city center. More and more people were walking in. Others had parked carriages, carts, and wagons in a semicircle around the plaza. Only one small opening remained, barely wide enough for her to squeeze the windstone vehicle through.

Several windstone vehicles were parked just beyond the carriages. Several people were watching the horses, but looking nervously at the center of the city, as if expecting something to go very badly.

Most of the carriages had at least one person nearby, as if someone (or many someones) were planning a hasty escape from the city. Maybe something like this had happened before.

No one seemed concerned with Barkson. Everyone was focused on that tower.

Maybe Rudolfo would have died this day, no matter what. She wasn't sure how large the Protectorate staff was here in Feltingham. Most local Protectorate offices had a minimum of twenty in the staff, but never much more than one hundred.

Many in that hundred were security, but that certainly wouldn't be enough to fight this rabble.

And some of the offices used locals as security as well.

She drove down a slight incline and immediately found herself in a different part of the city. Houses glistened behind pale brown walls. People were on the streets, carrying their weapons, robes swirling around them, but most of the people did not look like they belonged here.

She thought she saw guards near the gates around the houses, but she wasn't certain. Maybe the people she saw inside those walls were merely working their way out.

She exhaled. She wasn't exactly in the clear yet, but she was closer than she had been.

Barkson wasn't quite sure what she had seen, and she certainly didn't understand all of it. But she found herself wondering if Ghita and her children would have survived the day if Barkson hadn't shown up.

Not because they were Kirillis but because they represented the Protectorate.

Hundreds of people like that did not normally show up because of strong word of mouth. Something big had been planned, and Barkson had been on the edge of it.

She drove around the circular road near all the big estates. It took a few more turns into what looked like road but turned out to be blocked drives before she found the road she had been searching for.

The road that would take her out of Feltingham.

She wanted to get out of Feltshyon as quickly as she could, but there was nothing quick about it. Feltingham was in the south-central part of the country, and she still had a lot of travel to do before she crossed into Olyx.

At least in Olyx, she wouldn't be quite as conspicuous. They had actually asked for Protectorate help centuries before, since Olyx was between two countries that wanted their territory.

Olyx felt that Protectorate protection would allow them some autonomy, while maintaining their borders.

Although none of that mattered if Barkson couldn't get there.

She hoped the unrest she had witnessed was confined to Feltingham, or she might find herself in trouble ahead.

She had enough trouble right now.

She had to resist the urge to go to Chiedanna and wait to see if Ghita, her children, and the nanny made it to that inn.

Because that trip might not be as easy as Barkson had believed it would have been earlier that morning. She hoped that Ghita—or at least the nanny—was smart enough to travel as far from Feltingham as possible.

A strange feeling wrapped its way through Barkson as she drove.

It was only once she reached the farthest outskirts of Feltingham that she recognized the feeling for what it was.

Helplessness.

She could tell the Kirilli siblings to flee. She could make sure that they did.

But from there, the siblings were on their own.

Which she didn't like at all.

My dearest G,

There is unrest in Feltshyon. You will probably hear of it in the next few days. Because of the unrest, my task took on dimensions that I could not have anticipated.

I shall explain more in person. However, let me reassure you that Gh, the young ones, and one more are fine. When last I saw them, they were heading to a familiar and beloved place.

I am heading to my next stop, doing my best to stay away from the difficulties that have overtaken Feltingham.

I hope to have better news for you soon.

Your not-so-humble servant,

L.

SÉK

OLYX

OXECHANA

OLYX

CHAPTER
ELEVEN

The road that Barkson took through Feltshyon felt like something out of a dream rather than a drive in broad daylight. The road was one of the main thoroughfares to Olyx, paralleling the Hidden River, and meandering in and out of small villages.

There was scarcely any traffic moving in the same direction as Barkson. Instead, carriages, wagons, and carts headed toward Feltingham. Occasionally, Barkson had to slow down to another near crawl, because, as with the area around the plaza, the road was filled with people walking toward Feltingham.

She saw more weaponry than she liked. She did her best to remain inconspicuous but it was difficult in a windstone vehicle. So far, the ones she had seen the plaza had been the only windstone vehicles she had seen in all of Feltshyon.

The vehicle got a lot of sideways looks, but most people seemed more concerned with their walk than they were with a vehicle heading away from them. The conversations were long and loud enough to filter in through the windscreens.

Barkson drove carefully, feeling much too hot in her coat, but unwilling to stop and remove it. The air coming in through the vents, even with the small cooling rods, wasn't keeping up with the sunshine beating in through the windscreens.

Normally, she would drive with the windscreens down, but she wasn't about to do that until her vehicle was the only one on the road.

That took nearly two hours. She finally went around a hill, and down into a gully that led to yet another small village. As she drove past trees that seemed to form out of the river mud, she realized that she had seen no one for the past several miles. No carts, no wagons, and certainly no one on foot.

The landscape was still lush, but it had grown swampier. The road was built up on a berm because of obvious flooding nearby. She had driven this part of the road once before, and had noted that this part of Feltshyon looked a lot more like Olyx. If she hadn't passed some signage that had told her she had traveled into Feltshyon, she wouldn't have known the difference.

She drove the vehicle out of the gully to the top of a small rise. There was a turnout that was designed for people to stop and take in views of the river. Since there was no one else on the road here, she pulled over, and got out of the vehicle, hands shaking, not with fatigue but with the stress of that drive.

The air was hot and humid, swampy, and sticky. At least there was a wind, so there weren't a lot of bugs.

She pulled off her coat and set it in the vehicle. Then she took some of the food she had packed with Helia. Traveling with Helia had seemed like it happened days ago instead of hours.

The nap Barkson had taken on that part of the trip had done her good. She was too riled up to be tired right now.

She had some water in a glass jar. The water was warm, but it didn't matter. She used it to wash down some bread which was just a bit stale, and some very dry cheese.

That would carry her into Olyx. There, she knew, she would find some roadside fruit stands and strange little sandwich shops. If she had the time to stop.

Gussie had been the most worried about the next stop. Unlike his siblings, Benedeto did not own a permanent residence. He had money in trust for one, but he had not purchased one. Nor did he live on family lands.

Benedeto liked to travel—at least that was what Gussie had said—and he often stayed in one place until he tired of it.

Last she had heard, he had been in Oxechana, a strange little artist community on the river itself. Helia had heard the same thing, and had, of course, given Barkson a map.

What do I do if he's not there? Barkson had asked.

This map will tell you where he is, Helia had said.

At the time, Barkson hadn't believed it, but after all she had seen on this day, she believed it now.

She finished her small meal and resisted the urge to pull out the map. She didn't want to use too much magic, particularly magic that had originated with a Kirilli.

There were theories expressed at Serebro Academy that magic was traceable. There were even some scholars who believed that magic was unique to its user.

If Barkson activated Kirilli magic, then she might lead whoever it is—oh, if she was being honest with herself—the Fey, then to at least one of the Kirillis.

Barkson would use the magic if she had to, but she hoped she would not have to.

She took a few more minutes on that rise to write her letter to Gussie about Ghita. On the drive, Barkson had decided not to tell Gussie about Rudolfo's death. Barkson would deal with that later.

She had realized the farther she got from Trinovante, the less information she felt she should share with Gussie. Most of what Barkson needed to tell Gussie was best discussed in person—if, indeed, that would end up being possible.

Barkson was beginning to regret her own ego. She had thought she could do this trip on her own, without help.

But the incident at Dilshad's had made her realize how much help an extra person could be. And the encounter at Ghita's made Barkson feel even more alone.

If those men had attacked her or Ghita or the children, Barkson would have had her weapons and little else.

Barkson had taken on four men by herself in the past, but she hadn't had to be cautious because of the presence of children. She wouldn't have been able to be as ruthless as she needed to be.

And that worried her. She might need to be as ruthless as she could be to handle what was coming toward her.

She wasn't sure what that would be. All three of the remaining Kirilli siblings were unmarried, at least according to Gussie. But the three men also lived far from their father's reach.

Augustus Kirilli might not have been understanding of a match that fell outside of Qavnerian dictates. Barkson wouldn't have been surprised if Emberto or Corrin had found a companion that didn't quite fit into the dictates of a perfect Old Family match.

Her heart twisted a little. She hadn't seen Corrin in years, but the idea that he might have settled down stung.

She didn't know Emberto. She just knew where he lived. And part of her believed that anyone who lived that close to Mount Vitaki would want to live a life that was somewhat outside of the norm for a Qavnerian.

Benedeto was clearly living an abnormal life. Unmarried, without a home. That seemed strange for the eldest son.

But he was not the eldest child. Gussie was, and she too was unmarried. But she had a permanent home not far from her father's. It had been easy to see that she was the heir that Augustus Kirilli wanted, the kindred spirit that he felt would understand his life and the demands on a Kirilli.

The river glistened below Barkson, the sunlight slanting just a bit. The day was going to end by the time she got to Oxechana. And as welcoming as Olyx was for Qavnerians, Barkson wasn't certain she wanted to drive the poorly maintained Olyxian roads at night.

She would see what she could learn from Benedeto. Maybe he knew the best way to drive through Olyx. He had a wind-stone vehicle of his own, after all.

He was the first of all of them to get one. Barkson knew that much.

But the rest of what she knew about Benedeto had come from stories about him, not personal experience.

Gussie thought he was flighty. Helia had said he was the steadiest of all of them. And he lived an unusual life.

Barkson had no idea what she was getting into, but she knew

she had to move forward. The daylight was wasting, and Olyxian roads after dark were dangerous.

Oxechana was still an hour away. A long hard hour, on a poorly maintained road.

She patted the windstone vehicle, and promised it another cleaning when she stopped for the night.

If she stopped for the night.

If her information was right.

And nothing else went awry.

OXECHANA

CHAPTER
TWELVE

It was dark by the time Barkson reached Oxechana. The town was built on a cliff face that overlooked the Hidden River. There was a cove below, with some caves. Barkson only knew that because of the signs, written in Olyxyan and Qavnerian, warning of the dangers at river level. They included flooding, riptides, and the possibility of being trapped in the caves by high water.

The river was subject to flooding during heavy rains and spring runoff. Heavy rains happened in this part of Dorovich with startling suddenness. One minute, the sky was blue; the next it was stormy.

If the storm hit farther upriver, the rising water would have a major impact on all of the beaches, but worse along the coast here and a bit farther north.

The mountains that ringed the river were not really mountains. More like foothills for the mountain range ahead. This coastline was wild, with lots of dips and curves. The roads would occasionally fall away here, particularly after major storms.

That was one reason why a country as small as Olyx managed to hang onto its land on both sides of the river. Other countries saw it as less desirable.

Olyx was a place to travel through, not a place to reside, at least as far as the neighboring countries were concerned. Their prejudice against Olyx and the fact that most of those countries refused to give Olyx any assistance during the flooding years of the centuries past were the reasons why Olyx was happy to be part of the Protectorate.

Instead of losing power by becoming part of the Protectorate, Olyx had gained it. And some wealth as well.

Barkson was driving into one of the wealthier areas now. Oxechana was an artists' community. It had always been a strange little village, but in the past century, it had become a place where creative people and the wealthy from all over the Protectorate came to "escape" the rest of the world.

Whatever that meant. Barkson didn't believe anyone could escape the world. Eventually the world could find anyone, as the attackers were proving against the Kirilli family.

The city was lit with torches burning in clear ceramic baskets mounted on tall poles. The poles were on the sides of the street. There was no vegetation on these streets, although on the unlit streets, the vegetation grew wild like it did farther down the mountain.

The road was uneven cobblestone that covered an area the size of three roads in any other town. The top of the cliffside was completely covered in that cobblestone. The houses trailed down the other side of the mountain, which was softly curved, unlike the cliff face.

Here, stone buildings blocked the view of the river from anyone on the other side of the street. The backside of those stone buildings had patios and balconies that overlooked the river.

Through the middle of the wide avenue was a small raised area, filled with tables and smaller versions of the torch poles. People sat at those tables, eating and drinking, laughing as if they had not a care in the world.

Barkson drove past them. The side of the avenue farthest from the river also had stone buildings, some of them taverns and inns, some indoor markets, and a few looked like official government buildings.

She couldn't be sure of that, though, because she had no idea what part of the government was in Oxechana. Those buildings might simply have been built at the same time as many of the buildings that she considered to belong to the government.

On the outside of the taverns, candles in small glass holders were strung like fairy lights over the center of the stone. The effect was to make the entire downtown area lighter than it should have been with all of the torches, and yet, it still managed to create a lot of moving shadows.

The road was empty, except for people enjoying the evening out, at tables or talking to each other near the taverns. There were no other vehicles at all and, oddly, no one seemed to care about hers either.

She had given in about an hour back and looked at Gussie's instructions. The address that Gussie had given Barkson was for an apartment building behind the Hidden River Tavern on Fifth Street.

The Hidden River Tavern was the largest tavern in this section of road. The tavern actually divided itself into three parts —a part on the built-up berm, a part on the other side of the road, and a stone building overlooking the river. That part on the other side of the road had the largest patio, filled with the most tables. There was an entire circle of torches, each burning heavily.

The road beyond it was easy to see, although it dropped steeply off the hillside. Each road was marked with a number in a circle. The number five was white outlined in black, and reflected the light from the nearest torch.

She started to take that road, and then realized that what she had seen as steep didn't quite describe it. The road went so quickly downhill that she wasn't sure the windstone vehicle could handle it.

There was a carriage park across from the Hidden River Tavern, which, at the moment, happened to be empty of all but two horses. She parked near the main road, feeling uncomfortable about leaving the vehicle, but feeling like she had no choice.

She could, she supposed, pay someone to guard the windstone vehicle, but here, among all the people celebrating the evening, that felt like she was putting a big sign on her vehicle, telling would-be thieves that there was something to steal.

And there was a lot to steal, but most of her important items were in compartments that no one could open without knowing how. The vehicle itself was attuned to her and she hoped that would give it some protection.

Barkson got out of the vehicle. The air was cooler and

damper than she had expected. It smelled faintly of torch smoke, cut with some frying beef and the sickly-sweet scent of honey ale.

Behind it all was the smell of the river, fecund and fishy. It moved slowly through this part of Dorovich, unless the river was swollen from the rains or runoff. Otherwise, river plants from the shore could move into the middle of the water, stagnant on the sides.

This had to have been one of those times, because the slightly rotted smell was very strong.

She grabbed her coat, and actually needed it, unlike earlier in the day. She also grabbed her pistol and dagger. She preferred the dagger here. It was a quieter weapon. People would hear if she shot the pistol for any reason.

She closed the door to the vehicle, and waited to see if anyone looked at her or approached her. No one at the taverns or on the berm seemed to notice. She couldn't tell if someone inside the buildings was watching her or not.

People were laughing, though, and telling stories and having a great time. If something had gone awry here during the day, no one would be celebrating.

Barkson doubted there was much of this kind of conviviality in Feltingham on this night.

Even though no one was obviously watching her, Barkson didn't relax. She took a quiet breath, and headed down the side of the hill. There was a cobblestone walkway built onto this part of the hill, but she wasn't sure if that made the walk easier or harder.

Her boots clung to the walkway, but only just barely. She felt as if one false move would send her tumbling down several blocks. She couldn't see where the hill smoothed out. The bottom looked like a giant puddle of darkness.

The fact that the hill went down so steeply meant that the torchlight from the main part of Olyx did not reach the next road. Fortunately, this part of Olyx seemed to be laid out on a grid pattern.

The hill flattened and then crested again, but as it did, she could make out the shape of a large stone apartment building that looked like it belonged in Trinovante, not in the middle of Oxechana.

Even before she reached the building, she had a hunch that was where Benedeto was staying. People liked the familiar, although she was making presumptions about a man she'd only seen a few times and never really talked to.

But if he was anything like the rest of his family, he was Qavnerian through and through.

She walked around to the front of the building. The windows on that level all had curtains and they were all pulled, although behind some of them, lights flickered.

The main door had gaslights on either side of the frame. They were well maintained. No soot stains along the top, and the glass around the flame was clean.

She went to the door, hoping to find a list of tenants. Of course there wasn't one, but there was a bell pull. The pull was tucked into a notch in the wall, so that the wind (or some random person) wouldn't tug it automatically.

She tugged it, and heard a faint *bong* inside the building. Which meant that the bell wasn't that far from the door, considering how thick this stone was.

A curtain opened slightly to her right, sending a slice of light across the entry. Then the slice of light vanished.

A rectangle at eye level pulled to one side on the door, revealing eyes and part of a nose.

"What?"

The voice belonged to a woman, who was deliberately sounding none too happy about a visitor after dark. Maybe there were house rules.

"I'm looking for Benedeto Kirilli," Barkson said.

"He hasn't lived here in nearly a year," the woman said.

Barkson's heart sank. She had been worried about her ability to find all of the Kirillis, and now it had finally happened.

"Do you know where he might be?" Barkson asked.

"He took a room above Penderson's," the woman said, and moved away from the door.

"Wait!" Barkson said. "What's a Penderson's?"

"The tavern," the woman said as if Barkson was the stupidest person she had encountered in weeks. "On the river side. Mr. La Di Da wanted a view."

Then she slammed the rectangle closed.

Barkson stood there for a moment, feeling unsettled.

Almost a year ago, Benedeto took a room in a tavern here in Olyx. Gussie's address was old. And Helia hadn't said what the address she was using was, only that her map could track him down if need be.

Barkson walked back up the hill, slowly and carefully, picking her way along the cobblestone. She moved to the other side of the street, but the path was no better there, and the cobblestone on the street itself looked like it had been poorly maintained.

As the hill grew steeper, she heard music with a strong beat, the kind of rhythm people could dance to. The voices had grown louder and the laughter was raucous.

Living on that street would have been loud, but it would have felt like being inside the party.

She finally reached the top. It seemed like there were more lights than there had been. There were certainly more people at tables, and the scent of onions mixed with peppers and some kind of sharp spice made her stomach growl.

The windstone vehicle looked untouched, but she didn't stop near it. Obsessively checking it would have been another clue to a would-be thief that there was something valuable inside.

Instead, she walked past the carriage park, crossed the first part of the road, climbed up the berm, and threaded her way past tables filled with drinkers. A few of them toasted her. At least one man offered to get her a drink.

She ignored him, and walked down the other side, stunned that there still was no traffic.

The music had grown louder, but it mixed with some fainter music that was much more lyrical. That seemed to come from the river side of the street.

She didn't look for the musicians. Instead, she looked at the signage. Signs hung on poles above the doors, stating the name of the taverns. She saw several of the letters that composed Penderson intertwined on one of the signs two buildings down from the riverside Hidden River Tavern.

She walked in that direction. The music grew fainter here, but it still felt compelling, as if she really needed to dance.

She wondered if there was magic in it.

Several people sat at the tables outside Penderson's, but they were talking quietly. That they could talk quietly showed how far the tavern was from the noise emanating from the Hidden River Tavern.

Everyone was eating and the food looked similar. Different kinds of meats on skewers, some melted cheese over a flame to keep the cheese melted, more skewers, and chunks of bread on the tabletop. Near the bread were potatoes, celery, carrots and a bunch of vegetables she didn't recognize, as well as several different kinds of berries.

The conversations all stopped as she approached.

People also stopped eating, pulling their hands away from the piles of food.

She nodded at everyone she passed, gave them a small smile, and then went inside the tavern itself.

It was bigger than she expected and smelled faintly of woodsmoke. Beneath that smell was the sharp tang of a well-made cider, and the odor of cooking meats.

There was a heavyset woman inside, wearing a very modest shirt over some dark pants. Her hair was pulled up to the top of her head so that no strands would fall on the food. A younger woman stood near the long wooden bar, holding a tray.

"Help you?" the older woman asked.

"I'm looking for Benedeto Kirilli," Barkson said.

"Sweetie," the older woman said, "you look too old for Benedeto Kirilli."

Barkson smiled. She didn't mind the assumption.

"I've never met him," she lied. "I have a message for him."

"You clearly never met him," the younger woman said before the woman shushed her.

185

Which meant that Benedeto was somewhere nearby and Barkson had walked right past him.

"Which table is he at?" Barkson said. "I'll deliver my message and be on my way."

"I don't send people carrying pistols to my friends," the older woman said.

Barkson started. Most people never noticed the pistol beneath her coat unless she wanted them to.

"Well, then," Barkson said. "Give me a cider and some of that food which looks so good. I'll take a table in here and you can tell Benedeto that I have an important message from Trinovante."

"Oh, he won't like that," the younger woman said.

The older woman rolled her eyes and shook her head. "You want to keep working here, you'll learn how to shut your mouth."

"Sorry," the younger woman said.

"You deliver the message," the older woman said. "I'll make sure this one doesn't watch you."

The younger woman nodded. She set her tray on the bar, showing her newness. An experienced server would've made use of the trip, carrying a jug for refills, more food or more glasses.

The older woman led Barkson to a table deep in the back. Barkson sat with her back to the wall. She couldn't see the door, which made her nervous, but she had promised she wouldn't look.

"I have coin," Barkson said.

"I don't care," the older woman said. "If Deto comes in here, you'll get your meal. If not, I'm sending you out the back and you can eat at Hidden River."

She said that last as if she thought Barkson might poison herself by eating there.

"Fair enough," Barkson said.

She didn't say anything else, not how relieved she was that she had located Benedeto, not the fact that she had come a long way and had had a difficult journey already. She didn't ask the older woman's name or how she came to own this business—because the older woman clearly was the owner, or one of them.

After a moment, the younger woman came back inside, her mouth a thin line. She walked to the bar and grabbed a tray.

"I need three ales," she said as if she hadn't gone out of the tavern on a different mission.

"You'll wait," the older woman said.

Then a tall, thin man walked in. He wore black pants and a black shirt that was crumpled against his skin. He had a scraggly beard and his hair needed a trim.

He surveyed the interior until he saw Barkson in the back. Then he ran a hand through his hair and walked over to her.

Barkson braced herself. She wasn't sure what this man would want with her. Perhaps he had heard that she was interested in Benedeto.

It wasn't until he got close that she realized his eyes were just like Gussie's, filled with intelligence and a bit of wariness. Mixed into that was humor. He realized that Barkson hadn't recognized him.

"Lucinda Barkson," he said, his voice deep and warm. "I didn't expect you."

Her cheeks warmed. She hadn't realized that he knew her name. They had shared meals a few times at the Kirilli estate, but he had always treated her like she didn't matter.

He pulled up a chair, turned it around, and braced his arms on the back, looking at her.

"You can tell my father that I'm not coming home, no matter who he sends after me. He has Gussie, and they are aligned and he doesn't need me, no matter what tradition says."

Barkson's heart sank. She felt for Benedeto, because she was about to change his world.

At that moment, the older woman placed a plate of skewers in front of Barkson, as well as some cheese and cut-up vegetables.

"Ah," Benedeto said. "The house special. Allow me."

He reached into a pocket of that ragged shirt, and pulled out two gold coins, which was much too much money for this meal. Still, he handed it to the older woman, and she pocketed it as she walked away, giving him a slight smile.

Barkson finally understood. He was paying the woman for protecting his identity. He was also probably paying her to stay away, and not eavesdrop. Or paying extra in advance so that she wouldn't sell any information that she overheard.

The younger woman arrived with two ciders, two plates, two forks, and some empty skewers. The ciders steamed, the crisp scent making Barkson's stomach growl.

Then the woman returned with some kind of sauce in a bowl.

"This is how you eat it," Benedeto said, grabbing a loose skewer and poking a few of the vegetables. He dipped them, and put them on a plate, then grabbed a meat skewer and dipped it. He scraped the food off the skewers with the fork and took a bite, those eyes still on Barkson.

He did a lot of communicating without saying a word. He

was telling her that the food was safe, which was an interesting thing to communicate.

Barkson dipped a loose skewer in the sauce, then brought the skewer back and tasted it. The sauce tasted like sweet plums mixed with some kind of hot spice. It wouldn't be bad in small doses.

Then she took a meat skewer. The different meats were also steaming. She dipped it and set it on her plate.

Benedeto was eating his food, his gaze on hers, as he clearly waited for her to tell him what the meeting was about.

Barkson reached into her coat's upper pocket and removed Benedeto's letters.

"Gussie sent me," she said.

His face changed ever so subtly. The change was hard to see under all of that facial hair, but his eyes narrowed and the humor left them.

"Gussie," he said flatly, and with that one word, it became clear that he knew something had happened to his father.

"She told me to give you two letters," Barkson said. "This one first."

She handed him the thicker envelope with his name on it. He took it with his thumb and forefinger as if the envelope was going to cut him. It probably would.

He ripped the side of the envelope open and pulled out the two handwritten pages.

Barkson turned her concentration to her meal, to give him privacy.

She ate slowly, even though she was ravenous. The meat was better without the warm plum sauce. The meat had its own spices—different for the beef than for the chicken. There was something else here, lamb perhaps? And something gamey that she didn't recognize. The gamey meat tasted better with the plum sauce.

The vegetables did too, but the small berries did not. She didn't like them anyway—too tart. She had to eat more meat before she could sip the cider. She was afraid the tart berries would ruin the cider's bite.

It took a few minutes, but she realized that Benedeto hadn't moved. The letter was resting on his knee, and his head was bowed.

Barkson didn't want to disturb him, but she had to.

"I have a second letter for you," she said.

He raised his head, his gaze bleak. "I didn't expect this," he said.

"No one did," Barkson said, deliberately misunderstanding him. He had clearly been talking about the loss of his father so soon, and she was talking about the strange death.

Benedeto reached for his mug of cider, and then stopped, hand poised near the handle. He closed his hand into a fist and pulled it back.

"Is Gussie all right?" he asked.

"As of yesterday," Barkson said.

He nodded, as the words penetrated.

"You may as well give me the second one, then," he said.

She did. He opened it the way he had opened the first one.

She returned to her meal, which was probably the best meal she had had in a month. No wonder the locals ate here.

His second letter was very short. Through the light behind him, Barkson could see that the second letter was a single paragraph.

That made it shorter than every other letter Barkson had handed out so far.

He carefully folded the letter, and put it in his pocket.

"Did she tell you what she wants me to do?" he asked.

"No," Barkson said. "I only know vaguely what's in the letters."

"She wants me to go to Serebro," he said.

Barkson set down her fork. "I'm not going to advise you or discuss this with you," she said. "It's not my place. I still have to find Corrin and Emberto."

Benedeto's face shut down at her words.

"I'm not going to do what she wants," he said. "She needs me."

Barkson placed her hands on her lap underneath the table, so that Benedeto couldn't see her create fists. She wanted to tell him that he had no right to make decisions for Gussie, that Gussie was doing fine on her own.

But Barkson didn't really know that. She had left Gussie at the constabulary on the way out of Trinovante. For all Barkson knew, Gussie had returned to Barkson's apartment, closed the curtains, and crawled on the bed, not to get up again.

Although that didn't sound like Gussie. Gussie, the woman who saw the people who helped raise her slaughtered, who dealt with her dead father, and still managed to write letters to all her siblings and protect her family.

"What you do," Barkson said, "is between the two of you. She made her wishes clear. She's trying to protect all of you."

"She's overreacting," he said, but his words didn't have the sting that Nigel Netuno's had or even that a couple of Gussie's sisters had had. It almost sounded like Benedeto was asking a question.

"I wish she had been overreacting," Barkson said. "Helia and I managed to thwart an attack on Dilshad's home—"

"By whom?" Benedeto asked, loudly enough to attract the attention of the older woman.

Barkson waved a hand. She wasn't going to answer that yet.

"And," she continued a bit more forcefully, "Rudolfo died at his office this morning. His death might be related to unrest in Feltshyon or it might have come from the same attackers that went after your family in Trinovante and in G'zen. I didn't have time to investigate. I had to come here, and then I'll have to talk to your remaining two brothers. I have letters for them as well."

Benedeto let out a loud sigh. His gaze moved from side to side, almost as if he expected attackers here.

"Were you followed?" he asked.

"I don't think so," Barkson said. "But two of the attacks occurred when the attackers came out of portals."

"Who told you this?" Benedeto asked, loudly again.

She wanted to wave a hand, to convince him to be silent. But she didn't.

"A witness to Rudolfo's death," Barkson said.

"You've already stated that the information there can't be trusted," Benedeto said.

"*And*," Barkson said, "I saw one myself."

He let out another loud breath and leaned back. Then he closed his eyes, as if he was reviewing the information that she had told him.

Another smaller sigh, before he opened his eyes, and looked

at her. His eyes, which clearly held all of his emotions, now seemed dark and bleak.

"You said Helia helped you." He had lowered his voice. "What did she do?"

"It's a long story," Barkson said. "Suffice to say that she had a way of stopping the attackers that surprised us all when it worked."

He ran a hand over his mouth.

"In Gussie's letter, she speculates that someone might be coming for the Kirilli family." He looked directly at Barkson. "From the sound of it, her speculation is fact."

"It certainly seems that way," Barkson said.

"Then why does she want me to go to Serebro?"

"I don't speak for Gussie," Barkson said again.

"Yes, but you have a brain," he said. "You can speculate just as well as she can, maybe more so than in this letter, since you're in possession of even more facts."

"The Kirilli family has property in Serebro, do you not?" Barkson asked.

"We have property all over Dorovich," he said. "Just because I choose not to live in any of it means nothing."

That sounded like the echo of a fight with his father. Barkson decided to ignore the last statement.

"I seem to recall that the property in Serebro is extensive," Barkson said, "and it's related to the work your family has done with the Academy."

Benedeto frowned. It was a prodigious look, made more dramatic by the way that his beard and mustache moved with his mouth.

"A lot of the Old Families are connected to the Academy," he said.

"And a lot of the Old Families suffered the destruction of mementos," Barkson said. "Maybe even the death of one or two members of the staff. I'm not sure about that, because, as I said, I got on the road immediately. But it seems that there is something going on that will have an impact on all of the Old Families."

"Particularly the Kirillis," he said.

"Yes," Barkson said.

"We have a lot of staff in Serebro," he said, more to himself than to Barkson. "They keep the house ready at a moment's notice, so that anyone who has been called to the Academy has a place to stay."

"I remember," Barkson said quietly. She'd been to the Serebro estate several times. It was actually in the mountains between the city and the Academy. The estate was large, but the Kirillis called it a cottage. That was the first place she had seen Benedeto and Corrin.

Benedeto looked at her. "Yes, of course you remember."

He took a large sip from his cider, then set the mug down hard.

"You're telling me this has something to do with magic," he said.

"I have not used that word," Barkson said. "I will not."

"And my great-grandparents," Benedeto said.

"Again, I have not—"

"Said that, I know, and you will not," Benedeto said. "But you need to know that Emberto is living in their house across from Mount Vitaki. If there are items that are valuable to the family and the history of the Protectorate, you'll find most of them there."

Barkson felt a shiver run down her back. She hadn't known that about Emberto's home. All Helia had said was that he lived in a family-owned property.

The older woman was looking at them from the bar. The younger woman had five ales on a tray and was walking outside. Music from the Hidden River Tavern trickled in.

Barkson made sure her gaze met and held the older woman's. The older woman looked away.

"She's trustworthy," Benedeto said.

"Because you pay her to be," Barkson said. "All it takes is someone else to pay her more."

His eyes narrowed. Clearly, he had thought his gold coin moment with the older woman had not been something that Barkson understood.

"I need to go with you," he said.

Barkson let out a small laugh. "To protect me? Don't be foolish."

"You don't know what you're walking into at Emberto's," Benedeto said.

"I haven't known what I was facing all day," Barkson said. "I don't need you. Your sister needs you to go to Serebro. I'd listen to her."

"She doesn't know—"

"Maybe she does," Barkson snapped. "She's the one who dealt with this—admirably, I might add—from the moment it happened. She knows better than both of us what is going on. I'm here because she can't be spared. She needs all of her siblings to take action. That's why every one of you received the first letter, which is the same, and a second private letter with different instructions for each individual."

"What were the others told to do?" Benedeto asked.

She wasn't going to tell him. He was already failing one of her private tests, which was whether or not the Kirilli sibling listened to Gussie. He and Gussie were close in age, which was probably why he was less willing to listen, but still, he needed to pay attention now.

"I was not privy to those letters," Barkson said primly. She wasn't going to tell him that she was the only one who knew where the other siblings had gone.

"You said Rudolfo died," Benedeto said. "You didn't tell me about Ghita and the kids."

Barkson took a deep breath. She would tell him some of this. "They got away," she said. "Some locals were trying to harm them, and I stopped it."

"You," he said. Then he laughed. "Of course. You. You're the one Corrin couldn't tame."

Her cheeks flushed. No one knew about her relationship with Corrin. Not even Gussie.

"I don't like that word, 'tame,'" Barkson said. "If that's how you think about women then it makes sense that you're unwilling to listen to your sister."

Barkson wasn't going to let anything in this conversation be about her.

"You're not thinking clearly. First, you thought you needed to go to Gussie. Then you decided to come with me, uninvited, I might add."

"It sounds like Helia was with you," Benedeto said.

"Helia is with Dilshad and his family," Barkson said. She

could give him that much. "I watched them leave together. Filippa and her children have left their home as well. Her husband doesn't believe any of this is important, but at least he went to see his own family."

"But Rudolfo is dead," Benedeto repeated. Clearly he was just beginning to process this information.

"At work this morning," Barkson said. "I'm not sure if it's related. His job for the Protectorate made him very unpopular. It looked like there was some kind of planned uprising in Feltingham this morning. Thousands of people were pouring into the streets. I left as quickly as I could. After I made sure that Ghita and her children weren't being followed."

Benedeto stared at her. "But you didn't make sure, did you? You didn't go with them."

Barkson nodded. He couldn't needle her and upset her. She had done too much work over the years. She knew how to compartmentalize.

"If I had gone with any of them, I would have failed at my mission," Barkson said. "My assignment is simple: I will deliver letters to your siblings and make sure that they understand the letters, and hope that they follow the instructions in the second letter."

"Instructions are different for each of us?" Benedeto asked.

"Again," Barkson said, "I'm not privy to the letters. What I needed to do was make certain that no one in the family was easy to locate."

"I'm not easy to locate," Benedeto said.

"And yet, I found you," she said. "It wasn't hard. Your landlady from the apartments told me where you live."

He folded the second letter. "I will tell her to keep quiet."

"And thereby call attention to yourself and whatever problem is going on," Barkson said.

He tucked the letter in the pocket of his rumpled shirt.

"If, as you say, Gussie wants you in Serebro, you need to go," Barkson said. "It'll take at least a full day and night to get there."

"It's closer for her," he said sullenly. "She should have gone."

"For all we know, she has," Barkson said.

He looked up at Barkson, clearly alarmed.

"I wish you could tell me what is going on," he said, as if Barkson was holding out on him.

"I wish I knew," she said.

They sat in silence. She finished her meal, leaving some of the berries, since they didn't seem to go with any of the rest of it. She didn't drink all of the cider either, not because it was bad, but because it was too good.

The older woman behind the bar stopped watching them, but Barkson had the sense that the older woman was still listening. The younger woman was outside, serving drinks to people at the tables.

The music from the Hidden River Tavern seemed louder and more raucous. It was also less musical. Instead, it reminded Barkson of rhythmic shouting.

"You'll need to stay here tonight," Benedeto said after a long moment.

"I need to be on my way," Barkson said. "I told Gussie that I could make the trip in three days."

At the quickest. That was what Barkson had actually said. She thought it might take a lot longer. But she did need to hurry.

"Maybe," Benedeto said. "If there were two of you. But there aren't. You don't want to drive out of Oxechana at night."

She hadn't wanted to drive *into* Oxechana at night.

"And the drive to Corrin's is difficult. The trip to Emberto's is even rougher. You're going to need rest before you try any of that."

"I need to go as quickly as possible," Barkson said.

"You need to arrive safely at both places," Benedeto said. "I've made the trip numerous times. It takes a full day to get to Corrin's from here. It should go faster, but it never does. And it'll take at least a half day to get to Emberto's and that's if you're willing to drive like a maniac. I assume you have a windstone vehicle. You used to."

Barkson wasn't sure how he remembered all of this about her when she couldn't remember much about him at all.

"I do," she said.

"Then you definitely don't want to take the road at night," he said. "If you hit a rock, it will destroy some of your vents. And there are a lot of rocks. The road about five miles from here is broken into chunks and no one has repaired it."

She stared at him. He could be lying. But what would that gain him?

"That was initially why I thought I needed to go with you. It wasn't protection. It was local knowledge." Apparently her accusation stung. He was probably displacing a lot of emotion.

She decided not to take anything he said personally.

"I'm pretty sure there's an empty room here that you can take for the night," Benedeto said. "I'd recommend that you take it."

"There will be an empty room," Barkson said, "because

you're moving out tonight."

"I'm going to pack," he said. "I'll leave first thing in the morning. I won't sleep, I promise you, and you saw how they protected me. It'll be hard to get to me."

Barkson shook her head. "If I can find you—"

"I know," he said. "But I'm safer here. Trust me. I know this town. The rooms above this inn are private. The rooms in the other taverns are not. I've stayed in all of them. These are the only ones that feel safe."

He ran a hand over his face, then finished the last of his cider. He set the mug down hard.

"You have to tell me," he said. "Who do you think are after us?"

Barkson shook her head. "You need to discuss that with Gussie."

"She won't know. You've seen these people. You said you defeated some of them." His fingers were still wrapped around the mug, but his knuckles were turning white. "There's magic involved, which confuses me. Does it have something to do with the Protectorate? With Rudolfo? He wasn't really ever part of the family. He was a real prick, you know?"

Like Filippa's husband. Apparently the girls were good at picking prime candidates for their spouses.

"You've asked too many questions," Barkson said. "I don't know the answers. I have guesses and they are worth nothing."

"The magic bothers me," Benedeto said.

"It should," Barkson said.

They stared at each other. Finally she put her hands on the table and leveraged herself up. She was going to take his advice and sleep here, at least until dawn.

"Is there a safe place to park my vehicle?" she asked. "I'm in the carriage park across the way."

"It'll do for the night," he said.

She nodded. The food hadn't helped her stay awake. It had made her even more tired.

"You will talk to me before you go," she said to Benedeto. She needed to know if he changed his mind during the night, although she wasn't going to say that. She didn't want to give him any ideas.

"I would rather not," he said. "I will pack and leave—"

"No," she said. "You will talk to me."

He stared up at her. She stared at him.

"Or what?" he asked after a moment. "You'll tell Gussie?"

Barkson didn't even crack a smile. That statement was a bit too close to the truth.

"I'm putting my life at risk to help your family," she said quietly but firmly. "The least you could do is cooperate."

The skin on his face and neck turned slightly darker. He flushed. She had managed to shame him.

"You're right," he said after a moment. "I'm sorry."

"No need to apologize," she said. "I show up and drop news on you and demand that you change your life. It's difficult."

"This can't have been fun for you," he said. "We all would have reactions to the news."

"Yes," Barkson said curtly. "You all do. But I can keep you focused. And now, I need to keep myself focused. You will talk to me before you go."

"I will," he promised, and this time, she actually believed he would.

SÉK

OLYX

OXECHANA

OLYX

CHAPTER
THIRTEEN

A knock on the door caught Barkson splashing cold water on her face. There was no running water on this level of the inn, but each room had a full pitcher and bowl that looked clean enough. Her room had one thin window that faced east.

So far, the sun hadn't appeared. It was just making the horizon look pinkish.

She had gotten six hours of sleep, which might have to do for the next several days.

She grabbed a soft towel off the rack near the mirror on the dressing table, and dried her face as she walked to the door.

"Lucinda, wake up, dammit. I'm leaving."

Well, that at least meant that Benedeto made it through the night. She had slept so soundly that someone could have attacked this building and she wasn't certain the noise would have woken her up.

At least she had set her internal clock for six hours and, as usual, that internal clock had not failed her.

She used the slide at eye level, pulling it back even though she knew that Benedeto was outside the door. She had to make sure he was alone before she pulled the door open.

Only one person stood in front of her, even though she couldn't get a good look at him. But his hair was the right color and his voice had sounded right.

More importantly than that, the sentiment had been right.

No Benedeto impostor would have talked to her that way.

She unlocked the door and pulled it open.

A tall, thin man stood outside it, wearing a pressed shirt under a short jacket, pressed pants and shining shoes. He was clean-shaven, and his hair was trimmed.

But the eyes looked wary and tired and sad. They also looked just like Gussie's.

"You clean up well," Barkson said and moved away from the door. She didn't tell him her other reaction: he would have been better off wearing his crummy clothes and keeping his beard and long hair.

No one ever expected a Kirilli to look like that.

"If I'm going to Serebro, I can't look like a degenerate," he said as he entered. He was carrying a single round pack over his left shoulder. The pack was big enough for clothing and a pistol or a sword. He had a dagger on his hip.

She wouldn't have called him a degenerate. He had looked like a man down on his luck, a man who might have been an artist. A man who cared nothing for himself.

He pushed the door closed and looked around the room.

There was nothing of her in here. The bed was made,

because she always did that. Her coat hung over a chair, but that was it. She had changed nothing else and added nothing else.

"You really do travel light," he said.

She didn't respond. She grabbed her coat off the chair, made sure she hadn't left anything else in the room, and tucked her coat over her arm.

"Are you telling me that you're going to Serebro?" she asked. "Or are you actually *going* to Serebro?"

He raised his eyebrows. "Did you just ask me if I'm lying about where I'm going?"

Yes, she had. But she decided to be a bit more polite.

"You were uncertain about what you were going to do last night," she said.

"Does that mean you want me to come with you?" he asked.

She glared at him.

He held up both of his hands.

"I'm going," he said. "You and Gussie seem to think I need to be there, so I'm going."

Barkson nodded. She didn't tell him that she wasn't as important as Gussie, because she didn't want him to back down from going to Serebro.

"Where is your vehicle?" she asked.

"Not far from here," he said. And then when she glared at him again, he added, "I pay to keep it concealed."

"Even though you told me mine would be fine," she said.

"I'm a Kirilli," he said, and then made that same motion with his hands again. "Meaning that I'm more afraid someone would have tried to break into my vehicle or steal something from me or damage it, because of my name. As you learned on this trip, the Kirillis aren't always popular people in the various countries of Dorovich."

She had nothing to say to that. She wasn't tired, but she was getting tired of him.

And she wanted to get on the road.

"I'll need to see you leave," she said.

"Because you don't believe me?" he asked.

"Because I promised Gussie," she said. That wasn't entirely true. Barkson could have trusted him to drive off in the right direction, but the fact was that she didn't trust him.

"All right," he said, as he moved out of her way. She checked the room one last time. "I guess it doesn't matter if you see where I keep the vehicle. I probably won't return here anyway."

She looked at him. He seemed sad.

"You don't own property here," she said.

"That's correct," he said.

"Yet you've been here for quite some time."

He shrugged. "The community suits me."

It seemed like more than that, but she decided not to ask. She needed to get on the road and so did he.

She placed her gaudy key next to the wash bowl, and then let herself out of the room. She waited for Benedeto to walk out as well. He adjusted the pack as he headed for the stairs. She followed, putting on her coat as she walked.

The main floor of the tavern smelled of stale cider and spilled ale. The cooking smells had long since dissipated. The place felt like it had been abandoned, the way that taverns and bars usually did in the morning.

There was no light in here, except for some coming in under

the main door. Apparently, while Barkson and Benedeto had been talking, the sun had come up.

He walked around the large bar and headed into the back. She followed. The back had a mishmash of things, from containers filled with ale, full wine bottles on their sides, and a table that was clearly for food preparation.

A chill came from Barkson's left. She glanced toward it, saw a big solid stone door, and realized she was probably looking at a room that doubled as ice storage. She'd seen the like in several places, particularly farther north.

The people in the warmer climes seemed to like their food chilled or stored cold. Ice came at a premium, and apparently the wealthy in these places liked to pay that premium.

That, more than the design of the tavern itself, told Barkson there was a lot of money here.

She followed Benedeto through a corridor, and realized they were going slightly downhill. He pushed open a large wooden door to reveal a gigantic room, with big wagons parked against one wall and an ornate carriage in the center.

In front of it all, near a set of large double doors, was a gold windstone vehicle that looked like an early model. Its roof was down, and there was an extra set of seats behind the front seats. Barkson had never chosen that option for her vehicles.

"That's yours?" Barkson asked.

"That's mine," Benedeto said, threading his way past all of the wagons and equipment.

"Does it even run?" Barkson asked.

"It did a few weeks ago," Benedeto said.

He put his pack into the back seat, then wiped his hands on his pants. He turned toward her.

"I'm feeling leery," he said. "I don't just want to drive out of here. I'd like to see if the main road is empty before I do. This little parking area is secret for a reason."

"You could have told me about it last night," she said.

"I could have, but strangers aren't allowed to park here," he said. "This belongs to the inn."

"How early do people in this town arise?" Barkson asked. She couldn't imagine that it was very early, considering how late everyone had been up the night before. The music was still playing as she let herself fall asleep.

"It's not the locals that I'm worried about," he said, which was the first time she got the sense that he actually believed her about the threats.

She nodded. He led her back inside the tavern. It was definitely cooler in here than it was in that indoor storage area. Barkson pulled her coat tighter.

Benedeto pushed open a door that led into yet another storage area, this one for flour and sugar and canisters labeled with the names of various fruits and vegetables. Here, the air smelled of ginger, cloves, and cinnamon, which were probably in one of the various ciders that was offered at the bar.

Benedeto skirted around some barrels and waited for Barkson. She arrived a moment later. He unbolted the door, and was about to push it open, when she put a hand on his arm.

"Let me go first," she said.

Her job was to protect Kirillis, after all. He looked like he had been about to shove the door open and step outside quickly. The last thing she needed him to do was to step outside and draw an attack.

He gave her a surprised look, one that said, *You think you can handle an emergency better than I can?* But fortunately for him, he didn't say that.

She pushed past him, and then eased the door open just a hair.

The door opened on the side of the building, the crack facing the street. The street was quiet, unlike the night before. There was a slight wind.

The sun had just barely come up, sending gold and rose light across the patio. The tables had been pushed against the building, chairs upside down on top, legs to the sky. Weirdly, the tables were chained to the building, as if they were prisoners.

That told Barkson that theft of major items, like furniture, wasn't uncommon here, which made her deeply uncomfortable about having left her vehicle in the open.

The road seemed empty. Certainly no traffic was going by, which was unusual in most villages, cities, and towns. There were always the day workers in the cities, and in the villages, a lot of the farmers would be driving their wagons toward the daily market.

But not here. It seemed like dawn didn't matter at all in Oxechana.

She slipped through the door, and still saw no one. She beckoned Benedeto who started to say something. She touched his arm lightly, hoping he would understand.

She stopped near the tables. She could finally see diagonally across the street, where the carriage park was.

Her heart leapt up, adrenaline starting even before what she had seen had registered.

Two people, standing near her vehicle. They were tall and

thin, wearing leather jerkins and pants, daggers and swords around their waists. Their knee-high boots were travel-worn.

She put a finger to her mouth so that Benedeto wouldn't speak, and then she pointed.

His eyes widened. He fumbled for his own dagger. She grabbed her pistol, but as she did so, light reflected around her vehicle.

Light the size of a doorway.

A portal.

The two people conferred. One of them patted the hood of her windstone vehicle, and the other person laughed. The sound echoed in the early morning stillness.

Then the first person walked into that light, followed by the second. The light grew slowly narrower until it vanished altogether.

Benedeto cursed quietly. Barkson shot him a dismissive glance. At least he would believe her now.

He started to say something else.

"Shut up," she hissed. "We have to get you out of here now."

"But they found your vehicle," he said, "not mine."

"Yes, they did," she said. "There could be a variety of reasons for that. They might think it yours. Everyone knows that the Kirillis have had windstone vehicles for years. Or these people are tracking me somehow."

"If I leave now—"

"You might get away before they find you," Barkson said.

He drew himself upright. "Those are the attackers?"

She nodded. "They came through a portal like that at Dilshad's."

She didn't tell Benedeto that she had killed the person who came through that portal.

"They don't look like they belong in Dorovich," he said.

"No, they don't, do they?" she asked. "Let's get back inside. Now."

He didn't have to be told twice. He pulled open that side door—apparently he had never completely closed it—and slipped inside. She followed.

He started to walk toward his vehicle.

"Faster," she said as she jogged past him. He ran to catch up. She was the one who got them to the vehicle storage.

It looked no different, but she could feel the urgency. She had to get Benedeto out of here quickly.

His damn vehicle had better run.

She wended her way around the large carriage and the wagons. He followed.

"Is there a way out of here that doesn't take you on the main road?" she asked.

"There's the cliffside road," he said. "It's not stable."

"It'll be better than encountering those two again," she said.

He walked to the driver's side. "Maybe you should come with me."

"Maybe you should stop trying to change the plans," she said.

He opened his door, and got in.

"You're going to put up the roof and have your windscreens closed," Barkson said. "You're going to drive as fast as you can, and you're going to avoid any city or town that has Kirilli property. Do you understand me?"

He nodded, then twisted in the seat, reaching for the roof.

211

"I've got it," she said.

"How are you going to get out of here?" he asked.

"I'll drive," she said. She wasn't going to tell him that she might have to wait, especially if those two and their portal returned.

"You're not telling me something," Benedeto said.

Time to be honest.

"I'm not telling you many things," Barkson said. "I'm not authorized."

She grabbed the roof and tugged it, helping him activate it. It was old enough that it didn't slide as easily as her roof did.

"You weren't going to tell me that those people are Fey?" he asked.

She started, and hoped he didn't notice.

"I studied alchemy, thaumaturgy, and ancient magic," he said. "Not to mention art history. And I saw a lot of the possessions my great-grandmother brought back from Mount Vitaki. Those were Fey."

"Possibly," Barkson said. "I haven't been able to verify anything, and I'm not going to."

"But you're proceeding as if they are," he said.

"I'm proceeding as if you and your family are facing the worst threat of your lives. I just wish you'd take me seriously."

She snapped the roof in place, then patted the side of the windstone vehicle, commanding him to start it.

He did.

She walked over to the gigantic double doors, and removed the bolts before moving them enough so that she could peer out. A large path went uphill toward the main road. A smaller, extremely narrow path curved behind the tavern and down the hillside.

So that was the cliffside road. She was happy she wasn't going to drive it.

She pushed the doors the rest of the way, and Benedeto drove through them. He stopped at the fork, and she pointed to the downhill route.

He made a face, then eased the driver's side windscreen down.

"You be careful," he said.

"I'm not the one they're after," she said, wondering if that was true after her experiences with Dilshad. Had someone seen her kill the person who had come out of that portal on Dilshad's property? If so, she was in as much danger as Benedeto.

She tapped the side of the vehicle again.

"Get out of here," she said.

He nodded, pulled up the windscreen, and turned onto the smaller, narrow road, driving so slowly she could have walked past him.

Her heart was pounding hard. She turned and went back inside the tavern, hoping he was going to make it.

He was now no longer her responsibility.

And for that, she felt ridiculously relieved.

OXECHANA

CHAPTER
FOURTEEN

Barkson made sure the double doors were closed tight and the bar that prevented anyone from opening them easily had been replaced. It barely looked like anything had changed inside the large storage area. That windstone vehicle had seemed small compared to the wagons and the carriage.

She was glad of the storage—at least for Benedeto—and she hoped his vehicle would make the journey. She had no idea how old that model was, but she wasn't sure she had ever seen one with that configuration.

She couldn't think about it. She needed to make sure that no one followed him.

So she ran through the hallway and back to the other storage area. She wouldn't be able to lock this door behind her. She hoped that the tavern owner would forgive her.

Barkson pushed open that side door again, as slowly as she did the first time. There was still no one on the main street, although farther down the way, a couple walked hand in hand to a railing at the edge of the cliff. Barkson suspected they were tourists, waiting for the town to wake up.

She didn't want to wait for the town to wake up. She eased out the door and pushed it closed, fingering her pistol, but not pulling it out. No one stood near her vehicle this time, but she had to be on the alert.

If the attackers were looking for her, they would probably recognize her in an instant, particularly with her long flowing coat. She didn't dare take it off, though, because she needed both of her hands.

She crossed the first half of the strange road. The tables in the berm in the center were also chained in place. Benedeto liked this town, but the chained tables made Barkson realize that she didn't like Oxechana at all. She looked both ways, and then did a slow circle, before crossing the second part of the road and making herself walk like a person in no hurry at all to the carriage park.

Besides her vehicle, there was one small but ornate carriage toward the back. It had clearly arrived after she had.

The air here tingled. She recognized the feeling, even though she hadn't felt anything this strong in months.

Residual magic. The kind that came after a powerful spell.

She made herself move even more slowly. She didn't want to walk into some kind of trap or into another portal as it started to open.

The air felt even more tingly as she got closer to her vehicle.

And, as she suspected, someone had put a barrier around it.

She didn't have the magical ability to crack the barrier, but she did have a pretty educated guess about what would happen when she did.

She wished now she had some of Helia's little weapons. Barkson could have used them.

She pulled out her pistol and primed it. Then she picked up some rocks along the side of the road, and crouched, trying to remember exactly where that portal had appeared.

She could go around the vehicle, feeling the magic and where it had gotten stronger, but she wasn't going to do that. She needed to be prepared, not surprised.

Then she tossed the largest rock at the barrier. The barrier flared purple, gold, and some kind of blue, with sparks that flew in all directions.

The rock went through, and bounded off the side of her vehicle. She silently apologized to it, waiting to see what would happen next.

Nothing did, so she threw another rock, farther this time. It bounced near the passenger side of the vehicle.

This time, a thread of light appeared, as tall as a person, exactly where she had seen that portal.

Her heart pounded.

The light grew wider and brighter, and someone started to come through.

She shot, the pistol's bark even louder than usual in the silence of the morning.

The person fell backwards, into the portal, which she knew would cause some kind of confusion.

Now that they knew she was here, she didn't have any reason to stay.

She sprinted to the driver's side, feeling her skin burn as she scurried through that barrier.

The portal wavered, as if it couldn't hold its shape.

She pulled open the driver's door and was about to get inside when the portal solidified. Another person started to come through.

She had no shots left, so she grabbed her dagger with her left hand and threw, aiming at the center of whatever was coming through. The dagger seemed to connect and again, the portal wavered.

This time she didn't wait.

She got into the vehicle, pulled the door closed, and moved the driving sticks, backing out and praying that her vehicle would be able to get through that barrier.

But there no longer seemed to be a barrier at all, or maybe the metals of the vehicle negated it, something she hadn't thought of.

Iron protected against magic and she knew that some parts of the vehicle had bits of iron built in.

She drove away, heading deeper into Oxechana than she wanted, going down a hill away from the cliff face.

She would find another way out of the city.

She just needed to be unpredictable at the moment.

She didn't want the attackers to follow her, and she knew they might.

She had no idea if they had spelled her vehicle.

But Oxechana was a wealthy little town. There had to be other windstone vehicles here.

She wondered if she could buy one. She had enough gold, although it might tap her out.

Although, it would be worth a try.

OXECHANA

CHAPTER
FIFTEEN

It didn't take Barkson long to find a place that sold windstone vehicles. It was tucked in the intersection of a tiny side street and what had to be the main road for locals. Lots of businesses ran along that road, but most of them were the kind locals would use, from some indoor markets to repair shops.

The side streets, like the one that held the windstone vehicle sales office, had some more upscale stores. Some sold locally designed art, others sold furniture, and still others jewelry.

There was a carriage repair shop not too far away, but nothing for carriages or wagons near here. Just the windstone vehicle sales area.

Four vehicles were parked at angles on a gravel lot. A two-story stone building stood behind it, with a small sign over the door from the lot.

Barkson walked over to the sign. It had the name of the busi-

221

ness and actual hours posted. The place wouldn't open until the afternoon.

She let out a frustrated breath. She was convinced that her vehicle had been spelled. She had no idea what kind of spells existed, whether or not the attackers could track her vehicle, but it was clear they could put some kind of notification barrier around it.

They had shown up faster than she expected when she broke that barrier. And they had come out of the portal quickly.

Fortunately for her that portal had closed. She had left most of her weapons in the compartment of the windstone vehicle.

She wished she had been able to ask them if they were following her because they recognized her from Dilshad's or if they thought the vehicle belonged to Benedeto.

She wanted to believe it was because of Benedeto, but she had to act as if the attackers were tracking her now. And if that was the case, then she would lead them directly to Corrin and Emberto.

She walked around the windstone vehicles. One was older than hers, maybe the same model that Benedeto had. It had that same back area for passengers rather than compartments for storage.

Another one of the vehicles was just like the first model she'd had. She'd loved it at the time, but she later realized how heavy it was. It was too low to the ground to handle the roads as Benedeto had described them. The bottom would have been scraped off before she got too far from here.

The other two looked newer, and neither had a back area for passengers. She crouched and looked underneath the one closest to her. The vents glistened, just like hers had when she bought the vehicle.

A new windstone vehicle, without residual dirt and debris coating the interior of the vents, could almost fly down the roads. It would also seem lighter, because more wind would fill the vents.

She stood, and walked to the remaining vehicle. It looked similar to hers, but had some scratches along the side. Clearly it had been used before.

She stared at it, feeling unsettled.

The sun was still low on the eastern horizon. The morning was still new, and in a town like this, people wouldn't get moving for hours.

This place didn't open until the afternoon. In Trinovante, a place that didn't open until afternoon would have lost half of its business.

She crossed her arms and thought for a minute, looking back and forth between her potentially compromised vehicle and these four newer ones. She knew how to break into a windstone vehicle. It wasn't hard, although with some of the earlier models, driving could be difficult. The older vehicles seemed to know the quirks of their owners.

The newer ones didn't have that issue.

If she left her vehicle here, along with some coin in payment, the owner of the business might not be satisfied, but her conscience would be.

She really wanted the newest one; that way she wouldn't have the back passenger seat issue, and she wouldn't be taking on someone else's problem.

She took a deep breath, and looked around. The other businesses were closed as well and there still was no one else on the street. The fact that this town didn't arise until late worked to her advantage.

She went to her vehicle to remove the repair kit. None of the windstone vehicles had individual locks. They all had matching design, with matching locks. The picks that she would use to open her vehicle (if need be) were the same picks that she would use to open any of these.

Movement caught her eye. The door to the shop banged open. A man staggered out. He wore a loosely fitting suit with a tunic and had on expensive shoes. But he wasn't wearing socks and his hair stuck up in all directions.

He must have seen her or heard her from the upstairs in the building, put on clothing and hurried out the door.

"What are you doing here?" he asked.

"I was hoping to buy a replacement vehicle," she said, feeling a little more relieved than she expected. She really hadn't wanted to steal.

"We don't open until noon," he said.

"By then, I plan to be in Feltshyon." She lied about her destination. He didn't need to know where she was going.

"So what were you going to do? Break into one of the vehicles?"

Had she been that obvious?

She managed to make herself look indignant. "No. I was planning to leave and hope that my vehicle would make it back to Feltshyon. I got dust in all of the vents. I've blown them out, but they don't work to my satisfaction."

He blinked, as if she had surprised him.

"But you don't seem to want a sale, so I guess I'll take my chances." She put a hand on the driver's door of her vehicle.

"Wait," he said. "I'm sorry. You woke me up, and I had it in my head that anyone who was here at this time of day would be trying to steal."

"Yes," she said, "from what I've been hearing, Oxechana has been having a lot of trouble with theft."

She hadn't heard anything, but those chained tables had given her a clue.

He nodded, looking regretful. "It's a fairly new problem, but it's a bad one. And we can't locate the bad actors. They're stealing large things, which is even stranger."

Maybe taking those large things through portals, Barkson thought but did not say.

"Well," she said, "I'm not one of your thieves."

Although she probably would have been, if he hadn't seen her through his window.

She drew herself to her full height, which was slightly taller than his. "I would like to trade my vehicle for one of yours."

He took one small step back, as if she had surprised him. Apparently no one had offered to do that before.

"Your vehicle is newer than most of mine," he said. "Why would you want to get rid of it?"

"I've been driving for some time, and I can't seem to blow out the vents properly," she repeated.

"I'm sure I can find someone who would do that for you." His tone had become patronizing.

"I'm sure I could find someone on my own," she said. "But I don't want to be stuck here during the repair. Even waiting until this afternoon might be too long. I'm behind on my schedule, so I would like the best windstone vehicle you have."

She looked at the newest one.

He followed her look. "It's similar to yours," he said.

"It is," she said. "I trust it has a lot of storage?"

"I can show you," he said, immediately launching into sales mode.

He unlocked the vehicle using the same kind of picks she would have used. He pulled open the door, and then he unlatched the roof. With a practiced movement, he pushed the roof back and showed her the series of compartments in the back of the vehicle, compartments that matched hers exactly.

She said nothing, just let him run through his spiel. When he finished, she said, "I'll take that one, then."

He looked at her sideways. "I can't trade this vehicle for yours. Yours is, by your own admission, damaged. You've been driving it for some time. This one is brand new."

She looked at it. It had some visible flaws, probably from being driven to Oxechana. But she wasn't going to argue that.

She needed the new vehicle and she needed it fast.

"You could," he said when she hadn't responded, "take either of the older vehicles. They aren't as fast—"

"Nor do they work as well on the roads I'll be taking," she said. "I've owned those models."

He remained still, as if he was afraid he would harm this deal if he talked too much.

He wouldn't, but he didn't know that.

"I'm sure you don't sell a lot of vehicles here," she said. "You have these for the convenience of the wealthier tourists to Oxechana, am I right?"

She probably shouldn't have asked that as a question, but she couldn't take it back now.

"So, we're both at a bit of a disadvantage," she said. "I need a new vehicle, and you have one. You need a sale, and I'm willing to buy this vehicle, but I'm short on coin. What can we do?"

She was lying to him about being short on coin. But she did feel some compassion for him. If she succeeded in getting rid of her vehicle, he would receive one that wasn't just worn from the journey; it also probably carried some kind of magical marker.

He tilted his head as he clearly thought it through.

"The vehicle plus ten gold coins," he said.

"I don't have ten gold coins," she lied. "What I do have needs to get me through the trip. How about the vehicle plus two?"

"Eight," he said.

"Again, I don't have that much." She was used to lying in negotiations. "Three."

"Six," he said.

"Four," she said. "That leaves me very little to travel on."

He gave her a softer look. Clearly he believed her lies. When she first learned how to negotiate, the fact that he believed her would have bothered her.

These days, nothing like that bothered her.

"Done," he said, and patted the top of the vehicle. Then he gave her an apologetic smile.

She braced herself for some kind of surprise. That was what usually accompanied smiles like that.

"I require paperwork," he said. "I need to be able to prove you sold me your vehicle and I sold you this one."

She felt her shoulders relax. Paperwork like that was

common in Trinovante, but not in some other areas of the Protectorate.

"As long as you fill out copies for me as well, we should be just fine," she said.

He did that surprise blink again. Apparently few of his customers asked for that.

But given his need for paperwork, she could only guess how many times he had been bitten by some drunk rich young person, selling a vehicle, only to claim they hadn't done so.

"We'll fill out the paperwork inside," he said.

She almost glanced at her vehicle. She didn't trust it at all anymore. She worried that if she went in the building with him, she would return to see a portal opening near the vehicles.

"We'll do the work out here," she said.

He raised his eyebrows just a little, as if her insistence surprised him.

Then he nodded. "Out here it is," he said, and they got their business underway.

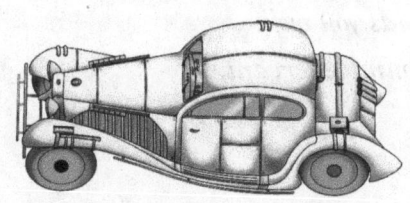

My dearest G,

I am dropping this at a Protectorate Mail Center on the outskirts of the town where you told me I could find B. I did, although B had relocated from the address you gave me nearly a year before.

After some discussion and a bit of wrangling, B is following your instructions. It would not surprise me, however, if B makes a short sideways trip to see you. B is quite worried, with cause, I might add.

I've had small troubles on this part of the trip. Nothing that you need to know until I return. I handled all of it.

You should know, however, that the threat remains. It is not limited to Trinovante. It has found its way to the hinterlands as well.

B informs me that I have a terrible drive ahead of me. I have not taken these roads before, so I must trust B's word. Do not expect to hear from me for some time after you receive this missive.

I would say that it'll take two days, but I am uncertain as to whether or not these letters reach you according to the same timetable that I send them on.

To recap, in case the timetable is different, I have to find the most distant two. The others have all taken your advice.

I hope this finds you well.

Your not-so-humble servant,

L.

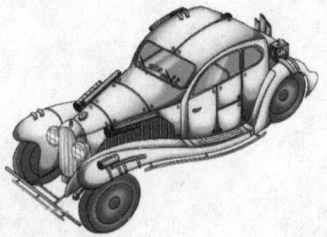

RAZBITAY

CHAPTER

SIXTEEN

Barkson arrived on the eastern side of the city-state of Razbitay after twilight. The city-state was as modern as Trinovante, with lightstone lanterns above each street instead of gaslight or regular torches. The buildings were made of riverstone, and the streets were either flat slate or flat cobblestone made of riverstone, wide enough to handle all kinds of vehicles, including windstone ones.

She had crossed into Razbitay from the country of Sék so that she avoided the Khēmían bureaucracy. The road from Sék into Razbitay was as wide as most of the roads in Razbitay and beautifully paved, clearly maintained by Razbitay instead of by Sék. Apparently the people of Razbitay, the Razbitios, preferred to travel through Sék when they left Razbitay instead of going through the rigors of Khēmían customs.

The official buildings of Razbitay were on the western side of the city-state, across the magnificent bridge. Some didn't trust the old bridge, called the Miracle Bridge, which had been in place for centuries, and instead traveled by punt or bateaux across the Hidden River itself.

Barkson hadn't traveled the Miracle Bridge in years and she certainly hadn't driven across it in a windstone vehicle. The winds on the bridge were legendary. The bridge's sides were built as high as most carriages so that they wouldn't get blown into the water.

But still, on extremely windy days, horse-drawn vehicles of any type could be extremely unstable. Windstone vehicles were lower to the ground, but they were subject to wind as well.

Barkson had heard tell of windstone vehicles that actually rose off the bridge and floated with the wind, never high enough to crest the walls and fall into the river, but high enough to crash into other vehicles.

Crossing the bridge wasn't something she wanted to do at night, either, although some enterprising souls had finally installed lights. They were brighter than she expected, which made the trip across easier than it had ever been.

The eastern side of Razbitay housed many of Razbitay's businesses, as well as government buildings for the Protectorate and the still-existing consulates for various governments throughout Dorovich.

Some of those consulates were for governments that still refused to join the Protectorate; others were for governments that were mostly unwilling parts of the Protectorate.

And then there were the agencies who occasionally hired people like Barkson.

She was going to stop at one of those on this night, before

she tried the address that Gussie had for Corrin. The address that Gussie had given Barkson had looked suspect from the start.

Barkson thought that perhaps there were apartments in that part of Razbitay, but if there were, no one in his right mind would admit to living there.

She suspected that the address was either a mail drop or a distraction, and she hoped she wouldn't have to find out in the morning.

She drove through the wide streets, happy to see carriages and other windstone vehicles and some guards in their red Razbitian security uniforms passing her on the road.

Razbitay did slow down at night, but not by much. It was probably the most active place she had ever visited and this night was no different.

The side street she wanted was in the center of the eastern side of the city. She rounded two cemeteries, went up a slight hill and found her way to a narrow passageway that in Trinovante would have been called an alley.

The passageway was too narrow for any vehicle—windstone or carriage—to pass through.

This was the oldest section of eastern Razbitay, built eight centuries before. The buildings had been maintained, but still showed their age in their narrow windows and main doors that were on the second story.

Before the bridge, before the Razbitios tamed the Hidden River, Razbitay had been subject to massive floods, particularly on what was called the lowlands, like this part of the city.

The locals had learned to put main entrances on the second

or third story, so that the actual living spaces wouldn't be flooded out. The lower levels were mostly columns and doors that could be opened like flood gates should the water's rise become truly threatening.

Barkson had to park her new vehicle on yet another side street, in a parking area built for windstone vehicles. Five were there now, parked haphazardly. She parked hers at the edge of the flattened area, so that if someone blocked her in, she could drive over the dying grass and get back onto the nearby street.

She fastened daggers to her hips, and made sure she had at least some coin. It wasn't unusual to see armed people in Razbitay, especially on this side of the river.

Then she set the windstone vehicle's locks and walked down the hill.

The hill was much steeper than she remembered it being. Maybe she had never parked on this road, or maybe she wore better shoes than these boots with an ever-so-slight heel.

Or maybe she hadn't been quite this tired. Or this hot. She almost felt like she had gotten off a boat, instead of spending all day on winding roads in the driver's seat of her vehicle.

She gratefully veered to the left, where the narrow road wasn't exactly flat, but it wasn't steep either.

The air here smelled of garlic and fry bread, something she hadn't had in years. Beneath that scent was the musty-iron smell of the river, so powerful it was almost like a spice in and of itself.

Voices carried across the neighborhood, having conversations and fights, some people laughing and at least one person crying. She had forgotten that almost everyone in Razbitay kept their windows open at all hours to deal with the sometimes stifling heat.

She had once drawn the suspicion of locals by having her windows closed on a cool evening. The open-window habit had become ingrained in the locals young, and they put up with discomfort in the cooler months unless that cool air was accompanied by one of Razbitay's legendary rainstorms.

Some windstone scooters were parked against the nearest building, and she veered toward them. She'd heard about windstone scooters, with their little narrow seats and handlebars and vents that ran beneath just like on the regular vehicles, but she had never seen one before.

They looked unstable and dangerous, and she supposed that was part of the appeal. They also looked like they'd be easy to maneuver in a city like this one, especially when carriage and wagon traffic covered the roads.

But she would worry about spooking horses and startling pedestrians.

Still, the scooters looked intriguing. She wondered how hard they would be to learn to drive.

Then she stopped. She didn't have time to investigate windstone scooters. They were a future problem or a future solution —she wasn't sure which.

She had to put them out of her mind.

She did, in a way. But they were indicative of this part of Razbitay. It was filled with people who liked taking risks, people who lived life on the edge.

She had spent more time here than she wanted to contemplate.

The narrow little road that she was on suddenly went steeply uphill. The stone buildings were built into the hillside, looking like they had grown out of it.

The lightstone lanterns that illuminated the streets below were missing here. The street lanterns were still gaslight, if they were on at all. Many of the lanterns were dark.

When she had lived here before, that darkness had been intentional. A lot of strange things happened in this neighborhood, and the cover of darkness protected those who participated in them.

This far back, the stone buildings were all multiunit housing. They'd originally been good-sized houses, but the city had allowed them to be carved up to accommodate the growing population.

The windows in all of the buildings had thick curtains. She could barely see interior lights through any of them.

The building she wanted was on an even narrower side street. That street had been built long before anyone thought to bring carriages up these hills. Horses or walkers, nothing more. Now, horses were banned this far up. The last stable on this road had closed just before Barkson had lived here for that short time, years ago.

The building was at the end of the street, pushed up against the hillside. The building had little to recommend it. It wasn't quite high enough on the hillside to give it a view of the mountains or the rest of the city.

The building was crammed between three others, and in some of the rooms, the only views were of the exteriors of the other buildings. Or the interiors if someone lifted those curtains, which happened rarely.

She was grateful for that. It meant she wouldn't be seen as much more than a shadow.

She reached the front door of the house, and used the only knock she knew—three raps, a pause, two raps, another pause, and then five raps.

It was the weekly signal from two years before, but it was the most recent that she had. She'd been in the house when someone used an old signal. It put everyone on alert.

If everything worked the way it had in the past, someone would be dispatched to the roof immediately. There should have already been a guard there, carrying a musket and looking for anything untoward. Whoever ran to the roof would inform the guard that they had a visitor with an old code.

The guard, if they were good, would belly flop onto the roof and peer over the edge, musket at the ready. If the person knocking was a known enemy, then the guard would shoot immediately.

If the person was unknown, there were other steps.

If the person was known, they still wouldn't be trusted. A lot could have happened since that person learned how to knock.

Barkson resisted the urge to look up and wave. She'd seen someone get shot at doing that very thing.

Fortunately for the person who had waved, muskets were not the most accurate guns. Only a handful of people could take their muskets and make them sure shots.

Barkson was not one of them, although when she had worked in and around Razbitay, she knew of a few people who would modify her muskets for accuracy.

She still had those muskets. The two she had brought on this trip had been modified like that. Her pistols were more accurate and easier to shoot, however. And she was deadly with knives.

Above her, a slight sound reached her, accompanied by the faint odor of beef stew. There was usually some kind of soup or stew cooking in this house, for any kind of late arrival.

Her stomach growled. The bread and cheese hours ago had not been enough to sustain her.

Still, she didn't move. She also did not repeat the knock, even though part of her—the exhausted part—wanted to.

Repeating a knock was the sign of someone who had never been part of this group. Repeating the knock often meant that whoever had gotten the code had gotten it through illicit or deadly means.

Verifying whoever was at the door took time. Any person who had lived in this house knew that.

To her right, a curtain in the nearest window bobbled. Most people would see that bobble as a draft as someone walked by or as quick little brush against a sleeve.

Barkson knew it for what it was; she had just been observed from the side. Next came the observation from the front.

The door slider would come next. For the person inside, the door slider, moving aside so that someone could see out just as the person outside could see in, was the most dangerous move of all.

Some attackers used that slide as a way to gain entry—shoot the person at the door through the face, and then take the moments of chaos inside to pick the door's lock from the outside.

Barkson made herself breathe slowly to keep herself calm.

She wanted to give off no hint of threat, even if the people inside did not know her.

The door slider pulled back, nearly blinding her with light that came from behind a shadowy face. The light was probably deliberate. She couldn't even see eye color. Heck, she really couldn't make out the eyes, just where they needed to be because of the eye sockets.

The person behind the slider said nothing. The slider closed.

Barkson's heart started pounding. Keeping calm was now proving impossible.

Then clicks and slams and thunks as various locks on the door opened.

Barkson stepped back. The door swung outward as forcefully as it always did. That swing often caught people by surprise.

Someone leaned over and said, "Inside, Barks. Now."

Barkson didn't have to be told twice. She stepped into the brightly lit room.

Lightstone lanterns stood on every available surface—tables, end tables, shelves, even a few chairs. The room was cool. The heat of the day rarely penetrated this place, probably because a large part of it was pressed into the hillside.

The door closed behind Barkson. She had to blink to make her eyes adjust.

The room itself was unchanged, but now it had an inordinate amount of furniture in the somewhat large space. Maybe a dozen straight-backed chairs, all pulled away from the tables, which were stretched across one side of the room.

The usual end table for keys and coins and other things that people normally kept in their pockets was on the right as she came in. A smaller table stood to her left. Above that table were hooks for coats and cloaks, not that anyone needed them on this warm day.

Her eyes finally adjusted. Maybe a dozen people stood in the room, most of whom she did not recognize. One young woman came running down the stairs toward the back.

She, apparently, had been the one chosen to head to the roof.

"Come with me," said a man to her left.

Barkson looked at him. He was tall and broad. His bare skull was perfectly formed, but his facial features were rough, almost like they'd been poorly sketched in.

It didn't help that he had broken his nose ten years before. Or rather, *Barkson* had broken his nose ten years before.

He didn't say her name so she didn't say his, because she didn't know what name he was using here.

The name he'd been using when she had first met him had been his own. Demos Rellis. Since then, he had used dozens of names. Barkson hadn't used that many in her own career, but she had used a lot.

He nodded at her, then pivoted, leading her to the back of the large room. They walked under the stairs into a small door that opened onto the windowless dining area just off the kitchen.

The kitchen was windowless too, but someone had thought that through, and vented the stove through its own pipe. A fireplace in the kitchen had a chimney that could be used to vent the kitchen as well.

The dining room, though, was always a bit stale and stuffy, and this evening was no different.

It did look oddly unproportional, though, because someone had removed the table. She had no idea how they had gotten the table out of this room into the main room, but they had.

Two chairs remained, both broken and stuffed in opposite corners. The built-in cabinets covered the wall between the kitchen and the dining room. The door to their left was closed tight.

Once the door under the stairs was closed, Demos's mouth twitched almost as if he wanted to smile and didn't quite trust himself.

"That knock is six years out of date," he said. "You scared the children."

By children, he meant the newest members of whatever he was doing.

"Five years," Barkson said, "and it was the most recent that I had."

"Which should have been a sign for you to stay away," he said.

"Yeah," Barkson said. "If I had the time, I would have tried for a meet somewhere in town or sent a message and followed protocol, although my knowledge of that is also five years old. So who knows what would have happened. However, I don't have time."

"You in trouble?" he asked.

"Technically, no," she said. Although for all practical purposes, she probably was now. She didn't want to go into depth with him, not that she thought he was associated with any attackers.

But Gussie hadn't given Barkson permission to talk with

anyone outside of the family, so Barkson was going to do the best she could by being vague.

"Technically?" he asked.

"I'll explain that in a moment," she said, with absolutely no intention of doing so. "I'm here because I need to find Corrin."

Demos's mouth thinned. "I'm sure you do."

Barkson had been expecting a reaction like that. On one of their last nights in this safe house, Barkson and Corrin had had a blow-out fight that had almost gotten them thrown into the street.

It was Barkson who stopped that disaster. She had reminded the house mother that the fight sounded like a domestic squabble, which would help the house continue to be seen as a quirky part of a quirky neighborhood.

Fortunately, that house mother had bought it.

Apparently, Demos had been in the house at the time (although Barkson didn't remember that) and hadn't bought that argument at all.

"I'm here because his sister sent me," Barkson said. "His father was murdered and she's afraid that the attackers might go after Corrin as well."

Demos rocked back on his heels, as if he hadn't expected that. He probably hadn't.

But a lot of people in Shadow Company, which this house was funded by, knew that Corrin's father, Augustus Kirilli, sometimes dabbled in shady business. There was talk that Augustus had encouraged his second son to get involved—as second sons of the Old Families often did.

Barkson had never asked Corrin, and he had never volunteered that information. He had seemed surprised, though, when he had first seen her in the community, and he had asked her in a sideways manner if she had known his father.

She had been new to the community at the time, and hadn't heard the rumors. So she had responded that she had met Corrin's father at some family gatherings, didn't he remember? Corrin had been at one of the early gatherings.

He had still been a child then, and Barkson had paid him no attention. At thirteen, she rarely noticed anyone who hadn't hit puberty yet. Corrin was three years younger, and as she had said to him once, the chasm between ten and thirteen was wider than the entire Forbidden Valley.

"Augustus Kirilli is dead?" Demos asked. "Murdered?"

Apparently the news hadn't traveled this far.

"He and his entire staff." Barkson had to think about the timing. The hours were blurring, which was telling her that she was tired. "Three days ago now."

"His staff at Kirilli, Capalidi, Konstandt, and B'Levin?"

Interesting question, and a revealing one at that. The firm handled accounting for high-level businesses within the Protectorate. Apparently, the firm handled other things as well.

"His staff at Kirilli manor," Barkson said. "I left before I learned the fate of anyone at Kirilli's firm."

Demos did not look mollified. In fact, he looked more uncomfortable than she had ever seen him.

"Corrin has nothing to do with the firm," Demos said.

Apparently, Demos thought she knew more about the firm than she did.

"Well, that's good news," Barkson said, "but it does not change my mission. I need to talk to Corrin."

"I'll take care of that," Demos said. "You can report to his sister that the message has been delivered."

Barkson let out a small laugh, designed to put him in his place.

"There's more to the message than I've told you," Barkson said. "I'm not supposed to read anyone else into this. I've already told you too much, but clearly I need you on this because I can't find Corrin without you. I'm assuming you're acting this way because you know where he is."

"I can find him," Demos said. Which was as much confirmation as she was going to get of her own assumptions.

"Then you need to tell me," Barkson said.

"Why did his sister send you?" Demos asked.

"You know Augusta," Barkson said. They had all gone to school together. "She doesn't really know much about Corrin's work or mine. But she knows I do occasional odd jobs for people."

"Is that what you call it?" Demos asked.

"I don't call it anything. She came looking for me. She has a big mess to clean up, literally, in Trinovante. She couldn't come this far north."

Demos absorbed that. It seemed to make sense to him. "So she paid you to come here," he said, almost as a test.

"Yes, she did," Barkson said. "And it was a good thing she chose me, because the address she gave me for Corrin put him in Razbitay, but not in a place he would ever be. So I assumed he was here or working on something shady."

Demos half-smiled at her. "I'd forgotten how good you are."

It was an acknowledgment of the fact that she had pulled a lot of information from him without giving much in return.

"It's public knowledge that Augustus is dead, isn't it?" Demos asked.

"I assume so," Barkson said. "He was killed on a public street."

"That's odd," Demos said.

"It's all odd." Barkson wished she could trust him. He might have insights into the Fey community in the Protectorate. Or in Fey-Qavnerian relationships, if there were any.

Demos was clearly thinking about all of this, weighing his oath to secrecy versus the potential threat against Corrin's life.

"You can verify if you want," Barkson said, and hoped he wouldn't choose that option. "But if you do, know that you might be costing Corrin his life."

"If whoever came after Augustus is coming after Corrin," Demos said.

"Yes," Barkson said.

"Do you think these murderers are attacking the Shadow Company?"

It was a fair question.

"Your guess is as good as mine," Barkson said. "It's not my concern, though. I have one job..." Another lie. "...and that is to find Corrin."

Demos frowned. He looked at one of the broken chairs as if he expected it to have repaired itself in the past few minutes. Then he sighed and shook his head.

"We're so far out here," he said, "that we don't get news from Trinovante quickly."

A small gift, then. He believed her, or he was going to believe her until he heard otherwise.

"I understand," she said. And she did. The fact that news

traveled slowly throughout the Protectorate sometimes caused a lot of problems.

"Did anything else happen there that I need to know about?" Demos asked.

"If you're asking me what else the Shadow Company needs to know, then I have to tell you that I don't know." Barkson knew she was being quite formal, but she really didn't have a lot of choice. "There appeared to be trouble brewing in G'zen that I think we'll hear about eventually."

Demos waved a hand dismissively. "Or not. There always seems to be trouble in G'zen."

His attitude made her decide not to tell him anything else. He might have been right about G'zen, but that crowd in G'Nzidia didn't seem like normal trouble to her.

She wasn't going to argue with him. She wanted to know where Corrin was, and she needed to focus on that.

She was about to restate her request when Demos said, "I have one last question. Were you followed?"

"No," she said, then held up a hand. "Before you quiz me further, I need to tell you I took every precaution. I switched vehicles in Olyx, and took roads I never want to see again as I traveled through Sék."

"You came through Sék? Via the Forbidden Valley?"

"Oh, no," she said. "I've taken those roads before. I went east, then north and finally I followed the border with Khēmía to get here."

"That seems out of the way."

She smiled at him, and opened her hands, letting her body language speak for her. *Yes, it was out of the way, Demos. Because I was trying to make sure I wasn't followed.*

She didn't want to call him an idiot, nor did she want to insult him, not when he knew where Corrin was.

"Procedure," was what she finally ended up saying.

Demos nodded. "Well, good," he said.

She waited.

He glanced at the chair behind him again, as if it could help him. For a moment, she thought he was going to leave the dining room to get an actual chair.

Instead, he shrugged his shoulders forward as if he was loosening the tension of out them, then took a deep breath. He looked down.

Apparently, this was Demos in the throes of decision-making.

It made Barkson want to punch him in the nose again. She had forgotten how very irritating he was, and how little self-control she'd had back in school.

She almost smiled at the memory of the incident: the provocation, her hand flying forward before she even realized she moved, and the satisfying *thunk* as her fist collided with his face.

He took another deep breath and looked up.

"Corrin is on estate duty," he said.

She knew what that meant: it meant that Corrin had just come off a particularly difficult job and he needed rest. So he was acting as a guard on one of the empty estates around Razbitay.

There were dozens of empty estates, estates that were second and third homes to the Old Families. There were also estates that belonged to Razbitay itself, and were used for visiting dignitaries but were shut down the rest of the time, with only a skeleton staff.

The idea that Corrin had estate duty made her very nervous.

"Is he alone?" she asked, hoping he at least had a skeleton staff.

"He has a small team," Demos said. "It's one of the larger estates."

Barkson didn't know if that was good or bad. Large might protect him. Large might not.

The fact that it was not his estate might protect him as well.

"Which estate is it?" she asked.

"Rezwell," he said.

She winced. She'd been to Rezwell. She'd worked a security detail there as a training mission. She'd been assigned to patrol the outside perimeter, and had done so, fending off all kinds of protestors and people who had looked, at least to her, suspicious.

She didn't like the idea that Corrin was there with a skeleton staff. The place was half the size of Oxechana. A skeleton staff would disappear in the leafy green trees and the reflections off the water.

"How long has he been there?" she asked.

"Ironically," Demos said, "three days."

That was good and bad. Good because Corrin hadn't been established there, so he hadn't had a lot of chances to interact with the so-called neighbors.

Bad because there was no one to help him if the attackers had found a way to open those portals near a Kirilli without a lot of footwork.

No matter who the skeleton staff was, they would be no match for the attackers coming out of those portals. Most of the members of the Shadow Company were anti-thaumaturgy, not realizing that once upon a time, their jobs had been created to *protect* the thaumaturgical.

Sometimes, the things that came out of the Purges made up seem like down. Barkson hated it all.

"I've been there before," she said, "but it's been years. So, please give me the instructions on how to get there quickly."

So Demos did.

RAZBITAY

CHAPTER

SEVENTEEN

T he Rezwell estate was in the far southeast corner of the city-state. Considered part of the city, the estate was more part of the "state" part of city-state. The estate's acreage was massive. There were some small countries on the western side of Dorovich that were smaller than the Rezwell estate.

Back when she guarded the estate, Barkson had felt like the estate was a city in and of itself.

She had seen larger estates since, but few that were filled with miles and miles of untamed wilderness, gigantic trees with flat palm-like leaves, more gigantic trees with ropy vine-like branches, and sandy black dirt that looked like nothing should grow in it, and yet everything stuck in it seemed to.

As she drove to the estate, with the daggers still on her hip, the gate code and extra key that Demos had given her firmly tucked in the pocket of her coat, along with the two letters,

Barkson tried to remember everything she could about the estate.

She hadn't been in the main building, which was the size of Qavner's Parliament in Trinovante combined with the Regents' Tower in Serebro. She would have thought, given the height of the two towers on the Rezwell estate, that the main building would be visible from both the road and the Hidden River, but it was neither.

Unlike most large buildings on most estates, the main building on the Rezwell acreage was lower than the other buildings, tucked against the foothills of the mountains, behind some stone formations that probably predated any civilizations in this part of the Forbidden Valley.

The estate's main building was hidden deliberately, and that gave her some comfort.

Usually, though, when someone was guarding an estate, they did so from one of the outbuildings. There were several on the Rezwell estate, from the guard tower off the main road to the housekeeping staff home near the main building itself.

There were some hunting shacks—the size of small houses in Trinovante—and the education garden, which wasn't a garden at all, but a school behind the tamed part of the landscape.

The estate had been built by one of the Old Families in Dorovich. The Rezwells had died off a century or two before, after bequeathing their estate to the city-state of Razbitay. The estate was used for visiting dignitaries or for private meetings with various government officials.

Sometimes other governments rented out the place so that

they could participate in peace talks or other delicate diplomatic discussions outside of the public eye.

Barkson had no idea who had been staying at the estate when she had been guarding it or if, indeed, anyone had. For all she knew, Shadow Company had some of its operatives doing some kind of play-acting while the trainees were on the property.

She just remembered the uneasy feeling that she had had because of the estate's size. In her opinion, there were too many ways that someone could enter the estate's grounds unseen, some of them from the Hidden River itself.

She had been told that it didn't matter; no one could easily breach the property or, from the unguarded portions, find the main building, which was always heavily guarded when someone important was on the premises.

She hadn't liked that answer, but she had been unable to do anything about it except make a mental note: if she was ever hired to guard a property like the Rezwell estate, she would make sure that all points of entry were covered, no matter how unlikely it was that someone would find their way to the important parts of the estate from there.

Then she had moved off of that kind of security and into things that were more suited to her skills, and she hadn't given guarding anything much thought.

Until now.

Demos seemed to believe no one was on the property except Corrin and the skeleton staff. That was pretty common for large estates. An operative who was exhausted and needed to recuperate from a tricky assignment often got what was considered an easy assignment by guarding an empty estate, making certain that it was in tip-top shape before the next time someone important had to use it.

Corrin didn't seem like a good candidate for that to Barkson, but then, she hadn't seen him in years. And if something had exhausted Corrin, then that something had had to be pretty extreme indeed.

Corrin didn't like resting and he didn't like being idle. Maybe he was reviewing the security for an upcoming visit. Or maybe he was guarding someone that not even Demos had known about.

After all, Demos was the house mother of that particular safe house; he wasn't in charge of operations in Razbitay.

Barkson didn't know who was in charge these days, which was one reason why she hadn't gone to that person first. Even if she had known that person, finding the local director of operations and demanding to know where one of their best operatives was for a reason that Barkson couldn't really prove wouldn't have gotten her much information.

It might have even gotten her in trouble with Shadow Company for not following protocol.

At least the roads between Razbitay and the estate were wide and smooth. The drive from the far side of the city to the estate took only an hour, and much of that time had been getting out of Razbitay proper.

When she got out of the city, the road became a dark gloomy corridor, heading down into the Forbidden Valley. No lights illuminated the sides of the road, and even the moon, which was heading toward full, didn't send its light into the valley.

It was as if light was forbidden in the valley, especially in the middle of the night.

The full lantern beams on the front of her vehicle kept her on the road, but also announced her presence. She knew from experience that lanterns and lights could be seen from the guard tower at the edge of the Rezwell estate.

But the only thing she could do to change that was something she was not willing to do—travel without lights. The moonlight wasn't powerful enough, and she didn't know this road, not well enough to keep the vents under her windstone vehicle from being shattered by an errant rock or branch in the road.

She reached the guard tower faster than she expected. She almost didn't realize what it was. The tower stood at the top of a hilly section of road. In the dark, the tower looked like a scraggly tree. She rounded five switchbacks before she realized that the scraggly tree she was aiming for was a bit too perfectly shaped.

Then the undercurrent of nerves that she'd been feeling since she had left the safe house turned into full-blown worry. That tower should have been flooded with light. There should have been light farther down the road, so that the people coming to the estate saw the road.

She had never been at the estate when it was supposed to be empty, though, so she didn't know if the road was supposed to be in darkness at times like this. But she always expected the tower to be filled with light.

Maybe that wasn't how Corrin did things. Maybe he protected the main buildings and not the grounds.

She rounded another switchback, and crested a small incline. The night was even inkier black than it should have been, and the blackness seemed to move.

She squinted, wondering if she was seeing storm clouds. The

Forbidden Valley and this part of Razbitay Mountains were subject to fierce storms.

A slightly bitter odor on the air caught her attention though. She sneezed, and as she did, she realized what she was smelling wasn't something bitter. It was smoke.

She squinted.

There were no lights around the tower, but there were yellow and orange dots on the hillside heading away from the tower. There were fires on the grounds.

She kept driving, but her mind took a mental pause. Maybe she should go back to Razbitay, to the safe house, and return with some support. Demos would help her if he knew that the estate was under attack.

But she didn't know if it was under attack or if those fires had been deliberately set by the grounds crew to refresh the land. Sometimes groundskeepers did that to get rid of pernicious plants, and sometimes groundskeepers did that to eliminate what the groundskeeper had done.

However, she had never heard of unattended fires, and she had never heard of any that had happened at night.

She was making an assumption, though, that these fires were unattended. She was also assuming that they could be easily doused. Some of the groundskeeper fires she had seen over the years had taken days to completely burn out.

Her mind was giving her logic, but her heart didn't want to believe any of it. It was true that she knew nothing about the maintenance of this estate, but it was also true that someone or something was after Kirillis.

What if that someone or something had found Corrin here?

She finally crested the hill. The tower loomed behind the

gate, no longer looking like a scraggly tree. The windows were open but in darkness. There was no covering on them, and no indication that a guard was in residence.

She parked in front of the gate, made sure she had the key and the code, as well as her daggers and the letters. She sat for a moment, looking at the darkness. She thought she saw movement to her left, but she wasn't certain.

There wasn't much wind, but there was enough to rustle branches.

Still, she had to be extremely cautious.

She let the light from the lanterns fade. She hoped there would be enough ambient light that she would be able to see the combination lock that was inside the gate. If not, she might have to input the code by touch, something she had done on other locks.

It wasn't ideal, but if she was lucky, she could take her time. She would be able to figure out how to get into the property without feeling any pressure at all, something that rarely happened for her.

She waited until her eyes adjusted to the darkness. It wasn't as dark now that the lightstone lanterns were off. There was some ambient light, mostly because the moon's light did reach this hilltop. The problem was the smoke. It acted like clouds occasionally blowing over the moon.

Still, there should be enough light for her to open the gate, return to the vehicle, and head into the estate.

She got out, and carefully closed the vehicle's door. Still, the sound thunked and echoed, which surprised her. There wasn't a lot of sound up here. She had expected more. When she had patrolled the edges of the estate in the past, there had been night owls, and shrieking hawks, the chitter of small animals, and the occasional rustle of wind through branches.

All of that used to make her jump because she hadn't had a lot of training, but her trainers had laughed when she mentioned it, telling her she had to get used to the fact that no place was ever truly silent, and that she, as an interloper, had to expect some kind of low-level noise.

But she wasn't hearing anything at the moment. Either the smoke and fires were driving the native creatures away or someone was nearby.

She scanned the area around her. It had a lot of people-sized shrubs of varieties she didn't know. Many of them had spiky green leaves, which would have been uncomfortable to hide near. Others had longer, flatter leaves. And some had so many branches and growths that she couldn't see through them at all.

If it had been daylight, she might have been able to note a color mismatch or some strange shape behind the shrubs, but she really couldn't see details clearly.

And the smoke was interfering with her sense of smell. If someone was near here or *something* was nearby, she couldn't smell it either.

Her stomach clenched. She wasn't exactly nervous, but she was on alert. She paused and listened.

She squared her shoulders. She could stand here forever or she could do her job.

She walked over to the gate. It had a dual lock, which was what she remembered from working here. First, she would unlock the front, which would reveal a little tube that had protruding numbers along it. Once she put in the code with the numbers, the tube would rescind the tumblers, clicking the firmer lock open and allowing her to push the gate aside.

She put her hand beside the first lock, the one that opened with a key, so that she could stick the key in properly. A sound behind her caught her.

Something had scraped against gravel. She started to turn when a hand covered her mouth, and an arm wrapped itself around her torso. The person held her tightly and started to drag her toward the bushes.

She didn't fight, not at first. Her left hand still had the key, which could do some damage, or she could drop the key and grab the dagger on her left side.

"Don't even think about it," a voice whispered in her ear. A *familiar* voice. A voice she used to love hearing.

Corrin's voice.

And dammit, it sent a shiver through her, just like it used to. Part of her wanted to lean into him.

She let him drag her all the way into the bushes. Then she moved her mouth against his hand. He'd known her a long time. He had to know that she would bite him if he didn't let go of her face.

"Don't say anything," he whispered. "Not yet."

His hand slid off her cheeks and down her chin, resting on her shoulder. His other arm still held her close.

"I wondered if the fires were a problem," she said quietly.

He let out a soft laugh that had a tinge of bitterness. "Problem?" he said in her ear. "I guess you could say that."

The arm he had around her waist loosened. She wanted to push away from him, but she didn't. Instead, she moved slowly, until she was close enough to hear him, but far enough away that he would have trouble grabbing her again.

He looked terrible. His dark hair was spiked around his face and clumped close together as if he hadn't been able to wash it. He had a two- or three-day stubble, which was not at all like him. His shirt was covered in leaves and dirt, and his pants looked like they could stand on their own. His boots were filthy.

He had daggers around his waist as well. They gave her a small start. He was as good with knives as she was.

If Corrin had thrown a dagger first rather than seeing who she was, she wouldn't be standing here. She would be dead now.

"You want to tell me what's going on?" she asked.

"You want to tell me why you're here?" he asked.

"You first," she said, "since you could've killed me, but clearly chose not to."

The right side of his mouth twitched as if it wanted to smile and the rest of his face disagreed.

"You were lucky," he said. "You sat in that expensive vehicle long enough for me to realize who you were."

"If I had gotten out right away, you would have killed me?"

"In my defense," he said, "I would have regretted it."

She had to stifle a laugh. Leave it to Corrin to make her laugh even when things were tense.

"And," he added, "in my defense, the attackers so far haven't come in vehicles."

She almost said, *Let me guess. They've come through portals.* But she didn't. She wanted him to tell her what was going on.

"How did they get here?" Barkson asked.

"I didn't know at first," he said. "But there's magic afoot, Barks. A lot of it."

262

She let out a small sigh.

"Your turn," he said.

"You really haven't told me anything yet," she said.

"Yeah, but you showing up in Razbitay is unusual these days, and then you coming out here meant someone broke the code of silence. I'm not going to ask who it is, because Demos has always had a soft spot for you, which is why, I'm guessing, you broke his nose."

She wasn't going to be sidetracked. The story of Demos and his nose didn't belong in this moment.

"Gussie sent me," Barkson said.

"*Gussie?*" Corrin asked.

Barkson nodded. "I have two letters for you from her. She wants you to read them right away."

"Here, in the dark, while I'm under attack." He shook his head. "Give me the gist."

She had so far resisted doing that with the other Kirillis, but she knew Corrin.

"I can't give you the gist of either letter," Barkson said. "I haven't read them. I know this, though. The first letter is the same as the one I've delivered to all your siblings except Emberto."

Corrin straightened. He clearly hadn't expected that.

"And the second letter is different for each one of you," Barkson finished.

Corrin glanced around, then peered over one of the shrubs. He was looking toward the fires.

Whatever he saw seemed to mollify him, because he turned back to Barkson, with a deep frown creasing his brow.

"What's Gussie about?" he asked. "This doesn't sound like her at all. Unless..."

The frown grew deeper. His face, which had been unlined when Barkson had last seen him, had furrows everywhere. He had clearly been under a lot of stress.

"My father's dead, isn't he?" Corrin asked.

Barkson knew better than to lie to Corrin about anything.

"Yes," she said. "He was murdered three nights ago now."

"Murdered." Corrin looked past another of the shrubs. "Three nights ago."

Then he peered around another shrub, as if he expected to see something important.

Barkson continued to look around as well, but she wasn't being as obvious about it. She kept her back to the shrub that he had hidden them behind, and looked down the road she had come up on.

After he finished looking this time, he focused on her.

"This started three nights ago," he said.

"What is this?" she asked.

"What seemed to me to be random attacks," he said. "People would appear, and break into the estate or go after one of the guards, and then they'd disappear again. I thought they were stealing some of the objets d'art, and we stopped them from some of that, but mostly, things got broken."

Barkson nodded.

"You're not surprised," he said.

"I'm not," she said. "Your entire family has been under attack. The only real loss so far has been Rudolfo, and I'm not sure if his death was tied to this or his position in the Protectorate."

"Rudolfo is dead." Corrin repeated that information without any emotion at all, as if he was trying on the thought for size. "Can't say as I'll miss him."

Which was Corrin-speak for *what an ass.*

"The only reason Rudolfo had a position with the Protectorate is because my father pulled some strings," Corrin said. "Father wanted Ghita to have the position, not Rudolfo, but Ghita wasn't interested. Which is probably a good thing now."

"Why would your father want someone in the Protectorate office in Feltingham?" Barkson asked.

"My father wanted Kirillis in all of the positions of power throughout the Protectorate," Corrin said. "He didn't succeed in that. Most of us didn't listen to him."

He paused, clearly thinking, but whether it was about his father or the Protectorate or positions of power, Barkson couldn't tell.

"Maybe I should have listened to him," Corrin said quietly.

"Gussie said the same thing," Barkson said.

Something popped loudly down the hill. Corrin put a hand on her arm, as if he expected her to run toward the sound.

All Barkson did was peer around the shrub, looking for the source of the sound. There seemed to be a lot more smoke, but she wasn't sure if that was from the sound.

Then she saw a tree going up in flames.

"We have to get you out of here," she said.

Corrin shook his head. "I have people down there. They're defending the estate."

"The estate doesn't matter," she said. "You do."

He whirled on her. "I don't think you heard me, Barks. I have *people* down there."

"If they're your people," she said, "then they're going to be able to take care of themselves."

"They're my people," he said tightly, "which is why I have to get them out."

"Maybe you should read the letters first," Barkson said.

"Letters. From my sister." His tone was sharp. "The first one tells me how my father died, and what it might mean. The second probably tells me to get my ass out of wherever I am and protect myself until she tells me it's safe."

"I don't know," Barkson said.

"But that seems likely, doesn't it?" he asked. "Because that was the mission for the others, wasn't it? And Gussie wants you to keep track of everyone so she can give us the all-clear when... what? She catches the perpetrators?"

"We didn't get that far," Barkson said. "She knew I had to find all of you, so we got me out of Trinovante as fast as possible."

He stared at Barkson. "She knows what you do?"

"Some of it," Barkson said. "She knows I live what she calls an adventurous life. She knows I take what she considers to be odd jobs. She knows I'm capable of defending myself."

His mouth thinned. "And that's all? You didn't tell her about me."

"About us?" Barkson asked.

He gave her a penetrating look.

"There is no us," he said, "as you'll recall."

"Rather hard to forget," Barkson said.

He grunted, looked at the burning tree. The air smelled of hot pitch and smoke and something a bit sharper. Sparks flew off the side of the tree.

The ground was damp here, so Barkson assumed nothing would burn. She hoped.

"Did you tell her," he asked slowly, "about me? About what I do?"

"I don't talk about you, Corrin." Barkson let herself sound as offended as she felt. "And if I did, I wouldn't break my oath. I'm as professional as you are."

He stared at her for a long moment.

"Then I don't need to see the second letter right now," he said. "She's going to assume that I am as incompetent as Dilshad."

Interesting that Corrin didn't say Benedeto.

Part of the tree exploded outward. The sound was deafening. Flames shot high into the night sky, illuminating the burning area around the base of the tree.

"How many people do you have here?" she asked.

"Ten," he said. Then shook his head. "Six now. Maybe. I haven't seen anyone in hours. I've been here, trying to see if one of Helia's devices worked as she said it would."

Barkson looked at him. "Helia's devices?"

"I don't know what you know about Helia," he said. "But she's—"

"I know about Helia," Barkson said. "She helped me save Dilshad's life, using one of her devices."

Corrin looked at her. "Now you tell me what's going on."

"I have no idea," Barkson said. "But I can tell you what I've seen. Will that do?"

"It'll have to," he said.

She kept it short. It was hard to condense the last few days, but she managed.

It helped that Corrin was a good listener.

"Portals," he said. "And the Fey, of all things."

"Yes," she said. "The Fey, of all things."

He rocked back on his heels, then sat down heavily. "We haven't fought them in generations. But we've been preparing. Did you participate in some of the seminars about the Fey at the Shadow Company?"

"No," Barkson said with a bit of a laugh. "You know how much I like history."

"Except this isn't history," he said.

"No, it's not," she said.

"I've been dealing with portals too," he said. "But more of them than it sounds like you dealt with. They appear and disappear all over the property. That's how I lost four of my people. It's almost like a sneak attack."

"Then what are the fires?" Barkson asked.

"One of the attackers, as you so quaintly call them, seems to like fireballs. So far, the attacker hasn't thrown fire at the buildings, but those fireballs have hit a few of my people. It's not pretty."

His voice went down for that.

"I have to get them out of here," he said. "I owe them that."

"I suspect they're only in danger because of you," Barkson said.

He shot her an angry glare. "That's not fair."

"These Fey are coming after your family," she said. "It might not seem fair to you, but it seems logical to me. If we get you out of here, that might save your people."

"And if you're wrong, they're on their own," he said.

"If they're your people, they'll be able to defend themselves just fine," she said.

"I'm not leaving, Barks," he said. "I'm not that person."

For a moment, she thought about continuing the argument. But he was right; he wasn't that person. He was going to drag everyone out of danger if it killed him.

He had always been that way.

"Why didn't you get them out of here sooner?" she asked.

"Because I thought the attack was on the estate," he said. "I never realized it was on me."

She nodded. She would have made that mistake as well.

"Does that mean they're all in the main building?" she asked.

"Yes," he said. "I had them spread out, but that was when I lost four. So I kept them close."

"Yet you're here," she said.

"Testing the device," he said. "I can't ask my people to use experimental magic and you know why."

"It seems counterintuitive to worry about violating laws written during the Purges when you might not survive otherwise," Barkson said.

"We have to work together, me and my people," Corrin said. "They won't listen to me if they think I have magic."

Then they're not very good people, Barkson almost said. But now was not the time for that argument.

"How do we get them out?" she asked. "Do you have carriages? Wagons? Windstone vehicles?"

"Boats," he said. "We get them to the river."

"That's ridiculous," Barkson said. "There's no easy route to the river from here. Better to let them return to Razbitay."

He stared at her for a long moment. Then shook his head.

"It's like we've never been apart," he said, and from his tone, she could tell he didn't think that was a good thing. "We still don't trust each other enough to let one of us lead."

"My mission supersedes yours," Barkson said. "I have to get you out of here, and then I have to get to Emberto."

"Emberto." Corrin's voice changed. "He's near Mount Vitaki, in our great-grandmother's house."

"So I've been told," Barkson said, "although I don't know why that's important. What's important is I have to get to him, and then my mission is done."

"Then go." Corrin sounded almost angry. "I can handle this."

She waved a hand at the burning tree, the glowing embers of other fires, the four dead people she had never met.

"It doesn't seem like you can," she said.

"I've been fighting off magical attackers for three days," he said. "I think I've got this."

"If you had it," she said, "you would have won already."

"Have I ever told you what a pain in the backside you are, Barks?" he asked.

"Almost every day we were working together," Barkson said.

He let out a small laugh. It seemed involuntary. Then his expression changed.

"You have to let me take care of this," he said.

"There is no taking care of anything if you die," Barkson said, but she wasn't sure about that. Maybe she didn't want him to die for selfish reasons, not because of her "mission."

"Barks, look—"

A portal opened behind him, looking just like the portals on

Dilshad's property. A figure inside the portal's opening raised his arms, long sleeves draped almost to his knees, a hood over his face.

Barkson didn't wait. She unsheathed a dagger and flung it in one fluid motion.

Corrin cursed, ducked slightly to the right, and then started when the dagger hit its mark with a solid *thunk*.

The person fell backwards, just like the one on Dilshad's property, only this time, the portal didn't close.

Corrin gave Barkson a startled glance, then whirled again, saw the open portal, and grabbed something from his pocket—a tiny little ball.

Barkson recognized it as the very same thing that Helia had thrown at the attackers on Dilshad's property.

Corrin did something to the ball and then whipped it at the portal.

The ball sped inside that portal, then seemed to stop in midair. Someone moved or something moved behind that ball, clearly reaching for it.

But the ball exploded.

The explosion sounded muffled. Red and orange and blue and green light expanded outward from the ball, and went deep into the portal.

The portal itself seemed to grow larger, opening wide like a hole in the sky. Then all of the light turned white, so bright that Barkson had to put a hand over her eyes.

"Look away," Corrin said, and she did. But she could still see the white light, getting brighter and brighter and brighter.

From far away, another explosion resounded. She couldn't tell if that came from the portal or deeper in the estate.

Sparks flew, like little white fireflies, illuminating the entire area, but no fires started here—at least that she could tell.

After a moment, the sky darkened, although she had spots in front of her eyes from the brightness of the white light and the sparks.

Cautiously, she looked up. Corrin was doing the same.

The portal was gone, but in its place, a rectangle the size of a door remained. It was black against the night sky, as if the door was actually there.

Then, ever so slowly, it decreased in size until it was just a small dot. Finally, that dot vanished as well.

"That's what you've been fighting?" Barkson asked.

"Yeah." Corrin's voice was flat.

"Do they all show up near you?" she asked.

"No," he said. "At first, they showed up all over the estate."

"At first," she said.

He nodded. "They appeared up here, and in some other parts of the estate."

His expression hardened. She recognized it. It was the way he covered emotion, particularly sadness. He covered it with anger.

"That's when I lost my people," he said. "They fought back, and most escaped, but the first two, they died when the portals opened near them. Just like I might have a few minutes ago."

That was as close as he would come to saying *thank you*.

"The light would have alerted you," she said.

"Maybe too late," he said.

The remnants of that light were fading from her eyes. She could see better now. She was glad he had told her to look away.

272

That white light might have given her even more trouble otherwise.

"That ball," Barkson said, "it was one of Helia's devices. I recognized it."

"Yes," he said. "We have—*I* have—maybe a dozen left. She worries about me. I thought she was being paranoid, but she wasn't. She said that she had seen some kind of vision where I needed magic of my own."

"She has visions?"

"Rarely," he said. "But yeah. My parents were repelled by that. Some of my siblings don't like it either."

"She led me to believe none of you accepted her," Barkson said.

He gave Barkson a sideways look. "That might be true," he said. "We take her help—some of us anyway—but she makes us all uncomfortable."

His words hung there for a moment. Barkson rose ever so slightly to see what the damage was from that portal.

The white sparks had burned small holes in leaves and left pockmarks on the ground, still visible in the not-quite darkness of the night. She didn't know if those pockmarks were damage too, or not.

"I didn't think to use a damn dagger," he said. "I thought the explosions were killing them."

Barkson eased back down. "They attacked Dilshad's place with a force of maybe ten. We closed the portal and he got out of there, so I have no idea if more arrived after that."

Corrin frowned at her. "If they're using tactical units like that, then I haven't been killing them. Just destroying their points of entry."

Barkson nodded. "After an explosion, have you had more time between attacks?"

"Yes," he said. "But the amount of time varies."

"So you are doing some damage," she said.

"Just not killing them, like you just did." He patted her arm. "Missed you, Barks."

She didn't respond to that. There was too much history between them for any kind of rational answer.

"The portals," she said, "after the first few where you lost people, have the portals opened near you?"

He frowned at her. "We were all gathered in the same place, in the main house, until I came up here."

"That's not an answer, Corrin," she said quietly. Although it probably was a yes. She just wanted him to say it.

"If they could find me," he said, still not answering her, "why would they open portals elsewhere?"

"I don't pretend to know," she said. "But, if Dilshad's place is any example, a portal opened far from the main house and the bulk of the attackers arrived there, fanning out to come at the house from the outside. Once they were nearly in place, then the portal opened near the house."

"But not in it," Corrin said.

"Not in it," she said.

"Even though Dilshad was inside."

She hadn't told him that, and it wasn't quite correct.

"What are you thinking?" Barkson asked.

"All of us have materials from our great-grandparents. My father spread out our inheritance, or so he said, and we have things that are...creepy, for lack of a better word."

Barkson peered around. Nothing was moving, but there still

was no animal, bird, or insect sound. Creepy was a good word for this place too.

"Did you bring some of those with you?" she asked. Because he had never traveled with anything like that before.

"No," he said. "But I had all of Helia's gifts. I didn't think it wise to keep them in Razbitay. I'm glad I brought them."

"You think that magic repelled them?" Barkson asked.

"You know as much about magic as I do," he said. "What do you think?"

She paused. She didn't know nearly enough about magic, and she might have to argue with him about knowing more. But she was too tired to argue, and getting more and more stressed by the minute.

"I don't know, Corrin," she said a bit more sharply than she intended, "and I think we're wasting time discussing it. Here's what I do know: the same attackers are after you as were after Dilshad, maybe after Helia. I don't know if they're the ones who murdered your father, and destroyed your family's estate, but I—"

"What?" Corrin asked. "You didn't tell me about the estate."

Barkson gestured at the Rezwell estate grounds. "A little busy here. I'm sure it's all in Gussie's letter."

Corrin stared at her. He finally said, "Good point. I'm sorry. We're reverting."

He was right. They were reverting to the couple they had been—not the fun young couple from the early months. The angry warring couple from the later months.

From the middle of the relationship forward, it had been a power struggle between them. It might even have been one from the start, but they'd been too wrapped up in each other to notice.

"We are," she said as calmly and gently as she could. "I asked about the portals opening near you not because I'm blaming you but because we need to know that from a tactical level. I might be able to get your people out easier than you will."

He leaned back a little. Maybe he heard that she was willing to sacrifice him. That's what the old Corrin would have heard. But logic didn't work that way. She had come here to save him, after all.

"Good point," he said with obvious reluctance. Then he nodded his head, as if finishing a conversation with himself. "We have four windstone vehicles."

"Four?" she asked.

"Four, down by the front of the estate house," he said. "I vowed I'd never use a carriage again."

She stared at him, torn between a dozen questions and plans. On the one hand, if they took the team out in carriages, the attackers wouldn't think it was Corrin. But that assumed that the attackers knew that Corrin was done with carriages.

Windstone vehicles were faster, but a lot more delicate. They broke down easier.

"Did you bring a vehicle up here?" she asked.

"No," he said. "I had someone drop me off and drive back down. If I failed at protecting the entry, I didn't want the vehicle trapped up here and unable to get back down the hillside."

"Good thinking," she said.

"How long is the window you usually get after attacking one of the portals?" she asked.

"Two hours, maybe less," he said.

"They've been appearing every two hours?" Barkson was stunned.

"There's no real rhythm to it," he said. "So I judge by the shortest time frame, not the longest."

Well, that wasn't helpful. Not in the planning stages anyway.

"Six people, plus you and me, five windstone vehicles." She was thinking out loud, but that used to work with the two of them. "Can all of your people drive?"

"Yes," he said.

"Then I say we hurry to the estate, and take all five vehicles out of here."

"Where to?" he asked. "If you're right, and they're coming after me, then we're in danger wherever we go."

"Yes," she said. "You and I are. But your people aren't. You send them back to Razbitay."

Corrin sat down heavily. "We'd be leaving this place unguarded."

"Yes," she said. "Think about this, though. Your presence here has already caused more damage than the usual guarding session."

"I hate it when you're logical," he said, and smiled.

She didn't smile back. She could feel the time pressure as if it were a living person, pushing her forward.

"We get your people out," she said, "then you go somewhere safe..."

"If what you're saying is true," he said, "there is nowhere safe. We have to obliterate the attackers."

She frowned at him. She didn't like to think of the implications of that. If he was right, and the attackers would keep coming after they had failed, then she might have sent Dilshad—hell, all of the Kirilli siblings so far—to their deaths.

Corrin seemed to understand her silence.

"It doesn't make sense that there's a full army going after Kirillis," he said. "If I were planning this, I'd have small tactical squads on each of the siblings. Or maybe even doubled up. So would you."

"Because we were trained by the same people," she said sullenly.

"And also because it's logical." He put a hand on her arm. "Your arrival got me thinking more clearly. I was reacting, not taking control of the situation."

"That's not like you," she said.

He sighed. "I haven't been thinking clearly for a while," he said. "This just proves it."

He squeezed her arm, and then let go.

"It's been a long time since you were here," he said. "Let me tell you the layout, where the troubles have been, and how I think we can get through them. We need to get to the people and then to the vehicles."

He almost sounded like he was asking her if he could lead this mission, which was decidedly not a Corrin maneuver. In the past, Corrin would automatically take control.

"I agree," she said. "I will need some of Helia's weapons."

He nodded. "You'll need another dagger."

"I have plenty," Barkson said, and hoped that was true. She had a feeling this fight would be harder than the others.

She wasn't exactly sure why.

THE HIDDEN

RAZBITAY

CHAPTER

EIGHTEEN

Barkson drove down the winding hill road toward the estate. She barely remembered this road. Mostly she remembered that it existed, but she hadn't traveled on it, back in the day. There were side paths that the staff used, that the guards used, just to make sure everything was safe.

Corrin had folded himself in the passenger seat, his legs tucked against his torso. The seat was a bench, which normally Barkson did not see as a problem, but she rarely had passengers.

The last had been Helia, and apparently they had been of a height.

Corrin hadn't complained. Nor had he complained about Barkson's driving, like he used to do when they were together. Maybe she had gotten better. Or maybe he had other things to think about besides torturing her.

Against his wishes, she was using the lightstone lanterns on the front of the vehicle. He was afraid the attackers would see her coming down the hill path. She was afraid that she would disable the vehicle by going off the road or hitting a large rock with the undercarriage.

He had assured her that the roads on the Rezwell estate were well maintained, but she wasn't going to trust the underside of her vehicle to his word.

He had broken it too many times with her already, always for reasons of expediency.

She could imagine him doing the same right now.

She had instructed him to watch for portals, and he hadn't disagreed with her. Maybe that was why he wasn't commenting on her driving.

Plus she was maintaining a speed that was halfway between terrifyingly fast and much too slow. Some of the corners she rounded hung out over some kind of ledge. The road had been built on the edge of the hill, not carved through the center of it.

Trees grew beneath that ledge, their pointed tops visible in the sweeping lights of the vehicle.

Twice, the vehicle had passed burning embers, which Corrin said tightly belonged to the first day of fighting.

As they passed the second pile of embers, he said quietly, "We managed to recover the bodies."

She wanted to look at him, but she couldn't. The road down was too treacherous.

She also didn't know how to respond to that statement. Of course, they had recovered the bodies. That was how the Shadow Company operated.

"Of the attackers?" she asked.

"No," he said. "Our people. To my knowledge, we have no bodies of the attackers. If we killed them..."

He shook his head. She wasn't going to exacerbate his feeling of failure by telling him she had abandoned an attacker's body at Dilshad's.

"What did you do with them?" she asked, hoping that she wouldn't be asked to remove bodies as well as living people.

"There's a crypt on the property," he said. "We placed them there, during a lull."

She almost said *good*, but caught herself just in time. There was nothing that she could say that would make him feel better, so she didn't try.

"You said there's a carriage house with the windstone vehicles in it," she said. "Where is it exactly?"

"We're not getting the vehicles first," he said.

There was the Corrin she knew. The one who argued and occasionally talked down to anyone else.

"I know." She kept her voice steady. "But I don't recall exactly where it is."

"We'll worry about that when we get to the estate," he said. "I don't want you to store this vehicle near the others."

They hadn't talked about where she would park her vehicle. That made her realize they had missed quite a bit of detail in the planning.

She didn't say anything more as the road leveled out. The estate grounds around them leveled out too, and become more formal, less overgrown with the plants that she had been unable to identify.

The lightstone lanterns were illuminating broad stretches of ground, which jogged her memory. Much of the ground here was not covered in grass or greenery, but in rich sandy dirt. The plants that grew down here were native to the region, and looked strong and healthy because of it.

They were also separated from the road by large rocks, almost human sized—too big to fit underneath a windstone vehicle. If one of those rocks rolled onto the road and she hit it, she would completely destroy the front of the vehicle.

"When these attackers came through the portal," she said, "they didn't grab carriages or wagons, did they? They had no conveyances, right?"

Because that was how it had been at Dilshad's.

"Not that we saw," Corrin said.

"Too bad," she said, eyeing the rocks.

She didn't say anything about blocking the roadway with them, even though that might have worked. It would have made leaving more difficult, though.

Ahead, she could see the roofs of several buildings. The roofs were made of red tubes, placed side by side, with slate underneath them. The rains here could be ferocious, and the tubes allowed water to stream off the roofs and onto the ground.

Each building had a runoff area that led to a couple of ponds, and beyond to the river itself.

She couldn't drive over those as she approached the buildings.

The big estate had some kind of small bridge over its runoff area.

Fortunately, it wasn't difficult to figure out which building was the main one. It was, as she remembered, in the middle of all the others, and four times their size.

She was not going to park around front, no matter what Corrin wanted. She parked about twenty yards from the back of the main building.

"We're not stopping here," he said.

"We are," she said.

"Then we have to run uphill to escape whatever happens," he said.

"Yes," she said.

She parked the vehicle in a small turnout. She didn't go nose-in. She used the turnout for its designated purpose. She turned the vehicle around so that it was poised to speed away should she ever return to it.

Then she leaned over the seat and grabbed two more daggers in their sheaths. That probably wasn't enough, but that was all she could carry.

"Give me some," Corrin said.

She grabbed two more by the sheath and handed them to him. He thanked her and attached them to his belt, struggling a bit to move inside the vehicle.

"Ready?" she asked. "We get out together."

"Yes," he said.

She grabbed the door handle, and shoved her door open as he shoved his open. They both got out, and closed the doors simultaneously. She hit the lock, and looked at the road.

It seemed farther than she expected to go down that hill. The roof of the main building was still visible, and the hill's grade looked a lot steeper than it had when she had been in the vehicle.

Corrin didn't say anything, though, and she was grateful for that. The old Corrin would have chastised her for the distance one more time.

Instead, he came around the front of the vehicle so that he was by her side.

She glanced up the hill that they had come down. The guard tower was not visible from here.

"All right," she said. "We're following the road because it's getting dark."

"I'll lead," he said, and for once, she didn't argue. In theory, he was familiar with this road, so he would be more sure-footed than she was.

He started down, only a foot or so ahead of her.

He came to the first switchback when another portal opened right in front of him. The person standing in the portal had their hood up, and long sleeves, just like the one Barkson had killed up top.

Only this person looked startled to see Corrin so close to the portal—or maybe startled to see Barkson.

Corrin reached for his dagger, and Barkson grabbed his arm, stopping him. Enough of the person's face was visible beneath that hood that Barkson saw a slight smile.

The person thought they (she? he?) had the two of them, and if that person decided to launch one of those fireballs, they just might.

Instead, they reached for something under their cloak as they stepped out of the portal.

That was when Barkson flung her first dagger, over Corrin's shoulder, and into the head of the person who thought they were going to attack.

The person did not fall backwards into the portal, but off to the side, just as Barkson had hoped.

The portal wavered, and then winked out, differently than the portal at the top of the hill had.

"What the hell did you wait for?" Corrin asked. He had one

of Helia's weapons in the palm of his hand. "I was going to throw this."

"I know," Barkson said. "But I've been thinking about it. I'm not sure that the weapon is helping."

"*What*?" He sounded offended.

"It took forever for that other portal to close," Barkson said. "And it gave off a powerful white light that I saw for some time. What if the magic you sent in there made everyone stronger, not weaker?"

"You have no basis for that speculation," he said.

"Except the fact that they've been coming for you nonstop for days, and even though you attack them, they don't seem to be getting weaker."

Barkson wasn't sure of her argument, but she knew something was off here. And she had an odd sense that whatever it was had something to do with the other weapons.

Corrin shook his arm out of her grasp. "Let's see if that attacker is dead," he said.

They hurried down the road to the attacker, sprawled on her back in the middle of the road. Her hood was down, and her dark eyes were open. She had the same upswept cheekbones that the other dead attacker had from Dilshad's, the same pointed ears, the same sharp facial features.

"This *is* a Fey," he said.

So for all of that discussion earlier, he hadn't believed her after all.

"Yes," she said.

"I've never seen one," he said.

Then he toed the body with his boot. The Fey didn't move. Anyone alive would have reacted to that shove.

"What was she grabbing?" he asked. "Do I dare...?"

He wasn't really asking Barkson, more like talking to himself. He used the toe of that same boot to pull back the edge of the cloak, revealing several pockets, all of them stuffed full of things.

"I don't know if we dare touch any of it," Barkson said.

"Yet if we leave it and they return, they have weapons—if, indeed, that's what these are," Corrin said.

She hated that argument, but it was a good one.

"We won't know what those things are or if they could hurt us," Barkson said.

"We'll set them aside," he said.

"And if the Fey can find her, they can find any weapons we set aside," Barkson said.

"Then let's set her aside, slow them down," he said.

Without waiting for a response, he pushed the body with his boot. Barkson joined him, and they shoved, pushed, rolled the body to the side of the road. The body tumbled down an embankment, barely visible from their spot on the road.

Corrin shoved some dirt over the side as well, spattering the body, making it less visible.

Barkson suddenly felt uneasy. Not because of the body—that Fey was clearly dead—but because she and Corrin hadn't attacked the portal.

It would reappear once the Fey regrouped.

"We have to go," she said.

He nodded, and together they hurried down the road to the main house.

RAZBITAY

CHAPTER
NINETEEN

"We're going to use the staff entrance in the back," Corrin said as he jogged down the hill. He was probably going slower than he normally would, thinking Barkson couldn't keep up.

She was keeping up just fine. She was staying behind him, with enough steps between them so that she wouldn't trip into him.

It had gotten a lot darker the closer to the main building that they got. Other buildings created shadows in the already dark back part of the estate. The trees and shrubs added more and, unfortunately, looked a lot like people, hunched or standing perfectly still.

The air reeked of smoke, but Barkson couldn't tell where the smoke was coming from. It might have been coming from the still-burning embers of the other attacks or that burning tree, but she wasn't certain.

It still seemed like a lot of smoke for old fires.

At least this part of the property looked somewhat familiar. She had gone in and out of those staff entrances at the back of the very large main building when she had worked here. What she had found unusual was how many staff entrances there actually were.

"Which one?" she asked.

"Near the kitchen." He sounded a bit breathless. "I told the team to wait there."

Barkson winced, thinking of Gussie's description of the murdered staff from the Kirilli estate. They had all been found in the kitchen.

But Barkson didn't say anything.

The road was leveling out. There should have been lights over the doors to all the entrances, front and back, staff and main, but there didn't seem to be any.

"You doused the lights," she said.

"I wasn't sure if that would give them an advantage or give us one," he said. "But I didn't want the property flooded in light the way it had been."

She could remember that too. The Rezwell estate had looked like a small city all by itself from the top of the hill when she had been here. It looked like dark abandoned buildings now.

She hadn't realized that until this moment.

Corrin stopped, put out a hand to effectively stop her. He pointed at something near one of the smaller outbuildings.

Barkson had to squint to see. The building provided a lot of shadow.

Then she realized that the shadows were moving, in a straight-line formation.

Military.

She put a hand on the hilt of one of her daggers. Corrin had done the same.

Together they crouched, heading toward the moving shadows. Corrin pointed again, then held up four fingers.

Four attackers.

Barkson nodded, even as she double-checked him. She could see four shadows as well, but she couldn't see where they were coming from.

She scanned back into the trees, realized that the burning tree was directly uphill from the attackers. Since Corrin had said that his people were in the main building, then the only reason that Barkson could think of for the tree burning was that these attackers had come through a portal, and maybe cleared the way with some kind of fire weapon.

She knew she was guessing, but it felt like an educated guess. She pointed to the burning tree, then moved her finger forward so that she drew the connection between the tree and the attackers.

Corrin nodded, then he hefted his dagger. With his other hand, he raised two fingers, then grabbed another dagger from his hip.

"On my count," he said quietly.

She nodded and pulled out two daggers as well. This wouldn't be as easy as nailing someone who was emerging from a portal. These attackers were moving, and there was no direct line of sight to their faces.

"We have to get ahead of them," she said. "We only get one chance at this."

He inclined his head slightly, and the two of them paralleled the attackers. It soon became clear to Barkson that the two of them wouldn't get ahead of the attackers, no matter how hard they tried—not and remain out of sight.

But she couldn't say that to Corrin. He was already getting farther ahead of her. Besides, from this angle on this part of the path, there were too many trees and shrubs in the way.

"Let them get ahead," she said softly. "Let's move laterally."

She wished she didn't have to speak. There once had been a time when she and Corrin rarely needed to speak to make their wishes known in a situation like this.

"The old routine?" he asked.

It took her a moment. They used to get ahead of their quarry, long ago, and then get the quarry's attention, and attack.

She nodded, hoping that was what he meant.

Together they hurried to the end of the road, then moved laterally alongside the building.

The attackers were moving directly toward the back of the building, slowing down as the second person in the line spoke and gestured.

Barkson didn't recognize the language.

The attackers were finally within range. Corrin moved one of his daggers to the other hand, then gestured with one finger, then two, then pointed to himself.

First two, me.

Which meant she was going for the second two. That made sense. She was slightly better at throwing across long distances than he was.

Or she used to be, anyway.

He put the dagger back in his hand, then stood in position. She mirrored him, spotting her two.

He whispered the count. She could barely hear him, so she knew the others couldn't.

Then he yelled, "Hey! Over here!"

All four stopped and turned.

Barkson couldn't see their features clearly in the dim light, but she could see the shape of their faces. Any hit in the face would cause enough damage to stop them, even if the hit didn't kill them.

She threw seconds ahead of him, because her daggers had to go farther, just like she used to do years ago.

Her first dagger hit the third attacker, who staggered backwards, but she missed the fourth, the dagger clattering against a tree.

Corrin hit the first attacker in the face, and they too staggered backwards.

The second one, the one who had been giving orders, spun. They might have been hit in the face, but that sort of reaction usually came when the hit was on the shoulder or arm or upper torso.

Barkson and Corrin ran toward the staff door. Barkson kept an eye on the attackers. The fourth attacker was reaching for some kind of weapon, but the second attacker slowly turned around, standing upright.

Barkson pushed Corrin to move quicker. They had almost reached the door when a ball of fire hit the ground beside them.

Barkson jumped back. The heat was instantaneous. Corrin was behind her somehow, even though she hadn't seen him jump either. The flames rose, blocking her ability to see the attackers.

"Now's the time for Helia's weapon," Barkson said. It had worked at Dilshad's. It would have to work here.

"I can't see them," Corrin said.

"When you can," Barkson said.

They were going to have to go to a different door. The fire was spreading toward the kitchen door. The manor was mostly made of stone—or so Barkson remembered—so it would be fine. But there was a lot of well-groomed tinder and brush along the paths.

She moved quickly toward the next door, with Corrin beside her. The smoke was thick and impossible to see through.

He reached the door and pulled it open. She wanted to snap something at him—that door should have been locked—but at the moment, it was lucky for both of them that the door had not been.

They stepped inside, breathing hard. The vestibule that they were in was tiny, more of a place to store coats than an actual door. A single lightstone lamp had flared when they had come inside.

"Two down," he said, and grinned at her.

"Their leader injured, I think," she said.

"Someone shot off that fire weapon," he said.

"We need to get your team," Barkson said. "There's a lot of doors in this place. We should be able to find a way out of here."

Corrin tapped her arm and led her to a door she hadn't even seen when she came in here. It blended in with the wall, hidden behind some thick coats.

He shoved the door open, beckoned her through, then followed her, yanking on the door handle to pull it closed. It squealed as it moved—not very secret after all.

They stepped into a corridor. A lightstone lamp hung from the wall, but the lamp was tiny. It didn't give off a lot of light, not that it needed to. The corridor was wide, but undecorated, clearly a staff corridor, built to carry things and to get people from one part of the large building to the other.

Corrin stopped near the light. His skin sagged just a bit. The shadows beneath his eyes were deep. He had lines near his mouth that Barkson had never seen before.

"All right," he said quietly. "Between the two of us, we know that we killed four of these attackers. You said there were six at Dilshad's, which should mean that the two who are still alive are the only two left."

"We can't know that," Barkson said. "And I have no idea if they tried to go after Dilshad and his family after I left. I don't know if the group who attacked your father and his estate are connected to these people or if there is some kind of small army here, trying to get to Kirillis. And I'm not even sure why they would go after Kirillis."

Corrin gave her a tired smile. "Way to take away a man's hope," he said, clearly only half-joking. "All right. We proceed as if there are many more of them than those two. Follow me."

He pivoted and headed down the corridor at a surprising clip. For a man who looked exhausted, he could move rapidly.

He backtracked past the door they had come through, weaving his way through the maze of branching corridors as if he had designed them himself.

In order to keep up, Barkson had to choose between moving silently in her heavy boots or moving quickly. She opted for moving quickly.

It took maybe three, maybe five minutes before they reached

the kitchen wing. They passed by the staff dining room, with its long table that had clearly once been in a more important room. The design was expensive, but the table itself had cuts and grooves and scorch marks from hot plates.

That room was empty. Corrin didn't even give it a second glance.

Barkson did, though. She wasn't sure where new attackers might be, and she didn't want to just hurry by.

There didn't appear to be a lot of room for someone to hide in that dining area. They'd have to hide beneath the table or the sideboards, and Barkson figured she'd see them. Or they would have started at the sound of her very loud boots.

As she and Corrin rounded a corner, she did see movement. Her right hand went to the hilt of one of her backup daggers, but Corrin didn't seem alarmed.

He raised a hand, putting a finger to his mouth. Barkson saw the movement again, registered it as someone's arm, and then realized that she and Corrin had finally arrived at the wide doors for the main part of the kitchen.

Unlike most kitchens in large estates like this, this one was not warm. There was no fire burning in the oven, and no strong smell of cooking foods or baking bread. Every scent here was old —a faint hint of oil, a touch of onion—or the scent came from spices—cumin and garlic and anise.

No one had actually lived and cooked here in a long time.

Corrin rounded a corner and entered the kitchen proper. Barkson followed. Six people stood around the working counter, all of them holding weapons. Most had daggers on their hips, but they all clutched either a pistol or a musket.

The man closest to the door was cradling his musket as if he had nearly used it. He was small and wiry, with corded muscles along his arms. His legs looked larger than they should have—probably more muscles.

"Smell of smoke is worse," the man said to Corrin.

"Fires outside," Corrin said, and then he swept a hand at Barkson. "This is Lucinda Barkson. Demos sent her."

Barkson nodded.

"She was to deliver a message," Corrin said. "Instead, she saved my life."

"More portals?" a woman asked. She had silver hair cut so short that it looked like feathers. She wore too many rings—at least two on each finger.

Barkson would have told her to lose all of them. Rings caught on everything.

"Two," Corrin said. "Maybe three."

"Hey, Barks," said a voice from the back. Another woman stepped out from around the table. Rea Gheen was tiny but lanky which made her look taller than she was. She had green eyes that seemed like glowing emeralds and a laugh that could be heard for miles.

But, at the moment, she looked like she hadn't laughed in a long time.

"Gheen," Barkson said. "I thought you got out."

They had worked together off and on during Barkson's entire time with the Shadow Company.

"He keeps pulling me back in," Gheen said. "Says I'm too good to sit on my butt."

Barkson nodded, feeling a slight and unexpected pull of jealousy.

"We'll have time for reunions later," said an older man. He

was hunched, his face scarred so badly along the chin and jawline that his skin was smooth and shiny. "Possibly three portals is bad."

"What's worse," Corrin said, "is that we have two attackers outside, and at least one of them is injured."

"I would think that part is good," another woman said. She was too thin which made her eyes seem too large and too round for her angular face.

"It's not, Enid," Corrin said. "That one appears to be in charge."

"We did kill four of them, though," Barkson said. "We know that for certain."

"Because Barks here," Corrin said, "is smart enough to use her dagger, rather than one of Helia's explosives."

Barkson noted that he didn't say anything about Helia's weapons possibly making the portals stronger.

"Told you we should just shoot them," Gheen said to Corrin.

"If we were better shots, I would agree," Corrin said. "But we're better with daggers."

"If only we had enough of them," said the sixth person, a round-faced man who seemed too young to be part of this team.

"There have to be kitchen knives," said the feather-haired woman that Barkson didn't recognize.

"You've never been trained on them, have you, Morwena?" said Gheen. Her tone was kindly, not sarcastic. "They have to be weighted right. You need to know exactly what you're doing."

The woman named Morwena frowned. "Pistols aren't exactly accurate. And they're tough to prime quickly."

"You throw one dagger, you've lost it," Gheen said.

"Stop," Corrin said. "We will take our weapons, but we're not going to fight."

"What?" the scarred man asked. "Why not?"

"Because we're leaving," Corrin said.

"Then who will protect the estate?" the scarred man asked.

"No one," Corrin said. "They're not after the estate. They're after me."

The scarred man glared at Barkson. "Did *she* tell you that?"

Barkson had no idea why he seemed to dislike her, but she didn't have time to care about it. She was about to answer when Corrin spoke.

"She told me that every one of my siblings has been targeted in the same way. She came to warn me."

The round-faced man grunted, as if that made sense to him. Gheen nodded. Enid frowned deeply.

The scarred man said, "It could be a ruse to get rid of us."

"It could," Corrin said, "but it's not. It explains why the attacks follow me."

"They don't..." The scarred man stopped, paused, and tilted his head as he thought about that. "The portals. They do open near you."

"Except the first few," Gheen said.

"That's right," Corrin said. He looked at his team. "Now that we have settled that, we need to vacate this place. Counting Barks' vehicle, we have five windstone vehicles. We're going to drive out of here at the same time. All of you are going back to Razbitay."

"Where will you go?" Morwena asked. "You're not going to be another diversion, are you? From the smell of that smoke, the first one didn't work."

Corrin didn't seem to mind the criticism. Barkson didn't remember that about him either. He used to get defensive.

"It didn't," he agreed. "I was grasping, trying to figure out what to do. Barks knows what to do. We're going to use her method."

"Which is to run?" the scarred man asked.

Barkson had had enough of him. She shifted, about to say something, when Corrin put his hand on her arm.

"We gain nothing from staying here," he said. "You'll head back to Razbitay and have Demos send someone else to watch the place. If I stay here, there will be more destruction."

"Maybe some of us should stay," Gheen said.

Barkson hadn't thought of that. She wanted to object, but she wasn't sure if her reaction was because the scarred man had irritated her or if she had an actual objection.

"If we're wrong," Corrin said, "then you'll probably die here."

"We might die anyway," Gheen said.

"Yes," Corrin said. "That's the risk."

"Our job isn't to protect you," the scarred man said. "It's to protect this place."

Barkson had had enough. "Then you protect it by getting Corrin out of here. We don't know what exactly is going on, but you've been under attack for days. Retreating is fine right now. It'll probably save the estate."

"You base that on what?" the scarred man asked.

Barkson stepped away from Corrin, so that she wasn't quite pulling her arm from his grasp. She was easing her arm away, in a manner that she hoped looked a little less petulant.

"These are magical attacks," Barkson said. "I've been dealing with them ever since I left Trinovante—"

"So they're after you," the scarred man said.

"Shut up, Stevens," Enid snapped. "We've been fighting for days. She just showed up. Use your brain for once."

"I'm not going to argue," Corrin said. "You can stay if you want, Stevens. Anyone who agrees with him can stay. Tell me now, though, so we don't plan on you."

He looked around at his team. If, indeed, they could be considered a team. Right now, they seemed ragged and tired and unwilling to listen.

Demos had said they were just babysitting the estate. They had all probably come off different missions and had been exhausted when they arrived for what they had thought was going to be a restful few weeks.

Instead, they encountered this.

"Anyone?" Corrin asked.

No one spoke up. No one even looked at Stevens.

"Looks like if you stay, you're on your own, Stevens," Corrin said.

Stevens nodded. "If what you say is true, then I'll be just fine. I'll start the cleanup."

It sounded reasonable. It might actually have been reasonable. But Barkson wasn't sure how the Fey would react.

This Stevens person must have seen doubt flit across Barkson's face, because he glared at her.

"You want us all to leave, don't you?" he asked. "You want something off the estate."

"Yes," she said. "I do want something off the estate. I want

Corrin off the estate. He needs to get as far from here as possible. I don't really care about the rest of you."

She inclined her head toward Corrin.

"He cares about you. He should have left with me up by the gate. Instead, we're down here, wasting time. We've weathered two attacks already because he wants you to get out of here alive. The fact that you're fighting him now only shows how petty you are. No wonder he's considered a leader in the Shadow Company, and the rest of you aren't."

"Barks," Corrin said, trying to stop her.

"If I were him, I'd leave right now, without a plan. But he's a better person than I am." She waved a hand at the group. "Clearly, he's a better person than all of you too."

"Barks," he said again.

She whirled on him. "They're not worth your time, Corrin, and they're not worth mine. I can't leave until you do. That's my mission. But after this little scene, I'm going to bodily carry you out of here if I have to."

Someone snorted. The man who had spoken first. He grinned at her, then nodded.

"We're leaving," he said. "Even Stevens. Because he's good with a musket, and we're clearly going to need that."

He looked at the group, meeting each person's gaze one at a time.

"You're not going to argue with anything. We know that for now, they're not attacking us in here, but it's only a matter of time. So rather than give them the time, we're going to sketch out the plan, and then we're getting out of here. Fast. Got that?"

Each person nodded. No one argued.

"You were wrong," Corrin whispered quietly. "I'm not the leader. I never was. That's Nofre's job."

Apparently, Nofre was the one who had been speaking first.

"Well," Barkson said, a little louder than necessary. "Let's hope he's good at it. Because we just wasted fifteen minutes we didn't have."

Nofre put up a single hand, gesturing downward, as if he was trying to calm Barkson. Nothing would calm her. She needed to get Corrin out of here and she needed to get to Emberto.

It was clear they were all running out of time.

"We know how they attack," Nofre said. "We're going to use our weapons to kill anything that comes out of the portals, right?"

He looked at Corrin.

"Right," Corrin said.

"And we're going to drive out of here faster than we've ever gone before. You first, Corrin," Nofre said.

"No," Barkson said. "We're last. Corrin wants you all to survive. They're coming for him. They'll attack him—me as well, because he's riding with me."

"Barks," Corrin said.

"The rest of you, no matter what happens to us, will keep going. You got that?"

She used the same technique as Nofre. She looked at each one of them. They all met her gaze and then looked at Nofre.

He nodded.

"You heard the plan. Those who are most accurate with either a dagger or a pistol are riding in a passenger seat. Everyone else is driving." He clapped his hands together. "Let's go."

RAZBITAY

CHAPTER
TWENTY

The six people that Corrin cared about too much were heading out different doors. All six of them had the same goal, though. They were heading to the carriage house where, stupidly in Barkson's not-so-humble opinion, they had placed all four windstone vehicles.

Clearly no one had expected an attack. Escape vehicles—the only escape vehicles, since the carriages here were old and there were no horses—should have been stored on different parts of the property.

She kept telling herself it wasn't her concern. But the look in Corrin's eyes, when he realized that all of his people had to funnel toward the carriage house no matter what door they left from, was a look that Barkson recognized.

He wanted to fix that.

She wasn't going to let him.

Two of the team—even though it really wasn't a team—were going to leave by the same door that Barkson and Corrin had entered through. Corrin believed, and he probably was right, that the attackers were either waiting for them there, or somewhere near it.

He wanted to throw one of Helia's weapons out the door first, but Nofre vetoed that. Each team of two had only one of Helia's weapons. Corrin had kept the rest.

He hadn't told them how many he actually had. He figured —Barkson figured, really—that they might need them on the drive to Emberto's.

If they managed to get out of this estate alive.

The door Corrin had picked to get them out of the main building wasn't really a door in the conventional sense. The building had a large cellar for food storage. Apparently the ground here was cooler than the air, and a lot of buildings used an underground area to store items that did better out of the heat, like potatoes and carrots and apples, as well as some fruits that Barkson didn't recognize.

Corrin carried a lightstone lantern through the underground cellar. The air down here was cold against the skin. The floor of the cellar remained flat, which bothered Barkson, since they had left the vehicle up the hill.

She shouldn't have worried. They reached the back part of the cellar. Stone steps led up to a wooden door reinforced with iron bars.

Corrin went first. He reached the top, where the door rested at an angle. A wheel served as the latch, which probably kept the door locked from the inside out, maybe even protected others from accidentally falling into this part of the cellar.

He handed Barkson the lightstone lantern. She did as he had instructed and set it as far from the stairs as possible. The problem with this type of lightstone lantern was that they couldn't be shut down. They had to fade when they were no longer in use.

Normally, Barkson would have covered the lantern with a cloth but there was nothing nearby.

So she set it far back down the path, and scurried back to the stairs. She had already counted them, so she knew how many she had to go up when the time came.

"Ready?" Corrin asked.

Barkson nodded, not sure how well sound carried through that closed door.

The problem, he had explained to her, wasn't just the light. It was the sound of the door opening. If someone was close, they would hear a small popping sound as the door unstuck from its moorings—at best, anyway. At worst, it would bang open or dirt and grass would fall off the top, making their own little crashing sound.

Corrin grunted as he tried to turn the wheel. It wasn't budging. Barkson was about to go up to help him when it finally let loose. Corrin nearly fell down the stairs. Only his grip on the wheel prevented it.

He placed his feet firmly on the stairs, his shoulder against the door, and one hand remained on the wheel. With the other hand, he beckoned Barkson.

She came up the stairs in the fading light, crouching so that she was as close to him as she could be.

Then he straightened, pushing the door open.

It did make a popping sound almost as if the door was a jar that had been stuck closed, and finally managed to let loose. Then debris showered onto Corrin and Barkson—dirt and leaves and twigs and clumps of something that smelled slightly foul.

Barkson brushed it off as she stood upright. The light from the lantern was still visible but faint, and it didn't seem like it was strong enough to escape the cellar.

She made herself look at the edge of the door, worried that if she actually looked up, she would get more debris in her face.

Corrin was still pushing the door open. He was going as slowly as he could so that it wouldn't bang against anything.

Finally he managed to lay the door flat. The inrushing air was warm and smelled faintly of the river, which wasn't that far away. Voices had some kind of heated interchange in the distance.

Barkson felt a thread of irritation. She hoped that it wasn't Corrin's people.

He climbed out of the cellar, crouching as he did so in case someone saw him and decided to attack. His posture was one he and Barkson had agreed on, just like they had agreed that they'd keep one hand on the hilt of a dagger as they left the cellar.

The night was even darker than before—or maybe that was just this part of the estate. Large trees grew around the door, as well as some human-shaped shrubs.

No matter what anyone said about the cellar being used for storage, the protections around this door to the hillside showed that someone believed that the cellar was also an escape route from the estate itself.

The voices grew louder. Barkson couldn't make out the words, but they sounded like commands.

She stepped out of the cellar, and Corrin gestured at her,

showing her the edge of the door. It took a moment for her to realize that he wanted her to help him close the door.

She grabbed her end, and together, they wedged the door back into place. If he wanted to replace the dirt and debris, she wasn't going to let him.

In his tiredness, his focus seemed to vacillate between his team, the estate, and getting away. She knew him well enough to realize that part of him believed he was wrong for trying to leave without the team.

She wasn't sure how to fight that.

One shot echoed across the grounds, followed by another. Someone yelped, and another person screamed. Light flared down the hill.

Corrin started toward the sounds, but Barkson grabbed his arm.

"You did what you could," she said. "They know what they're up against. We all agreed on this plan. We have to stick to it."

She had been planning that speech since they hit the cellar. She had hoped she wouldn't have to use it because she wasn't sure it would be effective.

He yanked his arm away from her. She reached for him again, worried that he would hurry down that hill.

But he didn't. He stood for a moment, looking sadly at the lights below, and then he squared his shoulders.

He didn't say a word. He just trudged toward the turnout where they had left Barkson's windstone vehicle.

They crossed two more rises, hurrying past trees that loomed like attackers in the dark.

Barkson had to focus hard on what was in front of her. The

ground was uneven, the shadows at her side seemed almost insurmountable, and the road was farther away than she thought.

Corrin didn't scurry like he had before. He climbed, almost as uncomfortably as she was.

They finally crested another rise when another shot echoed from below. The sound seemed bigger than the previous ones, almost overwhelming. And that was when Barkson realized that there had been no voices in the last several minutes.

Or, at least, nothing she could hear.

She had hoped that by the time they reached the windstone vehicle, she would have heard the crunch of wheels on the unpaved road. But nothing.

The silence after the shot was overwhelming. Once again, there was almost no sound around them—no night birds, no insects—only her boots crunching on leaves, and Corrin's occasional grunt as something scratched him.

They finally reached level ground. The road gleamed before them, even though there was barely any moonlight in this part of the estate, and beyond it, Barkson's new vehicle gleamed as well.

She hoped it wasn't glamoured. But it didn't matter, not really. She and Corrin had to take it anyway.

She hurried to the driver's side and unlocked it. Then she beckoned Corrin to get inside the vehicle.

She wasn't about to get in until he did. If he tried to bolt down the hill, she would tackle him.

She wasn't going to fail at her mission of saving Kirillis just because Corrin decided to be some kind of ridiculous hero.

But he didn't hesitate. He opened the door and slipped

inside the vehicle. Then he eased the door closed so that it would make a minimum of noise in this much-too-silent night.

She got in as well. The seat felt familiar and a little uncomfortable. She'd been sitting in this vehicle too long already on this day.

Now she would have to wait. She hated this part, even though she had designed it. It made her nervous.

The other vehicles should have been on their way now. She and Corrin had figured out that a direct route—no matter what direction someone took out of the main building—would take less time than going through that cellar.

Three shots. Barkson hoped that meant three attackers had died. But she hadn't liked the screams.

Corrin shifted in his seat. He leaned forward now, as if moving enabled him to see clearer through the darkness.

There weren't a lot of trees here, and the shrubs didn't really block the view of the road. But the path down the building was hilly, and most of the road wasn't visible.

Still, Barkson and Corrin should have been seeing vehicle lights by now.

Unless the windstone vehicles were so old that they didn't have exterior lightstone lamps. That mean that the older vehicles would travel more slowly at night, and their trip would be a lot more dangerous.

Just as she had that thought, lights rose and fell in the distance, the way that lightstone lamps did on the front of a vehicle.

Barkson couldn't count how many lights she was seeing, but she doubted it was four.

"They're coming," she said. "Does every vehicle have lights?"

"Yes," Corrin said tersely, as if the conversation would get in the way of anything he saw.

A vehicle rounded the nearest rise and drove past them so fast that it kicked up dust. Barkson wasn't even sure the driver had seen her vehicle in the turnout. Not that it mattered.

She left her own lights off.

Then another vehicle climbed the rise, and drove past. More dust, enveloping Barkson's vehicle like a wave.

Corrin leaned even farther forward, his face almost pressing against the windscreen.

One more set of lights—at least that was what it seemed like to Barkson. Just one.

She didn't say anything, hoping she was wrong.

The third vehicle crested the rise and then stopped, sliding on the road. Gheen leaned her head out of the passenger side.

Barkson pulled down her driver's side windscreen while Corrin was still fumbling to get his down. She said, quietly, "I've got this."

She leaned her head out. The air was filled with dirt and dust and the stench of smoke.

"Stevens is staying," she said. "We couldn't talk him out of it, and Nofre decided it wasn't worth trying. If you go back for him, we'll all be angry."

"We're not going back," Barkson said.

"Good, because half the grounds down there are on fire." Gheen grinned. She had more energy than she had had earlier. She actually seemed to be enjoying herself. "I think we killed three of the attackers, all from portals. None of us saw the two you mentioned."

Barkson wondered what happened to them. And what they were planning.

"Thanks," Barkson said. "That it?"

"That's all I know," Gheen said. And then she tapped her hand on the windscreen. "We're heading to Razbitay. We won't tell Demos where you are. I suspect he'll be back here with as many folks as he can find."

"Good," Barkson said. She leaned back into the vehicle, not because she felt like Gheen was done briefing her, but because Barkson felt if she asked another question, they'd be in this spot much too long.

Corrin had leaned over so that he could hear. He looked disappointed when Gheen put her head back inside the vehicle. He reached for his windscreen as if he thought he could get it open before Gheen's vehicle left.

But he didn't. The moment Gheen's windscreen went up, the vehicle continued up the hill, leaving clouds of dust and dirt in its wake. Barkson was glad her windscreen was up.

"Stop fiddling with the windscreen," Barkson said. "You let that crap in and we'll choke."

He opened his mouth as if he was going to say something, maybe even something about going back to the building.

"Don't even think about going back," Barkson said. "He made his choice. We're following the others."

Corrin's mouth thinned. He clearly disagreed with her.

She hadn't remembered Corrin being this unfocused before. But, then, she'd always been with Corrin on a mission, not at one of these guard-the-estate-while-you-rest things. Maybe he was different during those.

She held up a finger. "You're not saying any more. Or if you are, I won't listen. Got it?"

She didn't even wait for the answer. She started the vehicle. The lights came on, revealing even more dust and debris. It was almost as if they were in the middle of a massive dust storm.

Barkson didn't like that. She needed to be able to see—not just the road, but if any attackers lurked nearby.

She wasn't going to get that choice, though. She had to get up that road and off this estate.

She moved the drive sticks, felt the wheels turn underneath the vehicle, and glanced at Corrin. He was leaning back in his seat, finally, but his mouth remained in a thin line.

He didn't like this.

Neither did she. These attackers—these Fey—seemed to be closing in on the family.

And she was worried now, because of the conversation she'd had with Corrin, that the other siblings, the ones she thought she had rescued, had simply moved from one dangerous area to another.

At least they were informed now. At least they knew they were in trouble. Dilshad and Helia, in particular, knew what they were facing. Barkson couldn't vouch for Ghita and Filippa, although she figured they could probably take care of themselves.

And Benedeto was on the move, so he was probably all right.

But Emberto still didn't know what was going on, and if Corrin had been fighting these attackers for days, then there was the possibility that Emberto was under siege as well.

Barkson had waited as long as she could. The dust wasn't

really settling. In fact, it seemed thicker now. Maybe, given the rising smell, what she was seeing was no longer dust but smoke.

Gheen had said that the lower part of the grounds was on fire.

That must have been a hell of a battle. Barkson had no idea how Stevens thought he could survive anything like that or protect the estate all by himself, but he wasn't her concern.

Corrin was.

And she wasn't going to discuss anything with him, not yet. They were just going to drive.

She bumped the vehicle slowly toward the road, barely able to see through the thick clouds of debris. She probably should have let him drive, but she didn't trust him to leave the estate.

She found it odd that this man, one of the most competent people she knew, had become someone she didn't trust.

She went slower than she wanted, but she was driving by the light of the lanterns, and they only revealed the road a few feet ahead. Some of that was the black cloud they found themselves battling, but some of it was the way the road twisted and turned.

It seemed even more treacherous on the way up.

Corrin didn't say anything to help. Instead, he stared sullenly out the side windscreen.

Then he turned and faced Barkson. "Give me the damn letters."

Giving him the damn letters meant she had to take at least one hand off the drive sticks, which she was not willing to do.

"When we stop. You can't read them in here anyway. It's too dark."

He flounced back as if he was a teenager being told he

couldn't go to some party. Even though Corrin had never been that kid.

"Watch for anything strange," she said.

"It's all strange," he said.

That made anger flare through her. "You know what I mean."

He shifted again and leaned forward, as if he was trying to peer through the cloud.

It had gotten thinner, or maybe it had less smoke than it had down low.

The vehicle crested a rise and then another. The road was starting to feel familiar.

"Slow down," Corrin said, startling her.

She did. "Do you see something?"

"No," he said. "But we're getting near the gate, and it feels like we're being watched. Do you have that feeling?"

"I don't," she said, "but that means nothing."

They rounded another corner, and the guard tower rose ahead of them, dark against the dark sky. But there was sky, which meant that the dust cloud was easing.

He grabbed one of his daggers and rested it across his lap. She couldn't scan the area around them and concentrate on the road ahead. It was too dark, and the situation was too weird.

"We didn't discuss whether or not to leave the gate open," he said. "We should have discussed that."

"I'm sure they were driving too fast to even consider closing it," Barkson said. "They knew we were coming."

"No one is supposed to leave that gate open for any reason," he said. "It just depends on whether or not they have decided to follow orders."

The guard tower grew larger. The tree that had been burning when they went down the hill was embers now, the same kind of embers that Barkson had seen when she arrived here.

That bothered her as well, but she didn't have time to think about it.

"Stop!" Corrin said. "Stop now!"

She did. The brakes didn't grab immediately, and the vehicle skidded on the road's slick surface. She had to turn into the skid. The vehicle spun. She fought to keep control of it, so that it didn't fall off the edges of the road.

Then the vehicle stopped and rocked. Barkson's heart pounded.

"What the hell?" she asked.

"It looks like the last vehicle is near the gate," he said.

She twisted so that she could see. Something was near the gate, something whitish and windstone-vehicle shaped. But something about it looked odd.

Dust from her spinout still floated in the air. The back windscreen was so dust-covered that it was almost useless.

"It looks strange," she said.

He peered at it. Then he cursed.

"You're right," he said. "It's too wide."

"I thought it was too tall," she said.

They glanced at each other, both obviously unsettled.

"Can magic make something out of nothing?" she asked.

"You mean can it make a phantom vehicle?" he asked. "Some, I think. The Fey? I don't know. But they're much more magical than the rest of us, so if we can, then they can."

"Can we?" Barkson asked. She wasn't going to make a decision on supposition.

He shrugged. "We need Helia."

Barkson stared at the strange-looking vehicle. It glowed, even in the dust.

"So we have no idea if the gate is open or closed, and the only way to find out is to go near that thing," she said.

"Yeah," he said.

"There's no other road out of here?" she asked.

"There is," he said. "But it'll take time to get there."

His words hung in the air. Barkson had been clear about the lack of time they had. But she didn't want either of them to approach that thing. And she was worried that if they drove through it, then they might hit the closed gate and destroy her windstone vehicle.

"Is there a gate where you're planning to go?" she asked.

"I wasn't planning," he said.

"Is there a gate?" she asked through her teeth, so frustrated that she wanted to shake him.

"Yes," he said. "Of course. We have to get out somehow."

"I don't remember this exit," she said. She was supposed to have been monitoring all of the exits back in the day.

"You will when you see it," he said. "I want to tell you not to use the lightstone lanterns, but that's not practical."

"None of this is practical," she said. "I suppose we head back down the hill."

"Yes," he said. "Take a right when I tell you to."

Since she had spun the vehicle, it was now facing the correct direction for their retreat. She hated thinking of it that way, but that was exactly how it felt.

She moved the driving sticks, pushing the vehicle to a higher speed than she had used coming up. She told herself that she was doing that because she already knew the road, but that was a lie.

The phantom vehicle up near the gate—or whatever it was—was a warning and part of an attack. She had no idea what would have happened to her when she got out of her vehicle to see what had been going on with the phantom vehicle, and to open the gate if she needed to.

Her heart was pounding. She clutched the sticks tightly, preparing to turn when Corrin told her to.

He had his hand on windscreen in front of them as he peered into the darkness. The lightstone lanterns were making a bit of a dent, but not a lot. At least the dust cloud was fading a little.

And, Barkson reminded herself, she was creating a dust cloud behind her, so that if the attackers were following, then they would have been as blinded as she was coming up.

"Now," Corrin said. "Turn right now."

Barkson barely saw an opening in the trees, but she took it. The light from the lanterns swept the trunks of the trees, which almost seemed to be part of this road...if, indeed, it could be called a road at all. It was barely wide enough for the vehicle, which meant that most carriages could never have taken it.

As she had that thought, the road proved her point. It bumped along beneath the wheels, narrowing as it went.

"This thing better not take out the vents," she snapped at Corrin as she struggled to keep a grip on the sticks.

"I haven't driven this road," he said.

"Now you tell me," she said. "Watch for rocks."

He grunted, which she took as an assent.

"And," she added, "tell me when we have to turn again."

"We don't," he said. "We're going to start going up and then you'll see the main road."

Somehow Barkson didn't think it would be that easy, but she didn't say that to him. She bit her lower lip, concentrating, trying to see movement in the trees.

Once she had turned the vehicle onto this road, the attackers had to know where she was going. If they were familiar with the property.

They had been here for three days. By now, any good military leader would have learned the property.

The road started angling upward. The vehicle bounced, the wheels catching on large rocks and tilting the vehicle sideways.

"All the rocks seem to be on the edges of the road," Corrin said as if he wasn't noticing anything amiss. "Almost like someone put them there to prevent a vehicle from going over the side."

"Which I assume is bad," she said.

"If this were daylight, you would see that the road rises off the hillside almost like a bridge."

"You could have told me that," she said.

"And what would you do?" he asked. "Find another route out of here?"

His tone was as sharp with her as hers had been with him. He was still braced, the dagger in its hilt across his lap.

Barkson was almost seasick, given the way the vehicle was rocking. Her shoulders hurt from the tension of hanging onto those driving sticks. She had never driven a windstone vehicle over something like this.

The road started going steeply uphill. The trees crowded in even further.

Even with the light from the lanterns, Barkson could barely see what was ahead of her.

"I trust this is nearly the end of this damn road?" she asked.

"The gate is just ahead," he said. "Last I saw, it was open."

"And how long ago was that?" she asked.

"When we arrived," he said. "Weeks ago."

"And none of your people would have thought to shut it?" she asked.

"I..." He sighed. "Nofre was in charge."

She cursed, using words she hadn't thought of since the last time she saw Corrin.

She finally got ahold of her emotions. "Do I have a place to park this vehicle while we open the gate?"

"It's...um...no," he said. "You'll have to keep it on the hill."

"You know these vehicles don't stay parked on hills." It was one of their flaws. There was no brake that held a parked vehicle on an uphill or downhill slope.

"I...forgot," he said.

"What the hell is wrong with you?" she asked. "You've been fighting me all the way, forgetting things, and not thinking tactically. You were never like this before."

"Yeah." One word, short. She recognized the tone. He wasn't going to tell her anything.

She cursed again, not that it mattered. He was hunched, as if her words couldn't reach him at all.

"You're going to have to stay in the vehicle, foot on the brake, while I open the gate," he said.

"You can't get out of this vehicle," she said. "In case you forgot, *you're* the one that they're trying to kill."

"I haven't forgotten," he said. "I'll be quick."

The vehicle finally reached the top of the hill, the right front wheel resting on a rock, and the left back wheel resting on a rock, almost balancing the vehicle.

If Barkson had known about the situation before they got up here, she would have suggested putting rocks behind the wheels so that the vehicle wouldn't slide, but that would require someone to get out as well.

The gate was in front of them, narrow, made of iron, with some scrollwork. The gate was closed. On either side were stone pillars almost as tall as the trees. The rest of the wall was made of the same stone.

There was no going around that gate.

Barkson settled the vehicle between the two rocks, on what she hoped was the flattest part of the road. The vehicle wobbled. She wasn't sure if Corrin could even get out safely.

"You have maybe a minute before this vehicle starts going backwards," she said. Not to mention the attackers. If they were here, then she wasn't sure what would happen next.

"Then just drive forward a little," Corrin said as he grabbed the door's handle.

"I'm not sure I can even get traction on this rise," she said. "I'm not sure I'll be able to drive us out of here now."

"You will," he said, with a confidence that it was clear he didn't even feel.

He clutched the hilt of his dagger in the other hand, and eased the door open. So far, no one was around—at least that Barkson could see.

He stepped out, and the vehicle rocked even more. It started to slip, just as Barkson worried, so she moved the sticks. She wasn't sure she was making things better. What she wanted to do was turn the front wheels sideways, but the rock she was braced against up front wasn't allowing that.

He pushed the door closed—smart, since even a move of that could overbalance the vehicle—and then he crouched at its side.

If she had shut off the vehicle, the lightstone lanterns would fade, but she hadn't been able to shut off the vehicle. So instead of fading, the lanterns were growing brighter, just like they were designed to do.

Barkson couldn't see Corrin, but she could see that gate. It was latched. Part of her had hoped it wouldn't be, that someone would have left it partially open, but no one had.

Corrin ran for the gate, still crouched, but very visible in the light. He lifted the latch and pushed the gate back. Apparently this one didn't have that elaborate code. Maybe whoever built the estate had thought that other people couldn't find this entrance.

Or maybe it was an oversight based on the gate's age.

Corrin struggled to push the gate back against the fence. Apparently, even the gate was uphill. But he managed. Then he hooked the latch to the side, and started back to the car, when a movement caught Barkson's eye.

Arms swirling in the darkness. What she thought were some trees far beyond the road weren't trees at all, they were attackers.

And one of them let out the coldest, most chilling war cry she had ever heard.

Fear ran down her back until she reminded herself that cries like that were supposed to induce fear and terror. The arms continued to swirl.

Corrin came down the hill toward the vehicle, his feet sliding beneath him. He glanced toward the sound of the cry, which seemed to unbalance him further.

The arms came together, and between hands that were suddenly visible, there was a ball of fire.

The hands attached to a face she thought she'd seen before, but she didn't get a good enough glimpse. Apparently, Corrin did, though, because he threw his dagger as the attacker threw that fireball.

The moment Corrin released his dagger, he scurried for the vehicle. The fireball landed, rolled and missed him, leaving flames in its wake.

Corrin opened the vehicle's door, and jumped inside.

"There's more than one," he said. "We have to get out of here."

Barkson looked at the road ahead. It was on fire. She couldn't see the gate any longer.

But they had no choice. They had to drive through it.

No matter what happened next.

THE HIDDEN

RAZBITAY

CHAPTER

TWENTY-ONE

The flames ahead of the windstone vehicle went from small licks to a tower of flames within seconds. Instantly the air grew warm. It would be unbearably hot soon.

Barkson couldn't see the fence or the gate beyond the wall of flames. Nor could she see the attackers.

"Go! Go! Go!" Corrin said, as if he thought she wasn't going to move.

She adjusted the sticks, then took her foot off the brake. The vehicle slid backwards.

Corrin cursed.

"Let me drive the damn thing," he said, as if they had time to switch places, as if they had time for him to get his hands on the driving sticks, as if they dared risk unbalancing the vehicle even more than they had.

Trees around them were catching fire. The underbrush was completely engulfed. Soon Barkson would have no choice. She would have to drive them back down the steep road she had just come up.

That got her moving or maybe she had just adjusted the sticks properly. The wheels caught, the vehicle lurched forward, and got caught on the rock under the right tire.

"Go faster," Corrin said. "That'll get you off that rock."

She knew better. She eased up on the sticks, felt the vehicle slide back just enough before she tried again.

And this time, she used a slightly slower rate of speed, to accommodate the smoothness of the rock.

Her maneuver worked. Both sets of wheels—front and back —got over that rock.

Suddenly, though, she was speeding up much faster than she expected. The wall of flame looked intimidating, but it couldn't be very wide, not yet, anyway. If she got through it, she would be out of the gate and down the main road before the attackers even knew what she was about.

She sped up, bumped over the broken road and hit the wall of flame.

Corrin shouted something—she didn't know what, and she didn't care. The vehicle had to go fast because the wheels weren't made of stone and they were her biggest problem. Once she got off the flames, the wheels would put out the fire on their own wood simply by going across the road.

Or, at least, she hoped she was right about that.

She couldn't think about fire or burning wheels or anything. She had to bump her way out of this mess.

The air inside the vehicle got extra hot, and she suddenly understood what Corrin had yelled at her.

He had told her to close most of the vents.

She hadn't thought of that. The vents were open to the ground below.

The flames were coming through. There was no air left in the vehicle at all, just smoke and something hot licking at her boots.

She had to get past the fire now, because she had made that mistake. She needed fresh air in this vehicle and she needed it now.

The flames completely surrounded the vehicle. She concentrated so that the vehicle wouldn't change course.

One move in the wrong direction and she would hit the gate or the pillars or the fence itself.

The nose of the vehicle finally emerged out of the flames, but there was still smoke blocking her view. And that smoke had seeped inside the vehicle.

"Open your windscreen," she shouted. Just doing that made her chest hurt. She wasn't getting enough air. Her eyes burned, and now her throat did too.

She couldn't tell if Corrin had listened to her or not. She was too busy driving to pull down her own windscreen, even though she needed to.

The road bumped beneath the wheels or maybe the wheels were disintegrating. She couldn't tell. She couldn't see anything. And then the road smoothed out.

Cool air hit the side of her face, and even more cool air came up from underneath.

She wanted to stop, but she didn't dare.

"Turn right," Corrin said. He might have yelled it, but his voice was so scratchy that the words were a mere rasp.

He did know this road, and he knew where they were going.

She turned right and suddenly, the vehicle was headed downhill at a faster clip than she wanted, given how hard it was to see.

It took her a second to realize she wasn't driving through fire. The windscreen ahead of her was scorched. The lights were dim, probably covered in soot, if they existed at all.

"Think we can stop?" she asked.

"There's a turnout not far from here." Corrin had shoved his head out of the vehicle and was giving her directions that way. "I don't see any attackers. I don't think they believed we would make it."

Barkson hadn't been sure either.

"Turnout on your right," he said. "In three, two, *turn*!"

She did and hit the brakes. The vehicle slid again. If those wheels weren't damaged by the fire, they were probably damaged from the way she was driving on them.

The vehicle stopped and rocked. Barkson opened her door to let in fresh air, then put her face in her hands. Everything smelled of smoke. A headache that she hadn't even realized she had pounded at her skull.

"This is flat, right?" she asked. She couldn't really tell.

"Flat enough to get out," he said.

And so she did, half as a roll and half standing at the same time.

The night sky was clear. There were no trees nearby. Behind them, though, she could see flames working their way up the hillside.

Corrin peeled off his shirt and walked to the front of the vehicle. He wiped the lights, and they instantly got brighter. Then he worked on the windscreen.

Barkson gulped cool, fresh air. Her heart was racing. She had driven in some difficult situations, but never anything like that.

And she didn't have time, really, to take care of herself here. She had to keep going.

Provided the wheels were all right. The wheels and the vents.

First, the wheels.

She looked at the two on her side. The front wheel seemed fine. The back wheel looked too thin and very fragile. Finally, she understood the extra on the back. Provided it survived, of course.

She walked behind the vehicle. The extra wheel looked fine, but the wheel on Corrin's side had burned unevenly. The top seemed thick and fine, the side facing her was barely the size of one of her fingers.

Two damaged wheels meant she was going to have to stop somewhere and replace one of them. She couldn't go all the way to Mount Vitaki on damaged wheels. She wasn't even sure she would get down this road.

She walked past the open passenger door and looked at that front wheel. It was fine, although scorched.

Corrin wiped his face with the shirt, managing to smear more soot on himself.

Barkson was probably covered in soot as well.

"Where's the vent release?" he asked.

Vent release. He was right. The vents were probably filled with debris and dirt and ash.

She walked around the front, saw that he had cleaned up the lightstone lanterns better than she had thought possible, and then reached the driver's side.

Near her door was a hidden release that would clear the

vents, at least minimally. Later, she could actually clean them. If she had been closer to the river, she might have tried it now. But she wasn't. And they didn't have time.

She glanced over her shoulder. The entire side of the road above them was on fire.

"We have to get back into the vehicle," she said.

"Not yet," he said. "Clear the vents."

"If you change your back wheel," she said.

He grinned at her. He seemed elated. He probably was. They had just survived something awful—at least for the time being. When the euphoria left, he would be even more exhausted than he had been before.

"You always give me the tough jobs," he said.

Because you deserve them, she used to say in response. But right now, she wasn't up for banter.

She nodded, then worked on the vents. At least the side of the vehicle was cool. One of the benefits of windstone. That kind of heat wouldn't linger. If the vehicle had been in the fire too long, she would have been in trouble, but it had probably been only a few seconds.

It usually took two or three pulls to completely empty a vent. Then, the prescribed method was to scrub them. She couldn't scrub them.

She closed the release and walked around back. Corrin had removed the wheel and tossed it on the turnaround. The wheel was missing almost all of its spokes.

The wheel itself had been mostly ash. Parts of it had crumbled where he had thrown it.

Barkson hoped that the other back wheel was in better shape. She wasn't going to look, because she couldn't do anything about it. She also was afraid that if she looked, she might change her driving, ever so slightly, to accommodate the problems.

Corrin was attaching the other wheel. His movements were quick and efficient. He had clearly done this a few times before.

He stood, then peered at the road. Flames still licked their way forward, catching on underbrush.

"We don't have a lot of time," he said.

"I'm ready," she said. "How far is the nearest town?"

"Rezwell has a village nearby, attached to the estate. I'm sure there's a smithy." Corrin headed back into the vehicle. "I don't know distance, from here. Not far, though."

A smithy. It would have to do. She could at least replace the back wheel.

She hoped none of the attackers would follow.

She had no idea what kind of conveyances they used or if they always just traveled by portal.

Her tired brain didn't want to think about it.

She needed to get to that village. It would take all of her focus.

"Let's go," she said, and climbed back into the vehicle, praying it would stay in one piece for this last part of the drive.

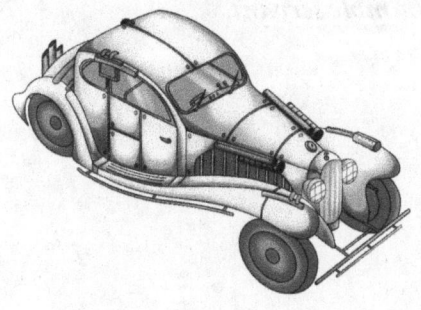

My dearest G,

I am writing to you after a very eventful evening. C is with me. We barely escaped a group of attackers with our lives. Some of C's colleagues were not as lucky.

The attackers are getting bolder. I am acutely aware that I need to hurry to get to E. I will do my best to arrive swiftly.

But first, my vehicle needed repair. We literally drove through fire to get away from the attacks. I will explain when I see you.

I am now concerned that the attackers might try multiple attacks against all of you. I hope that you are still safe in the place where I left you and that you have some assistance.

I comfort myself about the others with the knowledge that you and I informed them of the danger. They're all smart; they will do what they need to.

I should be leaving here shortly. The vehicle repairs were important, but they're not time-consuming.

Do not worry about us. By the time you read this, we will have moved on and probably reached the end of the mission.

I have hope that it will all go well.
Your not-so-humble servant,

L.

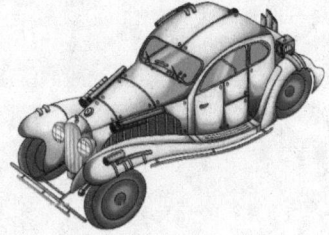

EMBERT

THE HIDDEN RIVE

CHAPTER
TWENTY-TWO

Barkson finished signing her name on this latest letter, and couldn't quite bring herself to look up. The smithy was loud and hot, voices echoing over the forge. Corrin and the smith were working on the spokes for the wheels.

Corrin wanted to replace all of the wheels, and Barkson was letting him. The new wheels were made of both wood and iron, which was a little less flexible, but probably wouldn't break as easily.

Barkson had let Corrin handle the wheels. Barkson herself removed the vents from beneath the vehicle. The vents were soaking in water right now, with some kind of solvent that the smith said would remove soot and ash from anything.

Since his business was all about soot and ash, Barkson had to believe him.

They had barely limped into the smithy just before dawn. There was no windstone vehicle shop in the village mostly owned by the Rezwell estate. There was a store which doubled as a post, and a lot of little houses for people who worked on or for the estate.

The smithy was the closest thing the village had to a business that would repair a windstone vehicle. This wasn't the first windstone vehicle the smith had seen, but it was the first one he ever touched.

He was a large man with the widest shoulders Barkson had ever seen. The muscles in his arms were so large that they almost looked like he had stuffed them with round balls. His hands were thick and covered with burn scars.

He was maybe fifty, with salt-and-pepper hair trimmed short. He seemed a friendly sort, wanting to chat, which neither Barkson nor Corrin felt like doing.

Which was why Barkson let Corrin work on the wheels. Barkson didn't want to make idle conversation. Corrin was good enough at it that he would be able to deflect the smith's questions, and keep the man interested enough to work fast.

Barkson had pulled the vents and soaked them in tubs that stood near the door. Some of the tubs were extras that the smith normally used to cool hot metals. All of the tubs had burn marks.

The main forge was outside, but there was a smaller one inside for rainy days. Lots of weapons and pipes and bars and poles littered the floor. After Barkson had finished pulling the vents so that she could soak them, the smith gave her a small space on a workbench far in the back to write her letter.

Using the workbench had seemed like a good idea, but it wasn't. It was exceptionally hot in the back, the kind of heat that felt like it had lingered from the night before or maybe even weeks before. Any smells that Corrin and the smith created—

and they had created a few as they molded spokes for the wheels —not only floated to the back, but stayed there, sometimes making Barkson's eyes water.

She didn't write a lot in the letter. She hadn't been writing a lot in any of the letters. Somewhere along the way, she had moved from being vague to actually lying to Gussie. As in this letter.

That last bit, the bit about hope, had been a lie. Barkson had a bad feeling about the last part of the trip.

The attackers had gotten very bold with Corrin. There also seemed to be a lot more of them than Barkson realized.

She sealed the letter in an envelope and addressed it. Then she stood. As she did so, she remembered that Corrin still hadn't read his letters.

She looked across the smith. The smith was assembling one of the wheels. Corrin was watching, arms crossed. His hair was sticking up at all angles, and his clothes were torn and singed.

He looked as disreputable as she felt.

"Corrin!" Barkson beckoned him.

He looked over at her, his eyes red-rimmed from smoke and exhaustion. Then he sighed and walked over.

"I'm going to mail my letter to Gussie and see if that store is open and get us something to eat. Before I go, I'm going to give you Gussie's letters. You need to read them."

He stared at her. "This isn't the time."

"There's no good time, Corrin," Barkson said. "I have no idea why you're putting it off, but you can't any longer."

She went over to the poor vehicle, which was sitting on blocks. The sides of the vehicle were scorched, and the undercarriage looked naked without its vents. She carefully pulled open the driver's door and leaned in, grabbing her coat.

She had taken it off when she realized how hot it would be in the smithy. She debated for a moment as to whether she should put the coat back on, then decided against it.

If the attackers found them here, then she would have to hurry back to the smithy rather than try to defend herself on the streets of this small village.

She pulled Corrin's letters from the upper pockets. Then she went back to him.

He was standing where she had left him, looking disgusted.

She handed him the first one.

"I'll give you the second one when I return," she said.

"I'll take them both now," he said.

He could be so controlling, especially when he was tired.

"I'm going to follow Gussie's instructions. She's the one who hired me."

Now Barkson didn't dare leave the second letter here. She folded it and tucked it in the back pocket of her pants, still clutching the envelope for Gussie.

"You can be unreasonably stubborn," Corrin said.

"So can you," she said.

They really had gone back to where they had been in their relationship. They had been well matched, and then they weren't. Or maybe they were too well matched.

She left without seeing his reaction. She hoped he read the first letter while she was gone.

She knew him well enough to know that he wouldn't read the letter while she was there, watching him. That would prove to him that he had lost the fight.

The store had barely opened. It was small, but well stocked, smelling of flour and sugar, which surprised her. She placed her letter in the post, then picked up fresh bread, more cheese, and quite a few different fruits, including some she didn't recognize.

Then she bought three pieces of a spice cake for herself, Corrin, and the smith.

She was gone for maybe ten minutes. By the time she got back, the smith had finished all but one of the wheels—the replacement wheel.

She didn't see Corrin at all. She whirled around, letting her eyes adjust to the smoky interior again, and finally she saw him, in the back near the workbench.

He was hunched over the letter, his shoulders shaking. It took a minute for her to realize that he was sobbing.

She had never seen Corrin cry like that. She hadn't realized that he and his father were close. Corrin never had much to say about either parent. When Corrin did discuss his family, it was always with a tinge of sarcasm.

She put most of the food in the vehicle, then took one of the cake slices to the smith, who thanked her. She carried her slice and Corrin's slice to the workbench.

She set the food down near him, but didn't say anything.

Corrin didn't even notice her. His sobs were silent. She doubted that the smith even knew that Corrin was in any kind of distress.

She went back to the cast-iron sink on the side of the smith and used two battered mugs to dip out some of the fresh drinking water that the smith had pointed out to her earlier.

She carried the water to the workbench, set hers beside her

piece of cake, and then slowly, gently, touched Corrin on the shoulder.

He started like a child who had done something wrong.

He kept his head bowed, wiped off his face with his forearm, cleared his throat, and said, "What?"

"I have water," she said.

"Well, good for you," he said, but he sat up and took it.

She made a point of not looking directly at his face. He didn't really want her to know he'd been crying, so she wasn't going to know.

"I also brought something sweet," she said. "It looked good."

He grunted.

She reached into her back pocket and removed the second letter. "Also, you need to read this."

"I don't know what else she can tell me that she didn't want to share with the others." His voice was harsh, angry. He still wasn't looking at Barkson.

"It's not more information," Barkson said. "It's instructions."

"Like I take instructions from Augusta," he said.

"Please, read it," Barkson said.

He snatched the envelope out of her hand. For a moment, she thought he was going to tear it up without opening it at all, but he didn't. He tore off the end, pulled out the paper, and hunched over again.

Barkson took her cake slice and went over to the smith. The man was attaching the wheels by himself, as if he had done this a million times. He spun each wheel after he attached it.

She went to the tubs filled with the vents. The water was

black, with something slick along the top. Ash also floated on the top part.

She'd never seen anything that slick on water before.

The smith joined her.

"Is that normal?" she asked, pointing at the slick.

"It's my solvent," he said. "Looks like it pulled off all the damage from the fires."

He grabbed a couple of relatively clean towels, then reached inside the black water. Barkson almost cautioned him to be careful, but she stopped herself.

He knew to be careful. She didn't want to insult him.

The first vent he pulled up was cleaner than it had been when she bought the vehicle. He dried the vent, then handed it to her.

"I have no idea where these go or how they attach," he said. "I'll dry, you assemble."

She nodded, happy to go to work. That meant she didn't have to hover over Corrin.

She used a little half-cart that the smith had—a piece of wood with wheels that propped her up and slid her underneath the windstone vehicle.

The soot still lined the edges of the vehicle, making it black. She'd need to clean the whole thing when she arrived at the right kind of facility, whenever that would be.

She pushed the first vent he handed her into its place, and started to slide out. He was waiting with more vents.

She slid back under with one vent at a time, attaching them carefully, checking and double-checking to make certain that she had them in the right place and going in the right direction.

They all smelled faintly sharp from the solvent, a scent that dug into her nose and made her want to sneeze.

It took maybe fifteen minutes, but then she finished reassembling all the vents.

The smith had wheeled over the replacement wheel. He had waited until she was no longer under the vehicle before attaching that wheel into its place.

"Good as new," he said when he was done.

"Maybe better," Barkson said. "I have no idea why they weren't using iron spokes."

"Or iron wheels," he said. "Not complete thinkers, these designers."

Something tinged in her mind, and then she remembered. The Iron Tombs existed to keep the magical dead in place. Her stomach jumped a little. Had she harmed her vehicle by placing iron on it? Or had she finally gotten it some protection from the attackers?

"Let me drive it to make sure the wheels are straight," she said. "It's tough to line them up right without the vents."

That wasn't true, and maybe the smith knew that wasn't true, but he didn't argue. He had a way to remove the blocks that used an elaborate pulley system, the same way that he had put the vehicle on the blocks in the first place.

He looked concerned as Barkson opened her driver's door, and at that moment, she realized he was worried that she would drive off without paying him.

She reached into the pocket of her coat and removed a gold coin.

"Is that enough?" she asked.

"Too much, miss," he said.

"You saved us. Too much is just fine."

She climbed into the driver's seat. It smelled of solvent and smoke inside, two scents that made her eyes water.

She adjusted the sticks, then backed out slowly.

The vehicle handled better than it had before. The wheels felt more stable than they had. Apparently, the iron spokes caused no problems at all.

She parked the vehicle near the outside forge and went back inside.

Corrin was standing near the workbench, watching her. She recognized the expression on his face. He had thought she was leaving without him.

She walked to the back, grabbed her piece of cake, and took a bite. It tasted of ginger and cinnamon mixed with oranges and raisins. She hadn't expected the fruit.

She took a sip from the mug, and looked at him.

His eyes were swollen, his nose red.

"I was going to do this anyway," he said, shaking the letter at her.

"I wasn't lying to you, Corrin," she said. "I have no idea what either letter says."

"The first," he snarled, "goes into too much damn detail about my father's death. The second tells me to go with you to Emberto's because Gussie's not sure you can get into the house without me there."

Barkson had no idea why that would be, but she trusted Gussie. Barkson also knew that Gussie did not know of the past relationship between Barkson and Corrin—or at least, Barkson had never told Gussie.

"All right, then," Barkson said a bit more calmly than she felt. "That's what we'll do."

"No arguing?" Corrin asked, his tone still lacerating. "No demand to look at the damn letter?"

"No." Barkson's cheeks heated. She probably would have demanded to see the letter toward the end of their relationship, just to annoy him. Or maybe to prove to him that he was untrustworthy. She had been quite unreasonable toward the end. "I'm not supposed to look at the letters, so I won't. I trust you, Corrin."

"Well, *that's* new," he said.

She had to let that slide. She wasn't going to defend herself, not, she was sure, she was worth defending here. Nor was she going to agree with him. He was just trying to provoke her so that he could think about something else.

He was more upset than she had ever seen him, which she didn't entirely understand. He had already known that his father was dead. She didn't know why the letter would make that worse.

"I paid our host," Barkson said. "We're free to go."

Corrin didn't say anything. He just stalked forward, heading to the vehicle.

When he reached it, he walked around it, checking the wheels, the vents, and the vehicle itself.

Barkson took her time joining him. She knew he needed a moment.

She thanked the smith again, and then stepped outside.

"We're lucky we made it here," Corrin said. He wasn't looking at the vehicle any longer but at the discarded wheels.

They barely looked like wheels. They were missing parts and had cracks running along their frames.

They looked even worse in the sunlight than they had earlier.

"We are lucky we made it," Barkson agreed. She was beginning to think that luck had favored her throughout this entire trip.

Corrin still wasn't looking at her. He had hunched again, as if he was protecting his heart.

Maybe he was.

"What's going on, Barks?" he asked quietly. "Why are we being targeted?"

We as in the Kirillis, not *we* as in the two of them.

"I don't know," Barkson said. "This trip has not illuminated that for me at all. There are a lot of theories, but nothing that makes sense."

"Emberto lives in the house my great-grandmother built," Corrin said. "If these people are destroying things of hers, as Gussie said, then the house might be gone."

"You don't think that Emberto can defend it?" Barkson asked. "He is a Kirilli."

Corrin turned around slowly. He seemed to have gotten control of his face. His skin was still blotchy and his eyes were still red, but they looked clear now.

"Emberto doesn't have the training that you and I have," Corrin said. "He's like Helia."

"Helia killed a group of the attackers with one of her weapons," Barkson said, but she didn't add that the idea of their deaths had become some kind of obsession for Helia a few hours later.

"There's a difference between doing that once to defend yourself and doing it repeatedly to fight some kind of force." Corrin ran a hand over his face. "Emberto's alone up there. He wanted it that way. He's always wanted it that way. We should have gone directly there."

The smith was cleaning up his forge, his back to them, too far away to hear the conversation, thank goodness. Barkson had no idea what he would make of it. She had no idea what he had made of them.

Barkson said, "It was my choice to stop along the way. Mine and Gussie's. She could have sent two people on this journey, me and someone else, but I think she was too upset to think about it."

Or maybe Gussie didn't know anyone else, especially someone who knew how to drive a windstone vehicle.

"She should have come," Corrin said.

"She was in no shape to come," Barkson said. Even if Gussie had wanted to come—which she hadn't—Barkson would have fought that.

Corrin frowned. "Her letters seem fine."

"It took her an extra hour to write them." Barkson almost put her hand on his arm, then stopped herself. "I knew something was wrong the moment I saw her. She was a mess, Corrin. I'd never seen her look so sloppy or so tired or so sad."

His eyes teared up. He looked away, and clearly wasn't allowing himself to blink.

"Besides," Barkson said softly, mostly to distract him, "Gussie doesn't have the training that you and I have either."

He nodded and one tear slipped down his cheek. He started to reach up to wipe the tear away, then stopped himself.

Barkson wanted to put her arms around him and pull him close. His tears made her forget about everything between them. He had never cried before, not like this, not even when they had lost colleagues.

He hadn't cried when she ended things either, just stared at her, steely-eyed and angry.

He swallowed hard, then took such a deep breath that his shoulders rose and fell.

"You should have gone to Emberto first," Corrin said, his voice thick.

She couldn't tell if he was trying to provoke again or if he actually meant what he had just said. Or, maybe, he was trying to provoke *and* he had meant what he said.

"Going to Emberto first was an option," Barkson said. "But it wasn't a good one. I don't regret the choice I made."

He turned toward her. Apparently a tear had trickled down the other cheek as well, because there was a fresh track along his soot-covered skin.

He needed to wash his face.

They both did.

"You don't regret the choice? What does that mean? It's not your family we're talking about here. How can you 'not regret' anything?"

Definitely provoking now. And probably believing what he was saying inside his anger.

It was Barkson's responsibility to remain calm in the face of all of this. She couldn't get trapped in the spiral of accusations and denials that had marked their last few weeks together.

"I arrived at Filippa's before the attackers did. Who knows

353

what would have happened if I had gone there last. The children..." She didn't want to finish that sentence.

Corrin closed his eyes and tilted his head back.

"The children," he said more to himself than to her. "How could I have forgotten the children?"

"I don't think Gussie did," Barkson said. "My last three stops—you, Benedeto, and Emberto—there's no family at all."

Corrin nodded curtly, wiped his face with his right hand, and spent a moment using his thumb and forefinger to clean out his eyes.

He took another deep breath, one that seemed to involve his entire body.

Then he opened his eyes, his gaze finding Barkson. He smiled a half-hearted smile, something that was almost apologetic.

"It seems that Gussie handled all of this better than I have so far," he said.

"She was having her troubles," Barkson said. "She knew she only had a few hours of clarity before she would collapse entirely. What she saw—"

"Is worse than anything you and I ever saw," he said.

Barkson was about to differ when he held up a hand.

"Because," he added, "it involved people she loved."

His voice broke on the word *loved*.

"I'm sorry about your father," Barkson said.

Corrin waved a hand at her dismissively. "We were estranged. We never saw eye to eye."

"That doesn't make it any easier," she said.

He bobbed his head once. Then he looked down.

"I'll never be able to tell the son of a bitch he was right."

The words echoed. That was what was bothering Corrin, deeply bothering him.

"Right about what?" Barkson asked.

"The threats," Corrin said. "To the family, to my great-grandparents' legacy, to...everything he held dear. I thought he was a bit of a crank. I really did. I thought he couldn't let go of the past and that he needed to move out of the estate and he needed to move forward with his life. I blamed Mother's death for his irrationality, and Barks, he wasn't irrational at all. I think maybe he was scared, and I had no sympathy for it. I called him..."

Corrin choked, then shook his head.

Barkson waited. She hadn't known any of this.

"It doesn't matter what I said to him. I can't take it back. He believed Gussie would carry on his legacy, and he was right. The strength it took to write these..." Corrin waved the letters, crumpled in his left hand. "Strength and clear-headedness after a massacre."

"You could have done that," Barkson said.

"But I didn't, did I? I even fought you when you showed up. I'm sorry, Barks."

There was more to this than his father's death. Corrin had been acting strangely since she arrived. But she had to remember that he had been sent to the estate to rest.

"Something bad happened on your last mission, didn't it?" she asked.

"Am I not allowed to be upset about my father?" Corrin snapped.

"You are," Barkson said. "But you're..."

More fragile than usual...More fragile than ever...Not thinking as clearly as you usually do...

He was watching her discard each thought.

"More volatile than usual," she finally said.

He let out a bitter laugh. "You're not the first person to tell me that."

But he didn't elaborate. His gaze slid away from hers.

"We need to leave," he said. "They'd been attacking me for days. If they've been going after Emberto that long..."

Barkson nodded. She opened the driver's door, and climbed into the driver's seat, adjusting the sticks.

Part of her was relieved that Corrin was coming along, and part of her was worried that he wouldn't be able to handle what they might find.

And that marked the first time since she'd known him that she worried about Corrin. He was usually so competent and smart and focused.

He was still smart, but not thinking clearly.

She wasn't sure she could call him competent or focused right now.

"You should get some sleep," she said as he climbed into the vehicle.

"I don't think I can," he said, but leaned his head back anyway.

By the time they had left the village, he was snoring softly, and Barkson was left alone with her thoughts.

EMBERT

THE HIDDEN RIVE

CHAPTER
TWENTY-THREE

By the time Corrin woke up, they were deep in Khēmía, the second-largest country in the Qavnerian Protectorate. Barkson stayed in the mountains for two reasons: Khēmían customs were often closed on these roads, which was going to save hours, and more importantly, she wasn't exactly certain where the Kirilli ancestral home was.

She knew it was close to Mount Vitaki and Mount Vitaki was at least a day's drive on these roads, which were narrow and unforgiving, filled with switchbacks and inclines that made her worry the vehicle would lose traction.

She drove carefully, all the while wondering if she should have taken what some called the flat-land route, even though it wasn't really flat. That would have taken them through Lyoye, the capital of Khēmía, a sprawling city with roads as narrow as these.

Her memories of Lyoye were of dust and stench and unforgiving heat. She had also been trapped in a back alley one hot afternoon as she searched for the offices of the Forbidden Valley Antiquities Service, which was less of a service and more of a government entity.

The road she took kept her in the Forbidden Valley, which had its own history, some of it violent, much of it secret.

There had been wars here, fought between nations that were now long gone, subsumed Khēmía centuries ago. Then there were battles, still, with some of the countries that bordered Khēmía.

And the very famous ancient battle against the Fey, in the valley itself, near the Hidden River and, some said, near Mount Vitaki itself.

Corrin moaned and ran a hand over his face. His skin looked raw and not just from the tears earlier. He must have been a lot closer to one of the fires than she realized.

Sleeping in the sun that poured in the windscreen hadn't helped him any.

"There's water in jugs in the back," she said.

He turned and grabbed one almost instantly. "These were Helia's," he said.

"Refilled by me," Barkson said.

He drank, then offered her some, but she waved the jug away. She would need to stop soon, and if she remembered correctly, there was an old town just ahead, one that had been in the same place long before Khēmía claimed this part of the valley.

"We're not that far from Emberto's," Corrin said with wonder. "How long was I sleeping?"

"Not that long," Barkson said. "I thought it would take most of a day to reach Mount Vitaki."

Corrin gave her a cool glance. "Mount Vitaki is in the middle of the river. We're on the opposite side. It's a shorter drive here. I thought you knew that, given the road we're on."

She shook her head. "I just figured we'd stay in the Razbitay Mountains for this trip. I didn't want to go to Lyoye."

"Which is out of the way," Corrin said, "and dangerous for us."

"Still?" she asked. When she had been training, she was told that her light brown skin and her Trinovante accent, as well as her (then) unfamiliarity with Khēmíanì, the official language of Khēmía, marked her as an outsider—or worse, as a conqueror.

She hadn't understood the conqueror label back then. During her school years, she'd been taught that Khēmía had voluntarily become part of the Protectorate.

But apparently those who wrote the history of the Protectorate had a different definition of "voluntary" than most people did. After many prolonged battles, and a lot of destruction of important Khēmían sites, the Khēmíans chose to become part of the Protectorate rather than continuing to lose their heritage.

It had been an awful bargain. The historic and cultural sites remained, but many of them had been looted—or "liberated" by people like Corrin's great-grandparents, who had stolen so many relics from this land that some worried that the Kirillis could never be safe here.

Corrin might have been referring to the fact that Trinovantians were not safe in Lyoye, or he might have been referring to the Kirillis.

Either way, it was clear that Barkson had made the correct choice in taking these mountain roads.

"How far do we have left?" she asked.

"I thought you had a map," he said.

She couldn't tell if he was deflecting or actually interested. Corrin could be the most difficult when he was waking up.

"I have two," she said. "One Gussie drew for me."

"Which is useless," he said.

Barkson smiled. "Yes. The farther I got from Qavner, the more useless it became."

"Because Gussie hasn't been this far north since she was a child," Corrin said. "She had to rely on memory."

"Which is stellar," Barkson said.

"Except that a child's memory and an adult's memory are very different." He leaned his head back. "You said two."

"Helia gave me one," Barkson said. "It scares me."

Corrin grinned. "One of her magic maps?"

Barkson almost flinched at the word "magic." It was an old habit, but when applied to something like a map, it made her twitch.

"Yes," Barkson said. "I'm afraid it'll draw the attackers, if not to me, then to the person I'm seeking."

Corrin's smile faded. He nodded once, seemingly in acknowledgment.

"I hadn't thought of that," he said. "It might also lead the attackers back to Helia."

"Because I'm accessing her magic?" Barkson asked.

"Yes," Corrin said. Then he sighed and replaced the cap on the jug. "I'm only pretending to understand this stuff. But given the amount of magic we've been seeing, you were smart to be cautious."

"You know how to get to the house, right?" Barkson asked.

"Oh, it's more than a house," Corrin said. "It's a compound.

362

Once it was an offshoot of the Forbidden Valley Antiquities Service...or rather, it was where the service was founded."

Barkson knew some of that. His great-grandparents founded the service toward the end of their lives in Khēmía. They worried that others would mine the same riches that they had already stolen. The service ostensibly was designed to protect the antiquities throughout the Forbidden Valley from "foreign" interlopers and local thieves.

The actual foreign interlopers were from the Protectorate, and many of the local thieves were scholars of the region, trying desperately to retain their own heritage.

There was some kind of uprising or difficulty or skirmish— Barkson couldn't remember most of the details, except that Corrin's great-grandmother had been here alone at the time, and had barely survived.

Many said she hadn't been the same after that.

"How big is this compound?" Barkson asked.

"You'll see," Corrin said.

"Do others live there besides Emberto?" Barkson asked.

"I think my father tried to hire staff, but Emberto kept firing them." Corrin shifted in his seat. He was probably very uncomfortable, since he didn't fit well in the vehicle, and he'd been sleeping.

Barkson had chosen not to wake him instead of stopping to walk around. She hadn't needed the break, not with the intense sun beating in through the windscreen. The heat and the dust and the brightness had kept her alert.

She had a feeling that when they did stop, she would be staggering with exhaustion.

"So he's alone," she said.

"Last time I was here, yes," Corrin said.

"You're hedging," Barkson said.

"Because I don't know," Corrin said. "I told him he needed company. He was beginning to sound mad, crazy."

Barkson felt a chill. "Like your father? A crank?"

Corrin gave her a sideways startled glance, as if he couldn't believe she had said that. She couldn't either, really. He had said that in a private moment, and she had just flung it back at him.

"I guess so," Corrin said quietly. "Maybe. It's just he's so young and he was beginning to show signs of—I don't know— being strange. Scary strange."

"Scary?" Barkson asked.

"He wouldn't let me in two of the buildings the last time I was there," Corrin said. "And one of those buildings I had always considered mine. It was a little five-bedroom dormitory first built for the Practical Interns that my great-grandmother used to bring up from Serebro."

"And you couldn't even go in," Barkson said.

"He didn't even want me to walk past," Corrin said. "I had the feeling that he didn't want me to look in the windows."

"Could someone have been staying there?" Barkson asked.

"No," Corrin said. "There was no evidence of another person anywhere on that compound."

Barkson didn't reply to that. If the compound was as big as Corrin made it sound and if it was as isolated as Gussie had mentioned, then it was possible that others were there and Corrin had not seen them.

But Barkson would be speculating based on nothing more than a hunch.

"How long ago did you last visit?" she asked.

Corrin shrugged. "Before my last mission."

She was about to ask him to be more specific when she glanced at him. His mouth had thinned, and his forehead was furrowed. He was actually trying to figure out when he had last been to see his brother.

How long had that last mission been, anyway? And what was it?

She might need more information on that, given time. It was beginning to sound like that mission was more important than she had originally realized.

"I don't know," he said, as if he hadn't paused at all. "Maybe a year ago?"

He shrugged, then shrugged again.

"Time has truly lost its meaning," he said, more to himself than to her. Then he leaned forward. "I shouldn't have left him alone."

"Did someone put you in charge of Emberto?" Barkson asked. "I thought he was a man full-grown."

Corrin snorted. "He came up here ostensibly between his final year as an academy student and his first year as an advanced student. He was actually going to study our family or so he said and so he wanted to look at the historical record."

"Studying where?" she asked. "In Lyoye?"

Corrin raised his eyebrows in surprise, as if he couldn't believe she had actually asked that question. "Our family only goes to Serebro Academy. I think we would have been disinherited if we went anywhere else."

"Even though Lyoye has the best antiquities department in the Protectorate?" Barkson asked.

Now, he looked offended. "That can be debated."

She shrugged a shoulder. Education had been a necessity for her, not some kind of holy calling. She only knew what she heard about schools, not what really mattered about them.

"I forgot," she said to mollify him. "Your father was a regent."

Corrin cursed. "His seat on the board. We're going to have to do something about that."

Apparently, Barkson hadn't mollified him at all, just managed to remind him of his father's death.

"I'm sure Gussie has given it some thought," Barkson said.

"I hope so," Corrin said. "Our father always said the power in Qavner rested with the Regents, not with the government."

Barkson remained quiet. She tried to stay out of debates about things that did not concern or interest her. Where the power rested in Qavner had never interested her.

She wondered now, though, if she should have paid more attention.

Now the road cut through part of the mountain, part of an ancient road that dated from before the founding of Khēmía. Red rocks shored up the road on both sides, and above, there was more red.

Corrin was right; they were getting closer to Mount Vitaki. Barkson knew this because one of the things she loved about this part of the Protectorate was how staggeringly beautiful the sky was. The sky was a brilliant blue, despite the sun reflecting off the bare dirt around them.

It rarely rained here, and the air was dry, which made it very clear. The road was on a steep incline and the windstone vehicle shuddered slightly. She wondered if one of the wheels was improperly balanced.

That was something to look at when they stopped.

The vehicle crested a hill and the view made Barkson gasp. The sky opened in front of her, revealing the entire valley, the mountains, and the Hidden River, glistening in the distance. She thought she might be able to see the ocean, hundreds of miles away.

Corrin, too, was looking, but not at the entire view. Just at the needlelike peak to their left.

Mount Vitaki, looking like one of the pillars in the ancient carvings, only so high that it dominated all of the other peaks. Mount Vitaki had sheer walls and a pointed top that belied the fact that the top of the mount was actually flat.

Or so Barkson had been told. She had never climbed up to it. She wasn't a mountain-climber, and driving to the top of the peak was impossible. In some of the nearby villages, pilots rented their services to fly the adventurous to the top of the peak in their demigliders.

Barkson had never done that either.

She had heard that it was possible to drive halfway up Mount Vitaki, but she had no idea what the point of that would be. To look out over the valley? There were plenty of good safe places with a strong view. And if she really wanted to have the best view in the valley, maybe she would splurge on a demiglider trip.

She had heard that from the top of Mount Vitaki, a person could see the entire Protectorate.

Corrin sat up. "This view gets me every time."

Barkson nodded and tried to keep her gaze on the road. "The fork...?"

"To right," he said. "Away from the valley. You actually will return to the valley on that road, but most people don't know it."

"All right," she said, and eased the vehicle down the slight decline to the fork. The road to the right really did appear to be the road less traveled. It had the same kind of yellow dirt that she had seen on the road to Ghita's.

Barkson had been led to believe that the yellow dust had come from some local magic in Feltshyon, not from the Kirilli family.

Maybe the family used whatever it could for whatever it wanted.

Or maybe that yellow dust was native to this place.

Barkson wasn't going to ask Corrin. He seemed preoccupied with watching the landscape as if it would reveal its secrets. And his moods were still volatile, too volatile for her to feel comfortable with pushing him too hard.

She was worried about that dust, though. In Feltshyon, it had clogged the windstone vents. She didn't need that here. She had just cleaned them out.

The road wound through what appeared to be rolling hills, even though the decline had been a short one. This was some kind of mountain valley, at a much higher altitude than the Hidden River.

The land was brown and red, the yellow dust marking the road and nothing else. Tall cacti stood at attention near the rolling hills, sometimes surrounding them, almost like a group of sentinels protecting their land.

The even spacing of the cacti made Barkson wondered if someone had planted them instead of the cacti occurring naturally.

Small bristly plants covered other parts of the ground, with long branches that bloomed with pale purple flowers.

The smell of saffron and lavender filled the vehicle, and Barkson fought the urge to sneeze.

"How much farther?" she asked.

"Not much," he said.

The road veered sharply to the left now, going at an almost ninety-degree angle from their previous path. They were heading back toward the Hidden River. Mount Vitaki gleamed like a beacon in the distance.

Mountains rose on all sides of the vehicle, the road becoming a mountain path again, looking like it was carved from something ancient.

Barkson continued to have that thought until a perfectly carved tunnel covered the road. The tunnel used modern stone blocks and some kind of metal reinforcements to make sure that the arch stayed up.

The road also widened here. That tunnel clearly hadn't been natural.

Someone had carved it into the mountainside.

"A tunnel?" she asked Corrin, not wanting to say more, because she was afraid that she would reveal how uncomfortable going through it made her.

"Don't worry," he said. "It's short."

"It limits our escape options," she said, even though that wasn't really her objection to the tunnel. She was mildly claustrophobic, especially when it came to things inside of mountains like caves and naturally occurring tunnels.

This one made her even more nervous.

"The *road* limits our escape options," Corrin said, then

glanced at her. He suddenly seemed to remember her claustrophobia. "You want me to drive this part?"

That would be so much worse. She would lose control of her vehicle and therefore her ability to get out of that tunnel quickly.

"I'm all right," she lied.

The road dipped slightly ahead of the tunnel, and then the road's surface changed from the yellow dust to carved stone blocks, the same as the rest of the tunnel.

The wheels actually clacked against the stone, making the vehicle louder than it usually was. The clacks bounced off the tunnel walls as the vehicle went deep inside.

At least the tunnel was straight. And not very long, just as Corrin promised. She could see the opening at the other end almost from the moment she entered the tunnel.

But like most things in these mountains, the distance was deceptive. She drove longer and farther than she expected, before bouncing out of the tunnel into a wide flat area that looked more like a plateau than part of the valley.

"We're here," Corrin said.

Barkson didn't see anything. Not buildings, not vehicles, not people. Just flat brown dirt and the road, still made of carved stone blocks, slightly elevated as it went straight toward what looked like the edge of a cliff face.

"We are?" Barkson asked.

"Just wait," Corrin said. He finally sounded relaxed.

The vehicle bumped along the stone, seemingly hitting every crack and crevice, the clacking continuing. It was irritating enough to make Barkson clench her jaw, and slow down just a bit.

She was tired and dusty, her nose tingling from the lingering smells of saffron and lavender (which were gradually being replaced by the smell of hot dust). She should have traded off driving duties with Corrin several miles back, but she hadn't. She had let him sleep instead, partly because he had been annoying her, and she hadn't wanted to converse with him.

But this part of the road was challenging her and making her feel every inch of the previous journey. Maybe it was the idea that she was almost to the last Kirilli sibling. Or maybe the fight and the fires and the fear were catching up to her.

Maybe it was the growing heat inside the vehicle or the clacking, which was irritating her deeply.

"It looks like we're going to run out of road," she said to Corrin.

"Trust it," he replied.

Trust it. Trust it. She nearly mocked him. And then she got mad. Why the hell couldn't he just tell her what was going to come next?

She opened her mouth to snap that very sentence at him when the road ahead vanished.

"What...?" She gripped the sticks even tighter, prepared for something awful.

"The road continues," he said. "You just can't see it from here. But do slow down."

He didn't have to tell her twice. She slowed to a near crawl and finally reached the edge of the drop-off.

The rest of the plateau and the cliff were half a mile away or more. She still had a lot of land left before she literally drove off a cliff.

But she could finally see what he meant. She wasn't going to drive off a cliff. The road veered sharply downward, and seemed to go to a secondary plateau, one built on actual rock.

It was dozens of feet down, the downward angle so steep that the vehicle sped up on its own.

It took all of her strength to keep the vehicle under control.

She was watching the road before her more than she stared at the plateau. Her shoulders ached, and her hands were cramping from the force she used to hold the driving sticks.

Finally the road leveled and she looked up.

Corrin had been right; this place was a compound. She could see maybe a dozen buildings, some large, some small, all of them made of adobe. The tile roofs were made from the same red rock as some of the roofs in Lyoye, but the adobe seemed to be composed of whatever nearby dirt someone found.

Half of the buildings were unpainted, but the ones closest to the road were painted a blinding white. They all had spectacular glass windows that were not receded into the building the way that she had seen with other adobe structures.

The older buildings—and she was guessing at their age from their condition—seemed to grow out of the land. The newer ones were built on top of the land.

The road vanished.

"Drive between the second and third buildings." Corrin pointed to the right.

The second and third buildings were identically built bookends, painted white, both looking more like buildings from Trinovante except made of adobe than anything that was native to Khēmía.

She drove between them, carefully, expecting to see other parked vehicles or carriages or something.

But there didn't appear to be a stable. No horses meant no carriages. No carriages meant no carriage house, although a couple of the buildings had an extra-long roof, held up by two posts. Underneath at least one of them was an ancient windstone vehicle, maybe one of the very first models.

It had clearly not been used in years, if not decades. The wheels had fallen off, the roof was caved in, and only the body—the part made of windstone—looked untouched by anything except the ever-present dust.

Corrin saw her looking at it.

"My great-grandmother's vehicle," he said. "She used to go back and forth from here to the Serebro Academy in it. She taught there."

Barkson knew that. Everyone knew that. It was part of Protectorate lore. Kyra Rowe Kirilli taught at Serebro Academy for three months of every year, bringing her Practical Interns with her for six months to explore and, some said, loot the cultural treasures of Khēmía.

When the Academy threw her out for some kind of infraction that either had to do with practicing magic or failing to teach magic or failing to believe in magic or dabbling in arcane practices that endangered lives—depending on who was telling the story—she founded a training ground near Mount Vitaki, while her husband Magnus founded the Forbidden Valley Antiquities Service.

Later the Qavnerian government got involved in the service, although some said that Kirillis still ran it. Or at least, the Old Families did.

Most of the Old Families had sent at least one of their children from each generation to study with Kyra Rowe Kirilli near

Mount Vitaki. And after her mysterious death, they sent the children to study with her heirs—not necessarily familial heirs, but the Practical Interns who had stopped being interns and had become masters of one kind or another.

For some reason, Barkson had thought that the entire area near Mount Vitaki would look like a Qavnerian school, with a full campus and a lot of buildings of red brick, a clock tower in the center to chime out the hours, and a few surreptitious guards to keep the curious away from the libraries.

But there didn't appear to be a library here. There certainly was no clock tower, and there definitely was no brick.

"My father wanted to donate it to a museum," Corrin said, still talking about his great-grandmother's vehicle, "but curators told him that the vehicle couldn't be touched. It had to be in the same shape it was in when they found it. They didn't dare repair it. But without repairing it, there's no getting it off this mountain."

Barkson frowned. This family had such strange concerns.

"It looks to me like this entire place should be a museum," Barkson said.

"It's a working compound," Corrin said. "Or it's supposed to be."

He sounded haunted, the relief that had been in his voice when they got close to the compound gone.

"Over there," Corrin said, pointing ahead.

Barkson had to look to see what he was pointing at. It was the largest building she had seen so far. Its U-shape was the only thing that made it seem Qavnerian, although, from what she could tell, the U was backwards.

If she had put the building on the site, the long arms of the

U would have faced the cliff, the mountains across the Forbidden Valley, and Mount Vitaki.

Instead, the bottom of the U faced in that direction, and the long arms extended toward her vehicle.

As she got closer, she saw that the adobe in the arms was a slightly different color than the adobe in the middle. Not just that, but the adobe in the middle looked stronger, less vulnerable to the elements.

The materials marked the middle as something made a hundred or more years ago. There was a science to using adobe, and it included the materials. Some of the older materials were superior to the modern ones, but so much harder to find.

Either those materials weren't available here when the wings were built onto the main building, or whoever added the wings didn't care.

"Park over there." Corrin clarified, waving his hand at a building just beyond the U-shaped building.

Barkson could immediately see where he wanted her to park. It was underneath another of those extended roofs. She pulled in, and let out a sigh.

Every muscle in her body ached.

But she didn't have time for that right now. They had arrived at what looked like an empty compound. No one had come out of the large U-shaped building or any other building.

Certainly, if someone lived here, they would have heard the vehicle coming. The clatter from the tunnel alone would have reached this plateau. And then there was the road itself, which had enough stone blocks to make noise all the way into this part of the valley.

Windstone vehicles weren't generally loud, but in the relative silence of this place, even the crunch of wheels on dirt would have been audible from a distance.

"I don't think anyone is here," she said.

"Yeah," he said, "and that's a bad sign."

"Why?" she asked. "Maybe Emberto heard about the attackers from someone else in your family."

"He wouldn't have left," Corrin said. "Not without notifying one of us."

Barkson frowned. "Why?"

"We're not to leave this compound empty," Corrin said. "There's too much history here."

"Whose rule is that? A family rule?" Barkson asked.

"Is there any other kind?" Corrin asked, and let himself out of the vehicle.

EMBERT

THE HIDDEN RIVER

CHAPTER
TWENTY-FOUR

Barkson grabbed two pistols and made sure she still had daggers on her hips before letting herself out of the vehicle. The hot air hit her with physical force. She hadn't expected it, even though she knew that the windstone vents kept the interiors of the vehicles relatively cool.

She was instantly covered in sweat. She left her coat in the vehicle, figuring she could get it—and the letters for Emberto— once she needed them.

Insects chirruped in a regular rhythm, lulled by the heat and the sunshine. The smell of hot dust permeated everything.

Corrin hadn't gone far. He remained under the long roof, in the shade, and he was staring at the U-shaped building. It looked empty, although Barkson didn't know why she felt that way. The windows were clean and there was no dust buildup from the wind around the edge of the building.

"This doesn't feel right," Corrin said as she joined him.

"I know," she said.

She had been expecting to arrive in the middle of an attack as she had done twice before. She hadn't expected to arrive in a place that felt like time had forgotten it.

Corrin left the shade and headed toward the right side of the U-shaped building, near a couple of the other buildings. Barkson followed a few paces back, looking around to see if anyone was watching them.

The sun, now that she had stepped into it, was intense, almost burning against her skin. When she lived in this part of Dorovich she had tried to stay out of the sunlight from midmorning until sunset.

Some of the locals slept during this time or stayed inside to get work done or read. Very few did much of anything in the heat of the day.

She wondered if that was what was happening here. All of the nearby buildings on this compound looked empty. Some of them did have dust on the windows, and dust blown up against the doors, which meant the buildings had been empty for a long time.

Corrin stopped just as he was stepping around the bottom of the U. He beckoned Barkson to join him.

She did, and sucked in a breath, the hot air and dust filtering down her lungs. Ahead of her, there were long scorch marks and a fire ring near the front of the building.

The markings looked a day or two old, because a thin layer of dust coated them.

Corrin looked at the side of the main building as if it had answers. Then he looked at the other building to his right. Barkson did the same. Neither building had scorch marks.

For a moment, Corrin hesitated. Then he continued

forward, going around the edges of the scorch marks. He actually stopped and looked at them from his new position, and mimed tossing something.

Barkson joined him.

From this angle, indeed, it looked like whatever had created the scorch marks had either been ignited a few yards away or been tossed into the air a few yards away.

She couldn't tell which, but Corrin seemed to know.

He stepped around, careful not to touch any of the scorch marks, and stopped beside the fire ring. He bit his lower lip, as if something about it disturbed him more than the ring itself.

Something certainly disturbed her. There had been some kind of fight here. It seemed to have ended.

She didn't like how that felt.

She wanted to push ahead of Corrin, so that she could see the damage before he did. But she was hampered by the same desire to move cautiously.

Corrin raised his head, his face expressionless like it often was in the middle of a mission. She couldn't tell what he felt about all of this.

She was worried.

A dry wind came up, swirling the dust around her feet. Here, the air did not smell faintly of smoke from a fire that had burned long and hot. Here, the air had a tinge of decay.

She wasn't going to join him at the fire ring. Instead, she walked over to the corner of the wing, and her breath caught.

Bodies lay in the dirt, so many that she couldn't count them. A hand raised up here, and a knee there, a foot to one side. The parts all seemed to be attached, but the bodies were clustered together, some of them on top of each other.

Most of them were on their backs.

On this side of the building, the smell was stronger, although still not as strong as she expected, given the number of bodies that she could see without getting close.

She didn't want to beckon Corrin over here. She didn't want to know if these bodies belonged to Emberto and the others who lived in the compound. She didn't want to deal with the emotional fallout, although she knew she was going to.

She had a hunch this was going to be a lot harder than she wanted it to be.

She turned so that she could gesture at Corrin, but as she did so, she saw the long wall inside the wings. That wall wasn't made of adobe. It had been made of glass, and the glass had been shattered.

Dust and sand piled in the building.

Her heart rate increased.

She didn't like this at all.

Something about the broken glass and the untended bodies confirmed that the buildings were empty—at least for now.

She didn't feel like she had to remain quiet.

Still, when she said Corrin's name, she did so softly.

He raised his head. He was at an angle where he couldn't see the bodies yet.

He shook his head, as if he didn't want to join her.

"Corrin," she said again, more firmly, so that he would come to her side.

She couldn't protect him from this mess. Her work before had shown her that. It was better to do the hard things immediately, and let the other people involved deal with whatever it was however they could.

He came toward her, shaking his head, and then he stopped. He clearly smelled the death that was only a few yards from him.

His shoulders sagged.

She waved a hand at the glass first. He stopped and stared at it, his skin going gray.

Then he looked at her, and in doing so, saw the bodies.

He started toward them.

She put a hand on his arm and stopped him.

She was going to make sure they were going to go over there together.

He actually let her walk a few steps ahead of him. Maybe he thought that could soften the blow if his brother was actually in that mess.

But as Barkson got closer, she understood what she was seeing.

She had seen something similar at Dilshad's when Helia had flung her weapon into a group of attackers.

They had all died.

Barkson stopped at the edge of the pile. The smell was worse here, because the bodies were bloated. That meant they had died at least two days ago.

But the bloating was unlike any she had seen before. Some areas were distended, like stomachs, but arms and faces and anything exposed to the sun had hardened. The bloat seeped out in other places, like the chin, which hadn't been exposed to the sun at all.

At least, that was what the five bodies on top looked like. There were two more farther back, and several underneath.

Barkson knew that focus would keep her from getting overwhelmed by this scene. She focused on figuring out how many people were here.

She counted fifteen, based on the heads or necks.

Then she looked at Corrin. He seemed to be counting too. But he was looking at other things—arms, legs, clothing, weapons. He seemed to have gone beyond faces.

Her movement must have caught his attention, because he looked directly at her.

"Emberto?" she asked, because she couldn't put it off any longer.

Corrin shook his head. "I've never seen these people before."

Barkson crouched, and peered closely at them. Thin faces, upraised eyebrows, pointed ears. The clothing was different than she had seen before—flowing and what might have been white, looking a lot more like something worn in Lyoye than something unfamiliar.

But that meant nothing. If they had been trying to blend in, they would have changed the clothing first.

"They're Fey," she said.

Corrin nodded. "And all dead. I don't understand."

"You should," she said. "You used the same weapon."

"Helia's weapon," he breathed.

Barkson nodded. "Only you threw it into the portals. That might have happened in the portals."

"It might not have," he said.

"It looks to me like they had come here, and started an attack on this building," Barkson said.

"The house," he said.

"And then, maybe, Emberto tossed the weapon at them, and killed a lot of them at once," she said.

"Then where is he?" Corrin asked. "Why didn't he greet us? How come this place feels so empty?"

"Maybe he figured out what to do before I arrived," she said. "Maybe he left."

"We're not to leave this place unattended," Corrin said. "If someone had to leave, then they should have brought in someone else to protect the compound."

"From the family?" Barkson asked.

"Preferably," Corrin said. "But not necessarily. There's just too much here to leave..."

He pivoted and walked toward the broken glass wall. Barkson had to hurry to keep up.

"Let me go in there first," she said.

"In case we find my brother and he's dead?" Corrin asked.

She hadn't expected him to be so blunt. "Yes."

"I can handle it, Barks," Corrin said.

He hadn't been able to handle his father's death, and he hadn't even seen evidence of it. How could he handle his brother's?

"I'm sure you can," she said, careful that her tone wasn't placating. "But let me go first anyway. It's just—"

"No," Corrin said. "I've been thinking about this the whole way here. I was surprised by my father. He seemed...indestructible, even though I should have known better. And I left it badly with him. But Emberto, if he's dead, I'm not going to be surprised. He and Helia were always messing with things they shouldn't have. I expected both of them to have accidentally killed themselves by now."

Just because he had thought about that as a possibility didn't mean he would be able to handle the reality.

"That's different," Barkson said.

"I know." Corrin stopped and put his hand on her arm. "I'll be all right, Barks, really. I've thought it through. I'd been under attack for days. I figured there was a good chance that Emberto had too, and he was alone here. He's smart, but I don't know if he's that smart."

Corrin gave her a rueful smile, then let go of her.

"I'm going in," he said.

He didn't add, *and you can't stop me*, but the words hung in the air.

She couldn't stop him, even though she wanted to.

"There might be more Fey in there," she said.

"If there are, then they would have come after us," he said.

"Not if they're injured," she said. Or asleep. Or in a part of the compound where they hadn't heard the conversation.

"Barks, whatever happens, happens," Corrin said and stepped over the broken glass into the main building itself.

CHAPTER
TWENTY-FIVE

Barkson stepped through the broken wall. It wasn't so much a wall as large glass doors that covered two walls and clearly had been closed at the time of the attack.

What lay in the middle of the shattered glass surprised her. She had expected some kind of weapon.

Instead, she saw two large rocks, so big that she wondered at the strength of the person who carried them and the person who chucked them through the glass.

The shattering glass would have been loud. It would have caught the attention not only of anyone inside this building, but also in the nearby buildings.

She put her boot on as little shattered glass as possible, but the glass was littered all over this part of the floor. That argued for Emberto not being here, or at the very least, being injured and unable to tend to this.

Because the smell from the decaying bodies outside had pooled in this main room.

389

It was a beautiful room, with raised ceilings covered in wood that didn't seem native to this part of Dorovich. Stone counters that were gray and red and buffed to perfection lined one wall, forming an open kitchen. A fireplace had been built into that wall, and next to it, some kind of stove and oven, something she had never seen before. She didn't see a chimney, but that didn't mean there wasn't one.

A nearby table which had chairs for twelve was covered in glass.

On the other side of the room, pillows and couches and single chairs that looked like pillows mounted on some kind of round wood frame made an inviting grouping.

She knew without turning around that this section of the room had a view of Mount Vitaki and the mountains beyond.

It seemed that the building had been constructed deliberately to face Mount Vitaki and not the nearby hills or even the Forbidden Valley just down the cliff face.

"You coming?" Corrin asked. He sounded annoyed.

He had gone deeper in the room and stood near an archway that she hadn't seen. It was just beyond the furniture grouping, and led into a hallway that was on the attacked side of the building.

She started to follow him when she heard something.

"Wait," she said.

Corrin flushed. He started to speak, but she held up a hand.

Something moaned. Or cried. Or made some kind of wailing sound. It was faint but it was clear.

"Do you hear that?" she asked.

He shook his head, but came to her side. His expression was

focused, as if he could will himself to hear whatever she was hearing.

The wail faded, then rose, and then faded. It sounded far away, almost muffled.

Corrin held up a hand for silence, like he used to do.

The wail sounded thready. Weak. Fainter than it had a moment ago.

It might have been a cat in or near one of the other buildings. It was the wrong time of day for a cat to be prowling, especially if it was a female in heat, but that didn't mean it didn't happen.

Or maybe it was a trapped animal somewhere.

Or a person, injured and nearly dead.

The wail rose, louder, as if it couldn't be stilled.

"This way," Corrin said and walked directly for the furniture grouping. There didn't seem to be anything that way, but Barkson didn't protest.

Corrin had been coming to this place his entire life. He had to know it better than she did.

He walked to the edge of the stone countertop and reached underneath it.

A panel slid back silently, and the wail became a full-throated cry.

He stepped into the panel. He didn't say anything to Barkson, and she wondered if she should guard the door.

But her curiosity got the better of her. She gripped her pistols tighter, not sure what to expect.

What she saw were lightstone lanterns that triggered as Corrin passed them. The floor sloped downhill, and after a few minutes, it turned into stairs.

The cry become muffled, followed by a shushing, and then another wail, this one from a different voice.

Injured people? Children?

Barkson couldn't tell.

Corrin reached the bottom of the stairs, and Barkson had to hurry to make sure she arrived at almost the same time. She didn't want him to do anything rash, even though she wasn't sure what that would be.

They appeared to be in a natural cavern, but it had furniture and lights, and sections segmented off from each other, so that a group could hide down here for a long time.

Dried food stores were in baskets against the wall, along with jugs presumably filled with water.

"Hello?" Corrin said in his best non-threatening voice. "Emberto?"

Barkson didn't say anything for fear of scaring off whoever might be making the noise.

But the wailing increased with Corrin's voice. It didn't fade.

"Emberto," Corrin said. "It's me, Corrin."

Now, there was a tinge of panic in Corrin's voice. He looked around the cavern, as if he could see all of it from the stairs. He clearly couldn't—Barkson couldn't either—but he seemed to sense that whoever was here was nearby.

"Corrin?" A woman's voice answered. "The brother?"

"Yes," Corrin said. "I'm here with a friend. We're here because my sister Augusta sent us. Where's Emberto?"

"I don't know," the woman said. "But we're back here."

We. Barkson let out a breath. *We.* Maybe the other people who lived at the compound? Had they come down here when the attack started, and had been too afraid to leave?

The wailing had stopped but there was snuffling and little choking sounds, almost like sobs.

Corrin started forward, but Barkson stopped him. She hefted the pistol in her right hand.

Whoever was here might not have been friendly. These Fey attackers, they seemed to know who the family was.

If Barkson had been thinking clearly, instead of surprised by this underground cavern, she would have spoken first.

Corrin put a hand on one of his daggers. He went slowly, but Barkson stepped in front of him.

If anyone was going to get killed down here, it would be her. She hadn't gone through all of this to let a Kirilli die.

Particularly this Kirilli.

She stepped between two of the sections. On her right stood a woman with short, tangled hair, her face chapped, her clothing stained. Next to her were two bassinets. Tiny fists waved out of one of them.

The snuffling came from the other.

Babies. There were babies down here.

"Hi," Barkson said, unsure what else to do.

"Hi." The woman's voice wobbled. She had dark eyes that matched her messy hair, a pointed chin, and skin about two shades darker than Barkson's.

She looked like she hadn't changed clothes in days.

Half-eaten food, open water jugs, and baby supplies were strewn all over the tables behind her. A cot, with blankets pulled back, revealed where she had been sleeping.

"Who the hell are you?" Corrin snapped. He had come up behind Barkson.

The snuffles in the other bassinet became a full-throated

wail. The woman shot Corrin a look that parents had used from the dawn of time. It was the *dammit, see what you did? You woke the baby* look.

She bent over and picked up the baby inside the bassinet, cradling the infant's head as she picked it up. The baby instantly stopped crying, and grabbed a fistful of shirt.

"I'm Gianna," she said as if she expected Corrin to recognize her name.

"That tells me exactly nothing," Corrin snapped. "Where's my brother?"

Barkson put a cautioning hand on his arm. If he continued in this vein, she'd tell him in no uncertain terms to shut up.

"I'm Lucinda Barkson," she said. "This is Emberto's rude older brother Corrin. I don't know the family dynamics, Gianna. How are you connected to Emberto?"

"I'm his wife," she whispered. "He said you would know that."

This last she directed at Corrin, but Barkson answered, since Corrin was vibrating with anger.

"Corrin has been on a mission for most of a year," Barkson said, not caring if it was true or not. "He hasn't kept up with the family."

Corrin took a step toward Gianna. She backed away, hand still on the baby's head.

"Twins?" he asked, peering at the second bassinette. Fists still waved as if the baby inside the bassinet was directing a small orchestra.

"Yes," Gianna said, her voice filled with tears. "They're only three weeks old."

Barkson kept up with Corrin so she could get in his way if

she had to. The deeper she got into this part of the big space, the more it smelled of sour milk and dirty diapers.

"How long have you been down here?" Barkson asked.

"I don't know." Gianna wiped a hand over her face. "Three days? Four days? Emberto said he'd be back in a day or so, but I know it's been longer. It's just been me and the babies, and those evil people—they haven't come down here, but I don't know if they're upstairs."

"No one is upstairs," Barkson said.

"Where did Emberto go?" Corrin asked.

At least he didn't say that no one was supposed to leave the compound. Technically, someone was still here.

"He went to Mount Vitaki. He says there's a cavern there filled with his great-grandmother's things. He says there's some kind of solution in it, something that would stop these attacks?"

Barkson had a lot of questions, but she went for the easy one first. "There were more attacks?"

"He saw someone during the night, before the big attack. He thought it was locals." Gianna swallowed and juggled the baby as if the tiny child weighed too much for her.

"Would you like me to hold the baby?" Barkson asked.

Gianna's gaze went down to Barkson's hands and then back to her face. At that moment, Barkson realized she was still holding the pistols.

"I've got her," Gianna said. "This is Kyrita."

Corrin started. "A diminutive of my great-grandmother's name?"

"Yes," Gianna said. "We named her for your great-grand-mother, but not the same name, because Emberto said that might confuse the ghosts."

"The what?" Barkson asked.

"Don't even start," Corrin said quietly to her. "That's what he was trying to talk to me about the last time I was here."

Gianna lifted her chin, as if she hated what she had just heard from Corrin. She turned slightly so she was only addressing Barkson.

"The other baby is named for my great-grandmother, Irini. We didn't make her name a diminutive because Emberto said the ghosts had no relationship with her."

Gianna spoke as if what she was saying was normal, as if Barkson would understand.

Barkson realized that Corrin was right; this was not the time. So she just nodded.

Gianna shifted the baby again. Barkson set the pistols down. She wasn't comfortable holding them near the children.

"He's dead, isn't he?" Gianna asked. "That's why you're here. He's dead."

"No," Barkson said. "We came to warn him about the attackers. Obviously we were too late."

Corrin winced.

Barkson hoped he had heard Gianna, though. The attacks started about the time the attacks had occurred in Trinovante.

This was a coordinated assault on the living Kirillis for reasons that Barkson—and possibly the Kirillis—didn't understand.

"He put us down here. He said we had to wait. I have been and I've been getting worried. We won't run out of food, but I need to clean the babies and I'm scared to use the water down here. He told me not to drink any of the water in the stream, and I was afraid to use it to wash them. Can I use it to wash them?"

She looked at Corrin for that.

"No," he said. "But we can go back into the house. You'll be able to clean up there."

Gianna took in a shaky breath.

"We need to clear the compound," Barkson said to Corrin. "I'd like to do that before we bring babies into a dangerous area."

"You think the attackers are still here?" Gianna's voice rose.

"I doubt it," Barkson said. "We didn't see anyone." *Anyone alive, that is.* "But it's better for us to check."

Gianna nodded.

"Barks," Corrin said, "I think I need to stay down here in case...you know what happened at the estate. We're protected down here."

"How do you know that?" Barkson asked.

"Because those babies are Kirillis, aren't they?" Corrin's tone was a bit too pointed as he directed that question at Gianna.

"Yes." She held herself straighter. She was clearly beginning to dislike her brother-in-law.

"The fact that they're fine proves that this cavern is as safe as my great-grandmother always thought it was," Corrin said.

"She built this place?" Gianna asked.

"She didn't build it," Corrin said. "It's a natural cave, part of the system that runs underneath the Razbitay Mountain Range. I've heard tell that it also goes beneath the Hidden River, but no one that I know of has ever explored that."

Barkson looked at him. His gaze met hers.

"When I last saw Emberto," Corrin said, "he claimed that there were ghosts down here. Is that true?"

Gianna shrugged, her grip on the poor baby tightening as

she did so. "I've been here for days and never seen any. But he did."

Corrin started to ask something else, but Barkson touched his arm. He didn't need to harangue Gianna, not now.

"You were staying here the last time Corrin came to visit, weren't you?" Barkson asked. She remembered Corrin's story about not using the usual room in the compound.

Gianna nodded. "Emberto wasn't ready to introduce us. He said we'd meet after he talked with the family. But clearly, he never did."

Her voice had gotten thicker. Tears threatened.

Barkson didn't like the drama. She was beginning to think the Kirillis were all about the drama, which made her feel better about the end of her relationship with Corrin. Maybe it hadn't been her fault that the relationship ended. Maybe Corrin truly had been too much to deal with.

"You're going to stay here," she said to Corrin, "while I clear the compound. I'm going to make sure there are no attackers just waiting for Emberto to return."

She doubted that was the case—the attackers would have revealed themselves around Corrin—but she wanted to make sure there weren't more bodies here.

She wanted to be the one to find Emberto's body, not Corrin, and certainly not Gianna.

Besides, clearing the compound would give Barkson time to think.

She needed a plan, and she wasn't even sure what that would be.

CHAPTER
TWENTY-SIX

It took nearly two hours to clear the compound. Barkson went through each building, looking in every room, moving stealthily and carefully, worried that she might roust an attacker.

This place was larger than it seemed even at first. Buildings upon buildings, rooms upon rooms. Many of the rooms were small, confirming Corrin's comment that there had been some kind of dormitories for Practical Interns years ago.

Clearly, there had been a lot of Practical Interns, apprenticing at the feet of the master—Kyra Rowe Kirilli, before she got disgraced.

The abundance of small rooms made clearing the place harder.

Barkson's unwillingness to go quickly also made it hard. Because the floors of some of the dormitories were covered in a thick layer of dirt and dust, so someone lazier than she was would think that meant no one was in the rooms.

But she couldn't get the portals out of her mind. If all the attackers had to do was portal in, then they wouldn't leave footprints in the dust.

However, the air smelled dusty too as well as somewhat stale. She had a feeling that no one had been in some of these buildings for years.

She was the only person leaving footprints now. She walked through as much of the area as she could, and then she would go back outside and look around. The hot air made her feel sluggish; the exhaustion she'd been carrying slowed her down.

She had to be careful that she didn't lose track of what she was doing, because if she did, then she might open the others up to some kind of attack.

The farther along she got in this, however, the less likely an attack was. She found a lot of artifacts, some of them just sitting loosely on shelves. She found some abandoned notebooks. She looked at a few, and found they didn't belong to a Kirilli. The notebooks were often from Practical Interns who decided to abandon their degrees and return to Serebro.

Something about studying under Kyra Row Kirilli would anger them. Often that something seemed to be her husband, Magnus.

Barkson found it surprising that someone thought it wise to keep the notebooks out. Was that to discourage new Practical Interns or to test them? Was it just an acknowledgment of the history of the place or something more?

She didn't know the answer, and she wasn't sure she wanted to know. Her responsibility had expanded from Emberto to his entire tiny family.

She wasn't sure if keeping them here was the best idea or

letting them go to some other part of Khēmía. Or maybe to be protected in Razbitay proper, if that was even possible.

Then she stumbled on something strange.

She had gone inside a building with a large door that covered an entire wall. There was a smaller door on the side, which she used. She had also seen footprints leading into the small door, footprints no one tried to erase.

That bothered her. She entered slowly, expecting to find Emberto's body. Her reasoning for that was simple: aside from the marks from the battle near the main building, there hadn't been any footprints or indication of how Emberto had left the property—if, indeed, he had.

That either meant he was in a building somewhere or that he had carefully smoothed away every print he made.

Either the footprints here would lead to some other creature, hiding in the building or they belonged to Emberto.

He'd been gone for days, Gianna said.

If he had come into this building to get something and had been injured, then the likelihood of his survival after all those days was slim. Or he might have died here. Who would know? Gianna hadn't been able to leave that hidden area.

Barkson almost held her breath as she opened the door and slid inside that building. But she didn't, because smells told her things.

She didn't smell decay. She smelled the ever-present dust, and something familiar, like warm stone.

All around her, lightstone lamps illuminated. They were attached to the walls, flooding the large interior with extremely bright light.

There, in the center of the large floor, were three windstone vehicles. On the far side, there was room enough for a fourth. Given the fact that all three vehicles had been parked straight, with their noses in, Barkson guessed that there had been a fourth and it was gone now.

She stepped deeper into the large space. The vehicle closest to her was as old as the vehicle she had seen in Oxechana, as old as the decrepit vehicle that she and Corrin had seen when they first arrived here.

Only this ancient vehicle was clean and looked to be in perfect condition. If Barkson had needed to, she probably could have driven that vehicle out of here.

Next to it was a windstone vehicle that was old, but not ancient. The sides had actually been painted a bright yellow that had clearly faded over time.

But this windstone vehicle was as clean and kept up as the other, looking ready to leave the building at a moment's notice.

The third vehicle was old enough that it was considered obsolete, just like the first two, but new enough that Barkson had seen one at the Bekyce School. One of the older students had been lucky enough to have been given an old windstone vehicle for her final year at the school, and—at the behest of the teachers—she had let everyone in class try driving it once.

Barkson had begged to be allowed to drive it again. That was when she had learned that begging was never a way to get what you wanted.

Barkson walked around the vehicles slowly. Sure enough, on the far side of that third vehicle, there were wheel impressions in the dirt. More than that, there were tracks, made as the vehicle backed up.

The tracks went under the wide wall-length door and outside.

She stared at them for a moment, thinking.

The assumption she could make—that she really had to make—was that Emberto had taken that windstone vehicle to his great-grandmother's cave, whatever that was.

Barkson figured Corrin knew what that was, which was why she hadn't really asked about it.

But now that cave became a factor, because Barkson still had two letters to hand out.

She let out a breath, then walked around the remaining windstone vehicles. The yellow-painted one gleamed in the bright light. The other two looked fresh enough, but not as bright.

She found that she did not like the brightness at all.

She went outside through the small door, then walked around. She saw no tracks at all in front of the wide wall-length door, but the door had been smoothed over, the way a person would smooth dirt with a shoe.

She followed the brush marks until she reached some rocks.

There, on the side of them, were two shoe prints, probably not something the person who had brushed away the wheel tracks had noticed.

From here, the road was made of stone bricks, chipped and crumbling. This road was ancient, unlike the others around this compound.

It also did not register any wheel prints, and whoever had driven the windstone vehicle had known that.

She let out a breath.

That was not something the attackers would have known.

Nor would they have known about the windstone vehicles, unless they too had gone inside the large building.

She saw no evidence that they had.

And, given who they were, she doubted that they had ever tried to drive a windstone vehicle. She knew it was a possibility —she had learned in her training long ago not to underestimate her enemy.

She just wished she understood this group better than she did.

Still, it relieved her to see that one of the windstone vehicles was missing and someone had tried to cover his tracks. It was logical to assume that someone was Emberto.

If he had driven away, then that meant he could eventually drive back.

Barkson finished examining the remaining buildings on the property—a few storage areas and a toolshed filled with equipment she only vaguely recognized.

Then she returned to the main building, and went into the cavern.

Corrin was pacing. He stopped when he saw her.

"We were getting worried," he said.

Gianna sat near the babies and didn't nod as he said that. She looked so tired that adding one more worry onto her other worries seemed impossible.

"This place is big," Barkson said.

Then she pulled up a chair and sat so that both could see her. Instantly, the exhaustion that had been dogging her grew worse.

She probably should have remained on her feet.

"I found no evidence of attackers, other than the ones we see outside this place," Barkson said. "The area is clear."

"Good," Corrin said. Then he sat down. "And Emberto?"

Barkson pivoted in her seat so that she could see Gianna's face better. Barkson had a feeling—although she couldn't quite tell—that Gianna was now cradling the other baby, the one that had been waving her tiny fists.

This baby seemed more joyful, lighter somehow.

Barkson wasn't sure how she could tell that about an infant, particularly one that was only a few weeks old. But something about this one—Irini?—seemed very different from Kyrita.

"I think he drove out of here in a windstone vehicle," Barkson said. "I can't be certain of that, though."

Gianna's expression remained impassive. The baby clutched at her shirt, but she didn't look down.

"Is it possible to drive to your great-grandmother's cave?" Barkson asked Corrin.

"From here?" Corrin asked. "Yes. There's no good way to get to the cave, not from anywhere, but you can drive to one of the lower-level openings, or so I'm told."

Barkson frowned. "'Told?' You've never been there?"

"Oh, I've been there," Corrin said. "I just can't find the openings on my own, and when I try to go inside, something repels me and forces me backwards."

"What?" Barkson asked. "What does that mean?"

"It means he's not welcome," Gianna said. She sounded tired. "Neither am I, which is why Emberto went alone. He can see the reflection on Mount Vitaki. Can you, Corrin?"

Corrin looked at her, his expression sad. "No."

"Me, either," Gianna said. "But Emberto swore it existed,

often as the sun went down. He said the reflection was brighter than the lightstone lamps."

"He went to Mount Vitaki?" Barkson asked. "I thought he was going to your great-grandmother's cave."

"Halfway up Mount Vitaki," Corrin said. "You can drive halfway up or so, and then—I'm told—you have to go inside and walk the rest of the way."

"You're told," Barkson said.

"My grandfather," Corrin said, "he tried to take all of us there at one point or another to see if we could climb inside. Helia and Emberto could, but Helia ran screaming from the place, vowing she would never go inside again."

Barkson was intrigued. "And Emberto?"

"He was young enough to believe that what he saw were toys. Our grandfather took him inside, carrying him—because Emberto was that young—and Emberto fell in love the way only a child can with something strange and secret." Corrin glanced at Gianna.

She was watching him closely now. Clearly, no one had told her this story.

"Shortly after that, our grandfather died. Emberto hadn't gone back, until his last year at the Academy, after he decided to continue his education with advanced degrees." Corrin ran a hand over his face, that new nervous gesture that was beginning to bother Barkson. "Then he came here and never left."

"That's not true," Gianna said. "Your father made him work at the Forbidden Valley Antiquities Service. For years. I met him there, in Lyoye. He wasn't even living here. He lived in Lyoye then."

"What made him move up here?" Barkson asked, before

Corrin could say anything. He looked a bit thunderous, as if he wanted to disagree with Gianna but didn't know how.

Gianna looked at Corrin. Something in that look was accusing.

"Your father had hired someone to maintain this property. Emberto decided that the person was doing a terrible job, and fired that person. Then Emberto took over the property. By the time your father found out, Emberto had been here six months."

Gianna spoke with the confidence only experience brought.

"I was worried. I brought him food and supplies." She smiled thinly.

Corrin glared at her, as if he was going to insult her.

"Your relationship developed from there, then," Barkson said.

Gianna shook her head. "We had a relationship before that. I became his conduit to the rest of society, until I found out I was pregnant. I wanted to move back to Lyoye, and I begged him to hire someone again to take care of this place. But he said no."

Her gaze hadn't left Barkson's.

"I was stupid," she said. "I was in love. I thought we could do anything. I should have listened to myself. I needed to be away from here long before the babies were born."

"Being away from here probably would have gotten you killed," Corrin said.

Gianna shifted the baby in her arms. "Staying here nearly got us killed."

"But Emberto stopped them," Corrin said, almost as if he was defending his brother.

The tonal shifts that Corrin kept making startled Barkson. He used to be so calm.

"Yes, he did," Gianna said. "But I can't. And then we ended up trapped here without him."

"Why didn't you just drive out of here?" Barkson asked. "Those windstone vehicles work."

Gianna let out a small laugh. "How would you propose I do that? Put the babies in boxes in the back? What if I hit a bump? What if the vehicle rolled over? I can barely handle the two of them here, where there's no road and nothing to watch out for. On the road? It just can't be done, not by one person alone."

Barkson saw the point and was a bit embarrassed that she hadn't thought of that herself. She would have tried to get out of here, though. She had just been surprised that Gianna hadn't.

"I thought he was coming back," Gianna said into Barkson's silence. "I was going to give him maybe a week, and then I was going to figure something out."

"Where would you have gone?" Barkson asked gently. "Family?"

Gianna let out a half-laugh. "My family disowned me when I became involved with the colonizers. Their word. They hate the Kirillis. I can't go to them for help."

The baby's little fist had relaxed. She was clearly asleep.

Gianna stood and put the baby in the bassinet. Then she checked on the other baby before sitting back down.

"I was going over scenario after scenario in my mind, trying to figure out what to do. No one comes here. You were the last visitor, Corrin, until those attackers showed up." She took a deep breath and let it out slowly. "I was afraid we'd die here, if Emberto didn't come back. I was convinced we would. I just couldn't figure out what would be better. Dying on the road to somewhere or dying under the house here, with no one knowing anything about any of us."

Her words rang in the silence.

Barkson frowned at Corrin, who was staring at Gianna.

"He would have come back," Corrin said. "Eventually. But there might be a problem."

"What's that?" Barkson asked.

Corrin glanced at her, as if he had forgotten she was in the conversation. Then he turned his attention back to Gianna.

He said, "Family lore says time works differently in my great-grandmother's cavern. That you could go in on a Tuesday and leave an hour later, only to find you'd lost several days in there. Maybe that's what happened to him."

Or, Barkson thought, *he died somewhere between here and there.*

"Did Emberto know that?" Gianna's voice rose in a panic. She looked at the babies, as if, somehow, this last made Emberto's disappearance real for her.

"I don't know," Corrin said. "It's lore. None of us were ever in that cave."

"Not even Emberto?" Barkson asked, but she really wasn't looking at Corrin. She was looking at Gianna, whom Barkson believed actually knew what was going on.

"He never told me about that cave before," Gianna said. "I have no idea what his history is with it."

Corrin folded his hands across his stomach, as if he was pretending to be relaxed. He wasn't though. It was obvious.

"What made him decide to leave?" he asked.

"The ghosts," Gianna said. "They told him he could find even better weapons in the cave."

Corrin's frown grew deeper. "Ghosts," he said. "My brother was taking advice from ghosts?"

"They were the ones who warned us about the attackers," Gianna said. "The ghosts told him about them, and told him what weapon would work."

"You believed that?" Corrin asked.

Barkson was glad he asked, because she nearly said the same thing. Although part of her was deeply aware that Gussie had seen some kind of shade/creature/being who claimed to be her father, after he was killed. So there was strange magic around these places.

A tear rolled down Gianna's face.

"I come from magic," she said quietly. "My people, we believe in it. That's why my family disowned me. You colonizers, you don't believe. And out here, people think that the Purges weren't about magic, they were about getting rid of mixed-race people and non-Qavnerians, not about getting rid of magic."

Barkson stiffened. She had heard that accusation before as well.

"So a ghost, yes, I believe in ghosts. Especially when they showed him which weapon would work,"

"You saw them show him?" Corrin asked.

She shook her head. "I was here, with the babies. He told me."

"And couldn't he have remembered the weapon and decided to use it?" Corrin asked.

"Why would he lie about the ghosts?" Gianna asked.

Corrin sighed. "I don't think he was lying. I think..."

412

He bit his lower lip as if he was contemplating saying what he actually thought. Barkson didn't move. She wasn't sure what the right play was here, if there was a play at all.

Corrin glanced at Barkson, as if asking her permission. She kept her expression neutral. She was not getting involved in his part.

"He...um..." Corrin shrugged. "He...wasn't himself, really, the last time I saw him."

"You think he has gone mad," Gianna said.

"I don't know," Corrin said. "Do you?"

"Magic sometimes makes people seem crazy," Gianna said.

"Yes," Corrin said. "I know."

"And magic stopped those attackers," Gianna said.

"So it seems," Corrin said.

"So why not ghosts telling him to go to the cave?" Gianna asked.

Barkson's shoulders had grown tight from tension.

"For what reason?" Corrin asked. "To benefit him? Or to benefit them?"

Gianna sucked in air. "I've been wondering that too," she said quietly, as if she expected to be overheard. "Especially since he hasn't returned."

Barkson frowned. All they had was Gianna's word that Emberto had gone to that cave, and maybe he had. But a lot could have happened between here and that cave.

Barkson stood. "I'm going to go find him."

"How do you plan to do that?" Corrin asked. "*I* can't get in that cave, and I'm a Kirilli."

"Windstone vehicles are fragile things," she said. "I assume there's a lot of dust and rock between here and there. He might not have made it to the cave proper."

Or he might have died on the road or in one of the small villages. She hadn't liked that word *colonizer*.

"You'll bring him back?" Gianna asked.

Barkson gave her a thin smile. "I'm not going to promise anything. I told Gussie I would do my best to find all her siblings, and I haven't yet done that with Emberto. But I'm going to try."

"You'll need me to go with you," Corrin said.

"I don't need you, Corrin," Barkson said in her most dismissive tone. "I have never needed you. I do just fine on my own. *They* need you. You two are going to have to figure out where the safest place for Gianna and the children is. And you'll either need a plan to get them there or you'll need a plan for staying here."

Corrin's mouth thinned. She had made him angry.

"I should look for Emberto," he said.

"You understand Helia's weapons, and I understand there are some here. You know how to fight. You know this property. I know none of that." Barkson glared at him. "You are not going to fight me on this. I'm going after him on my own."

"You won't be able to get in the cave," Gianna said.

"I'm more worried that she will be one of the few who can," Corrin said. "She might not come out in a timely manner."

Barkson had thought of that. She hadn't promised that she'd stay away from the cave, but she could make one other promise.

"If I'm not back in five days," she said, "you're going to assume I'm not coming back. You'll make decisions with that in mind."

Gianna and Corrin stared at her in silence.

Finally, Corrin said, "I don't like that."

"I don't either," Barkson said. "But we have to be realistic. It's safer for me to travel right now than either of you, but it's still dangerous. Those attackers might be lurking, looking for anyone who is coming out of this compound. I might encounter a lot of other things. I trust you, Corrin, to make the right decisions and to keep these babies safe. Gianna has done a great job, but she needs help, and I can't provide it."

Corrin let out a small harrumph. Barkson recognized the look on his face. He was frustrated for two reasons: he wanted to be part of the action but he knew that Barkson was right.

"Okay," he said, as if he was the one who had to give her permission.

She decided to let the tone slide. She was tired, and ready to be done with this mission. It had too many twists and turns for her.

"I'm going to sleep so I can think clearly," she said to both of them. She also needed the sleep because she wasn't sure when she'd get another chance. "Wake me in six hours, and give me something to eat, as well as food to bring with me."

Then she turned to Gianna.

"If he makes any noises about taking my vehicle or the other windstone vehicles, you wake me. I'll stop him."

"You can trust me," Corrin said.

"When you give me your word," Barkson said. "You didn't."

His lip curled slightly. Then he nodded once in acknowledgment.

"I give you my word that I will do what I can to keep Gianna and the babies safe," he said.

"Not enough," Barkson said. "You will give me your word that you will stay at their side until they're safe."

He straightened, clearly irritated that she knew enough about his rhetorical games to force a better oath out of him.

"Yes," he said tightly. "I give you my word that I will stay by their side until we're through this crisis, whatever that means."

It was as good as she would get out of him.

"Thank you," she said, and went off to find a place to sleep.

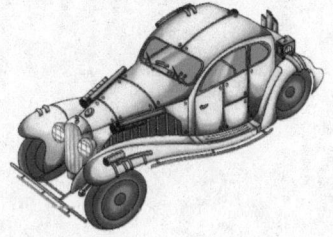

EMBERT

THE HIDDEN RIVE

CHAPTER
TWENTY-SEVEN

Dawn had started to pink the sky by the time Barkson left the compound. Gianna had given her a map to Mount Vitaki from the compound, since her knowledge of the drive was more recent than Corrin's. Besides, Gianna had been an adult when she had last gone there.

Corrin had not been to the mount since he was a child.

The drive was relatively simple. Down the mountain from the compound, to the Forbidden Valley. Then Barkson had to follow the valley road to the longest bridge in Dorovich.

The bridge crossed the Hidden River at a low point. It was also one of the wider points in the valley. So the area beneath the bridge looked like gigantic shallow puddles separated by large sandbanks.

The waterline on Barkson's side of the bridge showed that the river could rise, either with runoff or maybe from the sea. For all she knew, this part of the Hidden River was a tidal river, and actually filled with the tide.

419

Not that it mattered. The fact that the river was low here meant that long-ago engineers were able build large stone columns that supported the arches of the very long stone bridge.

This bridge seemed sturdy to Barkson. She even met oncoming traffic in the form of people on horseback as well as two small carriages, and she didn't feel squeezed.

She simply felt impatient. She hated going miles out of her way to get to a place she could see from the other side of the river.

Mount Vitaki loomed over everything here. As she drove across the bridge, she realized just how large Mount Vitaki was. She had to look away from the road to try to see the top of the mount, and even then, she was unable to. By the time she reached the bridge, the top of the mount had become enshrouded in clouds.

Corrin had warned her that might happen, even on a bright sunny day like this one. Mount Vitaki seemed to make its own weather. It even brought massive rainstorms to the other side of the river, which should have been impossible in this kind of high desert.

Barkson knew better than to question it. She had seen Mount Vitaki a handful of other times in her past, but never this close. She also hadn't known, until she got here, that one could simply drive up part of the mount. She thought the only way to the top was by demiglider or by rappelling its sides, something she would not have done, no matter how much Gussie would pay her.

The road on the other side of the river was narrower and older, the rock that composed it chalk-white where it had been broken off, gray everywhere else.

It was also uneven, which made her nervous, not just for her vehicle, but for Emberto's.

If Emberto had broken down anywhere on this side of the river, it would have taken him days to walk back to the compound, and that was if he started immediately.

He would have needed supplies as well, particularly water, since Corrin warned her that the water in the Hidden River was not safe to drink.

Barkson started watching the roadside for hikers on the compound side of the river. She saw none. She also didn't see anyone on the bridge, or, as she reached the other side, anyone walking there.

Perhaps there was a path that walkers knew about that kept them from this part of the road in Khēmía. Or perhaps walking here was frowned upon.

The road on this side threaded through a small ancient village, with buildings so old they were made of the same stone as the road itself. They had thatched roofs which seemed to be made of dry river grasses as well as some kind of cloth strap that held them down in the winds.

The villagers didn't look as carriages went by, but to a person, they all raised their heads when Barkson went by in her windstone vehicle.

She resisted the urge to blithely wave at them. She didn't want to insult anyone—not yet, anyway. She might need them or their expertise.

Gianna had told her that the road would start to go uphill at the base of Mount Vitaki, and she hadn't been kidding. As Barkson turned toward the river yet again, the road began a steep incline as it narrowed.

She couldn't even see Mount Vitaki. She was driving along its edge, in its shadow. The mount loomed over her, taller than the tallest building she had ever seen, taller than any mountain, maybe because the walls of the mountain were so very steep.

The road had been built into the side of the mountain with no protection on the cliffside. Her vehicle barely fit on the road as it was now, and if she had to go down, she might have to back up.

Ahead of her, as the road curved, she saw only far away mountain ridges and sky. Her heart beat in her throat. She wasn't sure she was up for this.

But she kept driving, glad she had gotten that good sleep so she was alert on this road. She was also glad she was driving during the day, because it would be impossible to drive this at night.

To her right, the side of the mount curved slightly—not yet straight up and down. The mountain's stone was actually black, unlike every other mountain in Dorovich, at least that she knew of.

Mount Vitaki almost looked like a pendant made of obsidian, rather than the side of a mountain. She wondered if it was some kind of obsidian, and then wondered if she would ever get the chance to ask anyone.

The road wound and wound and wound around the base, growing steeper the higher she went.

Eventually there would be no more road. The incline was already becoming impossible.

She rounded a final corner and saw a small flat area—not quite a turnout, more of a turnaround.

And parked squarely in the center of it was another wind-stone vehicle.

She pulled up beside it.

It was covered in dust. Someone had left the top down. There were prints inside as if someone else had been inside after the dust settled. Her heart pounded.

How would she know if this was Emberto's vehicle?

"Get out of the vehicle." A male voice spoke loudly.

She looked into her backing mirror, saw a tall thin man with skin as dark as Gianna's, holding a pistol on the vehicle. He had a pointed chin from which a braided goatee hung. His dark red clothing—a tunic over flared pants and sandals—reflected some of the outfits she had seen in the village below.

Barkson lowered her windscreen with one hand and grabbed the pistol beside her seat with the other.

"How about I just drive away?" she asked.

He seemed to consider it. Then he lowered the pistol.

"Go," he said.

She set her pistol on her lap, used both hands to move the drive sticks, looked in the mirror, and backed straight at him.

He cursed loudly in a language she did not recognize, and jumped to one side.

She spun around, engulfing him in a cloud of dust, and then stopped the vehicle close enough to him to drive over him if she had to.

He was on his stomach, looking startled, his pistol lost in the dust.

"Whose vehicle is that?" she asked.

"Mine," he said.

She pulled her pistol and pointed it out the windscreen at him. A shot this close would kill him, and they both knew that.

"Try again," she said.

"Mine," he repeated. Then he pointed at a sign that she hadn't seen when she drove up here.

It was written in two languages; one she didn't recognize and the other in Qavnerian.

After five days, abandoned vehicles will be sold and removed from the Mount Vitaki Landing.

Five days.

"You bought it when?" she asked, not moving her pistol.

"I'm taking it down to town," he said. "It's custom that whoever removes it owns it."

That made sense, considering how narrow this landing was.

"Who brought it up here?" she asked.

His mouth thinned. He knew, but he clearly didn't want to say.

"One more time," she said. "Who brought it up here?"

He visibly swallowed. "The colonist."

"I'm supposed to know who that is?" she asked, even though she was afraid she did.

"The Kirilli. Them what think they own this land, even though they don't."

Clearly this man was of the same opinion as Gianna's family about the Kirillis.

"Where is he?" Barkson asked.

"You know him?"

"No," she said honestly. "I do not. I was sent to retrieve him, though. Where is he?"

The man waved a hand at the mountain. "He went into the caves."

Barkson's heart sank. "And you sent someone in after him to kill him so you could get his vehicle?"

"None of us are stupid enough to go in there," the man said. "You can though."

Barkson looked at the black wall behind the landing. "Where exactly did he go in?"

The man hooted. "You don't see it, do you?"

"Not from here," she said.

"It's right in front of you," he said.

Then he picked up a rock. She cocked the pistol.

He held the rock and splayed his other hand, as if to say that he wasn't going to hurt her.

"I'm going to show you," he said.

He threw the rock at the mountainside. The rock should have hit the wall and bounced off.

Instead, it vanished and after a few more seconds, something clattered in the distance.

"You go in there," the man said, "you die. You die, I get your vehicle."

It was that simple to him, apparently.

She did some calculations. The vehicle had to be up here at least six days, from what Gianna had said.

"Why haven't you taken it before now?" Barkson asked.

The man's eyes narrowed, then his shoulder slumped.

"Tell you what," he said. "I'll find you a guide for the caves if you show me how to start the vehicle."

Barkson let out a small laugh. "You show me."

"I don't go in there. Too many never come back. Like your friend."

She let out a breath. She had a decision to make. She had promised Gussie that she would do everything she could to find Gussie's family, even risking her life.

But the idea of going into a cave that might or might not have magic, in which people vanished, in which time did not work properly according to lore, was too much even for her.

"Tell you what," Barkson said. "You get my guide and I'll show you both how to operate the vehicle."

The man shook his head.

"Come on," Barkson said. "You had to get up here somehow. You go back in whatever brought you and bring a guide. I'll wait."

The man looked at her warily.

"Or I'll just shoot you and go in there myself," Barkson said.

"All right." He held up his hands. "Can I get up?"

"Slowly. Hands in view at all times."

He did as she asked, then backed away from her, heading toward a small outcropping in the rock.

If he went into the cave, she wasn't going to follow. If he had compatriots, well, she had both her pistols and one dagger on the front seat.

He kept backing up until he reached the outcropping.

"You promised the vehicle to me," he said. "You remember that."

She hadn't done any such thing, but she wanted him to think that.

"I will," she said.

He slipped around the outcropping and her heart sank. If he had weapons there, she was in trouble.

But he came out, leading a very old horse.

"I want my pistol," he said.

"You'll get it when you come back," she said.

He glared at her, then mounted the horse. "You promised," he said. And just like that, he rode off.

She kept her pistol trained on him long after he moved to a range where the pistol was ineffective.

Then she got out of the vehicle and peered down the road. He was traveling slowly, but he was heading away from her, and he did appear to be alone.

She took his pistol and set it on the hood of her vehicle, uncertain what she would do with it.

Then when she was satisfied that he was nowhere around, she took that pistol (which was unbalanced and a little too heavy) and hers and looked behind the rock cropping.

There had barely been enough room for the horse. Barkson stepped out and peered at the landing. She looked up, and saw only the sheer side of Mount Vitaki.

She appeared to be alone here now.

She walked in the direction of the thrown rock. As far as she could tell, there was a sheer wall ahead of her.

When she reached it, she heard a slight buzzing. She grabbed another rock, a smaller one, and tossed it ahead of her.

It bounced back.

She moved it slightly to the right, and threw again. It disappeared into the wall. This time, she didn't hear a clatter.

The hair rose on the back of her neck.

She wasn't going to go in there alone, no matter what she

had promised Gussie. It would do no good for her and Emberto to die in there. He'd been gone in that cave system for almost a week.

Barkson wasn't willing to do that.

She walked back to her vehicle and leaned on it for a moment.

She had promised two things: she would do everything in her power to save Gussie's siblings and she would never read the letters.

Barkson wasn't sure what was in her power. She had done a lot, but she did not have the kind of magic that Helia had. Nor did Barkson have the ability to go after someone in what might have been a magical cave, filled with ghosts.

If she didn't go inside, then she was breaking one promise.

She turned, opened the vehicle's door, and reached into the back. She removed Helia's map from the compartment.

The map unfurled without her help.

On it, she saw an image of Corrin rise from the compound, floating markers that indicated the places Barkson had already been. Benedeto appeared to be on the road, not too far from Trinovante. Gussie was in Trinovante still.

Helia and Dilshad were together near the Hidden River in Feltshyon, and Ghita was in the small town she had said she would hide in. Filippa was in the Coastal Mountains.

This map was dangerous. It showed where all the siblings were.

All of them, except Emberto.

He wasn't on the map at all.

For the first time, Barkson wished she had used the map earlier to know if he had ever been on it.

She wasn't sure he had been.

Her hands were shaking. She grabbed the floating map and pulled it down, crumpling it.

It removed itself from her touch as if she had offended it, then rolled itself up and slipped back into the compartment all on its own.

If she had ever doubted that the Kirilli family had magic, those doubts were gone now.

And that also meant that the entrance to this cave was magical—a kind of magic that Barkson did not possess.

Still, she wasn't willing to leave without doing one more thing.

She pulled both remaining letters out of the compartment and looked at their markings.

She didn't have to read the first one; it was identical to all the others.

The second was the one that interested her.

She hefted it, feeling the weight of breaking this promise almost more than the weight of refusing to go after Emberto.

If she opened this letter, she would be done with her journey. She would have officially failed in her mission.

She would have found—and saved—all of the Kirilli siblings, but one.

She took a deep breath, looked around one final time, saw the black mountainside, the dust-covered vehicle, the unbalanced pistol, and the empty road.

Then she tore the second letter open, and began to read.

CHAPTER
TWENTY-EIGHT

E mberto,

      I'm sorry to ask you this on the heels of the news of our father, but I have no choice.

Our father told me a lot about the Kirilli Cave on Mount Vitaki.

So did our grandfather, although I'm not sure how well you remember that. You were just a boy when he took you in that cave. You loved it so. You talked about it for weeks afterwards.

Grandfather tried to take me inside.

I couldn't even see it, although he kept going in and out, trying to prove to me it was there. Rocks and toys and lamps could go in and out. Just not me, or Benedeto, or Corrin, or anyone else in the family.

Except Helia, of course.

Father believed that her trip into that cavern, much too young, warped her and made her slightly crazy. He never understood her magic. You do. We all do, even if we don't acknowledge it.

431

But she still has nightmares about that place. I cannot in good conscience ask her to go inside.

You, on the other hand, have always wanted to return. For all I know, you have returned, and you know all of the secrets.

Some are contained in Great-Grandmother's journals. Others are discussed in Grandfather's notebooks, or so I'm told. Father wanted me to read those notebooks but I never did.

He wanted me to understand a lot about the cave, even though I couldn't go in there. He said I needed to know, as head of the family and the next regent. I didn't learn it.

But one thing he did say to me stuck and stuck hard: the secrets to saving us from the Fey live in that cave. In the artifacts, many of which our great-grandparents removed, and in the cave itself.

I don't know what's in that cave that can save us. Maybe you do. I'm hoping you do.

I need you to go get whatever that is. I need you to bring it out so that we—and the other Old Families—can survive this attack.

I have done what I can for the other siblings. I asked Lucinda Barkson to get them to a safe place.

But if these attackers are as magical as I think they are, they will find all of us again. It's only a matter of time.

I'll be researching the artifacts and our options here. I'm sure Helia will use that strange talent of hers for making violent magic to keep the family safe.

But those are only short-term measures. I need you to find the real solution, the one that Father said lives inside that cave.

I know I'm asking a lot of you. I'm sorry to do so. I hope you take me up on this.

I love you dearly, Emberto.

I know you will make the right choice for yourself, for our family, and for the future.

With highest regard and affection,

Gussie

CHAPTER
TWENTY-NINE

Barkson stared at the letter for the longest time, reading and rereading what Gussie had written, stunned that Emberto had already followed the instructions.

Apparently, he knew what he was about, more than Barkson ever had.

Then she refolded the letter and stuffed it back in its envelope. She replaced the envelope in the compartment with the maps.

She would have to show the letter to Corrin and let him decide if Gianna needed to see it. Then the two of them could determine what they would do next.

If Gussie had to guess, they would remain at the compound until Emberto returned.

If he returned.

Her gaze floated past the mysterious wall that supposedly hid the cave opening from everyone except a chosen few and landed on the dust-covered vehicle.

When Emberto returned, he would need that vehicle.

She had no idea how long he would be gone, but she could buy a bit more time.

She removed her tools from the other compartment and walked over to the dust-covered vehicle.

She contemplated it for a moment, wondering what she could do that would keep the man she had met from stealing the vehicle.

He had said he didn't know how to drive the vehicle, which meant he didn't know how these vehicles worked.

She wouldn't be able to prevent him from bringing an expert up here to help him, but she could force him to make more than one trip on his elderly horse down that mountainside.

She took a deep breath, and then removed the tools for repairing the vents. She hoped that Emberto knew how to rein-stall windstone vents. If not, this would make no difference. If so, she would buy him another day or two.

It didn't take her long to remove all of the vents. She left most of them on the ground beneath the vehicle, but she dusted one off and placed it on the floor of the back. The vent would look like part of the vehicle to someone who was unfamiliar with it, but Emberto would know what it was.

Barkson hoped he would have enough time to reassemble the vehicle and get it down the mountain. With the right tools, it would only take a half an hour or so, but sometimes, in an emergency, a half an hour was too much.

Still, it was all she could do.

When she finished, she dusted off her hands, replaced her tools in their case, and put the case back in her vehicle.

Then she took the stranger's pistol and disassembled it. She placed it inside the back compartment of Emberto's vehicle, hoping he knew how to use a pistol like that.

If he did, he would have at least one more tool to save himself.

Then she gave the landing one last glance, peered at the mysterious wall, and still saw nothing.

So she got back into her windstone vehicle, started it, and drove down the mountainside.

When she reached the fork in the road that took her outside of the Forbidden Valley, she took that, not because she was leaving Corrin and Gianna behind, but because she didn't want to go anywhere near that village.

It would take Barkson a few more hours to return to the compound, but those hours might just be the difference between life and death—for her and for Emberto.

Barkson had done everything she could.

She only hoped that when she next saw Gussie, Gussie would understand.

My dearest G,

C came with me to the compound, as you requested. We found surprises there. It seems E has started a family and defended them well. When you read this, trust that they are safe. I will tell you more when I see you.

As for the other, E is doing as you asked. I did not remain to see if E is successful, but I did what I could to ensure success.

I hope that, by the time you read this, you will have already spoken with me. There is a chance, however, that I will be delayed.

I have chosen to write this missive in that case, so that I could put your mind at ease about the mission.

I have done all that I could.

The next part of whatever this is will be up to you.

Your not-so-humble servant,

L.

HEAR DIRECTLY
FROM KRIS

Sign up for the Kristine Kathryn Rusch newsletter and hear from Kris herself.

Go to kriswrites.com.

Get the latest news and releases from all of the WMG authors and lines, including Kristine Kathryn Rusch, Kristine Grayson, Kris Nelscott, Dean Wesley Smith, *Pulphouse Fiction Magazine, Smith's Monthly,* and so much more.

Go to wmgbooks.com.

You can also follow Kris on Bookbub.

We value honest feedback, and would love to hear your opinion in a review, if you're so inclined, on your favorite book retailer's site.

ABOUT THE AUTHOR

International bestseller Kristine Kathryn Rusch wrote seven books featuring the Fey before traditional publishing issues in the United States stymied her. The extremely popular series became a bestseller in multiple languages, including French, Italian, German, Polish, and Czech. When the first book, *The Sacrifice,* first appeared in the United States, it was hailed as one of the best fantasy novels of the year. Rusch took an unintended twenty-plus year hiatus from the Fey after completing the second full mini-saga. Spurred by a successful Kickstarter for a novella featuring the Fey, she dove back into the project. She explains her journey back to the Fey in *Lessons from the Writing of The Fey.* All seven of the books are back in print through WMG Publishing, and have garnered new readers worldwide. Rusch recently published the novella, *The Reflection on Mount Vitaki,* and has completed three new novels, with a fourth underway.

Rusch writes in many genres, from science fiction to mystery, from western to romance. She has written under a pile of pen names, but most of her work appears as Kristine Kathryn Rusch. Her Kris Nelscott pen name has won or been nominated for most of the awards in the mystery genre, and her Kristine

Grayson pen name became a bestseller in romance. Her science fiction novels set in the bestselling Diving Universe have won dozens of awards and are in development for a major TV show. She also writes the Retrieval Artist sf series and several major series that mostly appear as short fiction.

Rusch broke a number of barriers in the sf/f field, including being the first female editor of *The Magazine of Fantasy & Science Fiction*. She has owned two different publishing companies, and writes a highly regarded publishing industry blog on Patreon. She also writes a highly regarded weekly publishing industry blog. Find out more about her work at <u>kriswrites.com</u>, and more about the Fey at <u>WorldoftheFey.com</u>.

f facebook.com/kristinekathrynruschwriter

p patreon.com/kristinekathrynrusch

BB bookbub.com/authors/kristine-kathryn-rusch

www.ingramcontent.com/pod-product-compliance
Lightning Source LLC
Chambersburg PA
CBHW010731130726
47899CB00013B/3102